HIS FATHER'S GHOST

A Mina Scarletti Mystery
Book Five

Linda Stratmann

SAPERE
BOOKS

HIS FATHER'S GHOST

Published by Sapere Books.

20 Windermere Drive, Leeds, England, LS17 7UZ,
United Kingdom

saperebooks.com

ISBN: 978-1-80055-015-5

This book is dedicated to the Old Police Cells Museum Brighton, with special thanks to Ian for conducting a most enjoyable and informative tour
https://www.oldpolicecellsmuseum.org.uk

PROLOGUE

Brighton, 1872

It was midnight, and Franklin Holt, exhausted and restless, lay blearily awake in his bed, terrified to go to sleep. Despite the soft amber light of the streetlamp that spilled from the edges of the curtains, he was engulfed in an almost palpable darkness, a malevolent gloom that had been conjured only for him.

On the other side of the bedroom, his younger brother, Matthew slept peacefully, a contented expression on his disarmingly cherubic face, rumpled hair painting the pillow bronze after a boisterous day of fun and mischief.

There was no such peace for Franklin and had not been for some time. What should have been an easy drift into restoring slumber was instead haunted with half-sleeping, half-waking horrors. There was a presence in the room. It was always there, powerful and overbearing, but invisible. He imagined it as a grim dark cloud, lurking in corners, hiding, hovering, waiting. One day it would manifest before his eyes, and then it would swoop down and gather him up, drawing him swiftly to an unknown but certainly horrible fate. Insanity, death, and eternal torment awaited him, and that brief glance would doom him forever.

How he wished that his nurse was still there. He might have dared then to cry out for help, and she would have come to his side and smoothed the bedsheets and smilingly laid her hand on his brow. She had always spoken to him sweetly and been very kind and patient — not like his Aunt Marion.

Aunt Marion was horrid — worse than any threatening spirit. She had stormed into the house one day and sent the nurse away and told his mother not to trouble herself, because she would do everything. She had promised to look after Franklin and make him well, but instead she was angry with him all the time. She took him to task for being such a trial to his poor widowed mother and ordered him to change his behaviour. She read him stories of disobedient children and the cruel fates they suffered as a result of their wickedness, none of which sounded as bad as the misery Franklin endured. He would have done anything to change his ways, but how could he when he didn't know how, and his days were heavy eyed with weariness and his nights shrouded in fear?

When he finally lost the struggle and slept, he would sometimes wake to face still greater horrors. There were mornings when his body was cold and heavy as iron, his muscles rigid, and he could neither speak nor move his limbs. With tentatively opened eyelids he saw through gummed and gritty lashes the thing he had most dreaded; the creature standing at the foot of his bed. It was taller than any normal man, a solid shape consisting only of a head and enormous body, like a giant black bat enveloped in its own leathery wings. He would close his eyes, hoping that when he opened them again it would be gone. Sometimes when he dared to look again, it was no longer there, but there were also times when with a sick lurch in his chest he saw it still, and it had come closer, rising up to float in the air above him.

Although the apparition did not touch him, he could feel it as a heavy weight pressing down, so hard that he could scarcely breathe, and in those moments he really thought that his ribs would bend and crack and his lungs collapse and he would die. The creature stank of decay, like rotting seaweed that had dissolved into dark green slime. He might have cried out in despair, but his mouth and tongue were locked and immobile.

Aunt Marion had found him like that one morning when she came to wake him. She had shaken him and shouted at him and slapped his face, and then declared loudly that he was only pretending. When the sensation passed off, he had sobbed with fright and pain and relief, and she told him sneeringly that he was a bad, troublesome boy and had only got the punishment he deserved. Perhaps he did deserve it, but he could not understand why.

That night, at the stillest hour, he thought he was awake. Matthew slept on, his snores like the purr of a contented kitten, unaware of the grim horror engulfing his brother. But there were other, unearthly noises in the room, pattering footsteps circling Franklin's bed, insistent tapping, the beat of sinewy wings, and muttering voices.

The creature was there again. It stood watching him, faceless and menacing. He tried to address it, but his voice stuck in his throat. 'Who are you?' he wanted to say. 'Are you a ghost or a demon?', and although the thing did not speak, its reply was in his head and he heard the apparition say in tones that seemed to echo like the rumble of thunder in a stormy sky, 'I am your father!'

CHAPTER ONE

It had started quite innocently — a slight cold, a small but persistent cough. Mina Scarletti knew she had to guard her fragile health, especially from anything that might place a strain on her lungs, cramped as they were by the permanent snake twist in her spine, the result of scoliosis. Large gatherings of people were a particular danger, and to be avoided if possible, especially in the cooler months, when the atmosphere was almost visibly suffused with a cloud of myriad infections.

That March, the weather in Brighton had been marked by overcast skies, squally winds and chill mists that clawed at the throat. The barometer in the hallway wore a stern expression ordering Mina not to venture outdoors unless her visit was of vital importance. She had been unable, however, to resist spending an evening in the theatre to see her good friend, the actor Marcus Merridew, give his Hamlet.

When Mina and Mr Merridew had first become acquainted he was employed as a visitors' guide to the Royal Pavilion, his youthful career in the drama having faded to near obscurity. Lately, however, he had enjoyed a spectacular rise in fortune due to his masterful performance in an entertainment devised by Mina's brother Richard. In this creation, which had dazzled the Pavilion for just a single night, Mr Merridew, costumed as the Prince Regent, had defeated Richard's Napoleon, in a probably belated attempt to defend the honour of Mrs Fitzherbert. He was now constantly in demand for dramatic readings before gatherings of tea-sipping matrons and had ascended to be the shining star in the admittedly small firmament of the Brighton Theatre Company. No matter that

Hamlet was a man of thirty and Mr Merridew would not see fifty again. The years since his early triumphs had if anything mellowed and rounded the honeyed caress of his voice. On stage, his deportment was perfect, his energy unfailing, his every movement a study in elegance which drew sighs of admiration from the ladies who made up the greater part of his audience.

As the leading man he had availed himself of the opportunity to make some slight improvements to the Bard's play. The theatre was nightly roused to a pitch of frenzied excitement at the final duel in which Hamlet defeated the invader Fortinbras. Tears of joy were shed when it was revealed that the rumours of Ophelia's death were false, and she had regained her wits. The play ended in triumph with a glorious pageant, the wedding of Hamlet and Ophelia, jointly crowned King and Queen of Denmark.

Mina had cheered along with the enraptured throng, although she had been obliged at times to hold a herb-filled sachet to her face, breathing in its protective odour, since the man who sat beside her had wheezed noisily throughout the performance. On returning home, the Scarlettis' general maid, Rose, had fussed over Mina as usual, setting her before a blazing fire in the parlour and bringing hot drinks unbidden.

Two days later Mina awoke with a sting in her nostrils and a throbbing rawness in her throat. Rose, her every expression saying, 'I told you so,' brought her mutton broth and medicine, and when the cough started and refused to allow Mina any rest, Rose all but ordered her back to bed, and called Dr Hamid.

The wise doctor was proprietor of Brighton's most renowned Oriental healing emporium and was one of the few practitioners Mina trusted, since his late sister Eliza had also suffered from scoliosis and he had made a special study of the condition. Other less knowledgeable doctors encased their patients in steel corsets or plaster waistcoats, browbeat them into believing that the distortion of the spine was their own fault, and even advocated highly speculative surgery to sever their back muscles. Dr Hamid's treatments consisted of medicated vapour baths, soothing massages and stimulating exercise, his lady patients enjoying the sensitive care of his sister Anna. Mina would emerge from the baths where she made her weekly visit relaxed and refreshed and, for a time at least, free of the aches that were her daily plague.

Rose showed Dr Hamid to Mina's bedside where she lay bundled in blankets and shawls, a thoroughly unhappy and unwilling patient, since she found the enforced inactivity desperately frustrating. Although her mind insisted that she should be up and about and doing something interesting, her body was sending urgent messages that it was too weary to do much more than rest. She could not stop shivering, although the room was well warmed.

Dr Hamid used the time taken to approach her bedside to study Mina carefully. Their meetings, even those of a social nature, always began with a general enquiry after her health, but this time he did not ask, and she sensed that the look had told him all he needed to know. Although his greeting was friendly and sympathetic, he was unable to conceal a deep anxiety for his frail patient.

'It's only a cold,' Mina protested, defiantly, although it was a searingly wretched effort to speak at all. 'But I suppose I had better stay indoors for a while.'

'You certainly should,' he said. 'Do you have much pain?'

'Only when I breathe.' Mina coughed into a handkerchief and winced at a sharp stab through her breastbone. There was a rasping in her chest that was sounding like that of the man she had been seated beside in the theatre. She wondered if he was still alive.

'Rose, help me lift Miss Scarletti to sit a little higher. It will help ease the breathing,' said Dr Hamid. Each took an arm and raised her up with no more difficulty than settling a small child, and Rose plumped and rearranged the pillows. 'Is that better?'

Mina tried to catch her breath, failed, and nodded instead.

Dr Hamid placed the palm of his hand to her forehead for a few moments, said 'hm' then handed a thermometer to Rose and instructed her to position it under Mina's armpit — a procedure which involved much delving though layers of wool and linen. He took Mina's wrist in a firm grip and consulted his watch, then used his smart new binaural stethoscope to listen carefully to the action of her lungs. He looked at her once more, frowned, and made some notes in a little book, but made no comment concerning what he had observed.

'Plenty of fluids,' he said, with a nod to Rose, 'especially nourishing drinks such as beef tea. Warm linseed poultices on the chest, twice a day, and inhalations of hot medicated vapour whenever necessary. I will prescribe the drops you require and a mixture to soothe the throat. Miss Scarletti is not to be moved from her bed until I say it is safe to do so.' Rose retrieved the thermometer and Dr Hamid studied and noted the result. 'The temperature is slightly elevated but not dangerous.'

'Will I live?' asked Mina. It was not a frivolous question and she saw from his expression that he knew it.

'That is the intention. Try and keep your spirits up.'

'As I lie here idle? That will be hard.'

'I can imagine,' he said wryly. 'You may indulge in gentle amusements. Reading, and — well, reading. Poetry perhaps. Or sermons. But no excitement and no exertion,' he added firmly.

'I shall expect Rose to inform me if you attempt to go beyond my advice, and I will not be pleased if you do.'

Rose looked at Mina sternly and steadily. The reluctant patient was left in no doubt that the maid would attend diligently to Dr Hamid's directions.

Mina was left hoping for signs of improvement to appear soon, and eager to find herself restored to health in a few days at the most. She was all for indulging in a good book and Rose saw that she was suitably supported in a position to read and provided with a volume of religious essays. The next morning, however, Mina was feverish with a bounding pulse, and a cough that seemed to be trying to drag all her insides outwards. Unable to move, gasping for breath, she lay helpless, sunken into the pillows.

Despite this, Mina did not fully realise how ill she was until her mother arrived. Louisa Scarletti had spent most of the previous few months in London, acting as an ineffectual nurse, grim counsellor and general aggravator to her younger daughter Enid Inskip. Enid's solicitor husband was abroad on business and, having already been blessed with twin boys, she was anticipating an addition to the family, but not with any great pleasure. Once settled in, Louisa's main contribution to Mina's sickroom was to sit by the bed, her face buried in a handkerchief, whimpering, until Rose persuaded her to leave.

Dr Hamid visited twice a day, and soon after the arrival of Mina's mother he was accompanied by a young woman in a plain grey gown, a long white apron and a starched cap. 'This is Miss Cherry,' he said.

'Where is Rose?' asked Mina, in a breathy whisper.

'Rose is attending to Mrs Scarletti in addition to her household duties. You need someone experienced who can be by your side at all times. Miss Cherry is a nurse with the most impeccable credentials. I thoroughly recommend her.'

Mina looked at Miss Cherry, who was very tidy and had an air of quiet competence. 'Miss Cherry, I will try not to trouble you too much.'

Miss Cherry gave a neat bob of a curtsey.

Dr Hamid made the usual checks of Mina's temperature and pulse and listened to her chest.

'I am still feverish, am I not?' asked Mina.

He hesitated.

'I would prefer honest bad news to unrealistic reassurance.'

He smiled briefly. 'Yes, you are.'

'Then I may not be troubling anyone for much longer.'

'You must not lose hope,' he said. 'You are young yet.'

Mina burst into a new coughing fit and Miss Cherry acted at once, applying friction to her patient's back until the painful spasms subsided sufficiently for a teaspoonful of sedative mixture to be swallowed. She then poured water into a basin, dampened a cloth and applied it to Mina's brow and lips.

'I expected to die young,' said Mina, as she reclined on the pillows once more. 'I just didn't expect it to hurt this much.'

Miss Cherry said nothing, but as soon as Dr Hamid had left, she stamped her presence on the household. The Scarlettis employed a charlady to do the heavier domestic cleaning, and she did it well, but Miss Cherry did not consider this good enough for a sickroom. She therefore set about scrutinising every surface in Mina's bedroom, assessing each item therein for its cleanliness and suitability. Anything that might harbour dust or have an irritating scent was packed into boxes and stored away until the patient was strong enough to endure them.

There was some puzzlement over the small dumbbells that lay concealed at the bottom of the wardrobe and Mina was obliged to explain that she used them in the calisthenic exercises she had been taught by Anna Hamid. Miss Cherry commented dryly that they would not be needed for a while, rubbed them well with a cloth and replaced them. The little wedge-shaped cushion that Mina used to enable her to sit upright on chairs was taken away to be cleaned.

The fire was tended to give just the right degree of warmth, the upper window opened to admit fresh air without a draught. Brightness that did not tax the eyes, scents that soothed and an absence of the common odours of the sickroom were essential to Miss Cherry's way of ministering to her patients.

It was, thought Mina, a tremendous amount of fuss over a dying woman. And she *was* dying, there was no doubt about that. If not that day then another not too far off; if not from this illness, then probably the next one. And what, after all, she mused, did she have to live for? She would never have a husband or children. Her family didn't need her. Her stories, which she published under another name, did well enough but would never be accorded the status of good literature. Her life, she concluded, had no meaning and if she disappeared there might be a little brief regret and then the world would move on.

What would she miss, she wondered? The gentle friendship of Dr Hamid, the annoying but often amusing schemes of her quixotic brother Richard, and Brighton itself, the summer days when the sun gilded the town, and the scent of the blue-green sea as it washed over the pebbled beach. She was like a piece of limp bedraggled seaweed, drifting out with the tide.

As yet, she had not had a great deal of conversation with Miss Cherry, who discouraged her from speaking too much, and issued advice in the manner of a benevolent but firm command. That afternoon, Mina was trying to enjoy a cup of broth while her nurse inspected the medicines on the night table and made notes in a little book, but every so often Miss Cherry gave Mina a glance as if she wanted to make an observation but didn't like to.

'Please say what you wish to say,' Mina whispered. It was the only use of her voice that did not stimulate a fit of coughing. 'If I am not long for the world, I really want to know so I can make any arrangements.'

'Oh! No, that is not it, I assure you.'

'Then what is it?'

Miss Cherry hesitated then closed her notebook. 'I hope you don't mind my asking, but are you the same Miss Scarletti who has been mentioned in the newspapers? The lady who goes to mediums and finds out which ones are true and which false?'

Mina smiled slightly and nodded. 'I am.'

'I ask because there was a lady whose family I attended recently, and she said that she was about to write to you about a pressing question. I expect that she was not aware that you are unwell.'

'I have not received a letter at all for some days,' said Mina. She paused. *No excitement and no exertion*, Dr Hamid had said. Of course, she realised, if there *had* been letters, they would have been withheld from her. 'If you should see the lady, you must inform her that I am unwell,' she said. 'I will reply to her enquiry as soon as I am able.'

'I will do so, of course.' Miss Cherry opened her notebook and continued her work.

Mina laid her cup aside. 'Do you know what the pressing question was?'

Miss Cherry paused and frowned a little. 'I cannot reveal the secrets of the sickroom, Miss Scarletti.'

'No, of course not. I understand.'

'Although there *are* circumstances regarding the family that have already been published in the newspapers and are not secret. You must have read about it. The case of Mr Jasper Holt, the man who disappeared?'

Mina had lived in Brighton for three years but had never heard of this event. She might have been struggling to breathe but her curiosity and love of the *outré* were unimpaired. 'When did this occur?' she asked.

'In 1864. But of course, with recent events, it has become the talk of the town again.'

'Recent events?'

'Mrs Holt's remarriage. I am not a gossip by nature, but my mother works in Mr Grant's drapery shop in St James's Street, and she hears all the town news. It is a very superior establishment, and Mrs Holt was once a regular customer there. When the betrothal was announced there were many people in Brighton who recalled Mr Holt's disappearance, and they began to talk of it again. Mrs Grant especially; she kept all the newspapers and brought them out for her friends to look at. I saw them myself only the other day. All the old stories; the reports, the rumours and the suspicions have been dusted off and examined very closely. Of course, Mr Grant does not tolerate idle conversation, but much may be said over the counter while measuring ribbon.'

'I may have forgotten the details,' said Mina. 'Help me sit up a little more and tell me all about it.'

Miss Cherry complied. 'I read about it in the *Brighton Gazette* at the time,' she said, 'but somehow, it seems just like yesterday. It was July; the town was crowded with visitors, and it was a beautiful warm day with a calm sea. Not a hint of any danger. Mr Holt was a wine and spirit merchant, a family man, very well liked, and he wanted to take a trip on a yacht. He told the boatman that his doctor had recommended he should take the sea air for his health, and he thought he might purchase the yacht, but wanted to sail in it first. The yacht — it was a very small one — was called *Ocean Breeze*, and it was owned by a Mr William Sutherland. They took off near to the West Pier and lots of people on the shore saw them depart, and gave them a cheerful wave, and both men waved back. But when the yacht returned, some hours later, only Mr Sutherland was aboard. He was terribly upset and alerted the police immediately. He said there had been a tragic accident.'

Miss Cherry paused dramatically. Mina knew better than to interrupt and waited expectantly.

'Mr Sutherland told the police that once the yacht was on its way, Mr Holt said he wanted to sail to Shoreham, so he turned the vessel to the west. They had been going on well for about half an hour when there was a sudden strong gust of wind. Yachtsmen like Mr Sutherland know that this can happen from time to time in hot weather, but Mr Holt, not being an experienced sailor, thought that the vessel was in some danger. Mr Sutherland did his best to reassure him that all was well, but Mr Holt became very agitated. He rushed to the side to see if there was any assistance nearby, stumbled, and a sudden movement of the yacht threw him into the sea. This caused the yacht to roll most alarmingly, and Mr Sutherland had to work hard to avoid a capsize.

Mr Holt must have struck his head on the side of the boat as he fell, because Mr Sutherland saw him floating on the water unconscious, and tried to steer towards him to make a rescue, but he was unable to reach and recover him before he sank, weighed down by the sea water saturating his clothing. His body was never found.'

'His poor family,' said Mina. 'How old was he?'

'In his forties. And there were two young children. But there was more grief to come,' said Miss Cherry. 'It was found that Mr Holt's business was in terrible debt and was about to fail, something that he had kept very carefully hidden. In the week before he disappeared, he had insured his life with the Brighton and Hove Insurance Company for a very large sum. But the insurance company refused to make any payment. They said that there was no proof that Mr Holt was dead.'

'They suspected fraud,' said Mina.

'They did. In fact it was suggested that Mr Holt had planned the whole adventure, to make it seem that he was lost at sea when he was actually still alive and in hiding. Both Mrs Holt and Mr Sutherland were suspected of being involved, and they were questioned by the police, but they weren't charged.

So Mrs Holt's solicitor wrote to the newspapers saying that she didn't know anything about her husband's business affairs, and didn't know if he was alive or dead, but if he was alive, she begged him to surrender himself.'

'Who was her solicitor?' asked Mina.

'Oh — I am not sure, a Mr Phipps, I think.'

Mina nodded. Not her own solicitor, she thought, Mr Ronald Phipps, who would have been too young in 1864, but presumably a member of that partnership.

'Then Mr Sutherland's solicitor — I don't know his name — made a statement saying that he had told the truth about Mr Holt's fate and firmly believed him to be dead.'

'And has nothing been heard since?'

'Nothing. Mrs Holt's brother — he's Mr Gordon Saltmire — you might have heard of him, he has the porcelain business in

Hove — he engaged a private detective, but I never heard if anything came of that. And someone called 'Clarity' wrote to the *Gazette* to say that Mrs Holt was a highly respectable lady who would never tell a lie, and that Mr Holt's spirit had sent messages to say that Mr Sutherland's story was true.'

'I assume Clarity's testimony did not convince the insurance company to pay?'

'No. But seven years later with no sign of Mr Holt, a court declared him dead, and Mrs Holt married a Mr Vardy. But of course, that is only what was printed in the newspapers,' said Miss Cherry as she finished her story, and adjusted Mina's pillows. She had a superior knack in that skill which made Mina feel instantly more comfortable.

Mina, trying her best to control her surging interest, reflected that since her mother had been in London with Enid during the last few weeks there had been no teatime gatherings of ladies in her home, where such exchanges as this would have been relished. Town gossip was a tawdry commodity but if well sifted it could yield something of value. 'How very interesting,' she said. 'Is there more?'

Miss Cherry continued her pillow-smoothing which appeared to take rather longer than required, and Mina realised that she was thinking about how to respond. 'Dr Hamid has ordered no excitement and no exertion,' she said at last. 'I think I have said too much.'

'Then there *is* more,' Mina whispered hopefully, trying not to overtax her voice. 'Do tell. If the excitement should become overwhelming, I will let you know.'

Miss Cherry, who looked eager to tell her tale, despite the reservations imposed by her profession, drew up a chair beside the bed. 'I have been told that there have been letters written to the newspapers very recently expressing ideas about what

Mr Holt's fate might have been, but these letters were never published, because it would have been unwise to do so.'

'For fear of legal action,' said Mina. She had no difficulty in imagining what those letters might have said.

'Oh, there are a dozen different ideas about the true facts of the mystery. Much of it, I am sorry to say, is very unflattering to both Mr and Mrs Vardy.'

'Since the lady has remarried, she must now accept that her husband is deceased,' said Mina. Even as the sensible words left her lips Mina reminded herself that a second marriage where the first spouse was known to be alive was a circumstance that did occasionally trouble the courts. Without having met the lady in question she could not guess at her thoughts and motives.

'Naturally, Mrs Vardy has not discussed her private affairs with me,' added Miss Cherry, primly. 'I am not, therefore betraying any confidences.'

'It must be mortifying for her if she is aware that the whole town is discussing her situation.'

'She cannot be unaware,' said Miss Cherry.

A few moments passed before Mina understood the subtle meaning. 'You mean that Mrs Vardy has been receiving letters, too?'

Miss Cherry made no reply.

'And there must have been looks, and whispers.' Mina was very familiar with the stares and comments she attracted in town due to her unusual appearance, her twisted, child-sized body and ungainly lurching walk. But this was the curiosity of strangers, not the repugnance of former friends. 'And, I suspect, there have been fewer social calls and invitations.'

Still Miss Cherry said nothing.

'Why does Mrs Vardy think I can advise her?' Mina wondered. 'Perhaps she wishes me to recommend a good medium. I do have correspondence of that sort.'

'She visits a medium once a week and places great trust in her. It is a very select circle, and has existed for many years. The lady is quite old, and she has a remarkable machine, said to be the only one of its kind, that receives messages from beyond.'

Mina was about to comment but the effort of speech had been too much for her and she began to wheeze again. The air vanished from her lungs and the horrid cough came back to plague her.

Miss Cherry quickly leaned over and rubbed Mina's back until she had recovered her breath, then poured a glass of water. 'There now,' she said as Mina took small rapid sips. 'That is quite enough conversation for the present. Just rest.'

'What of the boatman, Mr Sutherland?' asked Mina — at least she tried to ask, but was prevented by a fresh fit of coughing which she attempted to stifle with a handkerchief.

At that moment, Rose entered with the poultice of boiled linseed spread on linen and Mina was obliged to submit to its application. Rose had a habit of making it a little hotter than necessary, presumably so it would last longer. Rose had to wait until Mina had coughed herself into a strained silence, then extracted the handkerchief from her grasp, inspected it and took it away for laundry.

'How is mother?' Mina gasped.

'Mrs Scarletti wishes you to know that she cannot come to see you today as she is prostrated by anxiety and exhaustion, but she prays for you and Mrs Inskip three times a day,' said Rose, tonelessly.

Mina tried to reply but unable to catch her breath, could only nod.

That night Mina's temperature unexpectedly soared again. In a clammy shivery haze, the plight of the unfortunate Mrs Vardy and the mystery of Mr Holt remained on her mind. She did not want to slip away from the world without knowing the answer; or would death provide her with all the answers she craved?

Her brow was glazed with perspiration, carefully blotted by a kind hand that seemed to descend from Heaven with a cooling cloth. Still, she burned and ached, and as her temples began to throb a spectre hovered before her, the figure of a man without a face. Somehow, she knew that he was Mr Jasper Holt, not a ghost, but a vision created by her fever, tantalising, beckoning, inviting her to find him if she could.

Every time she sank into sleep, she thought she might never waken again. When she opened her eyes, faces hovered over her and shapes moved quietly about the room, anxious voices whispering in case she overheard their dire predictions. The loudest voice was that of her mother, who sat at the foot of the bed like a marble monument of a weeping angel over a grave, bemoaning the sufferings inflicted upon her by cruel fate.

The spout of a feeding cup was presented to her lips and cool water trickled down her throat. A cold pack descended on her forehead and strong fingertips grasped her wrist. She felt her pulse flutter. Mina closed her eyes and tried to concentrate on the important thing that was now taking all her slight energy — breathing.

Consciousness came and went, and time passed. For a while, she believed that she was dead. She was floating like a wraith above her own body, which lay on the bed looking small and shrunken, drowned in a sea of flowers. Worse still, she thought she saw the young photographer Mr Beckler. She had met him last January when he had insulted her in a manner that was so distressing, she had spoken of it to no-one. In her imagination he had come to take a portrait of her corpse, hoping to capture on his glass plates an image of her angry spirit. In her vision, her dead eyes snapped open, creating alarm in the onlookers, and she returned to her body with a shock.

Slowly, Mina came to herself and found that she was alive. It was almost as if her desire to chase the elusive truth of Mr Holt was the only thing keeping her in the world.

She fell at last into a deep healing sleep.

CHAPTER TWO

When Mina next awoke, she was content for some time simply to take pleasure from the fact that she was not drenched in perspiration, her head no longer imitated the beating of a drum and her breathing while not precisely painless, was much less of an effort. She became aware that a hand was gently holding hers and opened her eyes. Sitting beside the bed was her younger brother Richard, the handsome scapegrace of the family. He usually lodged with their older brother Edward in London, and his visits to Brighton tended to be impetuous and unannounced. Exasperating as he so often was, it always warmed her heart to see him.

'Mina?' he asked, hopefully. She squeezed his hand, and he laughed in relief. 'Darling girl, you have given us all such a fright! How are you now?'

Mina considered this. 'Thirsty,' she whispered.

Miss Cherry was at her side in a moment, offering a cup, and Mina drank deeply, with only a slight cough marring the exercise, then sank back onto the pillows with a sigh. 'I think I would like to sit up.'

Miss Cherry placed a hand to her forehead and smiled. 'The fever is gone. Would you assist me, Mr Scarletti?'

Mina was carefully raised into a better position, then Miss Cherry went to refill the cup from the carafe on the night table, but there was not enough left. 'I'll fetch some fresh,' she said, and left the room.

'I suppose you know that Nellie is abroad at present?' Mina asked.

In the recent past Richard's visits to Brighton had by some extraordinary chance coincided with the absence on business of Nellie's husband, John Jordan, who was a partner in the fashionable clothing emporium of Jordan and Conroy. Richard and Nellie had been intimate friends before her marriage, and the friendship had continued subsequently to an extent that society would have considered inadvisable and a suspiciously jealous Mr Jordan unacceptable.

'I do, yes,' said Richard, 'She and her horrid husband are in Italy. Darling girl, I came to see *you*. Dr Hamid wrote and told us you were unwell, and I came as soon as I could.'

Mina was unusually touched by his concern. 'It was very good of you to come. I suppose Edward is occupied with business as usual?'

'Oh yes, he seems always to be working in that drab office, or talking about his wedding. He has almost no time for anything else. Miss Hooper has him well in harness, but he doesn't seem to see it. I never saw such a girl. She seems so meek, but she can crack a whip with a flutter of her eyelids.'

'I wouldn't insist that Edward abandons such a paragon,' said Mina, who, to her great shame, was rather fonder of Richard and his foolishness than of their sensible but duller older brother. 'I think if I was to find all the family standing in a circle about my bed it would not be a good sign. But, tell me, how is Enid? I assume there is still no word of Mr Inskip and when he might return?'

Richard rolled his eyes. 'No, and the matter is a constant trial to her, as it is to us all. I do try to be sympathetic, but it is very hard when so many of her woes she brought upon herself.'

Mina reflected sorrowfully on the tribulations of her vain and wilful younger sister and found it hard to disagree. Enid's husband, whom she had married on a whim and grown to despise was negotiating some property business with a Romanian count and had spent much of the autumn and winter hemmed in by snow and wolves and fighting an unnamed indisposition. Letters had been scarce, and he had not yet been apprised of Enid's blossoming condition which was incompatible with the period of his absence. The previous autumn Enid's undisciplined and selfish nature had led to indiscreet assignations with Mr Arthur Wallace Hope, the famous explorer and crusading spiritualist whose lectures had taken Brighton by storm. Too late, she had discovered that he had been associating with other foolish wives and cared nothing for any of his conquests. Some two or three months were required before Enid's delicate situation could be restored.

'She prays for her poor husband daily,' Richard added, with a meaningful look which suggested that Enid's most fervent wish was for Mr Inskip to continue to be abroad for as long as possible, and for preference never return at all.

'How long will you be able to stay?'

'Oh, Edward said as you were so ill, I could stay as long as I liked,' said Richard, airily. 'I could do with some sea air — anything that doesn't smell of ink or pencil.'

'Really? That is kind of him.' Richard, whose ambition in life was to become rich without it costing him any effort, had abandoned his recent attempt to become a playwright on discovering the profession to be both arduous and scant of remuneration. He had been working initially as a clerk and later a sketch artist for a ladies' magazine. The *Society Journal* was a product of the Scarletti publishing house, which had been managed by Edward and the senior partner Mr Greville since their father's death.

Mina was well aware that Edward had only offered Richard a position in the company from brotherly loyalty without any anticipation that he would ever discover the satisfaction of hard work. It was typical of Richard, she thought, that drawing, which had once been the idle amusement he had resorted to when bored by the clerkly tasks he was supposed to be doing had lost its appeal for him once it became his occupation. His extended absence from the office was unlikely to be a handicap to the business, which had however provided his longest ever period of gainful employment.

Mina wanted to question Richard further, but the conversation had taken all her slight energy, and as Miss Cherry returned to her side, she was obliged to accept that for the time being at least, her principal occupation would be resting.

The next morning, after a peaceful night, the sound of the postman's daily delivery alerted Mina's attention. 'Are there any letters for me?' she asked Miss Cherry.

'I don't believe so,' said Miss Cherry, but she turned her face away as she spoke.

'Not even one from Mrs Vardy?'

'I am sure I have not seen any letters at all.'

By the time Richard visited her again, Mina was quite certain that there were letters and felt frustrated at not being allowed to see them. Fortunately, Miss Cherry understood that Mina might wish to converse with her brother alone and went to speak to cook on the subject of chicken broth.

'Richard, tell me something,' said Mina, urgently as soon as the nurse had gone.

'Careful, my dear, Dr Hamid has said you are to remain very quiet and still, and not to worry yourself about anything.'

'And since when did I behave in such a way?'

'That is true, but he was very insistent.' He smiled and patted her hand. 'All right, what is it you want to know?'

'Have any letters arrived for me while I have been ill?'

He thought for a moment. 'I haven't seen any. There are none on the hall table. Why? Is something wrong, because if so —'

'No. I was just — I have been feeling very dull lying in bed all day long and was looking for something to read.'

'I could bring you one of mother's fashion magazines.'

'Something interesting.'

He nodded. 'I'll see what I can find. The *Gazette*?'

'I suppose I might be allowed that provided nothing remotely exciting has happened in Brighton in the last week.'

She looked so despondent that he leaned over and hugged her. 'Just get well, my dear.'

'And while you are here, why don't you go and see Mr Merridew, who gives his final performances as Hamlet this week? It is very entertaining. Perhaps you could make a sketch of the theatre and the stage and the actors in costume. Even people who scorn the theatre like to see pictures of it. Such a subject would be ideal for readers of the *Journal*.'

'Perhaps I could,' said Richard, looking unusually pensive. Mina was reminded that Nellie Jordan had, before her marriage graced the popular stage. A performance as Ophelia in a burlesque of Hamlet, in which Nellie had torn off most of her clothing during the mad scene was, so Mina had been assured, still talked about in certain circles.

Richard had been about to say more, when Rose arrived announcing the arrival of Dr Hamid.

'I shall go and sit with Mother,' said Richard, looking a little queasy at the sight of the doctor's medical bag. 'She will be overjoyed to know that you are better.'

'Try not to borrow money from her,' Mina pleaded.

He smiled. 'But if she offers, it would be such an insult to refuse.'

'Well this is quite a change!' said Dr Hamid, with the brightest and least forced smile Mina had seen since the start of her illness.

'I feel so much more myself,' she said, trying to sit up into something that approached an upright position. Miss Cherry returned and she and Rose hurried to assist. It was still an effort and her wretched chest would keep hurting, but Mina was feeling considerably less apprehensive about the prospect of a tragically early death.

An examination of her pulse and temperature confirmed that Mina was improving, and when Dr Hamid listened to her lungs, he was markedly less worried than previously. 'You are making good progress,' he said, 'but,' he added warningly, 'that is no reason to be complacent. You must still take great care and remain in bed for some little while longer until there is no further danger of a relapse. From now on we must concentrate on building up your strength.'

He delivered fresh instructions to Rose on the feeding of the patient, and supplied a small book on invalid diet, which he asked to be directed to the cook. Mina only hoped that cook would not find it too confusing as did any request to prepare something not in her usual limited repertoire. Mina was getting a little tired of insipid broths and would have preferred a refreshing drink of Dr Hamid's specially spiced aerated fruit beverage, which was available at the Baths, but that, like so many of the things she liked were currently denied her.

'What do you hear when you listen to my lungs?' asked Mina.

He hesitated, and she could see that he was debating with himself how much he ought to say. 'The sound initially was like the burning of a log fire, which is not what one normally expects of a healthy lung. But you will be pleased to know that the flames are much reduced.'

'I would improve much faster if I had some occupation for my mind,' she hinted.

'Well, we must think of something, then. Do you like acrostic puzzles? I can have some magazines sent over to you.'

'I would rather study the household accounts. I haven't seen them in over a week.'

'Oh, that is out of the question. But I understand that your cook is managing things from day to day for now, so you need not worry about that. She is a trustworthy woman, is she not?'

Mina was obliged to admit that this was the case.

'I have a little book of readings,' said Miss Cherry, helpfully, producing a small volume from her apron pocket. '*The Young Woman's Companion*. It is a treasure trove of useful information. I read it to all my lady patients.'

'That would be far more suitable,' said Dr Hamid.

'I would prefer it,' said Mina, trying to insert a little bite into her weakened voice, 'if you would allow me to see any letters that have arrived since I became ill. I am sure there have been some. In fact, if you were to tell me that there are none, I would refuse to believe it.'

'Hmm,' said Dr Hamid, crossing his arms and tapping his fingers on his sleeve indecisively.

'Many of the letters I receive are very amusing,' Mina went on. 'I could do with some amusement. And there is family news as well. My brother Edward often writes to me from London. I worry about my family all the time. You know I do, and I would only worry more if I had no news.'

'I suppose,' Dr Hamid said reluctantly, 'that I might agree to the letters if only to prevent the possibility of your getting out of bed and trying to retrieve them yourself.' He made the decision. 'Very well. But we will take this slowly. Rose, on my instructions, has been keeping back any letters addressed to you, but if you have another comfortable night, I will approve your seeing them.' He turned to speak to Rose. 'If Miss Scarletti continues to improve, then tomorrow morning you may bring her letters, but you must only allow her to see them one at a time. Once Miss Scarletti has read the first one, you and Miss Cherry must judge if it is safe to allow her the next, and so on.'

'Thank you,' said Mina. 'How is Mother?'

Dr Hamid closed his medical bag with a snap. 'Your mother will live to be a hundred, but I cannot persuade her of that. I fear that I must now make another attempt.'

Once he had gone, Miss Cherry settled herself in a chair beside the bed and, opening her little book, proceeded to read selected portions aloud, regaling Mina with such essential subjects as the cultivation of the pansy, the habits of birds and how to make ornamental papers. She would not, however, permit Mina to read it for herself, and Mina suspected that even in such a turgid volume there might be matters considered too stimulating for an invalid. She longed for something more diverting but dared not say so.

Mina's family were under the impression that her main amusement was writing gently moral tales for children under her own name, brought out almost as an act of indulgence by Scarletti Publishing. Her writing career had certainly begun in that way, with heart-warming stories designed to ease the gentle soul of her younger sister Marianne, who had died from consumption at the age of fifteen. In recent years, however, she had found her true vocation as a prolific author of bone-chilling adventures featuring ghosts, demons and witches. These were published by the Scarletti Library of Romance under the pseudonym Robert Neil, and enjoyed some moderate success. Even her brother Edward was unaware of her secret identity since works of short fiction were the remit of his business partner Mr Greville.

Mina, with no interest in pansies, birds or ornamental paper, understood completely the necessity of guarding her weakened body from harm, but did not think her mind required the same consideration. She decided that when she was well, and able to sit at her writing desk, she would compose a tale of horror in which a book of anodyne advice for young ladies proved to be the work of an evil magician designed to lure weak invalids to a terrible doom.

Thankfully, she passed a restful night, and awoke to the encouraging prospect of seeing her correspondence. After a breakfast of toast soaked in milk, she submitted without protest to her morning ablutions, and waited expectantly for Rose to bring her letters.

There was a small but promising looking bundle of correspondence, and Rose and Miss Cherry stood by with expressions of great solemnity to observe her responses.

Mina was first handed an advertisement for a conjuror called The Great Mysterioso who claimed to be able to use his special mystical powers to reveal all the secrets of the spirit mediums. He was assisted in this endeavour by wearing a feathered turban and exotically patterned oriental trousers. He would be performing throughout the summer months starting in June, from 10am to 9pm in a booth on the West Pier at a charge of one shilling per visitor.

'That could be interesting,' said Mina, keeping her manner deliberately bright, 'I would love to know the secrets of the spirit mediums, and will certainly pay him a visit. Rose, please place it on my desk and bring the next letter.'

Miss Cherry nodded to Rose who complied.

The second letter was from Mina's friend Mrs Honeyacre announcing that she would be in Brighton all next month and would be holding a salon, which she very much hoped Mina could attend.

'What a charming invitation! I will send a reply saying that I hope to be well enough to do so,' said Mina.

Rose grunted. 'Are you supposed to be writing letters?'

'Dr Hamid did not forbid it, therefore I am,' said Mina firmly. Rose and Miss Cherry exchanged glances but conceded victory to the patient.

A letter from Italy was of more than usual interest and she opened it eagerly. It had been some time since she had enquired after Nellie's happiness in her marriage to Mr John Jordan, since to do so was to invite responses best left unvoiced. The marriage had been motivated by Nellie's wish to acquire a secure establishment, and Mr Jordan's admiration of her person, which he adorned with all the latest fashions in his emporium, thus making her a walking breathing advertisement. Admiration of the gowns was always encouraged, but not of the voluptuous wearer. He had once employed a detective to spy on his wife during his absence on business, and she had narrowly escaped discovery, but this time he had simply removed her from temptation.

Palazzo Hotel
Florence
March 1872

Dear Mina,

The weather in Italy is so pleasant at this time of year, neither too warm nor too cool. I do hope that Brighton is being kind to you.

As you may imagine John is very occupied here with visiting all the workshops that produce such beautiful fabrics, and he is sure to make substantial purchases. I can promise that there will be much to astonish the fashionables in Brighton. But I am not idle or wanting for company. There is a delightful English lady here with two charming daughters of about my own age and we go everywhere together. I shall have so much to tell you when we return, which will not be for a few weeks at least, and I will make sure that you have the very best and latest trimmings before anyone else, so you will be envied!

I am very well indeed, but poor Zillah is finding the diet does not agree with her. I hope she will become accustomed to it in time.

With fondest good wishes
Nellie

As ever Mina was obliged to interpret the letter and realised that not only was Nellie accompanied by her personal maid, Zillah, but her husband had, in the guise of ensuring her safety and entertainment, supplied her with a guard of ladies carefully instructed not to let her out of their sight and to keep gentlemen at bay.

The third letter was from Mina's brother Edward and was dated the day she had been taken ill.

Scarletti Publishing
Regent Street
London
March 1872

Dear Mina,

I hope this finds you well, and that the Brighton weather is more pleasant than that of last month. London is still unseasonably cold, and there are the usual coughs and chills about, so we must all take great care, and it would be best for you not to visit us at present.

My darling Agatha is like a spring flower, her beauty is admired wherever she goes. I am truly fortunate. We have decided on an autumn wedding after which if business permits, we will take a short tour of the continent.

Enid and Mother are both as well as they can be under the circumstances, but they cannot agree on anything, and for reasons which entirely escape me I am expected to settle their quarrels, which can be very tiresome. There are whole days when they hardly speak to each other, and that is a blessing.

Nothing further has been heard from Mr Inskip in recent weeks, from which we may deduce that he is either alive or dead, but we have no means of knowing which. Enid remains frantic about the prospect of his early return. She has been perusing the newspapers reading about storms at sea and attempting to divine the chances of passenger ships foundering with all on board, which to her taste were disappointingly slight. Mother keeps asking for my advice, but she never takes it.

I feel I should warn you that you may discover Richard on your doorstep in the near future. I am sorry to have to inform you of this, but his association with Scarletti Publishing is at an end. If he wishes to make money without working for it then our business is not for him. In fact, I can scarcely think of any business which is. You may think it a cruel thing to dismiss one's own brother, but sometimes one must be cruel to be kind.

While he has some artistic talent, he does not take the trouble over it that he once did, and I am frankly wearied of his petty excuses.

Likewise, I can no longer allow him to live with me without paying rent. Agatha has been looking over the house with a view to making preparations for our marriage and has made it clear to me that Richard's absence from the premises will be essential to her domestic happiness. He has therefore been advised to find fresh accommodation. I have not yet told Mother about these arrangements. I have quite enough to do without facing her displeasure with which I know she will regale me on a daily basis.

Your affectionate brother
Edward

'Are you alright, Miss?' said Rose, with a frown.

Mina realised that she had been perusing the letter rather longer than might have seemed necessary from its length. 'Oh — er — yes, this is from my brother Edward with so much interesting news in it,' said Mina, forcing a cheerful smile. 'Just think, he plans to marry Miss Hooper in the autumn. That is something to look forward to. Are there any more letters?'

'One more.'

'Please bring it.'

Saltmire & Vardy
Fine Porcelain
Hove
March 1872

Dear Miss Scarletti,

I hope that you will permit me to appeal to you since I am a mother in torment. I find my family afflicted by a very strange and disturbing plight which has at its centre my elder son, Franklin, who is aged just fourteen.

My first husband was Mr Jasper Holt, who died in a sailing accident in 1864. Sadly, he was lost at sea and since his body was never found, he has only recently been declared deceased. My younger son, Matthew is ten years of age and therefore does not have a strong recollection of his father, however Franklin has very fond memories of my late husband to whom he was very attached.

It is of course upsetting for any child to lose a beloved parent, and when I was finally granted a death certificate for Jasper and therefore allowed to consider myself a widow in law, Franklin felt, I believe, as if he had lost that parent for a second time, and the situation aroused old griefs. He was also unhappy at my decision to marry Mr Vardy whom I have known for three years and who has been a very good friend to my family.

Franklin has been receiving an excellent education at one of the foremost preparatory schools in Brighton, and some weeks ago a package was delivered there by a messenger boy. Unfortunately, the boy had vanished by the time the package was opened and all efforts to trace him have been unsuccessful. The package was addressed to my son and contained a watch — a family heirloom which was once the property of his father who had inherited it from his father before him. Franklin recognised it at once, and the engraving left us in no doubt.

For some years I have been attending meetings with Mrs Barnham the clairvoyant and spirit medium, of whom you may have heard. She is a lady of great wisdom and impeccable connections, having been a prominent person at the court of the late King William. I took the watch to her and when she held it in her hands she knew at once that the owner of it had passed.

This information has done nothing to quell a rising discomfort in the mind of my poor son, who has been afflicted with increasingly disturbing symptoms. He is under treatment from our doctor but has been unable to attend school for some time. The manifestations of his condition are highly unusual, and some of the things he says are such that I cannot commit them to paper. But he does claim to have seen his father's ghost and heard it speak to him.

Miss Scarletti, all that I have read about you in the newspapers encourages me to think that you will be able to advise me. What must I do? Is there someone I should consult? Or would you be willing to interview my poor afflicted boy and deduce what course of action I ought to take?

Assuring you of my very greatest respect,
Charlotte Vardy

Mina was quiet for a while, then she read the letter again. She looked up. Rose and Miss Cherry were gazing at her very intently, studying her for signs of incipient collapse. She took the deepest calmest breath she could muster. 'Rose,' she said, 'I would so enjoy a nice cup of tea. And could you bring me a small plain biscuit?' She turned to Miss Cherry. 'I assume that Dr Hamid has not forbidden tea and plain biscuits?'

Miss Cherry looked pleased and relieved. 'I expect he would be very happy that you have regained some appetite. This is the first food you have asked for since you became ill.' She nodded to Rose, who gave Mina one of her expressionless yet meaningful looks, then went downstairs.

'Miss Cherry,' said Mina, and the nurse, understanding her confidential tone, drew nearer. 'This letter is from Mrs Vardy. It is most probably the one she told you she was writing to me, and I believe that the contents will not be a surprise to you. Mrs Vardy has told me a great deal about the difficulties she is facing and is clearly eager to come and tell me other things that she feels unable to write down.'

Mina handed the letter to Miss Cherry who perused it carefully, then nodded. 'Yes, all of this I have been told or overheard.'

'Are you, in the light of this letter, willing to tell me more? I ask not out of simple curiosity but because I would like to help this poor afflicted lady and her family. I assume that your attendance at her home was in order to care for the son?'

Miss Cherry nodded again. 'Yes, it was. His symptoms were most alarming. Sometimes when he awoke there was a minute or two when he could not move and struggled even to breathe. But he also —' she looked pained — 'he also had the strangest fancies, which he did sometimes confide to me. He thought the ghost of his father was visiting him in the night. But the thing that most troubles Mrs Vardy,' added Miss Cherry, sadly, 'is that her son Franklin believes that she and Mr Vardy were responsible for the death of her first husband.'

Mina glanced back at the letter. 'But Mrs Vardy has only known Mr Vardy for three years.'

'That is what she says,' replied Miss Cherry, 'but who can prove it?'

When Rose arrived, Mina sipped her tea and nibbled the edge of the biscuit, then, having shown herself capable of reading letters without any harm to herself, she asked for a tray and some writing materials, and as soon as they arrived she composed a reply to Mrs Vardy.

Dear Mrs Vardy,

I am sorry not to have replied to your letter sooner, however I have been very unwell and am at present confined to bed under strict orders not to attempt anything that might prove to be too interesting for my slight energies to tolerate. I am eager to assist you in any way I can, and hope that in a short while it will be possible to arrange an interview where we might discuss your concerns more openly than letters will permit.

Assuring you of the strictest confidence at all times
Mina Scarletti

CHAPTER THREE

The news of Mina's improvement brought her mother to the sickroom for one of her rare visits. Now that Louisa Scarletti was less terrified of losing her eldest daughter, she was able to allow her displeasure free rein.

'You have frightened me so much!' she exclaimed, sitting at a careful distance from the bedside. Still nervous of infection, she clutched a lace handkerchief drenched in cologne which she held before her face. A comforting maternal embrace was clearly out of the question. Louisa was achingly thin and pale as a spectre, her eyelids flushed rose with sleeplessness and tears, but she was still in her mature years, a vision of porcelain beauty. A widow for more than two years, she had adopted the fashionable demi-mourning colour of deep violet, with a daring hint of white trimming. This allowed her to remain an object of sympathy while at the same time dipping her slippered toes into Brighton society where she best flourished. 'You were told not to go out in company,' she said reproachfully, 'Dr Hamid told you so and I told you so, everyone told you so, but no, you would not listen to good advice, and now see what is the result. You know how much I rely on you, Mina, and you must not upset me like this again!'

'I promise I will take more care in future,' said Mina, contritely.

Louisa was unappeased. 'You cannot imagine how I feel! What with Enid in her delicate condition, and Mr Inskip heaven knows where, and the twins have started teething again, and they cannot be kept quiet and my head aches without ceasing, and now this! I don't know what I have done to be punished so.'

'How is my dear sister?' Mina ventured.

Louisa uttered one of her long groaning sighs. 'I only hope and pray that she and the child will live. The doctor says we may expect only one this time, and for that at least, I am thankful. But your sister is a torment to me. She complains all the time, of this and that, and who knows what else, and it is as much as I can do to try and console her. Neither of us have any sleep. Neither of us eat. Oh, when will the agony end!'

'I imagine Edward is a great support to you,' said Mina, trying to sound encouraging. 'He is so very sensible, and reliable,' she added, naming the two qualities in which her younger brother Richard was notably deficient.

Louisa gave a scoff that was very nearly a snarl. 'Edward has his head in the clouds all the time, he does not see how I suffer. All his thoughts are for the business and Miss Hooper — Agatha as I suppose I must call her, but I cannot like the girl. She and her pretty books of pressed flowers. He praises her all the time, but I have seen her flowers and do not think all of them are as pretty as he likes to make out. Some of them are very strange indeed. I would not dare show them to you, the very sight of them would make you quite ill. Oh, I know she comes from a prominent family and will bring money to the match, but I sometimes think she has bewitched my boy who can see nothing but good in her, and he often forgets he has family of his own. I believe that if she so much as pricked her little finger he would fly to her side at once, while I am left alone to manage as best I can.'

'Is there to be a family gathering to celebrate the betrothal?' asked Mina.

Louisa's look of resignation revealed that the prospect did not please her. 'I believe so, but I am too upset to even think of it. Edward says he will delay it until you are well, and Enid is recovered from her confinement, whenever that may be. She cannot tell me the date; she seems very vague on that point, but I dare not press her because when I ask about it, she flies into a temper. And Edward does hardly anything to help me with her. Sometimes he just stands there with a ridiculous expression on his face and says nothing at all, and what good is that to anyone?'

'Poor Mother,' said Mina. 'I will try to get well as soon as I can.' She reached out to pat her mother's hand but thought better of it.

Louisa found a dry scrap of lace and carefully blotted her eyes. 'At least Richard is settled in his career at last. I always knew he would be a success. It was so thoughtful of him to ask to be spared from his London work so he could come here and be a comfort to me. But I have told him that once Enid is well and I am back in Brighton for good he must come and live here all the time to be near me, and he has promised me that he will. It will be no trouble at all for him to travel to the London office when he is needed. What else are trains for, after all? What a good son he is!'

Mina's heart sank. Richard was the only one of her siblings who in her mother's estimation could do no wrong. Louisa had always been confident of a bright future for him, and at present these thoughts were the only ones that could gave her any pleasure. Once again, a heavy responsibility had fallen upon Mina's fragile shoulders. During the current family upheaval, she was obliged not only to protect her mother from the dismal truth about her favourite son, but also to take steps to mend the situation.

Once her mother had left she requested her writing materials and composed a letter to her older brother.

Dear Edward,

I understand that you have been told of my indisposition. You will be pleased to know that I am improving, and Dr Hamid considers me to be out of danger, but I am still confined to bed, and may be for some time.

I have only recently been permitted to read your last letter. Richard, as you correctly surmised is now here, as is Mother. The situation is quite possibly beyond my strength to manage, but I must attempt it all the same. Dr Hamid has arranged for a nurse to tend to me and for that I am grateful.

I cannot think of any message to send to Enid which would not upset her further, but I do think of her constantly and hope that she can find some peace and comfort. I leave it to your judgement of her capacity to appreciate sympathy as to whether or not to pass my words to her.

I send my good wishes to you and Miss Hooper and look forward to knowing her better. I am eagerly anticipating being able to view her collection of pressed flowers,

Affectionately
Mina

Mina's appetite, which was always moderate at best, was finally returning, if her largely favourable reaction to the scent of cooking dinner was anything to judge by. This was just as well, since the aroma could not be prevented from floating upstairs and became apparent in her room every time the door was opened. She assumed it to be some kind of boiled joint with vegetables which would be reinvented as hash for the following day's luncheon. Rose eventually arrived with a bowl of meat broth in which a slice of bread was floating. Mysterious things lurked beneath like creatures in a pond.

'Cook says there's arrowroot pudding if you want it,' said Rose.

Mina prodded the bread with her spoon. Dark slivers of onion rose to the surface of the liquid and sank again. 'I'll let you know,' she said.

In the event, she managed most of both the broth and the bread and set the dish aside.

Rose had removed the bowl and Miss Cherry was in her accustomed place when Richard arrived. He had the contented smile of the recently fed and the cheerful step of a man who did not yet know the fate that Mina had in store for him.

He sat on the bed beside Mina, and Miss Cherry gave a soft cough. 'If you please, Mr Scarletti,' she said gently, 'do not sit on the patient's bed.'

He jumped up. 'Oh dear, I am so sorry, I didn't know it was a rule! That is very bad of me, and I promise not to do it again.' He drew a chair to the bedside, and once seated, fastened all his attention on Mina. 'How are you, my girl? I hope you managed to eat some dinner.'

'I did. It was — adequate.'

'Mother protested that she was unable to eat at all.'

'Did she eat?'

'Heartily. And two glasses of wine, which she claimed were for medicinal purposes. But I have come with some news. I was at the benefit performance of Mr Merridew's Hamlet this afternoon and very splendid it is, too. I especially liked the musical interlude and Polonius' comic dance. But I took the opportunity of speaking to him afterwards to let him know that you are unwell. You should have seen his face; it was like the two masks — you know — the ones you see in the theatre all the time, one moment distraught to know of your illness —' Richard made a comically mournful face — 'and then all smiles —' he reversed his downturned mouth into a joyous beam —

'to learn that you are mending. He has another performance tonight, it is the very last one, and he promises to call on you tomorrow. Oh — I hope that isn't against the rules!' Richard turned to Miss Cherry. 'Visitors are permitted, are they not?'

The nurse's watchful expression had softened considerably, and she smiled. 'I am sure that a special allowance can be made for Mr Merridew as long as he does not make noise.'

'He will certainly cheer me up,' said Mina, and now she thought about it there might be a way in which her actor friend could assist her in the case of the missing Mr Holt. 'The other thing that cheers me is that Dr Hamid has permitted me to receive my correspondence at last,' she added.

'Oh. That is good,' said Richard. 'I know how you like letters. Have you heard from Nellie? Is she well? How is Italy?'

'I have received a letter from her, and she is enjoying the fine weather and the company there.'

Richard was thoughtful. 'Are there mountains in Italy? I have feeling there might be.'

'There are, but I doubt that Nellie will be attempting them, although I am sure she would make an accomplished Alpinist if she ever took up the sport.'

'What about her nasty husband?' said Richard with a sour expression. 'It would be very convenient if he was to climb up to the top of a mountain and fall off. I wish he would.'

'I think that would be a very unpleasant circumstance for everyone concerned.'

'I doubt it.'

'But Richard —' Mina prodded his arm to get his attention — 'I need to speak to you now on serious family business.'

'Really?' he protested. 'Must you? Serious talks are such a bore.'

'Yes, I insist.' Mina turned to the nurse. 'Miss Cherry, if you could oblige us?'

The nurse understood and departed without raising an objection.

Mina took her brother by the hand. Her own hands, now she looked at them, were almost child-sized by comparison, and both together could not encompass his one. 'Richard I want you to concentrate very carefully on what I am saying. This is very important.'

'I always listen to you, Mina, you know I do.'

Mina gave his fingers an affectionate squeeze. 'You know how much I worry about my family. And there always seems to be so much to worry about. At present, however, Enid is as well as we can reasonably expect, Edward is thriving and looking forward to his wedding, and Dr Hamid has confirmed to me that Mother is in good health, and that I am on the mend, so —' she paused for emphasis — 'the only person I need to be concerned about is you.'

'Me?' Richard laughed. 'Oh, Mina dear, I assure you, you have nothing to worry about. I am well and happy.'

'And prospering?' she queried.

'But of course!'

'Does Edward pay you well?'

He shrugged. 'Oh, you know Edward, his is ever the closed purse, but actually I am beginning to think that all this business nonsense is starting to suit me. And it is the family business after all, so I will probably be made a partner one day.'

Mina knew that look from Richard — the bland, open-countenanced expression of a soul at peace with his conscience, the look that always told her he was lying.

'Richard,' she said softly, 'I know your situation. I know why you are here. I received a letter from Edward. He told me everything.'

It took several moments for denial and protest to cross her brother's features and scurry away in shame, then his posture slumped. 'I was going to tell you, really I was.'

'I assume that Mother doesn't yet know?'

He shook his head and tried to look at her appealingly. Mina believed that she was one of the few people in the world who was immune to this expression.

She patted his hand. 'Don't worry, I will say nothing to her for now. But it is not for your sake. I have no wish to conspire with you to keep your secrets, but Mother has far too much to concern her at present, with both her daughters indisposed, and I don't want to upset her any more. I will not, however, be silent for ever. I will allow you perhaps three months, to make some significant improvement in your prospects. By that time, I sincerely hope that Enid and her new-born and I will all be less of a trial to Mother. So I suggest that you begin looking for a new career without delay.'

Richard, as Mina expected, did not appear pleased by this demand. He withdrew his hand from hers and searched in his pockets, as he usually did when looking for the small cigars he favoured, but then he caught the look in her eye and desisted.

'There isn't anything else I am suited to,' he sighed. 'I had hoped to marry well, but the season is done here, so all the rich families with single daughters are gone.' He rested his elbows on his knees, chin in his hands. 'Why didn't Father leave me more money?'

Mina made no compromises with the truth. 'Because the value of his estate mainly lay in this house and the business. He left you enough to make a start in life, and you spent it.'

Richard gave a little groan and rubbed the heels of his hands into his eyes. 'If Mr Jordan would only oblige me by falling off a mountain, Nellie would be rich and I could marry her. I know she'd have me.'

'Richard, please be serious.'

'I am!'

'Then be practical. Find some occupation which will enable you to earn your keep; something respectable that won't have to be kept a secret from Mother, and then stay with it. That is all we ask of you.'

He pouted. 'You make it sound so easy.'

'Other people in the world achieve it. Richard, you cannot go on like this forever — living a life of pleasure on other people's money.'

Mina's heart sank, because from her brother's expression that was exactly what he thought he could do.

CHAPTER FOUR

Mina never felt weaker than after the regular bedding and nightdress change and tepid sponge bath, delivered with brisk efficiency by Miss Cherry, but it was a wonderful relief when it was over and she could sink at last into laundered linen and newly plumped pillows, feeling very much as a monarch must feel when lying upon what he suspected might turn out to be his deathbed.

Thus enthroned, she received the visit of Mr Marcus Merridew, the famous actor of Brighton.

Mr Merridew entered every room as if emerging from the wings onto a stage where he was the acknowledged leading man. It naturally followed that the mere act of his appearing made him the admired object of all eyes. On his arrival, he stood for a moment, framed by the open doorway, looking like the portrait of a great benefactor, and gazing upon Mina with a tender and wistful expression, before extending his arms and bowing with deep respect.

Mr Merridew, as Mina knew, had not one single hair on his head, which was as smooth and polished and pink as a sweet apple. In his recently acclaimed portrayal of Hamlet, he had been wearing a wig of long straight darkly melancholy locks but he was now displaying a torrent of golden curls that dipped almost to his shoulders, an echo of the long-departed wavelets of his youth that had once shimmered in the limelight, and made his legions of lady admirers sigh.

'Dear, dear Miss Scarletti,' he breathed, 'how delighted I am to see you again, although the circumstances of this visit leave something to be desired. I hope and trust that you will soon be in good health, and when you are, we must take refreshments together at one of the select establishments of Brighton and talk about the delights of the town. I cannot as yet entertain you at my apartments as they are being extensively decorated and are quite unfit for visitors.'

Miss Cherry brought a chair for the honoured guest and set it by the bed. 'It is a pleasure to meet you, Mr Merridew,' she said, a little shyly.

'Oh likewise,' he smiled. 'I am sure that your good care of my dear friend will soon restore her.'

Miss Cherry blushed at the compliment, and was unable to prevent herself from blurting out, 'My mother will be beside herself when she knows I have met you! She has seen all your plays!'

Mr Merridew, with practised ease, looked not one whit offended at this reminder of his antiquity. 'Please convey my very best wishes to your dear mother,' he said, as he took his seat.

'May I offer you some refreshment?' asked Mina.

'Thank you, but tonight I am attending a little soiree given in my honour, and I have been promised a veritable feast of delicacies. One must mind one's figure, I am afraid.' He patted his stomach, which still retained the lissom contours of his youth.

'You look so very well,' said Mina. 'The stage is such an arduous profession.'

'Why thank you, dear lady,' exclaimed Mr Merridew. 'She is indeed a demanding mistress but will not be denied.' He still knew how to make the curls ripple with a toss of his head and patted them every so often presumably to reassure himself that they were still in place. 'I have brought a little gift to cheer you.' He brought a prettily coloured envelope from his pocket and handed it to her with a smile and a flourish.

'Oh, what can it be?' said Mina. She extracted a photograph — a portrait of Mr Merridew as Hamlet, inscribed to herself. He was arrayed in the military costume he had worn in the last scene of the play, standing in a fierce yet noble posture, and brandishing the sword with which he was about to defeat the entire Norwegian army. He was not, fortunately, displaying the decapitated head of Fortinbras, a grisly object which had, on the night when Mina had been in the theatre, elicited shrieks of alarm from the audience and caused one large and soldierly looking gentleman in the front row to faint.

'How splendid,' said Mina, 'I must have it framed.'

'There will be more!' Mr Merridew promised. 'My audiences clamour for them, there can never be enough. I am about to arrange for a sitting at the newest fashionable establishment in town to create a set of beautiful portraits in my finest costumes. There will be something to suit every taste.'

'I will purchase them all, of course,' said Mina. 'And an album to put them in.' Mina knew enough of Mr Merridew's profession not to ask about his next dramatic offering in case he was to suffer the embarrassment of admitting that there was not one.

'And I have news. My next engagement will be a season of poetry readings at a salon in the Royal Pavilion, accompanied by light refreshments. I do hope that you will be well enough to attend.'

'I will be sure to do so if at all possible. The Pavilion is quite my favourite place in all of Brighton.'

'As it is mine.'

Mina seized the opportunity offered by this observation to discover more about the spirit medium who was being consulted by Mrs Vardy. 'Mr Merridew, you are so very knowledgeable on all matters concerning the Pavilion, its treasures, and most especially its history. I have a question to ask you. I have recently been told of a lady who resides in Brighton and who claims to have been a member of the court of the late King William. She is called Mrs Barnham. Can you advise me — is her claim true, or is she merely a pretender?'

Mr Merridew allowed a smile to slowly curve his lips and there was a teasing twinkle in his eyes. 'Ah yes, the once famous Mrs Barnham. She is included in a little work I composed on ladies of the Royal Court at the Pavilion. But I have not heard that name for many a year. Is she still alive? She must be eighty or more.'

Mina could not conceal her surprise. 'Then she spoke the truth? She was a member of the court? I ask because it is so easy for someone to make a claim of fame and position in order to advance themselves, when there are regrettably few means of assuring oneself of the truth of the story. It is such a shame when people allow themselves to believe whatever they are told.'

Mr Merridew was thoughtful. 'If this is the actual Mrs Barnham and not an impostor, I can tell you that she was indeed at court, but not under that name. Her attendance there was prior to her marriage. And before she graced the court of King William, she was also well-known at the court of King George.' He paused. 'Extremely well-known.'

The implication hung in the air during a long silence. Mr Merridew glanced at the nurse and then back to Mina, who understood his meaning, and mouthed a little 'oh.'

'Miss Cherry,' said Mina at last. 'I am not sure that Rose has been diligent enough in the soaking of the linens. I would be grateful if you could go and watch over her and see that she does it correctly.'

Miss Cherry looked put out. She stared at Mina and Mr Merridew as if they were asking to be left alone in order to flirt. She rose to her feet, awkwardly. 'I will do so, of course. But Mr Merridew, I feel it is my duty to advise you that Miss Scarletti must not be subjected to any excitement. She is still only recently out of danger.'

'You have my word as a gentleman,' said Mr Merridew, placing his hand on his heart, and giving the nurse a look that would have dissolved granite, 'that Miss Scarletti will be cared for as she deserves, as a very great treasure.'

'And now,' said Mina, once Miss Cherry had left the room, 'I wish to know all about Mrs Barnham.'

Mr Merridew smiled, and adopted a heroic pose, that of a man about to declaim a work of great literature from memory.

'In 1805' he began, 'the Prince of Wales, who was then forty-two years of age, and still, so we are told, in the prime of his health and vigour, became greatly interested in a young actress, a Miss Margaret Green. She was then just eighteen and was appearing on the stage of the Theatre Royal Covent Garden where she was performing in a comedy, *The School of Reform: or How to Rule a Husband* in which she portrayed the virtuous Julia. The Prince at once demanded, and of course received, an introduction.

'Miss Green's powers of attraction were singular and undeniable, not only for the beauty of her face and form, which were considerable, and the refined elegance and good taste of her attire, but also the wit of her conversation which made her company highly agreeable to those of both sexes. It was said of her that she could persuade even the least susceptible of men to accommodate her every wish and achieve that without him so much as being aware of having fallen under her influence. Miss Green soon became a great favourite at court since gentlemen admired her and ladies found in her a good friend and trustworthy confidante. It is believed that when the Prince was in Brighton, she had her own secret apartment at the Royal Pavilion to which he repaired nightly to receive the consolation of her company.

'Miss Green remained a constant presence throughout the Regency and was a particular comfort to the Prince during the long indisposition of his father. Unlike so many ladies of the court, she never clamoured for fame and position, and therefore never, as so many others did, fell out of favour. On the Prince's accession as King George IV in 1820 her general popularity secured her position. Her skill in conversation never declined, and she was also adept with playing cards, being much in demand by the ladies of the nobility for the telling of fortunes.

'On the death of King George in 1830 it was found that he had made arrangements for Miss Green to receive a small pension and his successor King William IV generously permitted her a minor role at court. This continued until King William's death in 1837, after which she was no longer seen in royal circles.'

'And Miss Green became Mrs Barnham?' asked Mina.

'She did. Our good and gracious Queen on her accession to the throne examined the royal finances and when she discovered that pensions were being paid to former mistresses, put an end to them. Miss Green received a small sum in lieu, and a letter to the effect that her attendance at court was no longer required. She was not in a position to protest. Soon afterwards she became the wife of Mr Barnham, a maker of ships' instruments. Their modest income was enhanced by her skills in fortune telling. And then came the fashion for table tipping and she saw her chance to make money from mediumship.'

'Then this lady may well be who she claims,' said Mina. 'But I am not sure that she still performs table tipping. I have been told that she has a machine that receives messages from the spirits.'

This was news to Mr Merridew. 'Does she now?'

'I would very much like to see something like that, but of course it is not possible at present. Perhaps — I hardly like to ask — but could you make some enquiries for me?'

'But of course, I should be glad to do so.'

Mina reflected that an unfortunate result of her reputation for exposing mediumistic frauds was that many mediums refused to admit her to their presence, whether they were conducting a séance or not, and disguise was for her, not an option. Was Mrs Barnham sufficiently confident of her powers to admit a sceptic to her circle, or could she even be, and this was a possibility Mina did not dismiss, a genuine psychic? Time would provide the answer.

'But I think it would be best if you did not mention my name. Yours opens doors, but in the world of the spirit mediums mine closes them.'

'I understand.'

Mina had a new inspiration. 'In fact — why not make it known that you are writing a book about life at the court of King William, and wish to consult her? Nothing is more probable, and she is bound to be flattered. You might even offer to dedicate the volume to her.'

'Flattery is one of the great arts,' said Mr Merridew with a smile. 'The sign of a true master is knowing when to paint it thick and when to brush it thin.'

'In fact, your book should be the whole of your story. When asked, its subject should come easily to your lips.'

'Have no fear, I will know my part well and perform it to perfection. But tell me, do you know anything to the detriment of this lady? Do you think her a cheat?'

Mina paused, as she was unsure how much she ought to reveal of her true interest in Mrs Barnham's circle. 'As to that I have no information,' she said. 'I wish to satisfy my curiosity, not only concerning the lady herself and her unusual methods, but also those who believe in her. Think of it as a study to amuse me in these idle times. I am sure it will do me good to interest myself in something.'

'Then I am content to be your eyes and ears.'

'Only I would prefer it if we did not speak of this matter in front of Miss Cherry or Rose. They might consider the question likely to overheat my brain and cause a relapse, which is nonsense of course. And say nothing to Richard. Not a word, or he will only tell everyone about it, and then he will be very sorry he did so, and it will be impossible not to forgive him.'

Miss Cherry returned reporting that she had made a careful examination of Rose's steeping of the linens and corrected her in her methods. She took her seat again. There was a look in her eye which suggested to Mina that she would be hard to remove a second time.

'And now,' said Mr Merridew rising to his feet in one elegant movement, 'it is with great regret that I must take my leave of such charming ladies. But do not fear, I shall return!' And so, with much bowing and gestures of appreciation, he departed.

Miss Cherry, still looking a little pink about the ears, although that might possibly have been the effect of the hot water steeping the linens, drew her book from her apron pocket and opened it. 'The History of Butterflies' she announced.

Mina leaned back on the pillows and allowed her mind to flutter pleasantly through speculation.

How, she asked herself, might someone alleviate the sufferings of Mrs Vardy and her son? Only one course of action came to mind. The situation stemmed directly from the disappearance of Mr Jasper Holt in 1864, and his unknown fate. The answer was therefore to discover the location and history of the missing man, thus putting an end to uncertainty, morbid fear and suspicion. The truth might prove to be mundane, scandalous or tragic, but Mina believed that if someone wanted the truth then they had to be prepared from the start to discover that it was not the one for which they had hoped. There would of course always be some people who even when faced with the undeniable truth would refuse to believe it and prefer their own creations, but she couldn't help that.

Mr Jasper Holt, like Mina's brother-in-law Mr Inskip, was either alive or dead, but unlike Mr Inskip it was possible for him to be both at once, since he was legally dead, but could be alive in fact. The combination of threatened bankruptcy and a recent and substantial policy of insurance strongly suggested that when he set out on his boat trip, he had intended either to end his life, or as the Brighton and Hove Insurance Company clearly believed, falsify his death.

Mina knew nothing about policies of insurance, but she thought it logical for a number of reasons that no payment would be made in the event of a death by suicide. If Mr Holt intended his family to benefit under the policy, therefore, his real or false death had to appear to be an accident. And he had to be demonstrably dead, rather than merely missing or he would be, as had been proven, a mystery without any solution other than a seven year wait.

The question therefore was how had Mr Holt planned to prove himself dead without actually being dead? A man in his profession would have had no bloated corpse easily to hand to impersonate him, so he was obliged to disappear under circumstances that led to the inevitable conclusion that he was dead. In other words, he needed a reliable witness to his demise. Enter Mr William Sutherland, experienced boatman, as either criminal accomplice or innocent associate to add veracity to the tale.

Mina reflected that she knew nothing about Mr Sutherland other than that in 1864 he had owned a small yacht which he was willing to sell and knew how to sail it. Mr Holt, if still alive would be in his fifties but she did not know Mr Sutherland's age, occupation or place of residence. These facts might be discoverable, but there were other things she might never know. What was the true character of Mr Holt? What for that matter were the true characters of Mrs Vardy and Mr Sutherland? Were their innocent faces merely masks of deception?

When Miss Cherry had finished the history of butterflies she was about to embark on the subject of fancy needlework, when Mina asked if she might have her letters to read again. The letters had been placed in a box on her desk, one that contained her personal papers, and to which only she had the key. Miss Cherry brought the box, and Mina once more studied Mrs Vardy's letter. What could she glean of the missing Mr Holt? His son was very attached to him, suggesting that he had been a kind father. His actions also showed that he was a man determined to support his family although whether from love, a sense of duty or both, was unknown. Not having the means to do so, he had undertaken a desperate plan to ensure their future comfort. If he had cared nothing for his wife and sons he would, as men sometimes did, have simply deserted them.

It could not have been any part of his plan for the insurance money not to be paid. Which left the question of what had the plan actually been? Had he intended a later return to his wife and children under another name? Was Mrs Vardy an accomplice?

The courts had been willing to believe that since nothing had been heard from him for seven years since his disappearance, he should be regarded as deceased. Would such a man, if alive, even if he was in hiding from fear of discovery and imprisonment for fraud, have found some means of contacting his family? Had he in fact done so?

Mina also meditated on the fact that young Franklin had received a good education, the kind his father would have wished for him. Yet without the insurance money the estate would have been worthless. How had the expense been met?

Then there were the newspaper reports mentioned by Miss Cherry, the details of which had been refreshed in her mind by recent gossip. Had Mr Holt been telling the truth when he told Mr Sutherland that he was advised to take the sea air for his health? And was there any significance to his proposed visit to Shoreham? Who was the detective employed by Mrs Vardy's brother and what, if anything did he discover? There was, she realised, one enquiry she could easily make from her bed. If Mr Sutherland still lived in Brighton, she had the means of discovering his address.

CHAPTER FIVE

Miss Cherry settled in her chair, opened her little book, and cleared her throat in preparation for a new reading. 'Sincerity,' she announced, but Mina quickly interrupted her.

'I am sorry, but I cannot help myself — I am so distracted and cannot attend to your reading — all I can think of is poor Mrs Vardy and the sufferings of her child. Please can you reassure me of something, and set my mind at rest and then I can be content, — since you were able to leave your duties and consign young Franklin to the care of his family, then that must mean that his health has improved of late?'

Miss Cherry laid the book in her lap. 'I am reluctant to say anything, since I don't want to upset you —'

'Oh, please, I beg of you, the truth. I will know if you are making light of it. Imagination can be more upsetting if the truth is hidden.'

Miss Cherry, bound to care for her patient, did not like to hear this. 'Very well. I do not believe that he has improved. Mrs Vardy has a sister, a Mrs Norbert of Southsea. She is a very organising kind of lady, who I am sure must be excellent in her own way, but despite understanding nothing of his condition she has taken it upon herself to know what is best for her nephew. I don't believe Mrs Vardy sent for her, but she arrived at the house one day announcing in a very loud way that her sister's troubles were over, as she had come to take charge. There was no denying her. Mrs Vardy was very apologetic, but I was informed that she no longer required my services. That is her choice, of course.' Miss Cherry's opinion of this development was very apparent from her tone of voice.

'Does Mrs Norbert have any experience of caring for invalids?' asked Mina.

'All mothers must do to some extent; as in the normal ailments of childhood. As far as I have been able to learn, Mrs Norbert has a husband who is a chandler, two grown sons in good health who assist in the business and idle hands. I very much doubt that she has ever had to care for a boy who is afflicted like Franklin Holt. I did happen to encounter Mrs Vardy quite recently and asked after Franklin, but it was clear to me from her manner that if anything he was more indisposed than when he was under my care. I think she would have liked to engage me again but feared offending her sister.'

'It would appear that Mrs Norbert has failed to work her powers of healing,' said Mina. 'When I am feeling well again, I will arrange to meet Mrs Vardy and I hope to be able to advise her on whatever it is she wishes to ask me.'

'But you are not nearly well enough for that,' said Miss Cherry, sternly. 'When such a meeting becomes possible, I will advise you of it. The poor lady, I do feel for her, but I am not sure how you might be able to help her.'

'If nothing else I can try and put an end to the cruel rumours,' said Mina. 'I could write a letter to the newspapers, perhaps, or put a word in the right quarters. I have friends in Brighton who would be sympathetic and could introduce Mrs Vardy back into good society. That might be all that is needed. And when she is more content, then her family will be too. Sometimes all that is required is a period of calm and a little common sense.'

Miss Cherry nodded and returned to her book. 'Sincerity,' she read, 'expresses a quality which belongs to the mind and the heart. Sincerity is —'

'But what can you tell me of Mr Sutherland, the boatman? He too must be suffering under a cloud of ill-informed suspicion. Does he still reside in Brighton?'

'I am not sure,' said Miss Cherry.

'Although he was not charged with any offence, there must be many who still think that he was not being truthful about what happened on the yacht and was Mr Holt's accomplice in a plot to defraud the insurance company. You know how people like to believe the worst, even when there is no evidence for it. I wish I could speak to him.'

Miss Cherry sighed. She was clearly regretting having raised the matter in the first place. A tale told of events that took place almost eight years before was one thing, but she had started a hare running that she now felt should not be encouraged.

'Please indulge me in this, 'said Mina, sensing Miss Cherry's reservations. 'My body may be weak, but my mind is still strong. It keeps me alive when all else fails. Thoughts are as good as breath to me.'

'Dr Hamid was very strict,' said Miss Cherry, with a frown, but she was wavering. 'I feel I have already said too much.'

'But you are here beside me to judge if I go too far. I will rely on you and take your advice, I promise. Will you tell me what you know?'

There was a silence then Miss Cherry slowly nodded.

'What do you know about Mr Sutherland?'

'Only that I heard he was a professional gentleman.'

Mina was surprised. 'So he was not a boatman by trade? I had imagined him as a man who took visitors on sea trips.'

'No, I think that was only his amusement.'

'What was his profession?'

'Something in finance, I believe.'

'I wonder if there was a business connection between him and Mr Holt?' mused Mina, but from Miss Cherry's expression she clearly didn't know.

Rose arrived with a copy of *Page's Directory* which Mina had requested earlier, and Mina carefully studied its lists of residents and businesses in Brighton and nearby towns, but there was no-one with the surname Sutherland. Mina leaned back on the pillows, suddenly wearied. Had she overtaxed herself? She placed the book by her bedside but when Rose wanted to remove it, Mina placed her hand on it and shook her head.

It was possible, she thought, that Mr Sutherland, if he was something in finance might be a London man who visited Brighton for the pleasure of the climate and fresh sea air and sailing his little yacht. There were many such visitors in the summer months, professional gentlemen taking time away from the cares of business. Unfortunately, there was no London directory in the house, and any requests she might make for one to be purchased could arouse the suspicion that she was starting another enquiry, or at the very least testing her strength beyond what Dr Hamid had thought advisable.

She mused again on what she had gleaned so far. Mrs Vardy's solicitor in 1864 was a Mr Phipps, presumably a partner in Laidlaw and Phipps. Mina knew that in recent years the firm had added two more Phippses, while Mr Laidlaw had recently retired, supposedly on health grounds, but in reality, to avoid a scandal which had connected the name of his wife to that of the handsome adventurer Mr Arthur Wallace Hope.

The newest Phipps partner, Ronald of that ilk, was a sensible young man whom Mina had consulted several times in the recent past. He shared her opinion of those spirit mediums who leeched on the bereaved so as to feed on their fortunes, and he had been of considerable assistance in her enquiries. Young Mr Phipps could well be a fruitful source of information, but what reason could she offer for wanting to see him?

'Sincerity is the foundation of honesty. Honesty is uprightness of act,' continued Miss Cherry.

'Help me sit up and bring my writing materials,' said Mina.

Reluctantly, Miss Cherry put the book back in her pocket and made a careful check of Mina's brow, which was warm and flushed. 'That is enough conversation for today,' she said. 'I am not sure if I should allow you to write a letter.'

'But there is no time to lose,' said Mina, urgently. 'I require a solicitor. I am going to make my will.'

Miss Cherry started in alarm, then relented. 'Very well, I suppose you had better do so if it sets your mind at rest. Is that what you have been thinking about? I could see that you were preoccupied.'

'When one lies in bed all day one has the leisure to think of so many things,' said Mina, innocently.

Miss Cherry set some notepaper, ink and pens on a tray and put them on Mina's lap. Then she stood back and watched her charge carefully.

As Mina composed her letter to Mr Ronald Phipps, she began to wish that Saltmire and Vardy were funeral directors as that would make her task so much easier. Then a thought struck her, and she picked up *Page's Directory* once again. She found a half page advertisement for Saltmire and Vardy Fine Porcelain, listing their main products, a full brochure available on application. She read the list and smiled. How she might arrange it she was not yet sure, but she could now see a chance that her plans might fall into place.

CHAPTER SIX

Mr Ronald Phipps was about the same age as Mina, twenty-six, but in his appearance and demeanour he was deliberately courting thirty-five and seemed excessively anxious to reach forty. He was always perfectly correct in his behaviour, stiff and dignified in deportment and immaculately groomed, the first qualities required in an aspiring young solicitor. Good looks were not an essential, which was as well, since he had a face like an unhappy horse. Somewhere, lurking quietly beneath the formal exterior was a sense of humour which was rarely glimpsed, and when it was, vanished before it could be held accountable.

Mina had first consulted him on the subject of Miss Eustace, a spirit medium who had once been fashionable in Brighton. This lady had used her formidable skills in both conjuring and persuasion to extract large sums of money from her admirers who included Mina's mother and her friends. Mr Phipps had proved to be an invaluable ally in Mina's campaign to expose these criminal activities before any of the victims were ruined. As a result of their joint endeavours Miss Eustace and her accomplices were now serving prison sentences for extortion, and Mr Phipps' career was ascending.

Mr Phipps was a single man. Whether he had any ambitions to change that state of being in the future was unknown. His most constant companion was an elderly aunt, a Mrs Phipps, who required to be conducted to every social gathering in town, where she would consume copious amounts of tea and cake and fall asleep. Mr Phipps took this duty very seriously, so seriously that the rumour in Brighton was that Mrs Phipps' late husband who had never been seen by anybody was an illusion, and had never existed, and that the young solicitor was actually the lady's natural son due to an indiscretion of desperate late spinsterhood.

Mr Phipps arrived to see Mina with a leather case of papers, and a worried expression which softened a little when he saw her sitting up in bed. 'Miss Scarletti, I trust you are improved in health? From your letter I assumed… Well, no matter, you are looking very well.'

'Thank you, I am better than anyone had a right to expect,' said Mina. 'I was extremely ill for a while, but I am told that if I am well looked after, which I am, I will recover. Miss Cherry has been extremely careful of my health.'

Miss Cherry brought a chair forward for Mr Phipps and allowed herself a little smile at the praise.

'We were to discuss your will, and I believe you have not made one before?'

'That is correct. I suspect that people of my age rarely make wills, but given the recent circumstances, it seemed prudent. I fear that our interview may take some time. There are many delicate matters concerning my family about which I wish to consult you.'

'Ah, yes, families,' said Mr Phipps, nodding sympathetically, but not elaborating on that comment.

Miss Cherry had returned to her chair, but now she understood the import of the exchange, and rose. 'If you don't mind, Miss Scarletti, I need to give Rose some instructions about what is required from the chemist.'

'Please do so,' said Mina. 'Would you like some refreshments, Mr Phipps?'

'No, that will not be necessary. Let us to business.'

Miss Cherry inclined her head and left the room. Mina noticed that the nurse had no difficulty in leaving her alone with Mr Phipps. Young, single and male he might be, but doctors and solicitors were in Miss Cherry's view a kind of priesthood, professional gentlemen in whom one placed one's trust and confidence absolutely. Mina felt confident that Miss Cherry would not return until the solicitor had departed.

'And how is your aunt, Mrs Phipps?' Mina enquired. 'My mother is back in Brighton now and is often quite melancholy due to her anxiety over my health. I am sure she would appreciate a visit from a friend. It would lift her spirits.'

'Oh, my aunt is well, although she is occasionally troubled with arthritis which is only to be expected, I suppose, but it does hinder her travelling about which she is determined to do for as long as possible. She goes to see Miss Hamid at the Baths who she says does her a great deal of good, and as you know, she likes to see her friends as often as she can, especially those who know how to set a tea-table. I will make sure she knows that Mrs Scarletti is returned and would like to see her.'

'Your devotion is admirable,' said Mina, 'especially considering your recent professional advancement which must demand so much of your time.'

'Thank you, but as her closest relative I know my duty. I have suggested engaging a companion, but she won't hear of it.' He puffed out a mournful little sigh as he opened his briefcase and extracted some documents.

Mina had actually given hardly any thought as to whom she might leave her small savings and other possessions. There was the sum she had received from her father's estate which she had invested wisely, her clothes, which would fit no-one but herself, a few family trinkets, and the value of her published works. Taken all together she was worth very little. Ultimately the discussion was mainly about the options open to her, and when it was complete it was decided that she would consider them, and they would meet again.

'And now the other matter you mentioned in your letter,' said Mr Phipps. 'Might I know your interest in the Holt case?'

Mina chose her words carefully. 'I have never met any of the persons concerned, and the events of that case occurred several years before our family came to live in Brighton. But there has been a great deal of talk about it recently because of Mrs Holt's remarriage to a Mr Vardy. It interested me as a mystery, as a puzzle. I feel so very idle lying here all day and I suppose it occupied my mind.'

'That is understandable,' said Mr Phipps, cautiously.

Mina waited for him to mention some obstacle to her exercising her curiosity, but he merely looked thoughtful. 'If I was well it would be another matter, but if I cannot go out and see what information I can discover, then the information must come to me.'

His expression did not change but his eyes glanced quickly at the chair Miss Cherry had recently vacated. 'I have the feeling that your nurse would not approve of you pursuing this interest.'

Mina reluctantly decided to follow the path of sincerity and honesty. 'No, she would not.'

'Nor your doctor.'

'You are correct.'

'And what of the family concerned? Is it not their private affair?'

'It is, but — this is in confidence, of course…'

'Of course.'

'I have received a letter from Mrs Vardy written before I was taken ill, in which she begged for my help. I do not feel able to refuse her.'

'And you believe that you can help her?'

'I don't see why not. I would like to try.'

'I see. What an interesting life you do lead, Miss Scarletti.' He gave the question some consideration. 'What is it you wish to know?'

Relieved, Mina consulted the sheet of writing paper on which she had assembled her thoughts. 'When Mrs Holt was married recently the newspapers said that the body of her first husband had never been found. Is that true?'

'It is. As far as I am aware the body of Mr Holt has not been found, or at least none of the bodies recovered from the sea since his disappearance have proved to be his, neither has there been any evidence that he might still be alive. Legally, however, he is dead.'

'Is it possible, do you think, for a man to fall into the sea and drown and his body not to wash ashore?'

To Mina's surprise, Mr Phipps did not need to give this question any thought. 'Yes, it is. We do a great deal of inheritance work, and we have dealt with cases of that kind in the past.'

'I have been told that Laidlaw and Phipps acted for Mrs Holt at the time of her husband's disappearance.'

'We did. I did not act in the case myself as I was then engaged in my studies and had not yet joined the firm. But in view of your interest I did take a look at the papers we have. Of course, there is much that is private, and above all — I am sure you understand this — I must protect the confidentiality of our clients. However, I do not believe I saw anything in our files that is germane to the solution of the mystery.'

'Did your firm also act for the owner of the yacht, Mr Sutherland?'

'No, he employed a London solicitor.'

'What can you tell me about him?'

This did result in a pause for thought. 'I have never met him, although my uncle did correspond with his representatives. The letters mainly indicate that the incident was not only very distressing for Mr Sutherland but a personal and professional embarrassment. There was no information that had not already appeared in the press or at the inquest.'

'Did Mr Sutherland appear to give evidence when Mr Holt was declared to be deceased?'

'There was no new evidence. Neither he nor Mrs Holt appeared. It was simply a question of going over the original statements and confirming that nothing had been seen or heard of Mr Holt since the incident in 1864. Mrs Holt had hoped it would be dealt with as discreetly as possible, and her wishes were respected. It did not attract press attention until she remarried. That was when the rumours started again,' he added with a wince of distaste.

'Were Mr Sutherland and Mr Holt business associates?'

'No. I think they met through a mutual interest in yachting. Mr Sutherland was a member of a club. I am not sure if it is still there, it was called the Brighton Yacht Club and it had rooms on Old Steine. Mr Sutherland had been a sailing enthusiast for some years, whereas Mr Holt, I think had only recently become interested in yachting. Though, of course, as it turned out —' Mr Phipps permitted himself a brief smile — 'he might not have been genuinely interested but only told Sutherland he was. Mr Sutherland lives in London, but he came to Brighton when he could and stayed at the club when he wanted a few days sailing. The club rooms offered meals and overnight accommodation for its members.'

'What is his profession?'

'He is a stockbroker.'

'Ah, yes,' said Mina, 'I can see that being questioned by the police over a death and being suspected of complicity in a fraud would have been especially embarrassing to him. Does his business still thrive? I ask because Mr Holt's scheme arose because he was in financial difficulties. I was wondering if Mr Sutherland might have been in a similar situation?'

'I have no information on Mr Sutherland's financial situation, either then or now. I suppose I could make some discreet enquiries. I do know, however, that at the time of Mr Holt's disappearance Mr Sutherland was engaged to be married. A wedding date had been set. The married state can be financially demanding even for a professional gentleman.'

So, thought Mina, even if Mr Sutherland's business was successful, he might well have been in need of money, but would that have been sufficient for him to be tempted to connive with Mr Holt in a fraud in return for a payment from the anticipated life insurance? So much depended on the character of the man.

'I assume,' said Mina, 'that a policy on someone's life will not pay out if the insured person commits suicide?'

'That is correct, or there would be many more suicides than there are. Insurance companies take an extremely poor view of being cheated, even by those extreme measures.'

'But now that he has been declared dead, will there be a payment?'

'I am quite sure that there will not be. His legal date of death is seven years from when he was last seen, and only one instalment was ever paid. The policy lapsed when the second instalment was not paid.'

'Yes, of course. I should have thought of that. So, in order to receive any payment on the insurance policy there would have to be incontrovertible proof that he died, but not by his own hand, and before the second payment was due?'

'Exactly.'

'Around the date of his disappearance.'

'Yes.'

'What sum was Mr Holt insured for?'

'Twenty thousand pounds.'

'That is a very large amount.'

'Indeed. More than sufficient to clear all his debts and leave his family well provided for.'

'But was there no difficulty in obtaining the policy, as he was not in good health?'

Mr Phipps looked surprised. 'Why do you think that?'

'I understand that he told Mr Sutherland that he had been advised by his doctor to take the sea air for his health.'

'Ah, yes, I recall that now. He may have said so, but it might not have been true, of course. The gentleman was very duplicitous. Maybe it was an excuse, a reason he gave for wanting to take up sailing. But I can tell you that before taking out insurance in such a large sum Mr Holt was examined by a doctor who certified him to be in excellent health for his age. The policy would not have been granted without it.'

'What was the name of the doctor?'

'Dr Thomas Crosier.'

'And Mr Holt paid the first instalment?'

'He did. Only the first.'

'Was it a large sum of money?'

'Two hundred pounds. There were to be monthly payments thereafter.'

'And he had the resources to pay that sum?'

'No. At that juncture his situation was extremely serious, and the bank would not have honoured a cheque on his account. He made no large cash sales of stock which might have alerted his creditors to his difficulties. He paid in gold, and we never discovered the source. We assumed that he must have borrowed it, but no-one came forward to say that they loaned it to him.'

Mina wondered about Mr Sutherland as a possible source of the funds if he was complicit in the fraud. A private loan, either from his own resources or from the business, to be repaid with interest when Mr Holt's insurance was received. Without knowing Sutherland or his circumstances she could not judge if he would be willing to take such a risk.

'If Mr Holt did try to defraud the insurance company and he was in such a precarious financial situation, that might not have been the only crime he committed, either alone or with an associate. There might have been irregularities in his business or personal dealings as well.'

'That is possible, although of course he was not there to be questioned and I don't think that was ever gone into. As you are no doubt aware the police did decide at the time that there were no grounds to charge either Mrs Holt or Mr Sutherland.'

Time passed as Mina collected her thoughts.

'Do you wish me to look into it further?' asked Mr Phipps.

'Yes, please do. And thank you for your help.'

Mr Phipps put his papers away and rose to his feet. He hesitated for a moment. 'Miss Scarletti, on another matter, I am still hoping to find a suitable nurse companion for my aunt.

75

Would you be prepared to recommend Miss Cherry for that position?'

'I would, certainly.'

'Thank you. My aunt is very particular, you see, but as her age advances the more assistance she requires. Whenever I suggest employing a companion, she protests that the usual nurses are too coarse or too strident. From my brief observation, Miss Cherry appears to be neither.'

'She is not. Her manner towards me has always been as you have seen. Her care has been excellent.'

'Perhaps when you no longer require her services —'

Mina suddenly sensed an opportunity. 'Oh, you need not wait that long. If Mrs Phipps approves, I can arrange for Miss Cherry to have a free morning or afternoon and then she can pay a call on your aunt and they can become acquainted.'

'That is very kind. Are you sure you can spare her?'

'I believe so. Our maidservant Rose can look after me for a short while, and I do not need as much attention as I did.'

'That is extremely generous of you, Miss Scarletti, I do appreciate it.' Mr Phipps, looking like a less unhappy horse, took his leave.

When Miss Cherry returned, Mina informed her of the enquiry made by Mr Phipps and the suggestion that she pay a visit to his aunt, both of which were received without protest.

Mina omitted to mention what she planned to achieve during her nurse's absence.

CHAPTER SEVEN

M. Merridew
Brighton
March 1872

Dear Miss Scarletti,
I hope I may be permitted to call upon you this afternoon as I have stories to tell which I know will amuse and invigorate you and are rather too long and far too interesting to commit to a mere letter.
Respectfully
Marcus Merridew

Mina eagerly anticipated Mr Merridew's visit. She was anxious for him to speak freely of the fascinating information he had acquired, but without alerting Miss Cherry to the fact that she was launching herself recklessly into a new investigation. If Miss Cherry suspected her for a moment, firm words would be said to Dr Hamid. Then Dr Hamid would fold his arms and look at Mina reproachfully, shaking his head in that way he always adopted whenever she did anything interesting.

Mina was obliged to lay careful plans. She first requested that cook prepare a modest tea party for herself, Mr Merridew and Richard, thus avoiding any concerns Miss Cherry might have had about her conducting a second private interview with a single gentleman in the theatrical profession.

With these arrangements in place, Mina next asked Miss Cherry to assist in a difficult and arduous task, attending her mother who had recently received a letter from Enid. According to Richard, the letter was no more than the usual miserable litany of Enid's numerous complaints but Louisa Scarletti had chosen to take the contents powerfully to heart and needed comforting, or at least the company of someone who had no option but to listen to her and make the appropriate noises at the correct intervals. Miss Cherry braced herself for the ordeal, hunted through her little book for an appropriate reading, and thus armed, departed to do her duty.

Mr Merridew arrived with his usual flourish, in a brand new suit of clothes and an auburn wig, while Richard, looking unsure as to why he had been summoned, slumped in a chair and fidgeted.

Rose brought in a small tea-table and a laden tray, which Mina inspected anxiously. Cook was a good plain cook. If asked for a pound cake or a treacle tart, or a boiled pudding, she would provide generously. Further than that she ought not to have gone, but often did. Whenever Nellie called to take tea, Mina sent to the pastry shop for her favourite treats; delicate wafers and sugar cakes; and the result was that cook sometimes tried to imitate them with indifferent success. Mina's appetite was still in question, however the gentlemen, who were less dainty and rather hungrier, unashamedly loaded their plates, and Rose saw to it that Mina was provided with a plain bun dipped in tea before she left them to their refreshments.

'Is your kind nurse not in attendance?' asked Mr Merridew.

'She is helping Rose look after Mother,' Mina explained.

'Miss Cherry will feel quite bereft at being sent away,' observed Mr Merridew, a little smile showing that he well understood why Mina had ensured her nurse's absence. 'She is dedicated to making your existence as dull as possible. Of course, one must know when to rest but it also important to know when to play.'

'Doctors and nurses can be so boring,' agreed Richard washing down a lumpy cake with a gulp of tea. 'All they want to do is stop you having fun. Miss Cherry seems like a good sort, but she has her stays tied too tight. So what is this all about?'

'You might know,' Mr Merridew explained to Richard, 'that my ambitions have recently taken a literary turn, and I am about to embark on a history of the court of the late King William, with particular attention being paid to his sojourns at the Royal Pavilion. A former member of that court, a Mrs Barnham resides in Brighton, and I have sought her out and was permitted to pay a call on her. The results were more than usually informative.'

Mr Merridew cleared his throat and began his tale.

'Mrs Barnham occupies a set of rooms on the first floor of a respectable lodging house, tidily kept but devoid of any hint of luxurious living. I was met at the front door by the between stairs maid, a small very pale girl hardly more than thirteen, all wispy hair and dry elbows, and looking in urgent need of a nourishing meal. In my life as an actor, I have often been obliged to take humble lodgings where such poorly remunerated and underfed maidservants endure a dismal existence devoid of hope of anything better, and her situation naturally provoked a deep sympathy.

I spoke to her kindly. Her name was Maggie, and she told me that Mrs Barnham is very elderly, and lives with her maid, Miss Stone. Maggie led me up the stairs, which were fragrant with the odours of cheap soap and cabbage, to Mrs Barnham's door. I pressed a penny into the poor child's hand and she scurried away like a little mouse.

I knocked on the door and after what seemed like two minutes it opened a little. 'Yes?' came creakily from within.

I took a good breath and used my chest voice to make a good address. 'It is I, Marcus Merridew,' I announced, 'to call on Mrs Barnham, as agreed.'

After a short pause the door opened fully. 'Please enter.' The woman who stood within was a sturdily made person of middle years. She wore a black gown, a white cap, and a patterned shawl. There was a lace veil draped over her head and falling on either side of her face, partly shadowing a heavily mottled skin. She turned her head aside a little, and I guessed that she did so to soften the blow of the curious stare her appearance usually invited at first glance. I did not flinch. In my years in the theatre I have seen every variety of colour and pattern of flesh that nature has created, and others that have been fashioned by accident and disease, such that I have long abandoned judgement by outward beauty and viewed all my fellow beings as God's creatures, however made.

Miss Stone, for that was she, stepped aside and I entered a very warm gas-lit sitting room. My hat coat and walking cane were taken and placed on a coat stand, giving me a moment to survey my surroundings.

There was a small round table in the centre draped in a paisley patterned cloth of faded red, two plain dining chairs, and a fireplace where logs and coals blazed in a narrow iron grate. On the mantel above was a row of glass display boxes in which brass instruments caught the flickering light, and a framed photograph of a heavily be-whiskered gentleman.

In one corner of the room was a square table which could not help but draw my attention. An object the size and shape of a circular tea tray standing on its edge appeared to be attached to the front of it. I could not see what the object was, since both it and the table were draped in a heavy black cloth.

The room smelled scorched like the fire, with notes of old furnishings, dust, rum, lemon and spice.

Two armchairs were drawn up before the fire, and in one of them sat Mrs Barnham, a lady of advanced years and large proportions. She was holding a pewter tankard and inhaling the fragrance of what lay within, one hand grasping a handle, the other pressed around the body of the vessel. Neither hand could be described as steady but between them they were equal to the task. A jug on the small table at her elbow promised further supplies of the delicious brew. Her hands were encased in black knitted lace mittens, and the angle of her reddened fingers revealed the ravages of arthritis. Nearby there leaned a stout walking stick, the wear on the handle indicating long use.

I have seen portraits of Mrs Barnham when she had been the comely young actress Miss Margaret Green. There was no doubt in my mind that this was the same person, some fifty years later. Much had changed about her, but sunken into the swollen flesh of her face there were the same knowing eyes.

I bowed. 'Mrs Barnham, it is my honour to make your acquaintance.'

'I could say likewise,' she replied. 'Please excuse me if I do not rise to greet you. I regret that my limbs are not as strong as they once were.'

'I understand, of course, imagine it done,' said I.

'Please take a seat. May I offer you some rum punch?'

'The smallest possible sip,' I said, holding an index finger and thumb tip just a whisper apart, and as I was seated, I was handed half a teacupful of the hot beverage by the maid, who retired to one of the dining chairs.

'So,' said Mrs Barnham, smiling contentedly though the pungent steam that rose from her tankard, 'tell me how I may assist you in your desire to immortalise the Pavilion in its last royal years?'

'If I am correct,' I said, sipping my rum punch with caution, since it was a powerful brew, 'you were once a prominent member of the court of the late King William. I am sure that you must have abundant memories of the scenes and events of his reign.'

'I was indeed an habitué of the royal court,' said Mrs Barnham, with a lilt of understated pride in her voice. 'The King — and I am sorry to disappoint you — the King was a plain, simple fellow. He was already an old man when he acceded to the throne. Really, he might have been a country squire who enjoyed nothing more than taking a walk about his estate. There was an army of children by his mistresses, but that is a fact well known. He married late in life, and took no mistresses after that, but no legitimate child survived him. Queen Adelaide — she was a kind soul. Court life was unremarkable.' Mrs Barnham gave a little chuckle. 'I am afraid your book will make very dull reading.'

'It might at that, but of course the public has always had a fascination for kings, and his is a neglected reign amongst historians. And after King William's demise? Did you continue at court? Surely you must have some tales to tell of that time.'

'Not at all. Our revered Queen, and may the Almighty bless her in her sorrow and tribulation; she was young then and took a stout broom and swept away all that had gone before. I was one of her sweepings. It was shortly afterwards that I married Mr Barnham. He was a good man.'

I glanced at the portrait of the be-whiskered gentleman, but Mrs Barnham did not trouble herself to do so. 'I have been told that you were for a time a spirit medium,' I ventured. 'Did you use your powers at court? Did the King or Queen consult you?'

Mrs Barnham favoured me with a sly look which told me that she had recognised the meat of the discussion. 'I may have done, but there are some matters it would be unwise to disclose to the public, even now.'

'Of course. I understand. You might prefer me not to make any mention of it in my book. In any case, I hope you will give me permission to dedicate the volume to your good self.'

'That is so very kind. You may refer to my little spiritualistic gatherings at court, I think. A light touch, perhaps, without names. That will suffice.'

'But I assume that you no longer have contact with the spirits?'

Mrs Barnham was savouring her rum punch but lowered the tankard and raised an eyebrow. 'Why do you assume so?'

'There are a number of mediums at work in Brighton who advertise their services. You do not. I thought you had given up the practice. Am I incorrect?'

She gave me a shrewd glance, and one hand thoughtfully stroked the warm belly of the tankard. 'Have you ever attended a séance?'

I thought back to dull evenings spent in theatre dressing rooms which had sometimes been enlivened by the antics of animated tables. 'I have, although it was without the benefit of a medium, and there were never good results. I believe many of those present regarded it as no more than a diversion. And it was always a mistake to invite a conjuror to the circle. But' and here, I charged my voice with deep sincerity, 'I remain an earnest seeker after the truth.'

'It would be wrong of me,' said Mrs Barnham, 'not to use the gift I was given to alleviate the sorrows of others. I have a number of close friends many of whom have been visiting me for several years and we meet weekly. I do not advertise. I do not ask for money. It is enough reward for me that the bereaved can, through me, receive assurances of the eternal happiness of their departed loved ones, and the certainty that one day they will be reunited in heaven.'

I placed my teacup down and leaned forward. The time had come to adopt an expression of unfeigned eagerness, barely concealed. 'Have you made contact with the spirits of King William or Queen Adelaide? Or any royal or noble personages?'

Mrs Barnham allowed herself an indulgent smile. 'No, but then my sitters do not have such elevated connections, and they ask questions concerning their own families.'

'I confess that you have greatly excited my curiosity,' I said, breathlessly. 'How do the spirits pass on their wisdom? Do they appear before you? Do you and your sitters see them and hear them speak?'

'I regret that bodily manifestations only appear in very special cases. Neither do I or my sitters hear voices. No, the spirits send me messages. When they first started to come through there were simply raps or movements of the table. At first, they could only give us answers of yes or no, but then I devised a means of spelling out words. I would call out the letters of the alphabet one by one, and the rap or tilt would occur when I spoke the correct one. The method is slow, but the results are good. Some ten years ago, however, I gave a sitting to an American gentleman and he told me of a device he had seen, called a spiritoscope, which received the messages with much greater speed and clarity.'

'Clarity,' interrupted Mina when Mr Merridew reached that point in his account. 'She used that word?'

'She did indeed, most distinctly.'

Mina nodded, recalling the name given by the anonymous letter writer to the *Gazette* who had praised the virtue of Mrs Vardy. 'It is a very good word. Please do go on.' Mina glanced at Richard, who seemed only mildly interested and sat fumbling with the cigar case in his pocket. 'If you wish to smoke, Richard, you may do so, but not in here.' He took the hint and the last of the cake.

Mr Merridew continued, and it occurred to Mina that he, in his own way was a kind of medium, since his tone and gestures conjured up before her the face form and voice of Mrs Barnham.

'My husband,' said Mrs Barnham, 'was a maker of ship's instruments, and he was most interested in the device and asked the gentleman to describe it to him. From this description he was able to prepare a drawing of how it was constructed. Once the gentleman had left, he declared that such a device was very easy to make, and he built one for me. I have used it ever since.'

I glanced at the cloth-covered table with its mysterious disk in the corner of the room. 'Mrs Barnham, you would earn my eternal gratitude if I could see this device perform its miracles.'

She helped herself to more rum punch. 'Then you must call upon me at six o'clock tomorrow evening when my circle of friends gathers. You would be very welcome.'

'And so,' said Mr Merridew triumphantly, 'I am now *persona grata* at Mrs Barnham's select soiree, which I shall attend tonight, and which promises to be very fascinating. I will be your eyes and ears, but you must provide me with some clues as to what I am to observe. Surely you do not suspect the venerable lady of some crime? I am sure she does receive payment by some means or another, little gifts and favours, but her circumstances do not suggest that she is rich, far from it. And she must be more than eighty, now. Prison would not be kind to her.'

While Mina was considering her response, Rose came to remove the tea-things and since there was no more to eat, Richard removed himself.

Mina was about to protest that she had no interest in Mrs Barnham's séances other than curiosity about the spiritoscope, but that would not do. Mr Merridew was no fool, he would know if she deceived him and Mina felt she hardly had the energy to maintain the fiction any further.

'I do not suspect Mrs Barnham of wrongdoing,' said Mina. 'She may be genuine, she may be a fraud, but she brings comfort to her friends and appears to ask for nothing in return. What I would like to hear is your observations of those persons in her circle. Especially the ladies. I want to know more about them.'

'A study of character. Of those with tales to tell. Secrets perhaps,' said Mr Merridew with a conspiratorial smile.

'Perhaps,' said Mina.

'Character study,' said Mr Merridew, 'is my speciality.'

CHAPTER EIGHT

Mina, impatient to hear Mr Merridew's account of Mrs Barnham's séance, used the interlude to make the necessary arrangements for the next stage in her enquiries. There was an exchange of notes, the result being an appointment for Miss Cherry to have a free half day on the following Monday afternoon, so that she and Mrs Phipps could become acquainted. Mina suggested that it would be an opportunity for Miss Cherry to demonstrate her reading skills by taking her copy of *The Young Woman's Companion* for the entertainment of Mrs Phipps, reassuring the nurse that she could manage without it for a few hours. Miss Cherry instructed Rose on how to attend to Mina during her brief absence and prepared for the interview by purchasing a new bonnet.

Mina, meanwhile, composed a letter to Mrs Vardy.

Dear Mrs Vardy,

My health is very much improved, and I will be pleased to receive you on Monday afternoon at 2pm. I wish to keep our discussion confidential and I would therefore suggest a small and harmless deception to ensure secrecy. I hope you are agreeable to this.

When you call, please could you bring a business card of Saltmire and Vardy together with some samples of porcelain mourning brooches. I will tell my maid to expect a Miss Saltmire.

Yours in confidence
Mina Scarletti

Richard liked to call on Mina several times a day, if only for a respite from his mother's melancholy. Louisa Scarletti's doleful outpourings were particularly torn between Mina's close brush with death and Enid's forthcoming confinement, which she saw as tantamount to the same thing, but her mood always lightened when she clung to the arm of her handsome younger son, declaring him to be the best of the family, and their meetings always ended with tears of maternal pride and a small monetary donation.

On the morning after Mr Merridew's visit, however, Richard did not appear at Mina's side after breakfast and when his absence continued throughout the day she began to worry. Which was worse, she wondered, having him idling about the house or out in the town where she had no idea what he was doing?

Her worries were interrupted by the arrival of a letter from Mr Merridew.

Dear Miss Scarletti,

I could, if I were so inclined compose a sensational novel or a drama regarding my attendance at Mrs Barnham's circle last night. I am engaged for this afternoon and early evening, but if it is not too late, I will call on you at 8pm and tell you all.

Respectfully,
Marcus Merridew

As Mina replied to Mr Merridew's letter, she was doubly anxious for her brother to be home so she might converse with her visitor unencumbered, so it was to her considerable relief that Richard returned in time for dinner, and when he called on Mina he was all smiles.

'Mina my dear girl, you will be so proud of me,' he said.

They were alone since Miss Cherry had gone to get her dinner in the kitchen, and Richard took the opportunity to sit beside Mina on the bed which he would not have dared do under the nurse's sharp eye.

'You must never again say that I don't listen to your advice. Today, I have been all over Brighton, walking here and walking there, in the most desperate of weather, to see what employment can be offered to a man of my talents. The air is still far too chill for you to venture out of doors but there are a host of fashionable persons out strolling or driving whenever the sun chooses to appear and the whole effect is very colourful. And I have something for you.' He handed her a copy of the *Gazette*. 'There is nothing very interesting in it, I am sorry to say. Now that that awful poisoning woman has been declared insane, and we are disappointed of a hanging, the newspapers have wrung the case dry of all excitement and turned to politics. So that is Brighton scandal done for the year.'

'I hope you kept to the respectable part of town,' said Mina, receiving the gift eagerly. 'I read the most dreadful tales of beer houses as little more than dens of drunkenness and bad behaviour. I don't want to learn about your adventures in the police court column.'

Richard professed to be shocked at the suggestion. 'Would I ever get into trouble of that kind?'

'Yes, Richard, you would, and I am telling you not to.'

He put his hand on his heart. 'I promise faithfully to be a model of virtue. But there is news of another sort — would you believe I saw a friend of ours while I was out and about?'

'Oh?'

'I was in Ship Street when I chanced on Mr Beckler the photographer.'

Mina frowned but chewed her lip and remained silent.

'He was handing out cards to passers-by advertising his new business,' Richard continued. 'I stopped to say hallo, and he told me he is still trying to photograph ghosts but has made no progress with it. Until he succeeds, he has to rely on making portraits of the living or corpses. He makes them look so alike. He has a nice little shop of his own, very tidy and clean with portraits in the window of eminent persons. And you might be interested to know that he is displaying a very large one of his nefarious patron Mr Arthur Wallace Hope, who has just brought out another book, *Adventures with the Spirits*. I saw copies of it piled high in all the book shops and selling fast. And his *African Quest* has a brand-new edition.'

Mina did not care to be reminded of Mr Hope's self-aggrandising and best-selling publications but said nothing.

'You know I have often thought I ought to write a book,' mused Richard. 'It seems like a very good way of making a lot of money. I mean, you must do very well from all those stories you write.'

'Oh, if you only knew,' she replied.

'But you need not worry that you will encounter that creature again for some while, as according to Beckler he has just sailed for Africa again, determined to discover the whereabouts of Dr Livingstone. Really, a man as clever as Dr Livingstone must only be missing because he does not want to be found, at least not by Mr Hope. I suspect the good doctor would not wish to be advanced upon and browbeaten into spiritualism in the middle of a jungle where I am sure he has other things on his mind. I am pleased for Nellie's sake, too, that Mr Hope is gone, as she should not have to suffer that man's vile attentions again. I do wonder, you know, can Mr Beckler be aware of Mr Hope's reputation? Surely not.'

'Nowadays wealth and position excuse everything,' said Mina, coldly. 'I am confident that Mr Beckler is perfectly content to accept Mr Hope's patronage if it furthers his career.'

'My dear girl,' said Richard, in his most persuasive tone, 'I know you don't care for Mr Beckler, but I really do think he is fond of you. He was most upset when I told him that you had been unwell and said that he would like to call on you as soon as it was possible. Can I tell him you will receive him when you are better? I will be chaperone if you like.'

Mina, unable to look her brother in the face, tightened her grip on the newspaper. 'No, Richard. He is not to come here. I detest him.'

'I don't see why. He paid you some very nice compliments. I know you thought he was only flattering you to drum up business, but it was more than that, I'm sure of it. You should get to know him better.'

Mina steeled herself. Would it be wise to tell Richard the truth about Mr Beckler? Could it ever be advisable to share information of that nature with her affectionate, foolish, impetuous brother, who was a stranger to considered thought? She had hesitated many times before, and always felt unable to reveal what she knew, but perhaps, after all, now was the time. 'Richard, I —' she paused, groping for the right words.

'But here's the thing, my dear girl, he went and offered me a position, and I have accepted. So now I have respectable employment. With a salary. I have just told Mother and she is so very pleased. Do say that you are, too.'

Mina was momentarily speechless.

Richard chuckled. 'I can see you are surprised. You didn't think I could succeed on my own so quickly, but you always underestimate me.'

'But — you have no knowledge of photography,' she protested weakly.

'No, but I can learn,' said Richard with a dismissive gesture. 'I am quite clever with all sorts of things you know. And in the meantime, I will be busy handing out the advertising cards, making appointments and of course, flattering all the pretty ladies who are thinking of having their portraits taken.'

Mina groaned inwardly. Much as it pained her, she now felt obliged to remain silent on the horrid Mr Beckler and his unforgivable behaviour. 'When do you begin?' she asked.

'Monday morning, sharp. He has not abandoned his other business in Twickenham but leased it to another man. Here in Brighton he hopes to attract a more fashionable clientele. He's a coming man, Mina. You could do far worse.'

Mina took a few moments to calm herself before responding. 'Richard, I want to make this very clear to you. I neither need nor want admirers. I have no intention of ever marrying.'

He gave her an arch look, as if to imply that so firm a rebuttal was only evidence that she was about to change her mind. 'We shall see,' he said.

Mina was about to tell him the secret that so few knew, that on medical grounds, the role of wife and mother had been forbidden her. If she had any regrets, she had consigned them to a place in her mind where they could not trouble her. She consoled herself with the thought that by rejecting the roles assumed to be the most desirable and appropriate for women, she had found a better and more stimulating life, with avenues of achievement she could not otherwise have envisaged.

She could not allow herself any tender feelings other than those towards her family. Sincere friendships, she believed, could be better and more enduring than romantic illusions. Before she could reveal to Richard the truth that would put a stop to his constant and well-meaning hints, Rose came to the door and announced Mr Merridew.

Before long, Mr Merridew was once again setting the scene, ready to recount what he had learned.

'I arrived most carefully upon my hour. Little Maggie once again admitted me to the house, and I had brought a gift for her, a biscuit. She held it in her cupped hands and smelt it as if the baked aroma were the most heavenly scent in the world. For a moment I was afraid that she might actually faint, then she touched her lips to the edge of the treat and licked the sugar that clung to her mouth. 'Thank you, Sir,' she said, and then, in one undisguised moment, I saw a troubled look in her eyes.

I drew back a little so as not to frighten her. 'I mean only to be kind,' I said, gently, 'and if anyone is unkind to you, you must tell me at once.'

She nodded silently.

I was met at the door of Mrs Barnham's apartments by Miss Stone. 'Have you served Mrs Barnham for many years?' I asked as I handed her my hat, coat and cane.

She seemed surprised to be so addressed. 'I have. She has been very kind to me,' she whispered. 'Not everyone would have offered employment to a woman like myself.'

In the sitting room, which still had a lingering scent of hot rum, was a row of six straight backed chairs facing the cloth draped square table which had been drawn forward to change places with the circular breakfast table. Mrs Barnham was seated at the square table so that she faced the chairs, on the side opposite the disk-shaped device, the body of the table lying between herself and the visitors.

'Mr Merridew, how delightful to see you again,' said Mrs Barnham, as I greeted her before taking a seat. Miss Stone went to tend the fire. She did not, I noticed, stir it into a blaze, but banked it well so that it would need no further attention for a while, then she placed a guard, a strong sheet of embossed brass styled with a sailing ship, in front of the hearth so that the dim firelight cast about the room was soft and sheltered.

Two ladies arrived in company with each other, and I rose as they entered, making a deferential but not too extravagant bow and studied them as carefully as propriety would allow. I could see that they were friends, but from their appearance concluded that they were not related by blood. A tall lady, rather handsome, aged about forty-five was introduced as Mrs Vardy. She was well-dressed without being an ardent or frivolous devotee of fashion. Her companion, Mrs Wandle, was closer to seventy, shorter and stouter with features that were pleasant and regular although she could never have been a beauty even when young. Her gown was practical, and neither old nor new. Never having been kissed with fashion it was therefore impossible for it to be out of style. Despite their differences, I detected a close sympathy between the ladies, a sisterly affection, which suggested that each had suffered a loss that the other could understand.

I was introduced.

'Oh, Mr Merridew, it is such an honour to meet you,' exclaimed Mrs Vardy. 'The *Gazette* had high praise for your performance. Is your Hamlet still delighting and educating the town?'

'I regret that the final curtain has already fallen on that production,' I said, 'but there will be others, and I can promise you that they will be select and tasteful to a fault.'

We were seated.

'Mr Merridew is a man of many talents,' said Mrs Barnham, 'he is writing a book about the court of King William.'

Mrs Vardy produced a sharp inhalation. 'And might we expect to receive a message from the King? How wonderful that would be! Just imagine!'

'That is my hope,' I said, 'but I have never attended a séance of this nature before and I really cannot imagine what to expect.'

Mrs Barnham gave a soft chuckle. 'Then you must prepare to be amazed.' She beckoned to Miss Stone who shuffled over to the square table and carefully lifted the cloth away. 'Behold the spiritoscope!'

I pressed my fingertips to my chest and gave a little 'Oh!' of astonishment. Not all of it was counterfeit. 'How extraordinary! What a remarkable machine! I have never seen the like!'

'It is the only one in England,' said Mrs Barnham, proudly. Her voice admitted of no contradiction.

The first thing that came to my eye was the object immediately facing me, a vertical disk cut from a thin perfectly smooth sheet of metal. It was attached by a stout hub to a wooden frame which was fastened to the underneath surface of the table top, so that about a third of the disk was above the table's surface and the rest below. Around the outer circumference of the disk was a narrow strip painted white, on which the letters of the alphabet had been painted in black capitals.

While the letters were clearly visible to the sitters, a person seated at the table facing the row of chairs as Mrs Barnham did, would only be able to see the reverse surface of the disk. I could not help but wonder how the other side of the disk would appear to the medium. Was it like a piece of stage scenery, painted on one side for the enjoyment of the audience, but drab and unfinished on the other? Or did it have its own symbols, clues to what was on the side in view?

Attached to the hub of the disk was a metal device shaped like a hand, of which one finger, the index, pointed upwards, the others being depicted as curled into the palm. There was an elegance about the hand which invited admiration, a neat white cuff at the wrist, the suggestion of a sleeve, and the long finger like one of Mr Dickens's Christmas ghosts, indicating future fate. The pointing index was currently resting on an unlettered space at the perimeter.

A stout band was looped about the hub of the wheel. I followed it downwards with my eyes and saw that two of the legs of the table, those to the right of Mrs Barnham, ended in wheels connected by an axle, the band passing about one of the wheels. The other two legs were on castors. I am no engineer, but I am familiar with the action of stage machinery, and it was obvious to me that the whole table was able to move freely on its wheels and castors. When it did so, its motion would cause the painted disk to turn, and the pointing finger would rest on the letters.

I would have liked to see the other side of the disk, but thought it would be unwise to ask, since such a question, however much I disguised it as academic curiosity would suggest that I suspected Mrs Barnham of cheating and this might see me peremptorily ejected from the premises.

Miss Stone took up a notebook and pencil and placed herself on a chair near to the square table but facing it so that she could see the painted side of the disk. On the other side, conveniently to the elbow of Mrs Barnham, was a side table with a jug of water and a glass. This arrangement, I thought, served two purposes, it provided both assistance and refreshment to the medium and also prevented anyone from skirting around the table to look at the reverse surface of the disk.

Mrs Barnham extended her arms and placed her crooked hands on top of a small board that rested on the table before her, the distortion of her fingers meaning that not all were able to touch it at the same time. The board was supported on tiny castors, so that it could move easily across the table top.

'You will observe,' said Mrs Barnham, addressing me, 'that the table is free to move and as it does so, the spiritoscope will spell out messages. 'Miss Stone will make a note of what transpires. This board in front of me is merely the conduit through which the spirits send their influence, but see —' she propelled the board back and forth then side to side a number of times, the tiny castors sounding like glass marbles rolling on the varnished table top. The table itself did not move. She smiled. 'There can be no question of my being able to affect the table by muscular means. I know that it has been suggested in those cases where the medium and her sitters lay their hands directly upon the table, that one or more of them in some way, either deliberately or unconsciously create the movement. But that cannot be so here. In any case —' she held up her hands — 'you will see that I can be absolved of any suspicion in that area. I lack the necessary power.'

She gazed intently at me. 'Sir, I see in your expression a thousand questions you would like to ask me. Be assured that the spiritoscope was devised and thoroughly tested by an eminent gentleman, a professor of science, no less, a man who once argued most strongly against spiritualism. His object in constructing it was to test whether messages received during séances were sent by the spirits, and to remove absolutely any possibility that such messages could derive from an earthly plane. On attending many séances using apparatus similar to this one and subjecting the mediums to the most careful scrutiny he professed himself utterly converted.'

'How can one tell if the spirit is benign?' I asked.

She favoured me with a gracious smile. 'That is a good question. I have been told that there are such things as mischievous entities that spread false messages to the unwary, but have no fear, we can prevent their entering here by the power of our prayers.'

Another lady arrived and was shown to a chair. As she entered, the scent of camphor drifted in with her, and enveloped her form in an invisible cloud. She might once have been tall but had shrunk into something approaching a sphere, since she was both wide and round in all directions. Her age could not be determined, but youth had clearly fled some time ago, and the tight grey plaits wound about her head under a limp white cap were to my eye obviously not her own. Introduced to the company as Mrs Anscombe, she acknowledged all those present with a brief nod.

A gentleman was next to arrive, a Mr Eve. He was a very thin, stooped person of about sixty, with a grey beard like a bedraggled ruff about his throat. Like Mrs Anscombe, he seemed disinclined to exchange pleasantries with anyone, but nodded politely to Mrs Barnham and took his seat. He stared at me for a moment but said nothing and when he was introduced appeared not to recognise my name.

Mr Eve had an air of general dissatisfaction with anything that failed to suit him. When Mrs Barnham made the usual polite greeting, this impelled him into speech, informing everyone present that the weather was too cold, the air too thin, the street vendors too shabby and young persons too noisy. He was especially annoyed by beggars whose presence in any public thoroughfare was an insult to the town, and dirty ill-clad persons who defiled the streets. Mr Eve declared himself unable to understand why these monstrosities were not removed by the police. He offered no suggestions as to where they should be removed, the question clearly having no interest for him.

The roll of visitors was completed by a Mr Cobbe. He was a broad prosperous looking gentleman of about forty, with the confident air of a man who was used to commanding others and was well paid for his trouble. It was clear from the tenor of Mrs Barnham's greeting that he was a valued visitor, and that she saw his presence as a compliment to her skills. He showed no interest in the other visitors, but took his seat and waited, his posture suggesting that as far as he was concerned, the performance was to be conducted for his sole benefit.

'And now,' said Mrs Barnham, 'we are complete.'

There was something in her manner, the glint in her eye, the curl of her lip, or perhaps it was just the breathy pleasure in her voice, that made me shiver.

Miss Stone dimmed the gas lamps but only a little. There remained a soft golden glow, with a little dance of light from the fireplace. It was still possible for those present to see not only each other, but the table, the strange disk and its lettering. Miss Scarletti, you have told me of séances conducted in full dark, and the tricks that can be played on the unwary, but that was not the case here.

Again, Mrs Barnham spoke for the benefit of the newcomer. 'It will assist the spirits to communicate with us if we say a prayer to begin and then we should remain as quiet as possible.'

She pressed her palms together and began to intone a prayer. The company followed her lead, the words of worship uttered softly with piously bent heads. When it ended, all was still. The only sound was the gentle hum and crackle of smouldering coals and the flutter of wind in the chimney.

Mrs Barnham lifted her head, stretched out her hands, laid her fingers on the little board and closed her eyes. After taking a few moments to compose herself she said, 'If there be any spirits present please indicate the affirmative by causing the letter Y to come under the index.'

I watched with care, but as with a conjuror whose performance was being viewed for the first time, it was hard to know where best to direct my eyes to learn the secret. Was the spiritoscope more reliable than other methods? Did it ever fail to produce results? Or did Mrs Barnham's devout circle assemble in the certain knowledge that they would achieve communion with the spirits?

When I saw the first movement it was no more than a quiver, as if the table had been holding its breath all this time but had suddenly come to life. From the other sitters there was no more than a brief inhalation of pleasure. Success had been no surprise to them.

Mrs Barnham's hands remained on the little board, which did not move, but beneath it, the table began to shift in its entirety on its wheels and castors, and it did so the lettered disk turned. It was smooth, almost soundless, apart from a whisper of oiled metal, and when the pointing finger rested on the letter Y it stopped.

'Spirit,' said Mrs Barnham, 'please kindly let us know the initials of your name.'

There was no pause now, as the table moved again, more confidently this time, and spelled first C and then M. There was a slight shifting of persons, and I had the uncomfortable feeling that I was being observed by all eyes. Certainly, I was the only person in the room with the second initial M.

'Mr Merridew do you wish to question the spirit?' asked Mrs Barnham.

'I do indeed,' I said. 'Spirit, do you have a message for me?'

The table moved again, this time only a short way and then back, so the index once more rested on the Y.

'Is your surname Merridew?'

Again, the answer was yes.

I was now groping desperately and unsuccessfully in my memory for any knowledge of a relative with a Christian name beginning with C. I abandoned the search. 'Spirit, kindly spell out your first name.'

The table, moving swiftly and smoothly, obligingly imparted that the C stood for Charles. How it moved I could not detect, but even if Mrs Barnham had had both hands on the table, I felt sure that she could not have produced such an easy movement, and Miss Stone was too far away to have any effect. I had a clear view underneath the table and there was no space for any accomplice. No wonder the eminent man of science had been convinced.

'And kindly also indicate what relation you are to me,' I asked.

The table informed me that the spirit was that of my brother.

I now found myself in a dilemma. I do not have a brother. I am my parents' only child, having been born less than a year after their wedding, and my mother expired within weeks of my birth. My father remarried but the second union did not produce children. I was not about to mention any of this to Mrs Barnham. I glanced at her. Her eyes were open, and she saw my hesitation, and I felt sure that she had guessed the reason.

'Spirit,' she said, 'kindly tell me your age when you passed.'

The message was much longer this time, but spelled out adroitly, and each letter was carefully recorded by Miss Stone. When the table finally stilled, she read out the complete communication. 'I died before birth but am reborn in heaven.'

'I did not know that the souls of unborn infants receive names in heaven,' I said.

Mrs Barnham's features were wreathed in a blissful smile. 'Oh they, do, Mr Merridew, they do.'

This information had opened up a world of possibilities. Did I have an unknown half-brother, perhaps, never born, but conceived either prior to my father's first marriage or during the second? Or was Charles Merridew a mere invention? 'How extraordinary!' I exclaimed. 'The spirits are wise beyond men! These things must be true. They were not known to me, so no earthly being could have read my mind. A brother! I am happy that he is at peace.'

'Do you wish to ask another question?' said Mrs Barnham, pointedly, her tone suggesting that this was a good place at which to desist.

'I — let me consider — no, not at present.'

'I sense that this spirit has left us,' said Mrs Barnham. She did not encourage it to return. There was a pause, and some deep even breathing, as if the medium required a brief rest to restore her energy. At length, she spoke again. 'If a spirit be present please indicate the affirmative by causing the letter Y to come under the index.' To no-one's surprise there was, and this time, the initials were J H.

Mrs Vardy gasped as this was revealed, and convulsively clasped her hands together. 'Jasper, is that you?' she cried.

Again, the affirmative.

'Do you have a message for me or for your sons?'

Her rapid breaths could be clearly heard as the table moved and the disk turned. 'Do not fear. All will be well,' read Miss Stone.

'Oh Jasper, my dear, I have been so unhappy of late! People are saying such vile things about me. I beg you, tell them the truth!'

There was a tantalising pause before the table moved again. 'The truth will come from human agency.'

'But from whom? Who should I ask?'

'I cannot say.'

Mrs Vardy was almost grinding her teeth with frustration. 'But I suffer so!' she pleaded. 'Have pity on me!'

I saw Mrs Wandle reach out and place a calming and comforting pressure on her friend's hands.

'Do not question him further,' advised Mrs Barnham. 'The spirits have powers, but they do not fully understand them themselves. They cannot influence our mundane bodies. Neither are they all-knowing.'

Mrs Vardy subsided into a miserable silence.

The next message was from the late husband of Mrs Wandle, who said that he was happy with the way she ran the inn and that her old potman Henry who had passed away recently was with him in spirit. Mrs Wandle dabbed her eyes. 'It is so hard being a woman alone, but I have been fortunate in the help I have received. May the good Lord bless them both.'

Mr Eve was told by his late father that the rewards he hoped for would not be long in coming, news he acknowledged with a sceptical grunt, and Mrs Anscombe was reassured by her deceased husband that her sons would achieve worldly success and great respect. There was no alteration in her expression.

The next spirit bore the initials C C and was recognised with some enthusiasm by Mr Cobbe as his darling Caroline, his beloved daughter. From such an outwardly assured man, his response, conveying a deep emotion, was so powerful, that her presence in the room was almost tangible.

'Oh, my dear child, how I miss you!' he exclaimed. 'How I long for your light in my life!'

The messages provided by the table were rather longer, suggesting either a very active spirit or, I thought, the response Mrs Barnham felt necessary to provide for a prominent Brighton man.

'Kind father, do you feel my touch on your brow?'

He pressed his fingers to his forehead. 'I do, oh yes my dear child, I do!' he cried ecstatically.

'Do you feel my kiss on your cheek?'

A large palm cupped his larger cheek. 'Oh indeed, your sweet angel kiss, yes, yes I feel it.'

'Do not weep, I live in this celestial sphere as a moonbeam, in a place of love, where little children, happy and pure gather in joy.'

'Oh, if I could only see you, embrace you, kiss you, my dearest child!'

'You shall, Father.'

Mr Cobbe drew a substantial handkerchief from his pocket and buried his face in it, shoulders shaking. No-one said a word. It was several minutes before he recovered. 'Shall I see my darling girl?' he pleaded.

'I will call upon her spirit, and if the conditions are favourable, she may come,' said Mrs Barnham. 'We will pause awhile. Miss Stone, please attend to the lights, and bring refreshments, then we may proceed.'

Mrs Stone turned up the gas, inspected the fire, then departed.

'When we have had tea, we will hold a dark séance with prayers,' said Mrs Barnham. Mr Cobbe wiped his eyes and appeared very satisfied, returning to his previous equilibrium. I looked about me. Mr Eve and Mrs Anscombe appeared unmoved by their experience, but Mrs Vardy was trembling.

'All these years, and still no hint of the truth!' she exclaimed.

'Hush, my dear,' said Mrs Wandle, 'the truth must be known to someone, and you will receive it one day, I am sure of it.'

'Mr Merridew,' said Mrs Barnham, 'since this is your first experience of the spiritoscope, I would be interested to know your impressions?'

I chose my words carefully. I knew I must give no hint of scepticism, no suggestion that I felt sure that the medium's demonstration owed less to the spirits than a hidden mechanism that moved the table, but I also felt that too much enthusiasm might arouse suspicion. 'I have never had an experience like it,' I said. 'And I am extremely curious as to its operation. Do you know how the spirits are able to move something like a table? Even with the wheels and castors it would take an individual a little strength to move. But a spirit, as I understand it is an airy disembodied thing. Surely it can have no physical power. But please correct me if I am wrong. I only seek greater knowledge.'

'It is my theory,' said Mr Cobbe, using that tone of voice which gentlemen of authority like to adopt in every pronouncement whether it lies within or outside their expertise, 'that the spirits can by simple force of will, deprive physical bodies of their natural resistance to movement. It is a fact of science that all bodies must have this resistance, and it must be overcome in order to set them in motion.'

'That is true,' assented Mr Eve. 'I have read widely upon the subject and I believe that the spirits must use a special form of electricity, one which we as mere mortal beings cannot understand.'

'What does Mrs Barnham say?' I asked.

Mrs Barnham gave a little smile. 'Oh, I have been asked so many times to explain how the spirits communicate through me, but I am afraid I must disappoint you. That secret will only be apparent to me when I am a spirit myself. They have some means of taking possession of my brain and nerves, which deprives me of any control over my movements, and indeed once the séance is over my precise memory of the experience flies from me, so I could not describe to you how it feels to be so possessed, except that I am left with the impression that it is at once wearying and joyful.'

'I disagree with Mr Eve, on the subject of electricity' said Mr Cobbe. 'Sparks cannot move a table. Neither can a bolt of lightning, although it might break it. It is the association of the spirits with the special aura of the medium which gives activity to an effluvium which causes the phenomena of movement.'

'Ah, the gentlemen are all for explaining what is taking place without any thought as to the true value of what they receive,' said Mrs Barnham. 'You have witnessed proof that the mind never dies, that the spirit lives on, that there is no death. The man of science seeks fame and riches, but what is that brief pursuit of your earthly life in comparison to the ceaseless ages of your future existence with the angels?'

'Science means nothing to me,' said Mrs Vardy, harshly. 'And I shall know happiness when I see my dear Jasper in heaven. All I ask is to be released from this misery of uncertainty and suspicion, of the whispers and the horrid insinuations, so that others will come to acknowledge the truth and allow me to live in peace until I ascend. Jasper assures me that he has passed, he has assured me of that for many years, but when I tell that to the doubters I am not believed, and there are those who deny the spirits altogether. They tell me that I am a fool and a dupe. They say that all my impressions are a hallucination, but they will not come and see and hear for themselves. Messages to believers are all very well, but we do not need convincing. Why cannot Jasper send his messages to the incredulous, to those who insult me with their wicked accusations?'

'Alas,' said Mrs Barnham, with a sorrowful shake of the head, 'it is that very incredulity, the pernicious unshakeable bigotry that repels the spirits and in the presence of such persons they refuse to appear. Thus, it is only the true believers or those whose minds are open to receiving the truth who are granted messages of hope.'

'It is thought by some,' said Mr Cobbe, 'that there exists in certain persons a state which is the inverse of the medium's aura, one which neutralises it, and prevents it from activating the spirits.'

'There are such persons,' said Mrs Barnham, sadly, 'and they will never be admitted here, nor will their names ever be spoken in this house.'

I waited for some glancing allusion to you, Miss Scarletti, but before anyone could respond, Miss Stone arrived with a tea tray and a plate of bread and butter.

Mrs Barnham remained behind the table and accepted only tea.

Once the refreshments were consumed, and in view of the quantities provided this did not take long, Miss Stone quickly removed the tray, then ensured that the fire was more closely guarded, and the lights turned down to plunge the room into near darkness. Mrs Barnham invited her visitors to close their eyes and led them to pray for the souls of the departed, after which a hymn was sung by all, Mr Cobbe's voice sounding lustily above the others.

When they re-opened their eyes, a new figure stood in the room, facing the seated company. The height and form suggested a female child, and she was clad in long robes that shone like moonlight in the darkness. Her face was visible only through silvery veils, partly occluded by long strands of hair.

'Do not approach or touch her unless she invites you to,' warned Miss Stone.

I glanced at Mrs Barnham whose form was visible only in the spectral light. She was slumped forward, her head bent low. She appeared to be either asleep or in a trance.

'The spirit is formed from ethereal matter which has been drawn from Mrs Barnham's own body,' Miss Stone continued. 'Any undue interference would cause the material to rush back into the medium with such force that it might kill her.'

No-one moved. The child spectre paused and looking up and down the line slowly extended thin white arms towards Mr Cobbe.

'It is my sweet angel, Caroline!' he gasped. 'I beg you, come to your father's loving arms my dear child!'

She glided softly forward, making no sound on the carpeted floor. Trembling, he reached out for her, inviting her to him. Slowly, the spirit came nearer, and finally their hands touched. Mr Cobbe uttered a little moan, and gently drew her close until he was able to enclose her slight form in his arms and laid his head on her shoulder. He appeared to be weeping.

In the faint glow of spirit light I noticed the other sitters turning their faces away out of pity, or blotting their eyes with handkerchiefs, while Miss Stone looked only at her unconscious mistress. I alone gazed at the sight. I have met men like Mr Cobbe before, cruel men who hide their true selves under a mask of virtue, and I felt a great weight settle on my heart.

After a little while, Mrs Barnham began to groan and wail, and this seemed to be a signal for the ghost to depart. Reluctantly Mr Cobbe released the frail figure which backed away. Miss Stone rose to her feet, then Mr Cobbe rose awkwardly and abruptly left the room.

'And now,' said Miss Stone, 'I beg you to pray for the health of Mrs Barnham, that she may be restored to her full form and energy! Close your eyes everyone and pray!'

The voices all joined in prayer and no voice was louder than that of Miss Stone. As the prayer ended I opened my eyes, and the ghost had vanished. Miss Stone was giving Mrs Barnham a drink from her teacup which I felt sure was not tea.

'You deduced that the spirit of the child was none other than the little maidservant?' asked Mina, as Mr Merridew ended his tale.

'I am sure of it. There was every opportunity for her to be made ready by Miss Stone when she went to make the tea, and she was both brought in and removed while our eyes were shut. Our voices hid any noise of her coming and going.'

'And Mr Cobbe?'

'I think he is not what he seems. I mean to watch him.'

CHAPTER NINE

Mina's subterfuge to procure a private interview with Mrs Vardy was successful. There was a prompt reply to her letter agreeing to a call at the date and time proposed, and under the suggested conditions. When the time for their appointment came, therefore, Miss Cherry was absent on her visit to Mrs Phipps. Rose made Mina comfortable and showed the visitor into the room announcing her as Miss Saltmire.

The lady was, as Mr Merridew had described her, tall, with a good figure and handsome rather than beautiful, with a strong angular face, and expressive eyes. Although oppressed by many cares she nevertheless carried herself with strength and confidence. She had brought with her a little leather case of samples and a catalogue.

Mrs Vardy made the usual polite enquiries after Mina's health, tinged with a note of caution in case the visit itself should over tax the strength of the frail-looking lady sitting propped up in bed well wrapped in blankets.

'I am very much better, thank you,' said Mina. Her visitor's expression suggested that she hardly liked to imagine how Mina had appeared previously. 'I hope you don't mind the dissimulation concerning your name.'

'No, not at all, I quite understand; it was a wise precaution,' said Mrs Vardy with a wistful smile. 'There are times when I hardly like to own to it myself.' She sat down and held the sample case on her lap, clutching at it as if it was a support or a talisman. She made no effort to open it. 'The name Vardy has become notorious of late. I am being discussed all over town like a common criminal. I know it is just the fashion of the moment and I believe it will fade with time as these things do. I can bear it, but my poor boys should not have to endure this. There had been talk of them taking their stepfather's name, but it would be most unwise to do so at present. I do not —' she broke off for a moment in a burst of emotion. 'I do not want this suspicion to cling to my sons for the rest of their lives!'

'I am not sure I know precisely why you have chosen to consult me,' Mina began, 'but I promise I will do all in my power to advise and assist you.'

Mrs Vardy took a deep breath, but it seemed to hold itself in her throat and she was dangerously close to choking. There was a carafe of water and glasses by the bedside and Mina reached for them. 'Would you care for a glass of water? Or I can ring for refreshments to be brought.'

Mrs Vardy composed herself with an effort and shook her head. 'I will just take the water, thank you,' she whispered. 'Please don't trouble yourself, I will pour it.'

Mrs Vardy helped herself to the water and after slowly sipping it she appeared calmer. 'Forgive me, when I think of all that has transpired, it can overcome me. I have been through terrible times, and now, just when I had started to imagine that all could be settled in peace and comfort, and I might have some measure of happiness, it has begun again.' She put the glass down. Mina decided to wait and listen.

'My first husband Jasper Holt perished in an accident at sea almost eight years ago. There were aspects of the tragedy which led to suspicions such that it has not until recently been possible for the coroner to grant a death certificate. It was believed that Jasper had attempted to defraud an insurance company after taking out a large policy on his life, in order to pay off his business debts. Nothing has been heard from him since the last day he left our house, no note, no sighting. I admit that at first, I did entertain some hope that he was still alive, that he might write to me, or at least attempt to see his sons of whom he was very proud. But there has been nothing. Nothing at all. You must believe me, because I am sorry to say that there are many who do not.'

'I do,' said Mina, and Mrs Vardy with this assurance, continued.

'My brother Gordon actually employed a detective, a Mr Handley, to discover any news of Jasper's whereabouts but without success. I had previously been attending the readings of a very highly renowned medium, Mrs Barnham, regarding some messages I hoped to receive from my late parents, and when I consulted her about Jasper, his spirit revealed to me that he had indeed passed over. I begged him to tell me where his body could be found, but he could say no more than that the sea covered him. I doubt that any human agency could find him now, and I have given up all hope of granting him a Christian burial. We have said prayers for his soul by the seashore; that was all we could do. Of course, my boys, Franklin and Matthew, miss him terribly, but as time passed, we learned to be content in the family circle.'

She took up the glass and sipped more water. 'About three years ago, Gordon admitted Mr Silas Vardy to the company, and so valuable were his services that he was taken into partnership. I wish you to understand, Miss Scarletti, that there was at first nothing more than an acquaintance between myself and Mr Vardy, but that blossomed in time into a strong mutual regard. Mr Vardy eventually revealed that were it possible to do so, he would like to make me his wife.' She sighed. 'Did I do the right thing, I wonder? I could have refused him, saying that I could not in all conscience regard myself as a widow until the fact of Jasper's death was proven beyond all doubt, not only in the legal sense, that is. Courts can still be mistaken. But happiness in this world is such a fleeting thing, and one must grasp it when it is offered or risk losing it forever. Seven years had gone by since Jasper was last seen by anyone alive, and I therefore applied for a death certificate, which was granted. I was free to remarry.' She shook her head. 'There are days on which I wish I had not been so selfish.'

'Permit me to ask,' said Mina, 'how do your sons regard Mr Vardy?'

'They first encountered him when he was invited to family gatherings by my brother, and I believe they liked him very well. He has nephews and is therefore familiar with the company of children. When I saw him playing cricket with them at the company picnic, I suppose that was what decided me. I thought that he could be a second father to them. Matthew, who has little memory of his father, and is a robust child, was not affected, but for Franklin, when I told him, everything changed. It was as if the very act of finally and officially declaring Jasper deceased was tantamount to my destroying him, taking away any lingering hope that he was still alive. Worse still, I had ended the life of his father in order to replace him with another. I have been told since that boys of that age can be very sensitive.'

'How did his distress show itself?'

'At first it was long moping silences. He seemed to withdraw into his own thoughts and could hardly bring himself to talk to me or to Silas. I hoped that time would cure him, the maturity he would gain with the years, the better acquaintance with his stepfather which would earn respect at the very least, but it was not to be. Just as his temper began to improve, there was the incident of the watch.' Mrs Vardy unlatched the sample case and withdrew a gentleman's silver hunter-case watch and chain.

She cradled it in her hands for a moment then held it out to Mina. 'You can see the engraving on the reverse. F J Holt. It was a gift to Jasper's father from his associates when he retired from the wine trade. It is not of any great monetary value, but it had a sentimental attachment. Jasper was wearing this watch on the day he disappeared.'

'I see,' said Mina, 'May I examine it?'

'Oh, please do!' said Mrs Vardy, very eagerly, giving her the watch.

Mina read the inscription which was an appreciation from the Brighton Wine Sellers Association. 'May I open it?'

'Yes, of course.'

Mina's father had owned something similar, and she knew how to press the crown to open the case. The watch had been well cared for, recently wound and showing the right time.

'And you are in no doubt at all that he was wearing it that day?'

'None whatsoever. I remember he commented on the time he was due to meet Mr Sutherland and I saw him consult it when he was leaving.' Mrs Vardy gazed at Mina hopefully. 'Do you sense anything? Has it any meaning for you?'

Mina suddenly realised that Mrs Vardy thought she might be able to locate the owner of the watch simply by holding it. 'I am so very sorry, but no. I clearly have no abilities of that kind.'

Mina carefully closed the watch and handed it back to Mrs Vardy who did nothing to conceal her disappointment.

'But — forgive me — if your husband had indeed fallen into the sea and drowned as is supposed, how did you come by this?'

'It was delivered to Franklin's school, in a package with his name on it. It was not through the usual postal service but handed to the porter by a messenger boy. The boy has never been traced. The headmaster very sensibly called Franklin into his study and opened it for him in case there might be anything untoward inside. But Franklin recognised it at once, even after so many years. He was very fond of it, and Jasper often told him that when he was a man it would be his. He looks after it, now, keeps it polished and properly wound. It was quite hard for me to persuade him to allow me to borrow it for an afternoon.'

'Do you think your husband might perhaps have placed it somewhere for safekeeping before he stepped onto the yacht? And then someone found and recognised it and sent it to your son?' Mina ventured.

'That is possible, yes. But why the secrecy? How did the finder know that F J Holt was Jasper's father? How did he know where to send it? Franklin saw it as a sign. A sign that his father was if not exactly alive, but in some way communicating with him. The watch was trying to tell him something, but he didn't know what. He brooded on it for days afterwards. And then, quite suddenly, he developed the most alarming new symptoms. On waking up in the morning he found himself unable to move his limbs and he claimed that while in that state he could see the ghost of his father. He was afraid to fall asleep, and his appetite was severely impaired. He could no longer concentrate on his studies, and I was obliged to remove him from the school and keep him at home. The worst of it was that he became obsessed with the idea that either I or Mr Vardy or even both of us together were in some way to blame for his father's death.'

'Was Mr Vardy acquainted with Mr Holt?'

'No, they never met. I didn't meet Silas until three years ago. I tried to explain to Franklin how impossible his ideas were, but he will believe nothing I say.'

'I assume your son was seen by the family doctor.'

'Oh yes, Dr McClelland has been very good, but there is only so much he can do in cases like this.'

Mina recalled to mind the name of the doctor who Mr Phipps had told her had examined Mr Holt for the insurance company. 'I believe I may know Dr McClelland. Is he the man who is in partnership with a Dr Crosier?'

Mrs Vardy looked puzzled. 'No, I am not acquainted with a Dr Crosier. And Dr McClelland is not in a partnership.'

'Oh, then I must be mistaken. What treatment did he prescribe?'

'A light, nourishing diet, tonic mixtures and chloral to help him sleep. Franklin did not like the chloral, he fought against it and we had to give up on it. When there was no improvement Dr McClelland advised calling in a London man, a Dr Fielding who he said is a great authority in cases of this nature. He came and examined Franklin and asked him a great many questions, some of which I thought extremely indelicate. Eventually he said it was a case of mental shock, made worse by a generally sensitive disposition and my son's age. There is no cure, but there is the hope that with good care, he will mend with time. He requires nourishing food, fresh air, light exercise and pleasant companionship. There are some days when Franklin appears to be almost well again, but then he will relapse. He has to be watched constantly as there are fears he might injure himself. The worst of it is, he no longer trusts me to take care of him. His own mother!'

'This must be a terrible burden for you.'

'It is. Had we been without means my poor boy might have been locked away in some dreadful place, but at least he has been cared for at home, where there is a better chance of recovery. Initially we employed a daily nurse.'

'Initially? Then he must have improved such that he no longer needs a nurse.'

'He is a little better, in some ways, yes,' said Mrs Vardy with a hesitation suggesting to Mina that the improvement was more optimistic than actual, 'but my sister Mrs Norbert has come to stay and has taken charge. She is tutoring him, too. I fear it may be many months before he can be strong enough to attend school. He sleeps very poorly and still affirms that the ghost of his father comes to visit him, and to be honest, I have come to believe him. There are such things, I am convinced of it. Not all who see and converse with spirits are afflicted in the mind,' she added defiantly.

'Has anyone else seen or heard this ghost?'

'No. I was wondering if I ought to employ a medium, a sensitive.' She hesitated. 'I have heard say that you might be such a person.'

Mina was tempted as she always was to deny at once that she had made any such claims, but Mrs Vardy looked so hopeful, so plaintive, that she could not find it within herself to do so. 'I think, she said carefully, 'it is possible that because of the family connection, anything your son sees or hears will be experienced by him alone. But I shall give the question some thought. Perhaps if you have any further information to give me, I might be able to look at your situation and see if there is a way forward.'

Mrs Vardy looked disappointed but nodded. 'Very well.'

'On the occasions when you son sees the ghost of his father, is this only a vision, or does it speak? I ask because when

117

individuals are in poor health or experiencing grief, their sight may be affected; they see things that are simply products of the mind, pictures they have in their memory, images of people they know, either living or deceased, that will appear to them to be the actual person, real, and standing before them. It wants only a return to health to lay the supposed ghosts.'

Mrs Vardy bridled a little at the suggestion. 'It is the appearance of this spirit which is one of the things that convinces me that Jasper is deceased,' she said.

'But no-one apart from your son has seen it.'

'Not thus far, no. I do hope that in time perhaps Mrs Barnham might bring him to me, but at present it seems he only manifests to Franklin. My son is not insane, Miss Scarletti.'

Mina decided not to pursue that line of argument. 'Has this spectre spoken, or made a sign or imparted information to your son in any way?'

'If it has, I have not been told of it. Franklin tells me very little in any case, and my sister does not believe in the new spiritualism and dismisses it all as childish nonsense.'

'Your nursemaid did not report anything to you?'

'She witnessed a number of occasions on which Franklin awoke very distressed and unable to move his limbs. The episodes were brief but terrible and when the symptoms subsided, he said he had seen his father. He is sure that his father was attempting to tell him something very important. When the nurse told him that she could not see the ghost he suggested that it must be hiding behind the curtains. She looked and found nothing there, or at least nothing that she was aware of, but then she must not be a sensitive. I have considered bringing a medium to the house to hold a séance and try and contact Jasper, but I feel that it would only result in more upset for Franklin, and I have been advised that he needs to be kept calm.'

'For someone in fragile health séances can be very upsetting and are best avoided,' said Mina. 'That is my advice. I have seen harm come to some people because of them.'

Mrs Vardy reluctantly absorbed Mina's good counsel. 'I am sure you are right, but what can I do?'

'I think that regarding your son, your doctors are correct, this may be something that only time and good care will heal.'

Mrs Vardy gave a little groan of disappointment. She made to rise and leave. 'I see that I have troubled you unnecessarily.'

'Not at all. Please stay a little longer. There are more ways than one of solving a mystery.'

Mrs Vardy looked puzzled but sat down again.

'Tell me about the day you husband disappeared. How did he seem to you that day?'

The visitor's manner showed that it was a tale she had told many times before. 'He seemed particularly cheerful. I put it down to his looking forward to sailing in the yacht. The weather was exceptionally good.'

'You didn't think of going with him? He didn't suggest it?'

'No, but I am a poor sailor. He thought that in time it would be a fine thing for the boys. At least that is what he said.'

'He didn't plan to sail the yacht himself?'

'No, he had no experience of sailing. The vessel was owned by Mr Sutherland, who was to teach him how to sail it.'

'What can you tell me about Mr Sutherland?'

Mrs Vardy was surprised at the question, and not a little uncomfortable. 'Why, almost nothing.'

'No? You have never met him?'

'Never.'

'I had heard — please forgive me for mentioning it — that you were both interviewed by the police.'

Mrs Vardy clearly did not like to be reminded of this. 'Yes, that was a distressing time. And the suspicion against me remains in the public memory, and always will until the truth of what happened to Jasper has been revealed. I was interviewed at the Town Hall police office. There were men there who looked at me as if I was a criminal. I can't describe how I felt. Mr Sutherland might have been there at the same time for all I know, but if he was, he must have been in another room and I never saw him.'

'Perhaps you and he were kept apart as they suspected collusion.'

'I have no doubt at all that that is what they did suspect.'

'How did he and Mr Holt meet?'

'It was through business, I believe. Jasper was a purveyor of wines and spirits, mainly to the restaurant trade, but also through a shop premises. Mr Sutherland was the secretary of a gentleman's club whose interest was yachting. How many of the members actually owned yachts or even sailed I couldn't say. I never met any of them, and Jasper was never a member. But I believe he came to Jasper to arrange for wines and brandy to be served at their annual dinner.'

'How soon was this before your husband disappeared?'

'Not long before. I can't imagine that they knew each other well.'

'And did your husband tell you anything about Mr Sutherland?'

'No, he only said that he was thinking of buying a yacht for amusement, and was about to take a trip in one, to see if it suited him.' Mrs Vardy gave little wail of sorrow. 'How could I have known what he meant to do? The very act of him saying he wanted to purchase a yacht suggested to me that the business was doing well. That was all I knew; all I could know at the time.'

'But you found out more later?'

'Yes. His accountant, Mr Westbury told me. It wasn't Jasper's fault. There were other businesses that had failed, and they had no funds to pay Jasper's invoices. He had already supplied them with the goods which had been consumed and found himself unable to meet his own creditors. Cheques he had written were being returned by the bank and people were starting to talk. He had tried to persuade his creditors it was a temporary embarrassment, he even said it was a banker's error, but people in that line of business know each other and suspected that he was in difficulty. There had been talk of him declaring bankruptcy. None of this I knew until afterwards.'

'But he was able to take out insurance, was he not? In a large sum, so the newspapers said. He must have paid the first instalment at least.'

'Yes, just the first one. I suppose you want to know how he paid it.' Mrs Vardy gulped. A tear escaped one eye and trickled down her face before she could prevent it. She blotted it carefully with a handkerchief. Mina allowed her as long as she needed to recover. 'He took my jewellery, Miss Scarletti. Some of it had belonged to my mother and my grandmother. He told me he was having it valued for insurance, but that was a lie. He pawned it. How could he do such a thing? I suppose he thought that in time I would have the insurance money and be able to retrieve it, but of course that never happened. I have it back, now, through the kindness of my family. In fact, if it had not been for my brother, I would have been destitute. He and his wife gave a home to me and my children. They have not been blessed with a family of their own but are godparents to

Franklin and Matthew. My boys have had a good education and want for nothing.' Despite this proud statement she looked dejected. 'Have I wasted your time? I had so hoped…'

'Not at all,' Mina reassured her. 'You said you employed a detective?'

'Yes. I have all his reports if you would like to see them.'

'I would.'

'In fact, I will show you all the papers in my possession. Letters, newspapers. I kept them all.'

'That would be most helpful. I will write to you when I am able to come and see you once more.'

There was a knock on the door, and Rose peered in. 'The doctor is here to see you.'

Mrs Vardy rose. 'Then I will trouble you no further. Believe me, I would be so grateful for any advice you could give me.' She left quickly before the tears began again.

Once her visitor had departed, Mina looked in *Page's Directory* for a Doctor Crosier but found nothing.

CHAPTER TEN

Dr Hamid drew a chair near to Mina's bed and opened his medical bag. 'I hardly need to ask if you are feeling better as I can see it for myself. More colour in your cheeks, brighter eyes. So now you can see what sensible behaviour and plenty of rest can do for you.'

'I can indeed,' said Mina.

'And Rose tells me that your appetite is improved.'

'My appetite is as good as cook will allow it to be,' said Mina. 'Rose has been instructing her and she has studied your book on invalid diet, the result being that I have been presented with dishes which assume that I am either toothless or too weak to chew. Perhaps you could reassure her that she is mistaken in both suppositions. Not all meat has to be boiled for quite so long.'

He smiled. 'I will do so. As long as your digestion proceeds well.'

'My digestion is good, provided I take small meals, and no-one thinks I need to be fattened up.'

He extracted the stethoscope from his bag. 'Who is the lady I passed on the stairs?' he asked. 'She looked very upset. Was she visiting you? Her face looked familiar, but I couldn't quite place her.'

Mina could not avoid a slight hesitation before she replied. 'She is a representative of a porcelain company. I was looking at their catalogue of mourning brooches.'

Dr Hamid was about to don the earpieces of the stethoscope but stopped abruptly. A series of increasingly worried expressions crossed his features. 'Rose also tells me that you have been visited by Mr Phipps the solicitor.'

'Yes,' said Mina calmly, 'I thought it was about time I made a will.'

It was his eyes that first expressed alarm, and he swallowed convulsively, but then he quickly recovered himself. 'Of course,' he said steadily, in his most professional manner, 'that is a wise thing for most people to do, but they are usually at a greater age than yourself. I do hope that you are not becoming despondent. I have known patients who have concealed their unhappy thoughts and show to the world a good humour they do not feel. If you are in low spirits then I can reassure you that many patients who suffer from fever and breathlessness as you have done, will experience something of that nature, but I promise that it will pass as you become stronger. You are young. You must not give up on life.'

'Thank you,' said Mina, 'but I am simply being sensible. I do intend to recover my health.'

He did not appear entirely reassured. 'I am glad to hear it. But if you have any worries or concerns, anything at all that troubles you, you must tell me about it at once. I know how much of a support you are to your family when you are well, but there are times when you need to take care of yourself or have someone take care of you.'

Mina could only nod agreement.

'Now,' he went on, donning the stethoscope, 'breathe as evenly as you can.' Whatever the instrument was telling him seemed favourable. He gave a nod of satisfaction and made some notes before preparing to take her pulse.

'Speaking of my family,' said Mina, 'it has occurred to me that when I am well again, I should purchase some insurance. I would like to do something to assist them.'

'Insurance?' he queried. 'What kind of insurance?'

'I meant a policy on my life. Unless you think I am not worth insuring.'

'That is not for me to say.' He pressed his fingers to her wrist, which she thought, looked very thin and bone pale under his strong brown grip.

'I suppose if I was to do so I would be obliged to obtain a certificate of good health from a doctor.'

'That is usual, yes.'

'Would that be from yourself or another?'

'Insurance companies often prefer to appoint their own men.'

'Someone recently mentioned a Dr Crosier. Is he suitable?'

Dr Hamid paused. 'Crosier? Where did you hear that name?'

'I — er ...'

He released her wrist. 'Miss Scarletti, what are you doing? Because if your pulse rate is anything to judge by this is no innocent enquiry.' A thought crossed his mind. 'Porcelain mourning brooches, you said? Of course! Saltmire and Vardy. That was the new Mrs Vardy I passed on the stairs. She is an occasional client of my sister. That is where I have seen her before.'

'Yes, she brought a tray of mourning brooches for me to look at.'

There was no disarming Dr Hamid's growing suspicions. 'Did she now? What a curious coincidence that the very person whom all the town is discussing should happen to come and see you.'

Mina said nothing.

Dr Hamid completed his notes and closed his medical bag. 'Miss Scarletti, I know you far too well. I think that you are engaging in one of your adventures, even from your bed of sickness, despite all my warnings. I also fear that if I was to beg you to be sensible and stop, you would disobey me. Where is Miss Cherry? I need to speak to her.'

'She is not here; she has another appointment.'

'Really? How convenient for you that her appointment coincided with Mrs Vardy's visit. And I happen to know that if she had been here then Mrs Vardy and Miss Cherry would have recognised each other.' He pressed a hand to his forehead. 'Of course, I see the connection, now. I sincerely hope that Miss Cherry has not been saying things she ought not to.'

'Not at all,' Mina protested. 'Mrs Vardy wrote to me asking for an interview, without realising that I was unwell. She wants my advice. She has a concern that is very unusual. Miss Cherry's behaviour has been exemplary, but she keeps reading to me about butterflies and embroidery, subjects in which I have no interest. If I have too little stimulus in my life it will not help my recovery.'

He snorted with annoyance. 'So despite all our efforts to protect you, to prevent you sapping your energy so you can apply it solely to the recovery of your health, you have found yourself a mystery to solve.'

'Yes, I have,' Mina admitted. 'Or at least it found me.'

'And what has Mrs Vardy charged you with? If you don't tell me at once I will be sure to ask her myself. You see, I can make enquiries too.'

'Her elder son Franklin thinks that he sees the ghost of his father. Mrs Vardy read about me in the newspapers and they made her think that I was a sensitive who might be able to see and perhaps even question it.'

He looked alarmed. 'I trust you informed her that you could not assist her.'

'I can't, not in that way, of course, but it would be a nice thing if I could study the case and see if I can find an answer that would alleviate the family's suffering.'

'From your sick-bed?' he exclaimed.

'Why ever not?'

He sat back in the chair, shaking his head in exasperation. 'And was your enquiry about Dr Crosier a part of this?'

Mina toyed briefly with a number of explanations but decided that the truth was simplest. 'Yes, it was. He was the doctor who gave Mr Holt a certificate of health for his policy of life insurance.'

'I dare not ask how you came to know that. So you are dragging me into your schemes! Again! Without even telling me what you were doing.'

'I am sorry,' said Mina, trying to sound penitent. She was obliged to admit to herself that she had more than once asked him to go very close to the limit of what a doctor ought to do.

Dr Hamid rose from the chair, folded his arms and paced about the room. 'You are one of my most difficult patients. I hardly know what you will be up to next. You know you need to take good care of your health, but you insist on risking it at every turn.'

Mina watched him as he walked and thought his way through the dilemma.

He spun around to face her, accusingly. 'The visit from Mr Phipps, that was a part of it, too? I know he has helped you before.'

'Yes,' she conceded.

There was a long silence as he gazed at her. 'Well, at least I can see that you are none the worse for all this activity. If you were, if I thought for one moment that it was harmful to your health, I would insist that you be watched carefully night and day and receive no visitors apart from your family and myself. As it is ….'

'As it is,' said Mina, 'on your own admission, I look all the better for it.'

He sat down once more, controlling his irritation into calm and practicality. 'Very well. I will not prevent you from receiving visitors, which I can see will only make you more agitated, and even if I try, I suspect that you will still manage to find a way to flout my instructions, but I need to guard against your doing anything more dangerous than you have done so far. Please at the very least, promise me that you will obey very strictly all the most important rules that I have set for your recovery.'

Mina capitulated. 'I promise,' she said.

'First, and I insist on this, you must not go outdoors until I say that you are well enough to do so. The weather is still very inclement, and a chill may cause a serious relapse. Do I have that promise?'

Mina nodded, meekly.

'You will not try to get out of bed unassisted, and in any case not at all until both I and Miss Cherry agree that it is in order. Then, you will go no further than a chair beside the bed.'

She nodded again.

He took a deep breath. 'If you obey, but *only* if you obey, I will, within what is permitted by the rules of my profession, assist your enquiries. I will do so mainly because I think that you will become distressed if I prevent you.'

'Thank you,' said Mina, relieved. 'Does that mean you can tell me something about Dr Crosier?'

'Are you sure you want to go into this now?'

'Yes, I am.'

He looked uncomfortable. 'The name is familiar to me, but I will say no more of him until I am sure of my ground. I assume that Mr Holt was given a certificate of good health, or he would not have been granted the policy.'

'Yes, he was insured by the Brighton and Hove Insurance company, after being examined by Dr Crosier but he only paid one instalment before he disappeared.'

'I remember the scandal, of course. The company refused to pay. Quite rightly, too.'

'But he told the boat owner, Mr Sutherland that he had been advised by his doctor to take the sea air for his health.'

'That would not be unusual. Men of business who overwork themselves are often so advised. All they require is peace and quiet to restore themselves. It does not necessarily mean that he was suffering from any disease. It would not prevent him being granted the certificate for the insurance company.'

'I see. That does explain it. And as it later transpired, Mr Holt had serious business troubles he had confided to no-one, so he may well have been working hard, and must surely have been unsettled in his mind. Mrs Vardy told me that the family doctor is called McClelland and he called in a Dr Fielding from London to examine the son.'

Dr Hamid nodded thoughtfully. 'I know Dr McClelland; he is a highly regarded practitioner in Brighton. Fielding of London, you say? There is a doctor of that name who has a clinic for the treatment of insanity. He is considered a great authority on the subject. Given the nature of the son's indisposition, I am not surprised that a man of his expertise was consulted. But these are all medical matters. I really don't think it is a situation in which you can provide any advice or assistance to Mrs Vardy.'

'It may just be that having a sympathetic car will bring the lady some comfort,' said Mina.

Dr Hamid considered her again. 'You do look and sound much more like your usual self, and I am pleased with your progress, but I am not yet ready to allow you more freedom of movement. Too much exertion could prove harmful. Your lungs are not yet fully recovered. I will, however, advise Miss Cherry and Rose that some easing of the regime I prescribed is in order.'

'Thank you. I would like to be allowed to see any reading material I require.'

'You shall.'

'But I do miss my visits to the Baths. And I am afraid — '

'Yes?'

'I have heard of people who spend much time in bed and forget how to use their limbs which are almost wasted away from lack of use. And my limbs were never very large to begin with.' Mina looked at her hands, which now she thought about it were even thinner than she remembered them, like the claws of a small bird.

'A week or two of rest will not harm you, but if you are concerned, I will ask Anna to come and see you tomorrow morning and bring her massage oils.'

With that promise, Dr Hamid departed, but he was shaking his head as he went.

CHAPTER ELEVEN

Dinner was in preparation, but instead of Richard coming to see Mina after the meal, looking well fed and in good spirits, he arrived before it was announced, his expression piteous, and his posture suggesting the most profound fatigue.

'Oh, how exhausting work is!' he exclaimed, throwing himself onto the coverlet beside Mina with such a heavy thump that she almost bounced bodily out of the bed. He stretched out, sighing with relief.

Mina put aside her newspaper. 'Richard, please take your shoes off, or you will dirty the coverlet and Miss Cherry will be very cross with you.'

He pulled himself into a sitting position and obeyed, puffing with the effort, then tossed his shoes onto the floor and fell back again. 'Miss Cherry is a tyrant and I would dislike her very much indeed except that she has nice eyes. They are a very pretty sort of green.'

'But what can you tell me about your day? I would have thought photography was not to be numbered amongst the most arduous of occupations.'

'Oh it is, it is, far worse than anything that involves a desk. You would think it ought to be possible to make one's mark in the world without having to slave away for hours!'

'One has to be very rich in order to make money without labouring for it. Has your new employer been imposing upon you by making you work for your wages? How very cruel of him!'

Richard waved a languid hand. 'Of course, I knew I would have to do *something*, but I just thought it would be more fun, and less effort, especially as we are friends.'

'And what are friends for other than to appoint you to a well-paid sinecure?' she taunted.

'Well exactly!'

'But was the work not interesting at all? I can imagine it would be.'

'Sometimes it was,' said Richard, grudgingly. 'I'll say this for Beckler, he is always looking for the newest thing in photography. Did you know that there is a way of making the darkness as bright as day so one can take pictures where there is no light? Soon there will be no need at all to wait for the sunshine. There is a kind of ribbon, but it's made of metal, and you set fire to it. He showed me some. I wouldn't have believed it unless I had seen it demonstrated. It was just a tiny bit but the light it cast was extraordinary.'

'That should make séances more challenging,' said Mina with a smile.

'No, because Beckler says you could not use it in a drawing room, at least not for long enough to take a photograph, because it makes a lot of smoke, and everyone would choke on it, and then the carpet would be covered in ash which would not please anybody.'

'Were you not hoping to receive some lady customers so you might talk to them and brighten your wearisome day?'

Even this thought did not cheer her brother. 'There were some, yes, but the pretty ones mostly came with their husbands and armfuls of crying babies. I have found, however, that Mr Beckler is very adept at making portraits in which plain ladies look much better than they are, and so they are flocking to his door like an army of lost souls begging to be saved.'

Mina looked at him reproachfully. 'Richard, I hope you are not so shallow as only to find pretty ladies good company? There are many ladies who have not been blessed with beauty who are delightful companions, so much so that with better acquaintance they will become beautiful in your eyes.'

He pulled a sulky mouth. 'You can't blame me for my preferences. I am just a weak man and can't help but admire beauty in a female. It inspires me to gallantry, and poetry too, or it would if I only had the time to write it.' He rolled onto his side and gazed up at Mina. 'Mr Beckler thinks you are pretty, you know.'

'We won't discuss that.'

'And clever. And quite alarming, too. He said you threatened to hit him.'

'Richard!'

He sighed. 'All right, but you will come around in time I know you will.' He rolled onto his back and lay like a fallen marionette, gazing at the ceiling.' I think I may have made a conquest, but it is not one I would boast of,' he said gloomily. 'A Mr Hartop came in with his daughter to have her portrait made. She is shaped like a guinea-pig which she closely resembles. The lady is very excitable about everything, declares all she sees to be quite wonderful and expresses this emotion with a sound like the whistle on a railway train. It is a train that threatens to crush the spirit of any man foolish enough to linger in its path. She is single, which came as no surprise to me, although she must be thirty-five if a day, and I think her father hopes to entice a suitor with a flattering portrait. The portrait at least will be silent. When I wrote her name in the register of customers, she gazed at me as if I was a roast joint and made a strange little squeak. Before they left, her father asked for my card.'

'I didn't know you had a card.'

'I don't, I just gave him one for Scarletti Publishing.'

'That may have been unwise. They must now imagine that you are the heir to a thriving business. It makes you very eligible.'

'Oh dear!' said Richard.

'And what does Mr Hartop do?'

'I think he owns a number of lodging houses in Brighton.' Richard sat up and pulled a card from his pocket. 'Hartop and Co. North Street, Brighton. Superior accommodation. Unmarried daughter free on application.' He groaned and replaced the card. 'I should have told him I was penniless with no prospects.'

'Given what you have told me about Miss Hartop, he might not feel that to be an obstacle to the match,' said Mina, teasingly.

Richard groaned again.

'But apart from that, I can't imagine that your work was as arduous as you pretend. You are not frail. You have plenty of energy when you choose to employ it.'

'I suppose it was tolerable enough when I dealt with the clients,' he admitted, 'and I spent some time outside, handing out advertising cards to passers-by.'

'You didn't take any photographs?'

'No, he wouldn't let me. I wasn't allowed to touch the camera or anything!'

'That was probably very wise on your first day.'

Richard sat up again and gulped water from the carafe without troubling himself with a glass. 'Did you know the shop used to be the business of Mr Simpson the portrait photographer? Wasn't he the man who took the pictures at Enid's wedding? I thought it looked familiar. How mortifying it must be to have one's mistakes recorded for posterity. He passed away at the end of last year, and his son has just sold the whole business to Mr Beckler, including a great many old photographs. Oh, and there is a ghost as well. In Brighton every house of the slightest antiquity has to have one. It is the fashion. Old Mr Simpson is supposed to wander about the premises looking for something and muttering to himself.'

'I take it you have not seen him?'

'No. Beckler is hoping to capture his spirit in a photograph in order to please Mr Hope, but he hasn't succeeded so far. He is trying to mix new chemicals which the ghosts will find more to their taste. But it must be hard to photograph a ghost because you have to have a lot of light to make a portrait and everyone knows that ghosts only come out in the dark. As soon as you put the light on, they go away. He did it by accident once, but he doesn't know how it happened and he hasn't managed it since. His new idea now, is to leave the camera out all night with the lens cap off and hope to capture the ghost that way.'

'If he succeeds, I would like to see the picture,' said Mina, 'if only to find out how I might judge it to be genuine.'

'In the meantime, would you believe, he has tasked me with looking at all of Simpson's stock of photographs. There are whole boxes of the blessed things in the attic. Duplicates, I suppose, or ones that were never collected. I am to compose a list of the names of the subjects which are written on the back. Some of the portraits are very old, and I feel sure most of the people depicted are long dead. But Beckler thinks he can sell them as mementoes to the families. If you were to see them, you would think them a dreary assortment. The gentlemen in particular. It is a perfectly horrid display of beards and I would be ashamed to own up to any of them.'

'A beard is thought to be a very manly thing,' Mina objected. 'I admire a good beard myself if it is not over-large and tidily kept.'

'One like Dr Hamid's, you mean?'

'Something of that nature.'

'A large beard is only good to hide a weak chin,' said Richard, stroking the blond side whiskers which were all that adorned his face. 'And I think I have a rather good chin, which the world ought to see. But if I was to find that Miss Hartop detests beards, I will gladly grow one.' He lay back on the bed again. 'There must be easier paths to fortune. Are there no more rich widows in town? Do you know of any, Mina? They should be very old and easily flattered.'

'Only Mrs Bettinson,' said Mina, mischievously, naming a friend of her mother's whose main pleasures in life were gossip and consuming cake. 'But I don't think she is looking for another husband.'

Richard winced. 'Mrs Bettinson is a mountain I would rather not climb.'

'Then your future is clear. You must either work for a living or marry Miss Hartop.'

Richard buried his face in the pillow and whimpered.

Mina had never given any thought as to whether Miss Cherry had nice eyes or not, but now that her brother had pointed it out, she supposed it must be true. When the nurse returned early the next day following an afternoon in the company of Mrs Phipps, she did so with a smile that brightened her whole face including her eyes, which did appear to be green, and assured Mina that her visit had gone very well.

'At least that was my impression, but of course I have heard that the lady has in the past been considered hard to please so she may think differently,' she added modestly.

'I hope she enjoyed your readings.'

'She did, very much. She particularly appreciated the portion on the domestic use of starch, which she asked to hear no less than three times.' Miss Cherry took out the book, favouring Mina with an inviting smile, as if offering a great treat. 'I will read it to you now, if you like.'

'Thank you,' said Mina, hastily, but I must reserve that pleasure for another time. Miss Hamid is coming here this morning to perform an oriental massage.'

'Oh?' Miss Cherry was taken aback. 'Is that permitted?'

'Yes, it is on the instructions and advice of Dr Hamid. But you need not remain here for it. In fact, I would appreciate it very much if you were to accompany my mother on a little excursion she has planned. She has been disinclined to venture out recently but feels a little stronger today. Her intention is to visit the shops in St James's Street, and view the spring gardens in Old Steine. The fresh air will undoubtedly do her good, but I would feel so much happier if she was to be in sympathetic company, just in case it proves to be too wearying for her.'

Miss Cherry could do no more than put away her book and agree.

Mina did not mention this, but her mother, under the impression that Richard had been transformed almost instantly into an accomplished photographer, was considering paying an unannounced visit to his place of employment. It was therefore not entirely certain that the excursion would be an unqualified success, since it had the potential to reveal Richard's lack of any knowledge of or competence in the art of photography, but Mina had seen him talk his way out of such situations before and she supposed that he would do so again.

Miss Hamid arrived bringing a large stout leather bag from which she extracted a gift, a bottle of the herbal fruit mineral water that Mina particularly liked. She also imparted some good advice. 'There is too much emphasis on treating women as if they are made of something that will break if used,' she said. 'We need our vitality and our muscles just as much as men do, in fact sometimes I think we need them more. There are so many hard-working women and far too many idle men, who are only strong enough to lift a glass of beer but persist in thinking themselves the superior sex.'

She donned an apron, folded back her cuffs and made short brisk work of examining Mina's limbs. 'I am here not a moment too soon,' she said. 'Women should not lie in bed too long when they are unwell, or when their children are born, they should get up and walk. You have lost flesh which you cannot afford to lose, and I suppose you have not been allowed any exercise.'

'No, that is quite forbidden. I am hardly permitted to lift a book. Your brother said that I am not to get out of bed unassisted, and then I should only travel as far as the armchair, which is not a long journey.'

Miss Hamid permitted herself an indulgent smile. 'He means well, but he is a man. But he is right in one thing, you do need to take care. Work slowly and gradually, but you must work. I will show you some exercises which will firm your muscles, and which you can do very easily by yourself without any harm to your recovery.'

She pulled some fresh soft towels from her bag and laid them on the bed. They had the clean slightly spicy scent that transported Mina as if by magic back to the Baths, and its delicious vapours.

The simple act of being prepared for the massage was already making Mina feel better. She began to see the possibilities of writing a new story of adventure in which a humdrum item of textile was transformed into a flying platform by the application of special herbs and would take the inventor anywhere he or she pleased. Inevitably, since that was her usual way of thinking, she speculated on what might happen if the application dried out and lost its power during the flight.

The next item to appear from Miss Hamid's bag was a bottle of massage oil. It was one of Mina's favourites, sandalwood with hints of jasmine and other fragrant flowers, which both relaxed and invigorated at the same time. The masseuse carefully oiled her capable hands, and Mina nestled into the soft towels in pleasurable anticipation. 'I believe we have a mutual acquaintance, a Mrs Vardy,' she said. 'Your brother told me that she attends the Baths.'

'We do, although I only know her professionally,' said Miss Hamid, smoothing the oil into Mina's calves with firm fingers.

'Oh, well of course I wouldn't ask you to reveal to me what treatment you give her,' said Mina, quickly, 'I know that is confidential. But I am sure that what you do for her is very comforting. She has been very open with me about the trials she has to bear, and I feel that she deserves some peace.'

'She does.' Miss Hamid's face clouded a little with concern. 'I regret to say that certain of my clients have suggested to me that Mrs Vardy ought not to be admitted to the Baths in view of what they refer to as "her reputation". I have made it very clear to them that there is no proof that she is guilty of any wrongdoing. Some persons really have nothing better to do with their time than imagine themselves to be better than others.'

Mina understood what circumstances must have provoked that last comment, since the Hamids were of Anglo-Indian descent. She reflected sadly that while there were many who were happy to enjoy the application of the Indian *Cham-poo* as it was known, while visiting India, those same persons might have been less willing to avail themselves of the same treatment in Brighton. 'Does Mr Vardy attend the Baths?'

'No, I believe he has no requirement or interest in the healthful effects of the vapour bath, but he is perfectly content for Mrs Vardy to visit as often as she likes.'

'Does she ever seek treatments for her elder son, Franklin?'

Miss Hamid hesitated, unsure of how much to say.

'I am aware that he is in poor health, and is currently unable to attend school,' said Mina.

'Hm,' said the masseuse with a nod. 'From what Mrs Vardy has told me, I am sure that her son would benefit. In fact, I did offer to pay a visit to the house and see the child myself to determine what might be best for him, but Mrs Vardy said that her husband would not hear of it.'

'How curious!' said Mina, as Miss Hamid gently turned her over, 'so Mrs Vardy can avail herself of the treatments but not her son?'

'That is so. Apparently, the boy rests during the day and Mr Vardy does not wish him to be disturbed. That is the excuse at any rate. But there may be other reasons, their doctor's advice, perhaps.'

She said no more, but Mina detected in the firm hands that eased the strained muscles of her back that Miss Hamid was not comfortable with the explanation.

When Miss Hamid had departed, Mina was eager to follow the written instructions she had been given regarding the stretching and moving of her limbs. The ache in her twisted back was gone, and she felt if not exactly stronger, then ready and able to become stronger. She could for the first time since her illness confidently envisage a time when she would rise from her bed and walk unaided, dine with her family, pay visits to her friends, and go down to the seashore to enjoy the sound of the waves as they washed over the pebbled beach in the summer sun.

CHAPTER TWELVE

Over the next few days, Mina began to discover her strength again. Carefully but persistently, she undertook regular exercise, always when there was no-one else in the room. She would have liked to use her little dumbbells but felt that asking for them would be viewed with deep suspicion, so she made do with books. Miss Hamid had been right, of course. There were times when one was obliged to rest but after that, the best tonic was exercise. At last she felt ready to leave her bed, and so advised Miss Cherry and Rose, who to her great relief, did not disagree.

Mrs Vardy's eagerly anticipated second visit therefore found Mina seated in a cosy armchair beside her bed, swaddled in blankets. She hoped that the fact she was sitting rather than propped up made her look in better health and less like a *memento mori* photograph. She had not yet been permitted a mirror so felt doubtful on the subject. At least she wasn't surrounded by wreaths of fragrant flowers and her favourite books, with dark dots painted on her closed eyelids. She was alone, since Miss Cherry's meeting with Mrs Phipps had been pronounced a success. The nurse had accepted an engagement to accompany the lady on a visit to enjoy a light luncheon and listen to a recital of Shakespeare's poetry by Mr Merridew, both of which were keenly anticipated.

Mrs Vardy arrived carrying a portmanteau bag well stuffed with papers, which Mina thought looked very encouraging. She always felt a little thrill at the sight of a pile of documents, which held the rich promise of discovery, in much the same way as a hungry person might have regarded a plate laden with appetising food.

'I have brought you a portrait which includes my late husband,' said Mrs Vardy, 'It was taken the year before he disappeared. As you see we were a united and devoted family.'

She handed a photograph to Mina who studied it intently. It was a conventional family portrait, mounted on an embossed card, which was printed with the words *Premier Tintype Studio, St James's Street, Brighton*, and handsomely framed. The Holts as depicted were a proudly successful family. Mrs Vardy, seen nine years ago was immediately recognisable as a younger and rounder version of the woman who had called upon Mina. The intervening years had worn her with age and sadness. She was thinner and less fresh but had acquired in compensation a controlled dignity. Mrs Holt, as she was then, was portrayed seated on a straight-backed chair beside a round table that was draped in a fringed cloth and wearing what must have been her most expensive gown. She looked composed, confident, untroubled, proud. The elder boy Franklin stood in front of the table, stiff and serious in his best clothes, with straight hair in a severe centre parting, a poutingly sulky mouth and large eyes. The younger, a curly haired handful with a round face, plump cheeks and a mouth that looked about to break into a playful grin, was seated on his mother's lap, and must have been hard to keep still for the camera. On the far side of the table from his wife, Jasper Holt was standing in a carefully arranged pose, his hand resting lightly on the table top, shoulders well squared. At his fingertips was a cut glass decanter, a set of stemmed glasses and, to Mina's eyes, an unusually large wine bottle. Mina would have preferred to have seen an individual full face portrait of Mr Holt to gain a better impression of his features, but all she saw was a well-dressed stockily built man, his hair thick and brushed back from his face, worn short at the sides, and a beard of the most common cut. The chain of his father's watch was draped across the front of his waistcoat.

'You don't have a better picture?' asked Mina.

'No, there is only the wedding portrait. This is the best, the most recent one. It is how he appeared on the last day I saw him. I have a description here. Gordon took out an advertisement. We were still hoping, then.' She passed a printed paper to Mina.

'What date was this?'

'Gordon arranged it before those scandalous articles first appeared in the *Gazette*. I think Jasper had been missing for about a week. It was in all the newspapers, including *The Times*. That is one of the handbills Gordon had made. He had some posted up at railway stations. We thought Jasper might read one and then we would receive something from him, if only a note to say that he was well but had gone away for a rest.'

'You thought he might be in hiding?'

'I thought, perhaps that he had been working too hard and was suffering from nerves — that was all I could think of at the time.'

Mina studied the handbill.

MISSING

Mr Jasper Holt, of Holt and Co, purveyors of wines and spirits, St James's Street, Brighton.

Age 43. About 5ft 8 inches tall, strongly made, fresh complexion, hair and beard light brown, no distinguishing marks. Well-spoken. Smartly dressed and wearing a silver watch and chain, engraved with the name of his father, F J Holt. Mr Holt went missing after falling from a yacht on 18 July 1864, and was initially presumed drowned, but may have survived. A reward of £100 is offered by his family for any news of his whereabouts, either living or deceased. Details to G Saltmire of Saltmire Fine Porcelain, Hove.

'It says no distinguishing marks,' said Mina, regretfully. 'He has no scars, or blemishes upon him?'

'None of any significance,' said Mrs Vardy, 'although he may have had some afterwards — who knows what injuries he might have acquired in the accident?'

'And he was not troubled by poor health? Despite his business difficulties? There are men whose health would suffer in such a situation. You said you thought he was working too hard.'

Mrs Vardy looked wistful and Mina guessed that she was reliving the early days of July 1864, wondering perhaps if there was anything she ought to have seen or done which would have prevented the catastrophe. 'In the weeks leading to his disappearance he had been working much longer hours and seemed wearier than usual, but that is often the sign of a flourishing business, is it not? At least that is what I thought. How could I know differently? In fact, I recall suggesting to him that in view of how busy he was, he should think of engaging another assistant, but he said that it was only a temporary situation.'

'But what about his general health? Was that good, or did you have any concerns?'

'His general health was always good. I was worried about him for a time, since I knew that his father had died at the age of fifty-two from a failure of the heart, but Jasper reassured me that having observed his father's decline, he was familiar with the symptoms, and did not suffer in that way.'

'When he initially disappeared did you believe that there was a chance that he might have survived the fall in the water? Was he a strong swimmer?'

She smiled, and it was a proud, fond memory. 'Oh yes, very. In his youth he won prizes for it. Later he tried to swim whenever he had the chance, but of course he had not done so much in recent years because of the demands of his business. But from what I read in the newspapers the accident happened when the yacht was not far from shore. I would have thought a competent swimmer could have reached it. He might almost have floated to safety on the tide,' she added dreamily, as if conjuring up the scene in her imagination.

'I am told that according to Mr Sutherland he wished to sail to Shoreham?'

'So I understand.'

'Why was that, do you think? Do you have friends or relations there?'

'I don't know why. We know no-one who lives there. I asked Mr Benton, the assistant at the shop, if he knew anything, and he was just as mystified as the rest of us. He said that they had never done business with anyone in Shoreham. When Jasper and I were courting we took many excursions along the coast, and Shoreham was one of the places we passed through, but we never stayed there. I am wondering if Mr Sutherland's memory was faulty from the shock. Or maybe he misheard.'

Mrs Vardy took another packet of papers from her bag. 'There are letters here —business letters. I'm not sure what you will make of them. When Jasper disappeared, Gordon spoke to his accountant Mr Westbury but afterwards he told me not to trouble myself about it. He said that there were questions that only Jasper could clear up and he hoped that when Jasper returned all would be well.' Her lips trembled.

Mina received the packet and opened it. Inside, a bundle of neatly folded letters was tied in thin ribbon. She selected the top one and began to read.

Westbury and Graydon Accountants
North Street, Brighton
10 July 1864

Dear Mr Holt,

A serious matter has arisen concerning the accounts of Holt and Co, for the year ended 31 December 1863, which were completed and signed last month. Mr Livermore has been making some enquiries and received information which has caused him considerable unease. Since my signature is on the accounts I have been placed in a very difficult position, and I am quite unable to alleviate Mr Livermore's anxieties.

Please could you come and see me as a matter of urgency. I trust that there may simply have been an innocent error, which can be easily corrected, although Mr Livermore is putting quite a different cast on the situation and is insinuating that I not only knew of the irregularity but was complicit in its arrangement. Naturally I wish to resolve the question as soon as possible.

Yours faithfully
H Westbury

13 July 1864

Dear Mr Holt,

I am astonished to find that I have not yet received a reply to my letter of 2nd inst. I must emphasise that the matter is extremely urgent, and becomes more so with each passing day, as Mr Livermore has now consulted a solicitor. My clerk delivered a message to your place of business yesterday and found only your assistant Mr Benton on the premises who stated that you were not there, and he should look for you at home. My clerk then made enquiries for you at your residence only to be told by your servant that you were at your place of business.

I am extremely anxious to speak to you. If it is not convenient for you to come to my office, we may meet at any other reasonable location you prefer.

I should also mention that the cheque you used to pay my recent invoice has been returned due to an insufficiency of funds in your bank account, a situation which causes me considerable disquiet. If you wish me to continue to act for you, I shall first require payment in full.

Yours faithfully

H Westbury

'Who is Mr Livermore?' asked Mina.

'According to Gordon, he is a hotelier and was one of Jasper's most important customers. He was also one of Mr Westbury's clients. He loaned Jasper some money. At least I think it was a loan, but Mr Livermore claimed that it wasn't. He said that Jasper had approached him offering to make an investment for him as he had seen a good opportunity in the wine trade that needed to be taken advantage of at once.'

'And did he make the investment?' asked Mina, although she was fairly sure of the answer she would receive.

'It appears —', Mrs Vardy gave a soft unhappy exhalation, 'that he did not. He may have been intending to, of course. I would like to believe that he was. But he owed the bank a lot of money at the time, and they were sending him horrid letters demanding immediate payment, so it seems — I suppose the temptation must have been too much for him — it seems that he used Mr Livermore's money to pay off some of what he owed, just to gain time. There are so many conflicting stories and not one piece of paper to support any of them, that I don't know what to think.'

Mina was extremely grateful for the fact that since she came of age, she had insisted on managing her own modest finances. She would never be so bewildered as Mrs Vardy was, never be the victim of a husband who had promised to protect her interests but neglected to do so. 'Do you know what it was that Mr Westbury was concerned about regarding the business accounts?' she asked.

'Gordon had a long meeting with him after Jasper disappeared, and I did ask him to explain it to me. I think the suggestion was that Jasper had put some wrong figures in the accounts to make it look as if the business was doing well when it wasn't. I'm not sure why he did that, but Gordon says Jasper was hoping to borrow some money to keep the business going. Apparently, people will lend you money if you already have it, but not if you don't, which seems the wrong way round to me, but then I don't have a head for business. But Mr Livermore accused Mr Westbury of conniving with Jasper and for a man in his position that is a very serious accusation.'

Mina turned to the next letter in the bundle.

14 July 1864

Dear Mr Holt,

In view of your continued failure to meet either myself or any member of my firm, or to reply to my letters, I must assume that you no longer wish me to act on your behalf. My invoices remain unpaid, and I shall forthwith be placing the debts in the hands of persons who will be less accommodating than myself,

Yours faithfully
H Westbury

'As far as I know, that was the last letter Mr Westbury wrote to Jasper,' said Mrs Vardy. 'There were other letters addressed to him at the house after that, but I think he must have destroyed them. I only have those few because they were tumbled in with family documents, or I think he would have destroyed them, too. I believe that proceedings for debt were about to be taken against him, and then we would have had the misery and shame of bankruptcy. When Jasper disappeared and we didn't know his fate, all that came to nothing as his property could not be touched. After he was declared deceased the estate was valued, what little property remained was sold, and the proceeds used to pay something to the creditors. They received very little. Nowhere near what they were owed.'

Mrs Vardy handed Mina another bundle of papers.

'There are more pages from the newspapers, and letters from persons who claimed to have seen Jasper. One lady was convinced she had seen him in Australia which is ridiculous. He has also apparently appeared in Scotland, Cornwall and the Isle of Wight. But where the sightings sounded possible, Gordon did employ a man, a Mr Handley, to look into it. You'll find his reports there. I also received letters from clairvoyants saying that they could locate Jasper, but they always asked for money I didn't have. There was only so far that I could trespass on Gordon's generosity.'

'And you feel sure that Mr Holt is deceased?'

'Yes, I must accept it now. At least, what I mean is that his physical form is no more, although his soul, his spirit lives on. Mrs Barnham, the medium I consult has convinced me, and she has passed on many messages from him. He told me that his death was an accident, and that no blame is to be attached to Mr Sutherland. And he is happy and at peace and watches over us. But I can't make other people believe that, and they whisper against me. If I am sure of it, why is no-one else? Why do they deny the world of the spirit? Can you help me, Miss Scarletti?'

There was only one answer Mina could give. 'I will do my best. May I retain these papers for study?'

'Yes, if you have some secure place for them.'

They were too bulky for Mina's correspondence box, but she did have a lockable drawer in her writing desk which Miss Cherry had already explored and was unlikely to do so again. Here the papers were deposited.

As Mrs Vardy prepared to leave, she stopped and inhaled. 'There is a delightful scent in the air, but I see no flowers.'

'Ah yes, that is massage oil. Miss Hamid came to me this morning.'

'Oh, she is a wonder, is she not? The steam cure is so calming.'

'Perhaps Franklin would benefit from it?'

'In time, perhaps, but he sleeps so little at night that he rests during the day. My sister Marion is always there to watch over him, and she feels that the peace and quiet of that time is as good as any treatment and he ought not to be disturbed.'

Aunt Marion was a witch, of that Franklin was sure. He had read of such persons, not in anything his mother might have liked him to read, but one of the boys at school had a story called The Witch's Dark Spell, written by Robert Neil, which he had lent to him. It had been very frightening indeed and now he wished he had never read it, but it did answer all his questions. During the day Aunt Marion looked almost normal. He had always thought that witches were supposed to be very ugly, but he had learned from the story that they had spells that could make them look beautiful and made people trust them, even love them. Aunt Marion was quite good-looking he supposed, but when she snarled and snapped at him her face creased up and became quite twisted. That was her real witch face coming out, but no-one else but he was able to see it.

She didn't have a cauldron to mix her potions, but she had a little jug that she stirred things up in, some white powder and sugar and water, and insisted he swallowed a dose, saying that it would make him well again. He didn't like the potion, but Mr Vardy had insisted that he must take all his medicine, or he would never get better. It was as clear as plain water, but it smelt funny and stung his nostrils and tasted both sweet and bitter. Sometimes after taking it, his head ached, and he felt drowsy and sick. He was sure that he was being poisoned.

Franklin determined that if he was given the nasty medicine again, he would try and hold it in his mouth for as long as he could so the witch would think he had swallowed it, then when she had gone, he would spit it out into a handkerchief. If only he knew how, he would send a letter to Mr Robert Neil, telling him that he was a victim of a witch and begging for rescue, but he was friendless and alone, adrift in a sea of troubles.

CHAPTER THIRTEEN

Phipps and Co
Solicitors
Middle Street
Brighton
March 1872

Dear Miss Scarletti

I have made some further efforts to trace Mr William Sutherland but without success. Neither he nor his business are listed in any of the current London or Home Counties directories. Earlier directories show that at the time of the Holt tragedy Mr Sutherland was in partnership with a Mr Albert Fenwick, who I have traced, but he declines to make any statement saying simply that has not seen his former partner for several years.

I did however briefly correspond with a cousin of Mr Sutherland, who is an accountant residing in London. He has advised me that Mr Sutherland gave up his London office some years ago and is now in another line of business. I was not provided with an address; however, I was given to understand that he has no intention of discussing the disappearance of Mr Holt with anyone. The cousin could only say that there was no doubt in his mind that Mr Sutherland would always maintain that Mr Holt's death was an unfortunate accident.

I am sorry I could not be of any further assistance, but I will let you know if I hear anything further.

Yours faithfully,
R Phipps

The next time Dr Hamid called to see Mina he was unusually quiet and reserved. He studied her respiration and pulse stating that they were as good if not better than he had hoped but not as good as he would eventually like them to be, but more than that he seemed reluctant to say. His manner suggested that he was concerned to begin a new subject for fear of where it would lead him.

He was packing his medical bag and preparing to leave, when after standing up he paused, and abruptly sat down again.

'Thank you,' said Mina, who had been watching him carefully and understood the reason for his discomfort. 'What news do you have for me?'

The medical bag was on his lap, and he stared down at it, his hand wrapped reassuringly about the leather-bound handle. To any patient, anyone passing him in the street, it was a symbol of his profession. Mina felt suddenly guilty at how often she had engaged his help and pushed him further than he might have wanted to go. They had first met at a séance when Mina had been investigating the activities of Miss Eustace and he had been seeking answers in the midst of grief following the death of his wife. His eyes had been opened to the duplicity of mediums, but Mina knew that he had never lost hope.

Decisively, he picked up the bag, and placed it on the floor beside the chair. 'You are aware of course that many people come to the Baths not because they are unwell, but to restore and refresh themselves and therefore they cannot be regarded as patients but clients. We offer a service. It is not in any way a medical consultation.'

'I do appreciate that,' said Mina.

'If we can proceed with that understanding —?'

'We can.'

'Very well, I have examined all our records, and can confirm that Mr Jasper Holt, the missing man we have spoken of, was never a patient of mine. Neither did he ever ask me informally for medical advice. In fact, I don't believe that I have ever met him. However . .' He gestured uncertainly.

Mina smiled. 'Now that we have dealt with the question of patient confidentiality I would very much like to know about the '"however".'

'Yes. The thing is, Mr Holt did visit the Baths. He had an account and he used our services. This was not in the year before his disappearance, but prior to that, when I assume that his business was not in difficulties and he was more prosperous. It must have been his later financial situation that resulted in his giving up the account. But when he came, he took vapour baths and he also used the services of a masseur.'

'Is the masseur still employed by you?'

'He is, and I have spoken to him.'

'Since Mr Holt is legally dead, I don't think you need trouble about what either you or the masseur might have to say,' Mina hinted. 'Or do you think he may still be alive?'

'No, I think that he is dead. Although he did not consult me, he confided to the masseur that he had been having symptoms which had troubled him, and the masseur very sensibly advised him to see his doctor. Holt however replied that he did not want to see his family doctor — that would have been Dr McClelland — in case his wife was to learn of it and become anxious. The masseur then suggested that he consult another doctor, but of course he did not know whether Holt actually did so.'

'Could you discover anything about Mr Holt's state of health from what he told the masseur?'

'Never having examined Mr Holt, I can only judge by the symptoms he reported, but based on those, I think it is very possible that there was a weakness in the functioning of his heart, something for which there is no cure and would have shortened his life.'

'Ah,' said Mina, 'that is interesting, and I have learned something recently which strengthens that conclusion. I have spoken to Mrs Vardy again, and raised with her the question of Mr Holt's health. She knew nothing of any visit to a doctor, and although she noticed that her husband was tired, she assumed it was simple weariness from long hours of work, something that he claimed was a temporary situation. But she did mention to me that Mr Holt's father had died of a failure in the action of the heart at the age of fifty-two. Naturally she expressed concern about this to her husband, but he reassured her that he did not suffer in the same way as his father. But he could have been lying in order not to worry her.'

'He would not be the first man to do so,' said Dr Hamid, wryly.

'If we assume that Mr Sutherland's account of Mr Holt falling overboard is true, then Mr Holt might have died from the sudden fall into the water, creating a strain on his heart, whether or not he struck his head. In fact, now that I think about it, we don't even know for certain that he did strike his head, that was Mr Sutherland's assumption, which he based on the fact that he saw Mr Holt unconscious and then sinking very quickly. Under the circumstances is there any possibility at all that Mr Holt could have survived?'

Dr Hamid gave Mina's query some thought. 'That is not an easy question to answer. In such cases there are so many things to consider. Much depends on how good a swimmer he was, and how encumbered by clothing. There are also the weather and the tides to take into account, and how far from shore he was when he fell, whether or not he was injured by the fall, and how weak his heart was at the time. If he was unconscious, then probably not. If he was conscious, then panicked and struggled, I think not.'

'I understand that he was a good swimmer, and on that day the weather was good and the sea calm and the yacht not far from shore.'

'Then there was a slight chance. And in view of the attempted fraud the insurance company was quite right not to pay out on the policy, especially as there was no witness to the events other than the boatman whose account must be regarded with caution. Who knows, Mr Holt might never have fallen into the water at all, and was simply put ashore? But even if he had fallen and survived, his years of life were more limited than those of another man, and he was aware of it.'

'But do you think he had years, rather than weeks or months to live?'

'His general bodily health, according to the masseur, was otherwise robust, so yes, if he took good care of himself, he would have had several years.'

'Then is it possible that he is still alive?'

'I wouldn't rule it out. If I am pressed, I would say that there is a chance, just a very slight chance that he is still alive, but if so, I would be prepared to find him a very unwell man.'

Dear Miss Scarletti

Further to my recent letter I have been discussing your enquiries with one of the senior partners here who recalls the disappearance of Mr Holt and had some dealings with the estate. I do not know if this is of any interest to you, but the name of Mr Sutherland also came up in connection with a court case following events that took place in the previous year. It relates to charges of conspiracy to commit fraud levelled against the directors and officers of the Maritime Queen Insurance Company Ltd. Mr Sutherland was initially suspected of being involved in the conspiracy but after being questioned by the police it was accepted that he had only provided professional advice to the company in the usual way of business, and he was never charged with any offence. I don't believe his name ever appeared in the press in connection with the case.

Yours faithfully,

R Phipps

Dear Mr Phipps

Thank you for your letter. I was wondering if you could tell me more about the fraud case you mentioned. How did the charges come about? Who were the other defendants? Was there any mention of Mr Holt in connection with the case?

Yours faithfully,

M Scarletti

Dear Miss Scarletti

Thank you for your letter.

The Maritime Queen Insurance Company Ltd was formed in 1863 with its administrative offices at an address in Old Steine. The board of directors included a distinguished retired naval officer, Captain Horace Bulstrode, a highly regarded gentleman of impeccable reputation, who had served for many years as a Sussex magistrate. It was later established that Captain Bulstrode had had nothing at all to do with the conduct of the company and was a mere figurehead intended by the managers to provide an impression of respectability to their enterprise in order to attract wealthy investors. Two friends of Captain Bulstrode, retired military gentlemen who were not resident in Brighton were also, through him, drawn into the net, to the great embarrassment of all three. The other directors who were suspects in the fraud, included a Mr John Taylor, the secretary of a friendly society, Mr Walter Randall, a payroll clerk, and a Mr William Cobbe, bank manager.

Taylor and Randall had issued a false prospectus and a false balance sheet, the documents convincingly drawn up to persuade investors that the company had substantial assets, which was not the case. When the fraud was exposed the company was wound up with enormous debts and the investors lost all their money.

When the case finally came to trial in 1864, it was found that Taylor and Randall, each of whom had been bailed in the sum of £2,000, were nowhere to be found. It was eventually discovered that they had absconded and gone abroad, much to the distress of the friends who had stood surety for them in good faith. The other defendants were all acquitted.

I do not believe that Mr Holt was involved with the fraud, or at any rate his name has never been mentioned in connection with it.

Yours faithfully

R Phipps

William Cobbe, bank manager, thought Mina. *Could he be the same man who attended Mrs Barnham's séances, the man concerning whom Mr Merridew entertained suspicions?*

It was late afternoon, the time between luncheon and dinner, when the minds of English persons naturally turn to the subject of tea. Mina had just enjoyed a cup of milky tea and a slice of plain sponge cake and was comfortably settled in the armchair where she was now preferring to spend more of her time than in her bed. She was studying *Page's Directory* which Rose considered to be very peculiar reading indeed since it was only lists of names and advertisements. Every so often, Mina would look up at the window, hoping for a turn in the weather.

She was craving the brightness of the sun, warm breezes on her face, and the smell of the sea. Disappointed in the prospect of all three, she returned to the book, when there was a knock on her door, and she raised her head with a sudden realisation of how weary she was and rubbed her eyes.

Rose entered, thankfully without the hot poultice, which was now no longer thought necessary, bearing only a visitor's card which she was regarding with an expression of curiosity.

'It's a Mr Vardy, Miss. He presents his compliments, and good wishes for your health, and says that if you are too fatigued to see him, he quite understands, and if that is the case, he will depart without troubling you and come another time. Were you expecting him?'

'I was not.' Mina looked at the card, which advertised the company of Saltmire and Vardy, Fine Porcelain, but was also printed with the name S Vardy, managing director. 'Where is he now?'

'In the front parlour, Miss.'

'I take it he only wishes to see me if I am well enough to endure company?'

'Yes, Miss.' Rose gave her a hard look but did not express an opinion.

'Well I shan't disappoint him.' Mina decided that she ought to have another person present at her interview with a male stranger. 'Where is mother?'

'Mrs Scarletti is in the drawing room with Mrs Phipps and Mrs Bettinson and a great deal of cake. Miss Cherry is there too. She is wearing a new bonnet.'

Mina smiled. 'In that case I will not ask you to disturb them. Is my brother here? I suppose he is not back from his employment yet.'

'No, Miss.'

'Very well. You may bring some tea if Mr Vardy wishes it. And cake if there is any left. Don't bring the biscuits, they are only fit to make trifle. Since I am not acquainted with Mr Vardy, I will require you to remain.'

Rose departed, and Mina settled comfortably in her swaddle of shawls and wraps and scarves. The directory had already informed her that the Vardys occupied a family house in Hove, in one of the tall white terraces sloping down towards the sea, which proclaimed them to be comfortably off although not especially wealthy.

Rose appeared with Mr Vardy but no tea or cake. Mina reassured the maid that there was nothing more she required and there was a desultory arranging of the blankets about her shoulders which needed no arranging but served to enable Rose to stare closely at Mr Vardy a little longer before she settled into a chair in the corner and took out needle, thread and a handkerchief that required some attention to its edging.

Mr Vardy remained standing and smiled at Mina. He was clearly awaiting orders. 'Please do take a seat, Mr Vardy,' said Mina.

He bowed and drew up an armchair facing her. 'I am very happy to find that you are able to agree to my visit,' he said. 'I have heard reports that you have been extremely unwell, and I did fear that you might not yet be strong enough for an interview.'

'Rest assured that I am mending well, and my doctor advises me that I can expect a return to full health,' said Mina.

Mr Vardy smiled again. Mina studied his appearance and estimated that he was aged about thirty-five. He was above medium height, very well groomed with smooth dark hair and a short finely trimmed beard. It struck Mina that had she been writing a mystery story about a missing man who was rumoured to be dead, she might have devised a plot in which he returned under another name having changed his appearance in order to avoid his creditors, and remarried the supposed widow. This clearly could not be the case here, as Mr Vardy was too young, too tall and too robust to be the ailing and middle-aged Mr Holt in disguise.

He sat at ease his hands folded together. If he had ever worked with porcelain in his life there was no sign of it, none of the wear that would have imprinted itself on his skin. Mina guessed that he had always been an office administrator, more used to pen and ink than paste and kiln.

'I am so very glad that you are improving,' he said. 'I had better explain the reason for my visit. I have learned very recently that my wife has consulted you on two occasions — in fact she has taxed you with assisting her on private matters relating to our family. I cannot tell you how disturbed I was to discover this. First of all, her actions were taken without my authority or knowledge. I hardly need to explain to you my feelings on this. Also, of equal if not greater importance, I am very concerned for you, in case by her thoughtlessness, she has inadvertently caused a relapse.'

'There is one thing I wish to make clear,' said Mina. 'When Mrs Vardy sought to consult me, she was at the time quite unaware that I was unwell. There was no way she could have known, and if she had, I am sure she would not have written to me. As soon as I had recovered sufficiently to deal with my correspondence, I wrote to her suggesting a meeting. Whether or not she had consulted you, I did not enquire. It was not my place to do so. I can reassure you that there has been no detriment to my health, but even if there had been, the blame would have been all mine.'

'Well, be that as it may,' said Mr Vardy, unappeased, 'I have deemed it inadvisable for you to be troubled by matters that do not in any way concern you or your family, especially while you are still convalescent. If you were to suffer any harm by so doing, I would never forgive myself, and I am sure that Charlotte would be most distressed.'

Mr Vardy did not wear a wedding ring, but he had a gentleman's gold signet ring on the little finger of his left hand. It had an antique look, like something his father or grandfather might have worn. As he spoke, he held the ring between the thumb and forefinger of his right hand, and gave it a little twist, first one way, then the other.

As Mina saw Mr Vardy squeeze and twist the little ring, she suddenly became strongly aware of the packets of papers brought by Mrs Vardy on her recent visit which were locked away in her writing desk on the other side of the room where it faced the window. It took a considerable effort of will not to glance in that direction. He could not have known that she had the papers, or he would surely have demanded their return, and she did not want to provide him with any indication of their whereabouts.

'Thank you for your concern,' she said. 'I am already under a strict promise not to attempt anything too adventurous, and I know that my doctor would wholeheartedly approve of your warning.' There seemed to be nothing more to say, but Mina could not resist making an enquiry. 'Speaking of which, and please excuse this enquiry which is made with the best of intentions, I hope and trust that the health of your stepson is improving.'

Mr Vardy bridled a little at the question but retained his composure. 'He is in good hands. Franklin is a sensitive boy with a vivid imagination, which became overheated I believe by reading about the more turbulent episodes of English history which his school had seen fit to teach him. We are finding another school for him which will suit him better.' Another twist of the signet ring, left and then right. 'You need have no anxiety for him.'

'I am happy to hear it. If Mrs Vardy should wish to call on me again, if only to take tea and talk of uncontroversial matters suitable for ladies, I would be very glad to receive her. Does she take an interest in butterflies and the cultivation of flowers? I have been reading a great deal on those subjects of late.'

'She will not call again,' he said, with a little bite of determination at the end of the sentence. 'Conversation over the tea table might start as wholly innocent and suitable for someone like yourself who needs to conserve her strength, but I fear that Charlotte's anxiety might lead her to stray into areas that would be inadvisable. I have ordered her to pay no more visits to you. Please be assured, Miss Scarletti,' he added warmly, 'I only have your welfare in mind. All of Brighton knows that you are an ornament to the town. Your devoted studies, your passion for the truth, your appearances in court which cause the guilty to tremble with apprehension, you have benefitted so many by your efforts, that we would be desolate to lose you, and lose you we will, long before your time if you persist in activities which can only bring harm to yourself.' He gave the ring another twist. 'I speak as a friend.'

Once Rose had shown Mr Vardy out, she returned unbidden. 'Is he not to be allowed in again?' she asked. 'Only, he said he was a friend but —'

'We shall see,' said Mina. She had picked up the directory, but now she set it aside, lost in thought.

She had never yet seen a true ghost, although she knew from report that they were things of air and light. But there were ghosts of another kind, the past haunting the living who existed in a state of fear. What ghosts did Mr Vardy have? What was he afraid of?

'I would like to take a little nap, now,' said Mina. 'Please can you ensure that I am not disturbed. And if you could bring my chair around, nearer to my desk, so I can see out of the window, I would find that so very soothing.'

Rose gave an approving nod, did as she was asked, and made her comfortable. Alone, Mina was able to reach the drawer of the desk from which she extracted the bundle of Mrs Vardy's papers and read them once more.

Report of Jacob Handley, private investigator, Inspector of Police, Sussex, (retired).

In July 1864 I was engaged by Mr Gordon Saltmire to make enquiries concerning the disappearance of his brother in law Mr Jasper Holt wine-merchant of Brighton, on 18th of that month. On that date, Mr Holt had sailed from Brighton as a passenger on a small yacht in the company of the owner of the yacht, Mr William Sutherland. When the yacht returned to shore Mr Holt was not aboard and Mr Sutherland stated that Mr Holt had fallen from the vessel and drowned. He has not been seen or heard from since then.

I commenced my enquiries by interviewing both Mr Saltmire and his sister, Mrs Charlotte Holt. Mr Saltmire stated that that he had no information concerning the fate of his brother-in-law. Mrs Holt likewise had very little of any importance to divulge, mainly because of her husband's secretive nature concerning his business arrangements, and her own preference not to venture beyond the bounds of a woman's natural sphere.

I next interviewed Mr Holt's accountant, Mr Westbury, his bank manager Mr Cobbe, and Mr Benton the principal assistant at the wine shop, and become thoroughly acquainted with the missing man's precarious financial position. Here, I felt certain, lay the origins of the tragedy. I was therefore left in little doubt that when Jasper Holt stepped aboard Mr Sutherland's yacht he did not intend to return to his family, or at least, not immediately. As to what had transpired thereafter, I had only Mr Sutherland's word, and while his account was not beyond the bounds of possibility, there are a number of other explanations, none of them showing Mr Sutherland in a favourable light, which I was obliged to consider.

My initial enquiries concerning William Sutherland revealed that he was about thirty years of age, single, but engaged to be married, and a partner in a stockbroker's firm. The yacht had been purchased some three years previously, financed by a legacy from his grandfather. My interview with Mr Sutherland was brief and to the point. The man did not waver from the original statement he had made to the police and had nothing more to say. Shortly afterwards he returned to his business in London saying that he did not wish to be interviewed again. I continued, however, to request a second interview, in case Mr Sutherland should decide to change or add to his story. All such requests were curtly refused. My persistence arose from my many years of experience in the police force, and wide acquaintance with all classes of criminals. That experience told me that Mr Sutherland has yet to tell all the truth, and that a series of further interviews in which I make a close examination of his story will bear fruit.

At this stage in my enquiries I intend to redouble my efforts to interview Mr Sutherland.

Second report of Jacob Handley, August 1864

Since making my last report I have uncovered further information about Mr Sutherland which increased my disquiet. An informant has revealed that Sutherland was once associated with the Maritime Queen Insurance business, although in what capacity he was involved has never been proved. To be named in connection with two cases of financial fraud in two years looks highly suspicious, and it was not therefore surprising that he had been unhelpful.

I did not reveal my suspicions but continued to request a further interview, which was refused. A month after the disappearance of Mr Holt, however, a letter to Mr Sutherland's London business address was returned by the post office, undelivered. I made a personal visit, which revealed that it was being leased by another unconnected firm. I located and contacted members of Mr Sutherland's family, but none were was prepared to assist my enquiries.

Mr Sutherland had acted as secretary to the Brighton Yacht Club, and I proceeded to interview the members. None of them had ever met Mr Holt or could cast any light on the mystery. All had a high regard for Mr Sutherland, but told me that he had not attended any club meetings since being questioned by the police about Holt's disappearance and shortly afterwards he had handed in his resignation. The yacht had been put up for sale.

I traced the yacht, formerly called Ocean Breeze. It had been repainted and renamed Ocean Quest. I was permitted to examine it and did so minutely but found no traces of any crime or accident. The new owner told me that he had not discovered anything suspicious.

In the weeks that followed Mr Holt's disappearance many newspapers reported sightings of the missing man. Mrs Holt and Mr Saltmire also received numerous letters on the subject and I am grateful to them for preserving these and letting me see them.

All the letters had been written by people who stated that they had never met Jasper Holt, and simply said that someone answering his description had arrived in their neighbourhood behaving in a suspicious manner. Since the description of Mr Holt published in the newspapers could have applied to thousands of men, I did not set much store by these sightings, but I investigated them all the same. They came to nothing. Mrs Holt particularly begged me to look into the letters sent by spirit mediums, as she felt that the truth would be uncovered by those means, and I obliged her, though not with any confidence that they would provide an answer. These letters proved to be far too vague in content to provide useful material for investigation. Some claimed that Holt was alive and was living far away under another name. Neither the name nor the place, the two essentials for the statement to have any evidential value, were given. Most mediums, however, were certain that Holt was dead and that his body would be discovered in water. Since Brighton is a coastal town and Holt had last been seen stepping on a boat, it did not require the intervention of a spirit to make this a good guess.

I was left with only one definite clue. If Mr Sutherland was to be believed, and here there was some evidence that he was being truthful in one respect, Mr Holt had disappeared in a location to the west of Brighton. I therefore consulted a number of experienced yachtsmen, who provided useful guidance. Given the time of departure which was witnessed by a large number of persons, and the time that Mr Sutherland brought the yacht back, which was also witnessed, there was an identifiable area in which the event must had occurred. Allowing for the time taken by the journey, any delays due to the unsettled sea, the loss of Mr Holt and attempts to recover the body, I concluded that the yacht had sailed no further than Shoreham, the destination mentioned by Holt. I therefore intend to make further enquiries in the coastal villages west of Brighton and a number of locations inland.

Third report of Jacob Handley, August 1864

I have now completed extensive enquiries in the coastal villages, interviewing the inhabitants, especially fishermen and yacht owners. I distributed handbills with a portrait of Mr Holt, an engraving from the most recent photograph. I was able to eliminate from consideration any bodies that had been found on shore, and discoveries of male clothing. I also established that no-one in that part of the country had any family, business, or social connection with Mr Holt. I made particular enquiries concerning any strangers who had arrived recently matching Holt's description. There were a number of men of approximately the right age and appearance, but all were known to families living in the area.

I was left with the conclusion that Mr Jasper Holt had not come ashore on the day he disappeared, and his body, perhaps weighted down by clothing and anything he had been carrying upon his person, had sunk below the waves never to be seen again. That only leaves one question. Was the death of Mr Holt a suicide, accident or murder? Only one man knows the answer, Mr William Sutherland, and it seems that he has taken very great care to disappear.

Extract from the unpublished memoirs of Jacob Handley, private investigator, and Inspector of the Sussex police (retired).

Whatever people like to say about me, and people have said a great many things in my time, not all of them polite, I have never been accused of giving up on a case. I have already included in these papers the reports I made to Mr Gordon Saltmire in 1864, when I was engaged to discover the whereabouts of his brother-in-law, Mr Jasper Holt. Now, nearly eight years later, although I am no longer employed by the family, who have now accepted that the man is dead, and have a certificate to prove it, I cannot relinquish my curiosity. Someone, somewhere, I am sure, knows the truth of the matter. I am not a susceptible man, and rarely given to idle reveries and imaginings, but even so, there are times when I imagine, just for one happy moment, that I have solved the case and restored either the whole living man or a casket of his bones to the Holt family, only to awake to the disappointment of a dream.

This is no criticism of any of the suffering family, but I simply note that many of my cases tend to arise from facts which those closest to someone who has absconded or laid violent hands upon themselves, only discover to their shock and distress when it is far too late for the situation to be mended

I was and remain convinced to this day that the solution to the mystery lies with Mr Sutherland. That gentleman is of a class that believes he is more intelligent than a seasoned officer of the police. He might well be when it came to desk work, but he has yet to experience my methods of enquiry. If he ever does, he will reveal the truth. Over the years I have from time to time looked for notices of Mr Sutherland's marriage or death but found nothing.

Every day that Richard worked for Mr Beckler produced a fresh host of complaints, to which Mina listened with great patience. It appeared that the photography business had simply not been as much fun as her brother had expected, in fact the whole thing was pronounced to be 'a beastly disappointment'. Richard had assumed that what with Beckler being his friend, not to mention sweet on Mina, his days in the shop would entail only a few light duties, enlivened by amusing conversations with pretty ladies.

'I am being worked like a junior clerk!' he wailed after his third day of relentless toil. 'That dreary list of unsold photographs is thankfully almost done. Such a tedious waste of my time and talents, it's enough to make a man weep. I haven't been allowed to touch the camera or any of the chemicals. Instead I have been made to carry furnishings and some of the more robust and therefore infernally heavy equipment. And I know that if only I was given the chance to try photography the results would be marvellous.'

'Perhaps when you have more business experience?' suggested Mina, soothingly.

'Oh, he has promised me lessons one day, but when will that ever be? Do you know what he wants me to do tomorrow? I am to clean the glass plates. There is a box of old plates left over from Simpson's time, and while the glass is still good, the images are not, so I have to scrub them so he can use them again. I did think to suggest he employs a servant to do it, but then I thought, that in a way, I am that servant. It's a deuce of a downfall!' Richard buried his head in his hands and groaned. 'And while I am slaving at his command, what has Beckler been doing? He has been taking pictures of elderly ladies together with a large vase of flowers which to my mind would have been greatly improved if the ladies had been sitting behind the vase and not beside it.' Richard sighed. 'If only he was more adventurous. Why doesn't he take pictures of pretty French girls; a lot of gentlemen like that kind of thing. Oh, there's nothing wrong in it,' he added quickly. 'It's like art, you see paintings in the galleries all the time.'

Mina had noticed pictures of that description offered for sale in weekly newspapers. They were listed together with advertisements for cures for nervous debility and private diseases, neither of which she had ever had any wish to know more about. She had no idea if the girls were actually French and suspected that to the single gentlemen believed to be the purchasers of these pictures this description had an alternative meaning at which she could easily guess.

'But when I suggested it to Beckler he gave me such a ghastly look that I had to tell him it was just a joke.' Richard's expression was one of palpable disappointment.

'So your employer is determined to run a respectable business, in order to attract distinguished and wealthy clients, and create tasteful portraits,' said Mina, unable to conceal a smile.

She was obliged to admit to herself that Richard's disillusionment with the photography business was something of a relief. His expectations of a leisurely and lucrative career had been dashed, and it could not be long before he slid into his usual habits of neglect and be dismissed. She could only hope that he since he was personable and good natured, he would find some sinecure somewhere that would keep him out of mischief.

'You are much prettier than any of his lady customers, you know, even if you don't think so yourself. Beckler thinks so.'

Mina remained silent.

'I mean, you can be a bit frightening at times, and you are always so stern when you tell me what to do, but Beckler doesn't seem to mind that. I don't know if ladies admire Beckler at all. He does look like one of those black spidery creatures with long legs that one sees in the summertime. And the features of his face are very pronounced in a peculiar kind of way. Do ladies admire that sort of thing?'

'I really couldn't say.'

'But he knows his business, and works hard and makes money, so that has to be all right. Even Mother likes him. She has always said that you shouldn't marry, but perhaps she has changed her mind. The only person who seems set against the idea is you.' He paused. 'You are giving me that stern look again.'

Dear Miss Scarletti

I have recently had a conversation with one of the senior partners of our firm who recalls the Maritime Queen Insurance case I mentioned in my previous letter. When I last wrote to you, I had assumed that the two absconding officers of the company, Taylor and Randall, had not been found, but he has informed me that a few years afterwards both men were residing in Antwerp where they were engaged in launching a similar scheme. Fortunately, they were recognised and reported to the authorities before the intended victims could be parted from their money. There was a violent quarrel between the two, and Randall was later found dead in circumstances which suggested that he had been murdered, most probably by his former associate. Taylor escaped arrest and has not been seen since, although there have been rumours that he returned to England under an assumed name. I do hope that this is not the case as he is clearly a highly dangerous individual.

Yours faithfully
R Phipps

CHAPTER FOURTEEN

Miss Cherry had spent another morning with Mrs Phipps and returned from her expedition looking well and happy and a little flushed. She came to see Mina almost immediately and was too excited even to remove her new bonnet, which Mina could see was very handsomely trimmed.

'Oh, Miss Scarletti!' she began, and stopped short to catch her breath.

Mina laid aside her newspaper. 'What is it, Miss Cherry? No, let me guess. You have received an offer of employment from Mrs Phipps and wish to be released from the arrangement to attend me.'

Miss Cherry looked surprised. 'I — yes, if that is convenient.'

Mina smiled reassuringly. 'Miss Cherry, you have been a credit to your profession. I am profoundly grateful for your diligence which I know has gone a long way to ensuring my recovery. And I am delighted that you have been made such an excellent offer. Have no fear, I will set you free. I will also ensure that your account with us is settled without any delay. And I will happily include the free mornings and afternoons.'

'Why, thank you, that is most kind. But Miss Scarletti —'

'Oh, think nothing of it,' said Mina generously. 'I was wondering if you have seen Mrs Vardy recently? Have you heard anything of Master Franklin Holt? Is he well? I do hope so.'

'I have not heard that he is any better — but — Miss Scarletti —' Miss Cherry's eyes were wider and greener than they had ever been, and the earnestness of her manner commanded Mina's full attention, 'do you mean to say that you have not heard the latest news?'

'The latest? No. Only what I have read in the press. What has happened? I hope it is nothing bad.'

'Oh, but it is all over town! It is tremendously exciting! I heard it from a lady who came into the draper's shop and told my mother this morning. It's Mr Holt. He's come back!'

Mina struggled to make sense of this declaration. 'What? Mr Holt? Mr Jasper Holt? The man who was declared dead not so long ago?'

Miss Cherry nodded energetically. 'Yes!'

'But where? How? Is he alive?'

'Oh yes, he is very much alive. He just walked into the police office at the Town Hall this morning and said who he was.'

'Did this lady see him? How did he appear? Was he well or ill?'

'She didn't see him, but she knows a lady who did. Like an old tramp, so she was told, and very poorly. But well-spoken.'

Mina took a few moments to collect her thoughts. She could hardly think that this man could really be Mr Holt, although Dr Hamid had said that the missing man would probably be very ill if alive. If Jasper Holt had been hiding in frugal circumstances, or even living as a beggar, he might well appear old and dishevelled. Suddenly she thought of the broader consequences of this news. 'Has Mrs Vardy been told?'

'I don't know. I expect so. Poor lady, what a dreadful thing for her. I mean, she must be happy that her husband is alive, but — well — I can only imagine that her position is very complicated now. So as soon as I heard about it, I went and told Mr Phipps, and he went to tell his uncle who rushed away to see for himself. Then he came back and said that it was true

— a man calling himself Mr Holt was at the Town Hall and a correspondent from *The Times* was there, writing a report.'

'*The Times*? The London *Times*? That was very quick of them.'

'Yes. Apparently, the man came down to Brighton this morning to interview the new manager of the Aquarium and found a better story. I thought *The Times* only printed serious news. I didn't know it liked a scandal.'

'All newspapers like a scandal,' said Mina. 'I shall make sure to purchase a copy tomorrow.' She tried to think about anyone else from whom she could glean some news but realised that she would have to wait until Richard was home, unless any of her mother's friends should pay a visit.

'And I promise to call again when I can with any more information.'

'That would be appreciated. I am sure you will be calling here often in the company of your new charge.'

Miss Cherry smiled contentedly. 'I will. Mrs Phipps is a very nice lady and we suit each other well. She does so enjoy taking tea with Mrs Scarletti. I am only sorry that I didn't manage to finish reading *The Young Woman's Companion* to you. There were so many choice articles. Please say that you don't mind.'

Louisa Scarletti was not at home that morning. Her previous visit to the Ship Street photographic emporium had been pronounced a success. Entertained by a display of beautiful portraits, she had simply assumed that they were all Richard's expert productions and her confidence in her favourite son's artistic genius therefore remained undented. She had easily been persuaded to make an appointment to sit for a photograph, an event which had resulted in a flurry of decisions as to which would be the most appropriate gown to wear and the best accessories, a decision which had occupied

Rose's tireless energies for an entire day.

Louisa returned home in time for luncheon, fresh from the delights of being fussed over and flattered, declaring loudly that she hoped she would not look like a terrible fright in her portrait, but in a manner that showed that she was well aware of her refined appearance. Richard, she said, had attended her with such delicacy and expertise it had quite taken her breath away. He had been able to judge when the best moment was to operate the camera without even touching it, leaving the heavier work to his partner. Mr Beckler, she told Mina, was a young man of ability and energy who only wanted a good wife to complete his happiness. He was not handsome, but then it was impossible for a husband to have every virtue. Mina could only respond that she hoped he would find someone suitable.

'I am sure he will,' said Louisa, patting her hair, 'but Mina, you must have no ambitions in that direction, for the sake of your health.'

'I promise you,' said Mina sincerely, 'Mr Beckler is as far from my ambitions as it is possible to be.'

'And of course, you are needed too much at home. This is your proper place.'

'Is there any interesting news in the town?' Mina asked, hopefully.

Louisa gave a little gasp of disapproval. 'Oh, my dear, I must not say, it is far too alarming for you to contemplate. It almost verges on indecency and I cannot expose you to that. I am only surprised that Dr Hamid allows you to have newspapers, which are full of the most dreadful things. They would make me quite ill if I could bear to read them, so it is a wonder that you can manage. Why not write one of your pretty children's stories to amuse yourself?'

Mina was resigned to the fact that unless Richard had any news she would have to wait until Rose brought her *The Times* next morning.

'Have you heard the news about Mr Holt?' asked Dr Hamid later that afternoon. He looked not so much excited but anxious in case Mina was prostrated by the revelation. It was clear that he had rushed round to see her because he wanted to be first with the information in case she became so excited that medical intervention should prove necessary.

'Only that he has come alive again and is at the Town Hall,' said Mina, calmly. 'Is there more?'

He sat down, clearly relieved at her equanimity. 'You always seem to know everything before anyone else. I can never discover where you get your information from, apart from extracting it from me, that is. No wonder people say you are in touch with the all-seeing spirits.'

Mina laughed but didn't enlighten him. 'How did you learn of it?'

'I was passing through Bartholomew Square and saw a very substantial crowd gathered outside the Town Hall, and they were not there to purchase vegetables. Unusually for such assemblies the participants were both sober and respectable. Naturally I made enquiries and a gentleman told me that they were hoping to be allowed into the police office to speak to Mr Holt.'

'And he believed that the man is actually Mr Holt?'

'He felt sure of it. He has not actually seen him but like everyone else he is going by the description that has been bandied about, of a man of about the right age and build, and I suspect his own preferences. I was told that Mrs Vardy has been allowed in to see him, but she said that he was not Holt.'

'Then that should settle the matter. Surely she ought to know her own husband?'

'One would have thought so, but I am sorry to say that the men assembled outside the Town Hall refuse to believe the wife's statement.'

'Poor Mrs Vardy,' said Mina sympathetically, 'Is she not to be left in peace?'

'I doubt it.'

'But from what you say this is no idle rabble assembled out of curiosity.'

'No, they were tradesmen and gentlemen of the business class.'

'What interest or purpose can they have? I thought the estate had been settled.'

'I did wonder, since if they are Mr Holt's creditors, they can have no hope of retrieving their funds. But one of the gentlemen did introduce himself to me as Mr Stephen Westbury an accountant. His father, who is now retired from the practice once acted for Mr Holt, preparing the accounts of his business in good faith from the ledgers supplied. It transpired that Mr Holt's figures were false, his debtors fictitious, and his bank account augmented by borrowings which were made to appear as profits. Mr Westbury senior became embroiled in the scandal that followed Mr Holt's disappearance, and his reputation and business suffered badly since Mr Holt was not there to exonerate him from blame.'

'I can understand the son's anxiety for the father. So he just wants the good name of the family restored.'

'Some of them have less creditable motives. Revenge. They want to see Holt in prison.'

'How long did the crowds remain?'

'I don't know, I thought I should come and tell you what I know without delay, so I was obliged to come away. They were still there when I left. But your brother ought to be able to enlighten you.'

'Richard?' Mina found that news profoundly alarming. 'Was he there? How was he involved? What can his concern be?'

'I don't think he was directly concerned. I saw him handing out some advertising cards.' Dr Hamid adopted a cautious tone. 'I hope this means he has some respectable employment.'

'Oh, yes, of course, that must be it,' said Mina, relieved, 'he is working at a photographer's shop in Ship Street, that is hardly two minutes' walk away.'

'You mean the new business, Mr Beckler's?' exclaimed Dr Hamid, startled. 'Your brother is working for him?'

'Yes,' said Mina, with a sigh of regret. 'Mother is very pleased about it.'

Mina had never seen Dr Hamid look more awkward. 'Does Mr Beckler — er — continue his attentions towards you? When you first met him, I couldn't help but notice — not that it is any business of mine, of course, but I was not under the impression that you — and I do not think your health permits — I'm sorry but what I meant to say was —'

'My inclinations do not permit,' said Mina with a smile.

Mina was impatient to hear what Richard would have to say and spent the rest of the afternoon worrying that he might decide to dine out after the shop closed. In that case she would probably not even see him until next morning, when he would have a headache and be disinclined to hold a conversation. Fortunately, she heard him arrive home at his usual time, in that dull interlude after tea and before dinner was announced, and he called on Mina at once.

'There has been such excitement in town today,' he said breathlessly, 'The world of photographic art has never been more interesting! I now regret every wasted moment I laboured to make those drawings for the *Journal*. There is no doubt about it, the photograph is the future! It will take the place of the pencil, the pen and the brush. And today through the art of the camera, I have made my name!' He thumped his chest with a fist and looked very proud.

'So, sit down my dear, and tell me all about your day,' said Mina. She listened expectantly but her brother's announcements of this nature always provoked in her a sense of foreboding. 'I know Mother sat for her portrait this morning.'

'Oh yes, she was very pleased and is sure to tell everyone how well I did.'

'And Dr Hamid says he saw you distributing cards.'

'Yes — invitations to a special free exhibition. Portraits of the notable residents of Brighton, and a novelty, a picture taken inside a cave lit by the new metal ribbon that Beckler is so excited about.'

'Is the inside of a cave so very interesting?'

'It is not interesting at all. I can imagine all sorts of reasons why one might want to take photographs in the dark, but a cave is not one of them. Beckler, however is convinced that the public will flock to see the exhibition if he includes a demonstration of the action of the metal ribbon. They are bound to come even if only for the hope that he might set fire to himself.'

Mina smiled, but Richard, seeing that there was a tea tray nearby, inspected it, ate a stray biscuit, helped himself from the milk jug, and launched into his account which promised to be thirsty work.

CHAPTER FIFTEEN

Mina was unsurprised to learn that on leaving the shop with his bundle of cards Richard had not felt inclined to hurry about his task. There were some opportunities to hand out cards in Ship Street, a narrow busy thoroughfare, with its shops and inns and post office, but the traffic did not encourage idlers and strollers, so he had decided to cut through Prince Albert Street to Market Street, where there were butchers, bakers and fruit sellers, and the Market Hall, where there was sure to be a lot of people. There, he could dispose of the cards easily and quickly, leaving some free time to explore the more inviting possibilities of the cigar shop. He was approaching Bartholomew Square and its bustling vegetable market when he was attracted by the sight and sound of a large gathering of gentlemen outside the Town Hall and went to see what all the excitement was about.

'That is where the police offices are,' prompted Mina.

'Yes, they were all standing about the front steps, and there were any number of discussions and debates going on. You might wonder why they didn't go in but there were two constables standing on the top step guarding the doors. I think the constables had been specially chosen for their general largeness which was quite extraordinary and went in all directions.

On the other side of the square, people were going about their daily business at the vegetable stalls but they also kept watch on the unusual assembly and I could see them talking about it with lots of shrugs and amusement.

'Hallo, what's the to-do?' I asked weaving my way into the crowd. I tried to distribute some cards, but everyone was too engaged with other matters to care about photography, so I soon abandoned the attempt.

'Haven't you heard?' said a short man with a round hat. 'That miscreant Holt who ran off owing thousands and tried to pretend he was dead — he has just turned up as large as life and given himself up to the police.'

'And then his wife came and had a look at him and said it isn't him!' added another man. He had red whiskers like a wild boar which trembled with indignation, even when he wasn't speaking.

'Yes, she and her brother were both here,' said round hat. 'They were hardly inside more than five minutes. I don't think they looked at him at all. In fact, I think they made up their minds before they went in to say it wasn't him.'

'Oh, but do have some sympathy for the lady,' said a third man, imploringly. He was a nervous looking type with a stiff collar and thinning hair. 'If that is her husband then she is living in a sinful situation which she has not brought upon herself. I would not wish for any relative of mine to be placed in such a position.'

'I've no sympathy for her!' said round hat with a nasty sneer. 'If you ask me, she knew from the start that he was a cheat. I think she helped him run off, and knew he was alive all the time. And then what does she do? Maybe she thinks he isn't coming back, so first chance she gets she kills him off, legal-like, and takes up with some young fancy man. She probably got her brother to make him a partner in the business. That's women, for you! I think that's why Holt turned up again. To put her to shame.'

'Who are all these people?' I asked them. The gathering of men in their good suits looked like an outdoor business convocation.

'Why they are all those to whom Holt owes money or at least an explanation,' said red whiskers.

'I used to work for him' said round hat. 'He owes me a month's wages. Not that I'll ever get to squeeze it out of him.'

'And see that fellow over there?' said the nervous man, pointing out a young gentleman in dark grey. 'He is Mr Stephen Westbury the accountant. There were all sorts of nasty allegations against his father when Holt disappeared. He lost business because of it. He was never the same man after.'

'I still think old Westbury knew more than he was admitting,' muttered red whiskers. 'I wouldn't trust him.'

'See those two?' said round hat, pointing to a mournful pair of shabby gentlemen, talking in close proximity and glancing over their shoulders. 'Businesses collapsed when Holt's cheques weren't honoured. They'd punch him on the nose if they got close enough. Or worse.'

'What about Livermore?' said red whiskers. 'Holt owes him thousands.'

'And Cobbe, the banker,' said round hat. 'He won't feel friendly towards him. I think they're both here.' He craned his neck, and seeing both the gentlemen in question, nodded. 'Oh yes,' he rubbed his hands together and chuckled, 'this could get very interesting!'

'Oh dear,' said the nervous man. 'I hope things don't turn to violence.'

The I saw a man in a plain suit begin to push importantly through the crowd, creating a trail of annoyed exclamations, and when he reached the top of the steps, he tried to march into the Town Hall, but his boldness didn't help him. He was stopped by the constables before he could pass through the doors and interviewed very closely. It was a rapid conversation, with much energetic waving of hands by the man, and dignified tolerance from the constables, which I was too far away to hear. The result was that the man was very firmly motioned to leave. He protested, but the constables remained solid, like twin statues. Eventually he gave up and stamped away unwillingly, but he only went as far as the base of the steps. I saw him pull out a notebook and pencil and start writing.

'Who is that fellow?' I asked.

'*Gazette*,' said round hat with a snort of derision.

Well I had been thinking about this, so I had to ask, 'If Holt owes all these people money, does he have the means to pay them? Is that why there are all here?'

'No. Bankrupt,' said red whiskers, derisively. 'Not a penny to his name. I think his creditors would just like to see him in prison.'

'Or hanging from a nail,' said round hat and he laughed, but I don't think it was a joke.

'Oh dear!' said the nervous man again.

'Perhaps his wife has money,' I said.

'What do you mean?' asked red whiskers. 'If she does, then it would be his in any case. And the receiver would have found it and paid it out. She doesn't have anything.'

'It could be in a trust, locked up so he couldn't touch it,' said the nervous man. 'But I don't believe she came from that sort of money.'

'Oh, you know what ladies are like,' I said. 'Some of them when they get married, they don't like to give up all their fortune to their husbands. They can be very clever about it, too. I knew a lady once who had a whole box of jewels hidden

185

away. Worth thousands. She said her husband didn't know about them and would never get his hands on them.'

Round hat was very impressed by my story. 'You might have something, there,' he said. 'What if Mrs Vardy has something put away that Holt didn't know about?'

'She might do at that,' said red whiskers 'a woman of that sort, they'll stoop to anything. And if she does,' he growled, clenching a fist as if grasping hold of what he was owed, or maybe he was thinking of Mr Holt's throat, 'I shall make a claim on it.'

Well would you believe it, before I knew it, my comment had become the very latest news. It gained wings and flew about the crowd like a little bird, and as it twittered from mouth to mouth, it transformed in moments from idle speculation to a strong possibility and finally became an absolute fact. The man from the *Gazette* heard it and I could see him becoming very excited and scribbled even faster than before.

So now, the crowd, seeing the prospect of actual money, began to surge forward with fresh determination. Men were shouting, demanding to be allowed in and see the man Holt, and a whole forest of rolled up newspapers, walking sticks and umbrellas were being waved aloft. People cried out angrily at being pushed by those behind them and turned around to protest; quarrels broke out and there was a serious threat of fisticuffs. It was far and away the most interesting thing that had happened to me for weeks and I thought that if I had only had a sketch pad with me and if I had still been employed by Edward, I might have thought of recording the scene for the *Journal*.

And that,' said Richard, cheerily oblivious to Mina's expression of muted horror, 'was when I had my most brilliant idea. A sketch is just a kind of picture, and I knew how to produce a picture of another kind, or at least I know a man who does. So quick as anything, I turned and hurried back to Ship Street and the photographic shop, where Mr Beckler was just saying an obsequious farewell to a lady who was wearing a monster of a ruffled skirt train that was taking longer to exit the premises than she did.

'There's a bit of a disturbance outside the Town Hall,' I exclaimed. 'All sorts of fellows, bankers and accountants and businessmen, all of them demanding to see a Mr Holt. He was supposed to be dead but he isn't and now his creditors are all after him. It's getting a bit heated.'

Beckler's eyes lit up. He glanced at his watch. 'I've no-one for the next half hour and the light is —' he looked out of the window '— hmm, it might just be adequate if the clouds move off. Let us go and see what we can do.' It took only moments for us to gather a box of prepared dry coated glass plates, fold the camera into its carrying case with a spare lens, and close up the tripod. Beckler changed the sign on the shop door to 'closed' and burdened with the equipment we made our way as quickly as we could to Bartholomew Square.

By then, the noise of the disturbance could be heard two streets away. My comment had really excited the crowds, and there was a restless sea of business suits in front of the Town Hall. The man from the *Gazette* had been knocked over in the crush, and was trying to crawl up the front steps to safety, the policemen were trying to look taller, wider and more determined, and the vegetable traders had stopped work and were looking on like spectators at a circus where the lions had just escaped and were mauling their trainer.

Beckler stayed back and surveyed the scene from a safe distance. 'All I can reasonably see from here is the entrance and the front steps,' he said. 'It's like a battlefield. There is too much movement of the crowd to be sure of a good picture.' From his position at the far side of the square he selected the best vantage point he could find, set up the tripod and camera on top of an overturned vegetable box, checked the focus, slotted a plate into position, and waited his chance.

Then one of the gentlemen mounted the steps and instead of attempting to enter the building or speak to the constables, he turned and stood in front of the double doors to address the crowd, pleading for quiet. It had been a fairly dull day but as he stood there with arms outstretched, the sun, which was high in the sky, emerged from behind a cloud and he was suddenly illuminated in a bright golden light. I saw Beckler quickly remove the lens cap and replace it.

A respectful hush fell over the crowd, and the surging movement calmed to a breathless ripple. 'I think you all know me,' said the man, a prosperous looking individual in his fifties, 'but if you don't, you'll know my hotel.' There was a murmur of assent. 'Livermore's the name. Eight years ago, Mr Jasper Holt offered me an investment in fine wines, and because of our long business association I trusted him. I trusted his knowledge, and I thought him an honest man. But, as we all now know, it was a cheat, a calculated deception to take my money under false pretences. In fact, as I later found out, if he hadn't practised on me in that way, he would have found himself bankrupt six months before he actually did.' Livermore took a bundle of papers from his pocket and waved them at the crowd. 'Here are my documents, proof if it be needed that Mr Holt is my debtor for a very large sum of money.' He gestured towards the crowd with the papers. 'And I can see Mr William Cobbe over there, who can stand witness to the fact. His bank lost money over Holt's failure. And over there' he gestured again 'is Mr Stephen Westbury. The good name of his honourable father, Mr Henry Westbury, who has been a friend of mine for many years, has been dragged through the mud through no fault of his own. Now we all knew Mr Holt by sight, and unlike his relations, we have no wish to hide the truth.' There was a laugh and a rumble of agreement from the massed voices.

Livermore half turned towards the entrance of the Town Hall, pointing an accusing finger and moving it back and forth as if stabbing it repeatedly into the body of the despicable Mr Holt. 'If that man in there is Jasper Holt, we will recognise him, and we will speak out without fear!' He surveyed the throng once more. 'Now I know you would all like to go in and take a look —'

There were roars of 'Yes!' from the crowd.

'But of course,' Livermore went on, with a placatory voice and gesture, 'we can't all go in at once. I have no wish to inconvenience the police; they are a fine body of men who are only doing their duty, and to whom we should be grateful for keeping the peace in Brighton and making it safe for our visitors and therefore good for our businesses. So what I propose is this. With the permission of these brave constables, the guardians of our town,' he gestured towards the two constables who despite the warmth of the praise, succeeded in remaining as impassive as royal guardsmen, 'I shall enter the station, peacefully, quietly and respectfully, and ask to speak to the Chief Constable. I shall entreat his agreement to receive a small delegation to represent us all. I propose that the delegation should consist of myself, Mr Westbury and Mr Cobbe. Are we all agreed?'

Fresh debates broke out in the crowd, but no-one seemed inclined to oppose Mr Livermore's wishes.

'Are we all agreed?' he repeated.

There was a murmur of assent, and a few cries of 'Yes!'

'In the meantime, I would earnestly beg you all to keep calm. We don't want to turn into a riotous assembly now, do we?' he added with a playful smile.

There was some laughter.

'Is that agreed?'

The crowd indicated its agreement and Mr Livermore bowed and after a few words with the constables he was permitted to enter the police station.

'It sounds like Mr Livermore did the right thing,' said Mina, thankful that Richard's baseless speculation had not led to a murderous rampage.

'Oh yes, because everyone was very determined to go in and see the man, and not for any beneficial purpose,' said Richard. 'We made some good photographs of the commotion. I must say not all of the gentlemen there wished to be photographed, I really don't know why, but there is no reason why you have to ask them first.'

'And did Mr Livermore get his deputation?'

Richard grinned. 'Oh, my dear girl, what came next was the very best part of all!'

'Quickly, give out the cards!' said Beckler, losing no opportunity to set me to work while everyone waited for Mr Livermore to return. 'If they ask, say that I am photographer to the nobility.'

Round hat came and stared at the apparatus. 'You should go inside and picture the man in the cells. Then we can all see him and make our minds up.'

'Is there enough light in the cells?' I asked.

'Not nearly enough,' said Beckler, with a regretful shake of the head.

I had another inspiration. I have so many good ideas, Mina, you can't imagine! 'I know, we could burn some of that metal ribbon! Have you got any about you? I mean it works in caves, why not cells?'

To my surprise Mr Beckler did not think this was a good idea. 'That could involve damaging municipal property. It is not the kind of advertisement I was seeking.' He looked up at the Town Hall windows, and I could see he was thinking. 'But if they brought him out of the cells and put him near to a window with the sun coming through as bright as it is now, and I adjust the exposure time, I might be able to secure a passable image.' He nodded. 'Yes. It's worth trying. Come with me!' Beckler took up the camera and tripod and I picked up the case of glass plates, and we advanced on the Town Hall. Fortunately, Mr Livermore's speech had quietened the crowds, so it wanted only some care and politeness to be allowed through the mass of waiting gentleman. 'I hope they will admit us,' said Beckler, 'but all we can do is ask.'

The constables stared at us laden as we were as we mounted the steps. I arrived first, and Mr Beckler, who was more heavily burdened, which was his fault as he insisted on carrying the camera, brought up the rear looking like the porter of a foreign expedition. So I suppose the police thought that I was the man in charge. Before Beckler could say anything, I greeted the policemen with an extravagant salute, announcing 'Scotland Yard photographic department!'

'Do you have a note, sir?' asked one constable, staring at the camera.

'No time, I'm afraid, we just rushed here as soon as we could!'

The constables glanced at each other. 'All right, you can go in and see the sergeant.'

Inside, the tiled reception hall was quite handsome, but it smelt of old clothes and stale pastry. There was a small attendance of people sitting in rows on wooden benches looking very unhappy to be there. They must have been hoping to see the sergeant who was manning a desk, however it was obvious that Mr Livermore had already asserted his superior authority and had ignored the grumbling masses in order to take first place.

He was discussing with the sergeant his proposal to take a delegation down to the cells, and the sergeant was scratching his chin and pondering the request.

'Ah, my good man,' I said, approaching the desk, 'your troubles are over, we are here! I expect you are relieved to see us, eh?' Mr Beckler put the camera down and stared at me, mouth gaping open like a large fish. He was obviously dismayed at my boldness, which must have come close to impertinence, but unsure whether or not to interrupt as it seemed to be doing the trick.

'I don't rightly know who you are,' said the sergeant. 'Why are you here and who sent for you?'

'We are Beckler and Scarletti, photographers to nobility and royalty,' I said before Becker could reply. I still had some of the advertising cards in my pocket, so I took one, made a bit of a flourish with it, and handed it to the sergeant. 'Engaged by the special photographic department of Scotland Yard to make a portrait of your prisoner, Mr Holt. We received an emergency telegram, from someone very important, and we came here at once.' I patted my pockets as if looking for the telegram. 'I had it here somewhere. No matter. Do be a good chap and bring the fellow Holt or whoever he is up to the light so we can get a decent photograph.'

The sergeant frowned, but the card and the presence of abundant photographic equipment was proof enough. 'If I do, and I can't promise it, he'll be under close guard. Not that I think he'll run off. Docile as a lamb. You'd think he wanted to be locked up.'

Livermore had been watching us very keenly. 'There are a hundred men outside who would very much like him to be freed for an interview,' he said grimly.

'That I don't doubt,' said the sergeant.

I hardly dared look at Beckler, but when I did he was looking at me as if he couldn't decide whether to compliment me or dismiss me on the spot. Then I saw the professional gentleman assert himself once more. 'Is there a place near a window where we can have sufficient light for a photograph?' he asked.

The sergeant stared at him, then glanced at the card. 'This is that new shop in Ship Street?'

'Under the patronage of Viscount Hope,' said Mr Beckler.

The policeman considered this, and nodded. 'You sirs,' he addressed us, 'you can come this way. Mr Livermore, I will attend to you shortly.' We were shown to a private office at the front of the building, which was uninhabited, and left to prepare the room.

There was no time to talk about what had happened. I watched Beckler set up the camera on its tripod and then he threw back the curtains to admit the sunlight. When he did so, there was an excited roar from outside, which soon subsided as the crowds saw a very tall figure at the window, who was obviously not their quarry. I handed him a glass plate from the box, and he slotted it into place, then replaced the lens with the one he uses for portraits. I drew up a chair before the window and he positioned it where he judged that the light would best fall on the face of the subject.

When the sergeant returned, he was accompanied by Mr Livermore, Mr Westbury and Mr Cobbe. 'We are to be allowed to see the prisoner,' said Livermore, triumphantly. The members of the delegation ranged themselves against the wall facing the chair, and everyone waited expectantly for the appearance of Mr Holt.

The three gentlemen, Livermore, Westbury and Cobbe, stood in a row, fidgeting with anticipation, all of them eager and primed to see, hear and speak whatever evil they knew of Mr Jasper Holt, while the sergeant went to fetch the prisoner. Beckler's attention was directed solely towards his camera, and he circled about it, adjusting for the available light like a costume-maker dancing about a bride being fitted for her wedding dress. Several times he dipped his head under the black hood at the back, emerging with a dispirited expression, and increasingly rumpled hair, then stared disconsolately out of the window as if in the hopes of heavenly intervention.

He turned to me. 'Mr Scarletti,' he rapped, 'assist me if you please by sitting in the subject's chair.'

It was really more of an order than a request. I had the feeling that Beckler was not at all pleased with me for speaking out, which I thought he ought to have been, however I sat where directed. And now I was obliged to endure repeated and probably unnecessary corrections of my posture before Beckler once again retreated to the camera and threw the dark cloth over his head and shoulders.

I had once been allowed to look under the camera hood so I knew that Beckler was examining the screen to judge if the picture was sharp enough. I couldn't help wondering how a fellow was expected to keep his hair in good order with such a tiresome demand. Ladies much prefer gentlemen to have tidy hair and I am always careful with his grooming when going out, although now I think about it, Mina, you often take me severely to task for my appearance when I return. That is hardly reasonable; one can't expect a fellow to be perfectly coiffed with a clean collar after a night out. But perhaps,' Richard mused, 'some ladies like a little wildness about the locks. It hints at adventure, like the dreadful Mr Hope who so I have heard is very successful with ladies. I wonder if it would help my chances if I went to Africa, but it does seem like a lot of trouble.'

'Was it possible to take a photograph?' asked Mina, making an effort to be patient.

'Oh, yes, well, as I was saying, Mr Beckler emerged from the camera hood looking thoroughly dissatisfied, and started searching about the room, peering closely at things like wall plaques and a framed certificate. Eventually he found a battered tea tray on top of a cabinet, which he snatched up triumphantly as if it was a great prize. Then he handed it to me together with a polishing cloth from the camera case. 'Take this and rub it till it shines,' he said. The three gentlemen were all looking very surprised by this. 'It will serve to reflect the light' Beckler explained.

It was no occupation for man of my ability, but what could I do but obey, and think of what complaint I might make later. When I had completed this task as well as I could, Beckler examined the tray, then gave it an extra rub with the cloth before handing it back. 'Now, hold this, stand up and face the window. No — not there — there. Now turn. Turn more. Stop. Good, stay there. And hold the tray just so. Higher. Yes. And don't move unless I say so.' I felt less like a photographer's assistant than a performing animal.

At last, the door of the office opened, and the Chief Constable entered, followed by a constable and the sergeant, bringing with them the unexpected guest. The Chief Constable greeted the three delegates, shaking hands with them, and nodded to me and Mr Beckler, then stood beside the fireplace to keep a wary eye on the proceedings, taking particular care to place his body between the fire irons and the prisoner. The constable had stepped to one side so as to guard the door, and then came the sergeant, with one hand firmly on the prisoner's arm. The sergeant's hand was large with thick gnarled fingers. It went almost entirely around the upper arm of the prisoner, not tightly but admitting of no resistance, although the man offered none, and hardly looked capable of it. I realised that beneath his clothing the prisoner was thin almost to the point of emaciation.

At the first sight of the arrival, Mr Westbury impulsively tried to take a step forward for a closer look, but the sergeant thrust out his free arm, palm first, to dissuade him. 'Get back, Sir,' he said, but his words were hardly necessary. It was a strong arm and a firm palm and Mr Westbury stepped back. I admit I was lost in admiration. What would it be like to command men in that way, with a simple word and gesture? I thought if I became a policeman, then ladies would surely be impressed by my air of authority. Admittedly the uniform is not so good as a military one, but I think I might look rather handsome in it. Did you know, Mina, that I had once considered soldiering as profession? The uniform is so splendid, and all that marching about on parade looks like fun, but when I mentioned it to Mother, she had an attack of hysterics, and the idea had to be given up. Do you know how much policemen earn? Is it hard work?'

'Richard, did you pay any attention at all to the man claiming to be Mr Holt?' Mina demanded.

'Yes, I did, a great deal in fact, because I knew you would ask me about him and would be very cross if I had nothing to say. It's a pity you weren't there, Mina, because everyone has been trying to solve the question of who he is, and no one can but if you had seen him you would have had the answer in a trice. So I stared very hard at him, and tried to remember as much as I could, as if I was a sort of camera, only one that recorded colours and sounds and smells too, which someone really ought to invent one day. Well, perhaps not the smells.

The supposed Mr Holt is neither tall nor short, but he seemed shorter than the average size because he did not stand straight. His shoulders were held very rounded as if he was pressed down by the weight of misery. He was not old, nor very young, in fact it was hard to guess his age with any exactness, not that I could remember how old Mr Holt was supposed to be. His hair was thick and very untidy, more grey than brown, and rather dirty. It hung over his ears almost to his collar. He was heavily bearded, but not in the fashionable manly style; bearded as a result of long neglect. His clothes were worn; thinning at the elbows, baggy at the knees, with a ragged stained collar. I rather thought that the poor fellow must possess only the one suit of clothes which he wore every day and was never cleaned. But I could see that the garments had been good once, perhaps they had been given to him out of charity. The shoes were in a similar state, worn at the toes, unpolished, the upper starting to lift from the soles, but made from good leather.'

'Do you think he was a beggar, a man without a home?' asked Mina. 'Such a man might admit to anything just to have some sheltered place to stay.'

'He could have been a beggar, but there was no deeply ingrained grime that might have been expected if he had lived long on the streets. His hands were not clean, although there was some smeary evidence that they and his face had recently, probably that morning, been allowed to make simple ablutions, and there was a very determined blackening about the fingertips, as if he had rubbed the pads of his fingers in coal or something similar. He smelt unbathed, and as he moved further into the room, the air became pungent with it.

'No-one must approach the prisoner,' said the sergeant, firmly to all three witnesses. 'Now then sir,' he said to his charge, 'I see there is a chair set ready for you so please make yourself comfortable.'

The door was closed, and the constable stepped in front of it. No-one was about to try and make their way through either.

The prisoner shuffled forward but whether this odd gait was due to bodily weakness or the restrictions of his broken footwear was unclear. He eased himself carefully into the chair by the window, and sat very still with bent head, taking very little notice of those around him. The movement, seen from outside brought a fresh set of exclamations from the assembled onlookers in the square, and the voices of the constables who guarded the front door could be heard persuading them not to mount the steps.

'You couldn't close the curtains, could you, sir?' asked the sergeant. 'The crowds are getting very restive.'

'I'm sorry, but I need as much light as I can get for the photograph,' said Beckler. 'It will only take a few moments.'

'Be quick, then,' said the sergeant reluctantly.

I then studied the three witnesses. You see, Mina I do think of you! Mr Stephen Westbury was a rather young man who would have been better advised to wait another year or two before making another attempt to grow whiskers. His pale speckled chin was cupped in one hand, and he craned his neck forward and stared at the prisoner intently. Mr Livermore, his eyes bulging with intense concentration, was also leaning forward as much as possible to get a good view. Mr Cobbe, however, his jaw slackening, his eyes opened wide, looked like a man who had seen a ghost, and it was not the ghost of someone he wished to see. 'Oh!' gasped Cobbe, and he rocked back on his heels. The constable was obliged to take him by the elbow to steady him.

The other witnesses turned to stare at Mr Cobbe.

The prisoner raised his head and looked around, and something that might have been mistaken for a smile spread slowly across his face, parting the grey thatch around his mouth and revealing the tips of yellowed teeth. 'Cobbe,' he said, and the voice was weak as if rarely used. 'Have they got you, too? I suppose it was about time.'

Cobbe made a noise deep in his throat like a man who had swallowed too big a piece of steak and was about to choke on it.

'Well, he certainly knows you!' said Mr Westbury.

'What do you say, gentleman?' asked the sergeant. 'Is this Holt?'

Mr Westbury, who had seemed so determined earlier was now less certain. 'I'm afraid I only saw Mr Holt in passing when he came to the office to see my father,' he said, awkwardly. 'Unfortunately, my father is not in the best of health and I doubt that he would be able to identify him now. And of course, this man has clearly endured much and cannot be the same as he once was. But,' he took a deep breath, 'I see no reason why he cannot be Holt, especially as he seems to know Mr Cobbe.'

Mr Livermore nodded. 'He's older and greyer than I remember, but that's to be expected. The same in height and general proportions, allowing for the passage of time, of course. I would say he is Holt. What about you, Cobbe?'

Mr Cobbe was red in the face but gulped and nodded emphatically. 'Yes, that man is undoubtedly Mr Jasper Holt. I recognise him perfectly!'

'Well, well,' said the Chief Constable, 'So Mr Holt is alive after all.'

Unexpectedly, the man in the chair leaned back and gave a cackle. 'Oh indeed. Yes. Mr Jasper Holt is very much alive, and he sits before you now.'

'What about the wife, then?' said Westbury to Livermore. 'And the brother in law? Did they lie?'

'I wouldn't say they lied,' said Livermore, generously. 'They simply saw what they wanted to see. He's changed, of course, and that was enough of a reason for their mistake.'

'Just turn your head a little and look directly at the camera, sir,' said Beckler to the prisoner. 'Hold still please. Just until I say you can move.' The man, after his short bout of hilarity allowed his features to sink into the same impassive expression as when he had entered the room. He turned towards the camera but showed no further inclination to move.

Beckler took the lens cap off and replaced it but shook his head. 'There is really far too little light.' He removed the glass plate from the camera and slid it carefully into the carrying case, then replaced it with a new one. 'Just one more, sir. There will be a longer exposure this time. Scarletti, tilt the tray a little to your left.'

The sergeant looked at the proceedings with keen interest and not a little curiosity. 'Is that done?' he asked at last.

'It is. But I would like some more pictures if you please, to record this important event. Gentlemen, if you could come forward just a little more. Just to where the sunlight comes through the window.'

The three witnesses looked somewhat surprised, but obeyed, and with some repositioning of the tea tray they were immortalised on glass.

'And sir, if you would so kind?' he asked the Chief Constable, who happily adopted a dignified pose for his portrait.

The sergeant coughed. 'I'd like a picture to show the missus, sir, if that's alright,' he said.

'If you please sir, might I have one to show mother?' asked the constable.

The Chief Constable cheerfully gave his assent, and both the sergeant and the constable made the most of the remaining light.

'Thank you for your assistance,' said Mr Beckler, to the policemen. 'Mr Scarletti, we are done here.'

'In that case,' said the Chief Constable, turning to the prisoner, 'Mr Jasper Holt it is my duty to place you under arrest on a charge of attempting to defraud an insurance company. I advise you not to make any statement that might tend to criminate you. Now please accompany the constable back to the cells.'

The man's eyes glazed over, but after a pause, he made an effort and rose from the chair. 'It's no more than I deserve,' he said.

'And you gentlemen,' added the sergeant to the witnesses 'will oblige us by leaving the station now.'

'Shouldn't his wife be told?' demanded Livermore.

'You leave that to us, sir.'

So we packed away the equipment for transport back to the shop. As we left, Beckler turned to me and said, 'that was good work, alerting me to the circumstances. If the pictures come out well, they will be as good as an advertisement. Now let us see what we have!'

It was all done not a moment too soon, as dark clouds had drifted to cover the sun, and there was even a threat of rain.

'So Mr Livermore was the hero of the hour, and he came out with a big smile on his face and stood at the top of the steps and made a speech,' said Richard.

'What did he say?' asked Mina.

'Oh, you'll read all about in the *Gazette*.'

Mina gritted her teeth. 'The *Gazette* is a weekly publication,' she reminded him.

'I know. Oh, I see what you mean. Well as far as I could make out, he said that they had all recognised the man as Mr Holt who was now under arrest for fraud, and he would see his solicitor at once about claiming compensation and advised everyone else to do the same. And everyone cheered him, and people clapped him on the back. Then it started to rain, and they went away, and we ran back to the shop.'

'And the pictures,' said Mina. 'Were they good?'

'Oh yes, say what you will about Beckler, and I still don't understand why you won't entertain him, he knows his business. The likenesses are very good indeed and once they are properly mounted they will take pride of place in the shop window. The Chief Constable and his men look very smart in their uniforms. I wouldn't be surprised if all the police in town came to have their pictures taken, now.'

'I hope I will get to see this picture of the prisoner,' said Mina.

'Oh, I am sure you will one day, my dear!'

'What I meant was, I would like you to bring me a copy.'

'Oh, I see. Well, why not?'

Mina had a sudden thought. 'You told me you have been cataloguing a collection of old pictures?'

Richard grimaced. 'Oh, yes that is a beast of job, but it is almost done.'

'And the names of the people in the pictures are written on the back?'

'Yes.'

'Pass me a sheet of writing paper and pen and ink.'

Richard complied, and Mina wrote down a list of names, all the men who had been mentioned to her as possible associates of Mr Jasper Holt. She handed him the paper. 'Take this, and please don't lose it. When you are next at work on the list of pictures, I want you to look and see if any of the names are on this list. I want to see any pictures of the people named on this paper.'

'But that will take a long time! 'Richard protested, 'there are lots of them.'

'You have listed them in alphabetical order?'

He looked blank. 'Was I supposed to?'

Mina took the deepest breath of which she was capable. 'I'd like to say it would make sense, but obviously only to me. You'll do this for me, Richard, won't you?'

He nodded. 'Anything for you, my dear! Are they all friends of yours?'

'No, but I might like to know them.'

When Richard had gone to dinner Rose brought Mina a tray, the contents of which were more nearly like the meal her family was enjoying, although the meat and vegetables were cut very small as if for a child, either because they deemed her to be too weak to cut them herself or in danger of choking on anything not diced. She would have liked to write to Mrs Vardy asking how she had been so certain that the man in the police cells was not Mr Holt, but given Mr Vardy's manner on their one meeting she felt sure that if she did, the letter would not reach its intended recipient. Regrettably, she did not expect to hear from Mrs Vardy again by way of letter. Once she was well, however, a meeting might be carefully arranged, perhaps through the good offices of Mr Merridew.

Mina remained hopeful that if she was patient the mysteries that engaged her mind would eventually be resolved, but she was obliged to admit that the cultivation of patience was not amongst her most successful accomplishments.

CHAPTER SIXTEEN

When Dr Hamid called on Mina next day she was settled in her armchair deeply engrossed in the pages of that morning's *Times*.

MISSING BRIGHTON MAN BACK FROM THE DEAD
From our special correspondent in Brighton

Yesterday morning a man walked into Brighton police office at the Town Hall, Bartholomew Square, and announced that he was Mr Jasper Holt, the wine merchant, who was declared missing and presumed to have been drowned after a yachting accident in 1864. Our readers should be reminded that just prior to this event Mr Holt had taken out a heavy insurance on his life but due to some unusual circumstances which concerned both his finances and the supposed accident, the company, suspecting fraud, declined to honour the policy. Nothing has been seen or heard of Mr Holt for more than seven years. His reappearance has caused considerable consternation in the town, as he was declared legally dead at the end of last year, and his widow has recently married Mr Silas Vardy, a manager of Saltmire and Vardy of Hove, a firm manufacturing fine porcelain.

Several persons were in the police station at the time of Mr Holt's arrival, and a lady who happened to be there in order to complain of a nuisance from one of the town's beer shops, witnessed the entire transaction. She has described the man to our correspondent as middle aged, with a grey beard and hair, somewhat slovenly, not very clean about his person, and shabbily dressed. As far as it has been possible to ascertain there is nothing in that description which precludes him from being Mr Holt. He was in a state of nervousness and at first she thought he had come there to report a crime, but instead he advanced to the sergeant's desk and announced in a quiet voice that he was Mr Jasper Holt and he had determined to surrender himself to the authorities. He was taken aside for questioning, but the lady was able to hear him say that he was sorry for all he had done and wished to suffer the consequences of his actions.

As we go to press, our correspondent has reported that Mrs Vardy in the company of her brother Mr Gordon Saltmire has been seen entering the police station, and it is a reasonable conclusion that they have been called there to identify the man claiming to be Mr Jasper Holt. As Mr Saltmire entered the building he was overheard to make the comment that the man was undoubtedly an impostor or a madman and he was sure that the question would be settled very quickly. Mrs Vardy, who was heavily veiled, although onlookers declared that she could be none but the distressed wife, said nothing.

THE BRIGHTON SCANDAL

Further to our earlier report we must describe a very remarkable scene which took place in the normally respectable parts of Brighton yesterday. A large assembly of persons of the business classes gathered outside the Town Hall demanding to see the man who has declared himself to be Mr Jasper Holt. Our correspondent, who was present, states that the situation came close to an outright assault on the building, which had to be protected by officers of the law.

Our readers might wonder at this turn of events, since the former Mrs Holt and her brother have both stated that the man in the cells is not Mr Holt, and there the matter ought to rest, however he continues to insist that he is, and a rumour began to circulate in the crowd that there was some prospect of his creditors receiving their money.

Peace was restored when three gentlemen all of whom were acquainted with Mr Holt and were connected with him in business, were permitted to enter the Town Hall and see the mysterious resident of the cells. All three were able to confirm that he was indeed who he claimed to be, and he was at once charged with the attempted fraud on the Brighton and Hove Insurance Company. He remains in the cells waiting for a legal representative to be appointed. While he appears to be without funds, we have no doubt that in such a notorious case, there will be many in the legal profession who will see it in their interest to represent him, the public excitement his situation has aroused, and the constant speculation that appears in the daily prints being tantamount to a fee. He will probably appear before the police courts in the next few days when we will expect to hear that he has been committed to be tried at the next assizes.

We are advised that a special delegation from the photographic department of Scotland Yard was able to view the prisoner and portraits of him will be placed on display at a Brighton photographer's shop very soon, where we have no doubt that they will attract considerable public attention.

There followed a lively debate in the correspondence column under the general heading: MR JASPER HOLT:

TO THE EDITOR OF THE TIMES

Sir— I had occasion to be in the vicinity of the police station this morning when I heard that a gentleman confessing to be Mr Jasper Holt was being held there. I hope to be excused from any accusation of overweening curiosity on the matter, but I was some years ago a customer of Mr Holt's wine emporium and therefore I am in a good position to identify the stranger. I witnessed Mrs Vardy and Mr Saltmire going into the station and what was my astonishment to see them emerge less than five minutes later. I really doubt that they can have had any opportunity to view and question the individual.

I have since been advised that they were adamant that the man being held in the Town Hall is not Mr Jasper Holt. Would it be too bold of me to suggest that their minds had been made up before they saw him? To *identify the man as the missing Mr Holt would place Mrs Vardy especially in a very difficult not to mention delicate position, and I can well understand her reluctance to do so. I did approach the police to offer my services and was told that these were not required. I do think it is essential to have another view on the matter.*

   BRIGHTON RESIDENT

BRIGHTON RESIDENT TO THE EDITOR OF THE TIMES

Sir— there have been many persons amongst the residents of Brighton, especially men of business, who have long suspected that the disappearance of Mr Jasper Holt was a well calculated fraud, designed to cheat his creditors. I for one, have always believed that he was able to reach the shore safely and make his escape undetected, perhaps with the assistance of accomplices. I have my suspicions of who those accomplices might have been, but beyond commenting that one must have been a female, I decline to venture an opinion. And now he reappears, begging forgiveness! There are men in Brighton who came close to ruin or whose good reputations were unjustifiably sullied because of his actions and they cannot forgive him however much he pleads for mercy. Are the police taking no steps to place him under arrest? They had better take good care of him or he might run away again.

JUSTICE

TO THE EDITOR OF THE TIMES

Sir— Might I suggest that the person best placed to determine whether the man who claims to be Mr Jasper Holt is actually his family doctor?

COMMON SENSE

Mina pointed to the last contribution. 'People without information are often very free with their opinions. They think they have all the answers which other, stupider people have not thought of, and they never think to check if they have their facts right before writing their letters. As a result, their mistakes are immortalised in print for the world to see. This person who demanded that the family doctor should go and identify the man in the Town Hall was obviously unaware that Mr Holt was never examined by Dr McClelland. Dr Crosier would be a better man to consult.'

'Yes,' said Dr Hamid, thoughtfully, 'the man who examined Mr Holt for the insurance company.' He made a brief but attentive examination of Mina's respiration and pulse, and nodded satisfaction. 'Dr Crosier's name was familiar to me, when you first mentioned him, but I decided not to say anything at the time in case my memory was faulty. I did not want to risk criticising a man's character without good reason. I have however, been making some discreet enquiries on the subject, and I have at last discovered that Dr Crosier died two years ago at the age of eighty-four.' He made a pause that was so solemn and significant that he had all Mina's attention. 'But that was not before he had been struck off the medical register.'

'Oh? For what reason?'

Dr Hamid completed his notes. 'That I have not yet been able to establish. If I do, I will let you know. But my feeling is that it must have been something more serious than a decline in his faculties with age. Had that been the case; for example, had he been losing his sight, he would simply have been encouraged to retire from practice.'

'But if the answer does not lie with either Dr McClelland or Dr Crosier, you might be able to solve the mystery. Didn't you tell me that Mr Holt used to visit the Baths?'

'Yes, but I didn't examine him.'

'But your masseur might recall if there were any marks about him that would assist identification.'

'I will ask, but it seems unlikely. It was about ten years ago, and our records do not keep details of that kind unless they are relevant for treatments.'

'Did he ask for any special treatment?'

'Nothing out of the ordinary. Many gentlemen ask for a shoulder and back massage especially businessmen and shopkeepers. And the scalp as well, if they are afraid of losing their hair. I'm sorry, but I don't think I have any information which would assist the police.'

Mina pointed to the letter from JUSTICE. 'The veiled inference here is as clear as day. Even if the man is not Mr Holt, I fear that the suspicion that Mrs Vardy actually connived and colluded with her husband's disappearance will always attach to her. She will never be free of it.' Suspicion, she thought was like the corpse of a drowned man, one that had sunk below the waves, and then just as one hoped it had finally rotted away to nothing, it rose to the surface again, bloated by the foul-smelling gas of gossip.

'Oh, it may turn out to be much worse for her than that,' said Dr Hamid, regretfully. 'One of my patients was in the crowd yesterday and he tells me that someone had heard a rumour that Mrs Vardy had not been left destitute by her husband's loss, but had, unknown to him, been concealing some property, a box of jewels or some such, that she had held when she was single, and which by law ought to have passed to him on their marriage.'

'But the Married Women's Property Act —'

'It is not retrospective. And in my opinion does not go nearly far enough.'

'As if I needed another reason not to marry,' said Mina dryly. 'But the rumour cannot be true!'

'There will be some people to whom that hardly matters. Those who prefer scandal to the truth. But as you can imagine it has especially aroused the interest of Mr Holt's creditors, who suddenly saw a chance of suing him for their money.'

Mina realised that in her eagerness to solve the mystery of Mr Holt she had not seriously considered that in one sense it would never be solved. Even the production of a mouldering corpse wearing the last garments the man was seen in, or his living body recognised by his nearest and dearest would never for some people, be enough.

CHAPTER SEVENTEEN

Mina was eager to hear from Mr Merridew again. She had written to him asking him to observe Mrs Vardy specially at the next séance, saying that having read all about the recent dramatic events at the Town Hall she was concerned for the lady's wellbeing. She was delighted to receive his reply informing her that he had visited Mrs Barnham a second time and would call on her to make his report.

When he arrived and saw her no longer in bed but sitting in an armchair, he gave a little cry of pleasure and made a pirouette of joy, before joining her before a table where there was a dish of biscuits and tiny cakes, nicely arranged, and a carafe of refreshing mineral water.

'As you know,' he said, 'I was anxious about the behaviour of one of the attendees at the last séance, a Mr Cobbe. 'I am sorry to say that there are persons who take a delight in cruelty to others, especially those in a humble way of life, who cannot speak out in their defence.'

'Is that Mr William Cobbe, the banker?' asked Mina

'It is. Do you know him?'

'Only by name. I have sometimes read in the newspapers of people who treat their servants quite abominably,' said Mina, 'usually when they are facing judge and jury. Prison is the only place for them. Is he a creature of that sort?'

'I fear he may be. A man such as Mr Cobbe, who is very jealous of his reputation, dare not indulge his cruelty too openly,' observed Mr Merridew, 'but he will always find ways and places. I therefore took the opportunity to speak to little Maggie before I went up to the medium's rooms.'

Mr Merridew proceeded to describe everything that had happened when he reached the house:

As Maggie opened the door, I was struck once more how dreadfully thin and worn she was and could not help wondering if she might be a little older than she looked. I wanted to sit her down to a good nourishing dinner, but I doubted that Mrs Barnham would allow it, and there was also the concern that Maggie might well mistake my intentions. Some of these vile individuals earn the trust of their victims with outward kindness, which they soon abandon. I would not be able to help her if she were frightened of me. I asked if I could speak to her for a moment.

She agreed and paused in the dank hallway. There were the faded remains of flowered wallpaper and as she drew back towards the wall she seemed to be sinking into and becoming part of it. I asked her if Mr Cobbe would be there that evening. She seemed to shrink at the mention of his name, but she shook her head, telling me he had important business at the bank.

I was relieved to hear this since I had not yet formulated a design and did not want to confront Mr Cobbe until I had. But I felt that the little servant was shrewder and more observant that she was given credit for. And if she was regarded as a person of no consequence, what might she have witnessed or overheard and remembered? I said: 'You know, Maggie, although I have only met Mr Cobbe once, it is my belief from what I have seen of him that he is a very bad man. What do you think?'

Maggie looked down at the floor, and her fingers twisted together. 'I don't know. I'm not to say.'

'No?' I questioned. 'Well, tell me this, then; when he comes here, does he give presents of money to Mrs Barnham?'

Maggie looked up. She stared into my face, as if trying to fathom whether I could be trusted, and then made a decision and nodded. 'Not in the room in front of everyone, but later on, so the other visitors don't see. Mrs Barnham always tells people she doesn't take money for the sittings, but that isn't true. And he gives something to Miss Stone as well. But I don't think it's as much.'

I asked her if she also received presents from him and she told me he had given her a penny if she agreed not to say anything about what went on.

'How long has he been coming to these séances?'

'Not long. The last time when you were here it was the second time. He — he tells Mrs Barnham what he wants,' she added in a whisper.

'Maggie, I couldn't help but see that you were afraid when I gave you a present. But that was not for any bad intention, please never think that. I am not like Mr Cobbe.'

I gave her another penny. She took the coin and wiped a dry little fist across her eyes.

'I think I may have guessed something,' I ventured. 'When the ghost of the little girl appears at the séance, that is really you, isn't it? You are all dressed up to look like a ghost of a child, and you have been schooled about what to do and how to walk about without making a noise.'

She bit her lip.

'That's all right, you don't have to say anything, but I can tell. I expect it is Miss Stone who gets you ready to appear like a ghost? She does it when she takes the tea things down to the kitchen, and when we sing our hymns and pray with our eyes closed that is when you can come in and go away without our noticing you?'

Maggie nodded again.

'And you must pretend to be Mr Cobbe's daughter?'

'Yes, only —' she stopped.

'Only what, Maggie?'

She took a deep breath, and looked more bravely into my eyes, the penny clutched tightly in her hand. 'I heard Mrs Barnham tell Miss Stone once. Mr Cobbe doesn't have a daughter. He never has had. He's never had a wife, neither.'

'And yet he would have us all believe that he grieves for a lost daughter; he addresses you, embraces you as such.'

'It's play-acting. That's what Mrs Barnham said. But I don't want to do it. And if I was his daughter he —'

The child could say no more, and I did not press her further. How desperately I wanted to comfort the poor creature, but it was not my place. What she needs is a motherly figure, something neither I nor the women who have charge of her could ever be. 'Maggie, are your parents alive?' I asked.

She shook her head. 'Father was killed on the railway. I looked after mother till she died. Then Miss Stone saw me begging in the street and said I was just what she wanted.'

'For play-acting?'

'Yes.'

I smiled reassuringly. 'Oh, I have nothing against a little honest play-acting. I have been known to do it myself from time to time. If the audience is pleased with the performance and the actors are happy with their lot, there is no harm in it. It can be a highly respectable mode of living. But what if the actors are not happy? What if they are told to play a part that they feel is not honest and proper? What do they do if they have no-one to help them?'

Maggie shuffled her feet. 'I don't know.'

'Well, I will tell you. If they can, they find a friend. Now I know that Mr Cobbe is an important man in Brighton. A gentleman whose occupation commands respect. And if you were to say that you were not happy with the play-acting that Mrs Barnham asks you to do for Mr Cobbe, and he denied that anything was the matter with it, then it would be he who would be believed and not you. Isn't that so?'

She nodded.

'But I believe you, and I will be your friend.'

She gulped. 'Mr Cobbe told Mrs Barnham that he wants to take me away so I can be his maidservant. But I don't want to go!'

'Oh, I promise you,' I told her, very seriously indeed, 'that will never happen.'

I took my seat at the séance, hoping to see Mrs Vardy. This time, however, Mrs Vardy's companion Mrs Wandle came alone, and took her seat with an expression of profound sorrow. The fire burned brightly but she looked chilled.

'I trust I find you well,' said Mrs Barnham, letting the real question hang in the air unasked.

'I am well enough,' said Mrs Wandle, 'but I regret that my dear friend Mrs Vardy will not be able to attend today as she had hoped. The recent dreadful events have prostrated her. She is able neither to pay visits nor receive visitors.'

Mrs Anscombe grunted, although whether from sympathy or scepticism was unclear.

'I was in the square on that day,' said Mr Eve, 'since I acted for one of Mr Holt's creditors who was too elderly to attend, and a more disgraceful scene I never witnessed. Men of business acting like wild animals. Some fool started a rumour about Mrs Vardy which I cannot believe.'

'It is quite untrue,' said Mrs Wandle, firmly.

'Then we must all pray for her,' said Mrs Barnham.

The company prayed more devoutly than ever before, with special words said for the health of Mrs Vardy, and in the séance that followed, the spiritoscope spelled out its wisdom. I was honoured to receive a heartfelt message from the spirit of King William IV commending my intention to write a history of his court, and both Mrs Wandle and Mrs Anscombe were comforted by kind words from their deceased loved ones. To Mr Eve, there was a statement from a past associate, an appreciation of his good qualities, which he was assured, would earn him great gratitude in all his endeavours. There was even a message from an unnamed spirit advising Mrs Vardy to be of good heart.

For myself, given my concerns, I felt that I could do no more than endure the nonsense with a pretence of admiration until my business with the medium was done.

I may have dissimulated better than I imagined, since as I rose to leave, Mrs Barnham beckoned me towards her for a private conversation. 'Please, remain a little longer,' she said, and much as I wanted to quit the place, I decided to oblige and see what I might learn. We sat by the fireside and waited until the other guests had departed. Miss Stone draped the spiritoscope in its black cloth and prepared rum punch. 'How are you progressing with your book?' asked Mrs Barnham.

'I have made a beginning,' I told her, 'but it is painstaking work, and may not be complete for a while.' I declined the offer of punch, which I felt might choke me.

'It must be so reassuring to know that you have the approval of His Majesty. I will ask Miss Stone to make a copy of his message to you which should make a very nice frontispiece.'

'It will indeed,' I replied, summoning up a burst of enthusiasm, 'a blessing from the King himself, what could possibly be better!'

Mrs Barnham accepted her tankard and savoured the warm fragrance that rose from its contents. 'If you are interested, I could make a special arrangement for you that would greatly assist your work. I sometimes offer private séances to my most important clients. In such a séance you would undoubtedly be able to converse directly with the spirits of the royal court. Now that the King himself has spoken to you I am sure that others of almost equal note will follow. Of course, such a consultation will sap my poor energies somewhat, but I am able to recover my strength very quickly if I have the right medicine.' She drank deeply and smacked her lips. 'Unfortunately,' and here she gave a regretful shake of the head, 'the medicine is very rare and hard to obtain.'

I at once recognised her meaning. 'Its purchase will put you to some expense,' I said.

She leaned towards me, as if speaking in confidence. 'You know of course that I never ask for payment from my clients. I make no profit from my work. I hardly like to ask for a donation towards the cost of the medicine, but since it enables me to serve you better, it would be most appreciated.'

'I understand of course.'

'A single dose can cost as much as £20, but it will restore me to health immediately.'

'You need have no worries on that account,' I said. 'The arrangement suits me very well, and I am more than delighted to pay the cost of your medicine. I will consult my diary and propose a day when I will be free to interview the royal spirits. I trust that they will appear before me in person?'

Mrs Barnham hesitated, and her eyes narrowed. I don't believe she was expecting that. 'Anything is possible,' she said, cautiously.

'But that would be more tiring for you and require more medicine.'

She cheered up at once. 'Precisely. Perhaps two doses.'

On that understanding I departed. I had the horrid feeling that had Mr Cobbe been at the séance that evening then he too would have been offered a special individual service, something I would have moved Heaven and Earth to prevent.

CHAPTER EIGHTEEN

The morning after Mr Merridew's revelations, Mina paid special attention to the early edition of *The Times* which devoted considerable column space to editorials and correspondence concerning the Holt mystery.

THE BRIGHTON SCANDAL

The associates of Mr Jasper Holt, the gentleman recently declared legally deceased after having been missing for more than seven years, have been making vigorous demands that the Holts' family doctor should be requested to examine the man claiming to be Mr Holt returned from the dead, to establish his true identity once and for all. The man, having been identified by three respectable gentlemen with whom Mr Holt formerly had business connections, has been charged with fraud under the name of Jasper Holt. This despite the fact that Mr Holt's widow and brother in law have stated that he is not Mr Holt, and they do not know who he is. The town, especially in the business quarters, is in an uproar.

Our correspondent has been most diligent in his enquiries and secured an interview with the medical gentleman in question, a Dr McClelland. He discovered that the doctor had never examined Mr Holt, having only been concerned with the trivial and normal maladies of the children, when called in by the anxious mother. He has therefore declined to make any pronouncement on the man in the cells, or even to go and see him.

An enquiry was then made of the Brighton and Hove Insurance Company which arranged for the medical examination of Mr Holt in order to grant the life policy, which, we must remind our readers, was never paid out on due to the suspicious circumstances of Mr Holt's disappearance. We venture to suggest that had the payment been made the man in the police cells would be in an even more serious position than he is at present. The certificate of good health was given by a Dr Crosier, who is now unfortunately deceased. We hope and trust that the late doctor's notes will be examined to see if any information can be gleaned to solve this remarkable mystery.

Meanwhile general agitation remains rife. We hear that Mrs Vardy has been inundated with correspondence making the most unpleasant and ill-conceived accusations which we will refrain from printing here.

THE TRIUMPH OF SCIENCE

Once again, we must celebrate the valuable work of our men of science who have provided us with so many useful inventions. Not the least of these is the photograph, which has hitherto been regarded mainly as an item of amusement, and a method of recording the image of persons without recourse to engaging an artist, something that so many in our land are prevented from doing due to the expense. Thus portraits have become available to us all, and it is a good thing. The results are sometimes a little cruel, as the camera can show the sitter in the true honesty of their appearance, yet people flock to have their pictures taken, and even include them on cartes de visite, so not everyone is disappointed. And these images form treasured mementoes of those loved ones who have passed away.

More recently the photograph, being an accurate and unflattering portrait has shown its power to assist in the solving of a mystery. The man who is currently in the cells at Brighton police station awaiting an appearance at the police court, received a very unusual visitor the other day, a young photographer of the name of Beckler who has recently set up shop in that town. Entering the station with his camera and equipment and an assistant, he somehow, making a great show of audacity and confidence, managed to gain access to the prisoner and take a picture. (We had recently supposed that he was a representative of the Scotland Yard photographic department, but we were in error and must correct our earlier report.) *That portrait is now being displayed in his shop window in Ship Street. Several hundred residents of Brighton have now seen it, including men of business who were acquainted with Mr Holt and who all declare that he is the man, though undoubtedly fallen on hard times. We might wonder whether the fact that these individuals are owed money by Mr Holt has anything to do with the matter, but we are not in a position to speculate. Other residents of Brighton state that they believe they have seen the man in the streets of the town, but do not know his name or where, if anywhere, he normally resides.*

But as things stand, his former associates say he is Holt and he says he is Holt, and he has been charged with fraud under that name. The lady who has been his wife and then his widow and then the wife of another man, and now, we suppose, is his wife once more, has declined to comment.

For the time being, however, we believe that the artist who wields brush and pen need not be concerned for his profession which still has an essential place in our society.

TO THE EDITOR OF THE TIMES

Sir — forgive me if I state that I do not believe the Holt mystery to be very mysterious at all. Neither do I attach any blame to Mrs Vardy — or should I call her Mrs Holt? — or even to Mr Saltmire for failing to identify the prisoner. We have all read of cases where a body has been identified by distressed persons as that of a missing relative only to have that relative return home alive and well.

The lady was clearly under great emotional strain at the time of her visit, and she might not have dared to take more than a glance at the man. He was undoubtedly changed from the man she had once loved and called husband, and her natural disinclination to find herself in a dreadful situation did the rest. As for Mr Saltmire, I must assume that he found it best to simply agree with his sister.

I should also mention that according to reports Mr Holt was brought out of his cell and placed in a well-lit room to be photographed and identified. His three business associates would therefore have had the benefit of bright sunlight in which to view him, a commodity in which I understand the Town Hall police cells to be deficient.

COMMON SENSE

TO THE EDITOR OF THE TIMES

Sir — *It is said that one should never speak ill of the dead, however I feel that under the circumstances appertaining to Mr Holt and the gentleman currently languishing in the cells at Brighton, I should reveal what I know of Dr Crosier, who passed away two years ago at the age of eighty-four.*

I was once a friend of Dr Crosier, but with advancing age and the deterioration of both his hearing and his eyesight, his patients began to seek other medical advice, and his practice was greatly reduced. On the last occasion on which I saw him, I wished to be examined for an insurance policy and he told me that he was content to sign any paper required, for a fee, irrespective of any condition which might result in an increase of the premium, or even refusal of the policy. Naturally I declined the offer, but I was somewhat shocked by it, and on making enquiries found that other patients had been advised the same, although all had stoutly refused to take advantage of it. One gentleman said, and I hope he was joking, that for the right fee Dr Crosier would sign a paper to say that a man had two good legs when he only had one.

I was considering what to do with this information, but soon afterwards I was relieved of that burden on hearing that Dr Crosier had been struck off the medical register. The proceedings were never reported in the daily press, and I believe it was assumed that he had retired due to his advanced age, however I made discreet enquiries and was told that he had indeed been struck off for signing fraudulent certificates. Soon afterwards he suffered a fit and lost the use of one side of his body. He was never prosecuted for the offence and died about a year later.

    BRIGHT RESIDENT

TO THE EDITOR OF THE TIMES

Sir — Have your correspondents not considered that the gentleman claiming to be Mr Jasper Holt may be him in fact but at the same time, deceased? It is not beyond the bounds of possibility. I myself have attended many séances in which spirits of my departed relations have appeared to me. I recognised them at once, since they were exactly as they had been in life, able to move, and even warm to the touch, only they were now clad in glowing heavenly garments. I have even been permitted to embrace my dear mother's spirit.

    If this be the earthly reappearance of Mr Holt, then he has come to tell us of his tribulations and should be allowed to repent of his transgressions in order for his immortal soul to find the peace it craves.

    I suggest that the authorities in Brighton call in the services of a sensitive, who will be able to establish this man's identity beyond any doubt by viewing his aura. There is a noted sensitive residing in Brighton, a Miss S who surely ought to be consulted.

    SPIRITUALIST

When Rose brought Mina her daily post, it consisted not of one or two letters but several dozen. Mina had an unhappy feeling as to what the letters would say and on opening one of them found that her instinct was correct. The powerful hand of famed explorer, spiritualist and persistent roué Mr Arthur Wallace Hope who had so often insisted that Mina was a sensitive who refused to acknowledge her gifts, was reaching out to her even from across the sea.

'There are a number of persons outside asking to see you,' said Rose.

'Are they from the newspapers?'

'They don't say they are.'

'Then I expect they are. You are to admit anyone who is either a uniformed policeman or someone I already know. The others can leave their card.'

'That will be all of them, then,' said Rose.

CHAPTER NINETEEN

That evening Richard arrived home complaining of a headache and declaring himself too exhausted even to sample the delights of the town. Mina found herself unexpectedly transformed from patient to nurse as she asked Rose to bring her a cloth, a towel, and a basin of cool water with which to bathe Richard's temples.

'I now know exactly how many people live in Brighton,' he moaned, as he collapsed into a chair by her side, 'because every single one of them down to the last bootlace and match seller has been crowding into Ship Street, and most of them have come for just one reason, to stare at the pictures in the window of Beckler's shop. That is all very fine for him, I suppose, and he is highly pleased about it, but when will the chaos end? The street is very narrow as you know, but much used, so the crush has been preventing the movement of traffic. And the noise! There were frightened horses and barking dogs, quarrelling ladies and burst parcels all over the place. Two carriers started laying about them with whips, three shopkeepers came in to complain to us that they weren't getting their deliveries, and the only man who was able to travel from one end of the street to the other without hindrance was riding a velocipede.'

'Did anyone have any useful suggestions as to who the man in the police station might be?' asked Mina. 'Apart from Mr Holt's creditors, that is, who are all adamant that he is Mr Holt.'

'Everyone has an idea, but no-one could actually give him a name. He has been everything and everyone, a beggar, a fishmonger's delivery man, an escaped convict, a puppeteer, a famous private detective in disguise, and who knows what else, all in the course of one day. It is too much for anyone to endure!' Richard took the damp cloth from Mina and pressed it to his face. 'I need a brandy. I need a good smoke. I need a holiday. I need —' he groaned. 'I need Nellie. I wish she would come back.'

'Perhaps all these people think that they will get a reward, although none has been offered,' Mina suggested. 'Didn't someone start a rumour that Mrs Vardy has a secret cache of valuables, which has led the creditors to imagine they might receive their money after all? That is the person you should be blaming for the pandemonium.'

Richard peeped out one eye from under the cloth. 'It wasn't a rumour it was just idle talk, the sort of thing all fellows do. It might be true though. Married ladies are always hiding things from their husbands.'

'I won't ask how you know this, but it will certainly stand you in good stead when you marry.' Mina took the cloth and wetted it again, then dabbed it to her brother's forehead. 'Do you have any other symptoms apart from the headache?'

'Only misery and ennui,' he sighed. 'But I did find something you might like.' He sat up, produced a photograph from his pocket and handed it to Mina. 'Don't tell anyone but I have borrowed it. They look like a fine collection of walruses.'

Mina put aside the cloth, dried her hands and studied the picture. It was a card-mounted tintype of a group of six gentlemen standing about a table on which was displayed a handsome model yacht. She turned it over and written on the reverse of the card was 'Brighton Yacht Club, 1863, Old Steine, Brighton, Secretary W Sutherland.'

'Why was this not collected?' said Mina, 'or did Mr Simpson keep duplicates as samples for display?'

'Beckler keeps samples to show the customers,' said Richard.

Mina nodded. 'That must be it. To encourage other Brighton clubs to have their portraits made. But the individuals are not named,' she added, gazing once more at the row of faces. 'I wonder which of these gentlemen is Mr Sutherland? Is he even in the picture? If he is the secretary, then he ought to be.'

'That man is not Sutherland,' said Richard, pointing to a portly figure with a heavy moustache. 'He is Mr Cobbe the bank manager. I know that because he was at the Town Hall when there was all that excitement. He was one of the men who identified Holt. In fact, he looked quite frightened to see him. And Holt certainly knew him. He actually thought Cobbe was there because he was under arrest, too. I don't know why.'

'I think I can guess,' said Mina. 'There was some sort of scandal about an insurance company in that year. Maritime Queen, I think it was called, but it was all a fraud, a false company that did no business but was designed to cheat the investors out of their money.'

This aroused Richard's interest. 'Really? How does that work?' he asked, siting up.

'It doesn't and the perpetrators were caught and had to flee the country and one of them murdered the other,' said Mina, before Richard could give the concept serious consideration. 'I think Mr Cobbe was one of the accused, but he was acquitted. I didn't know he was a member of the yacht club. Who are these other men? I wish I knew.'

'I have seen a picture of that fellow at the shop,' said Richard, pointing to a man who was rather older than the rest. 'He was in some sort of a uniform. Naval, I think.'

'I may know who he is,' said Mina. 'Bring me my correspondence.'

Richard wiped his face once more, tossed the cloth into the basin, dried his hands and grinned, all his sorrows suddenly forgotten. 'You have that look in your eye,' he said as he brought the box of letters.

'I don't know what you mean,' said Mina.

'And I know now what I shall write my book about. It will be called, "Miss Mina Scarletti the Famous Lady Detective of Brighton." It will be a big success and I shall be very rich.'

'I look forward to reading it.'

'I know!' he exclaimed, 'You're the real writer in the family. Why don't you just write it for me, and I'll put my name on it? It wouldn't take you long.'

'Only if I can keep all the money from the sales.'

He scowled. 'That's not fair! It was my idea!'

Mina left him to ruminate on this claim, and soon found the letter from Mr Phipps about the Maritime Queen scandal. 'Yes, I was right, he is Captain Horace Bulstrode.'

'That was his name, yes. What did he do?'

'He was a director of the company that collapsed due to the discovery of the fraud. But he was just an innocent dupe, brought onto the board for his name and reputation, to give confidence to the investors. There were two others, friends of his, I think, retired military men, though the rest of the men in this picture are far too young to be either of them, so I doubt that they had any connection with the club. The other members look to be no more than thirty.'

Mina looked carefully from face to face, seeing proud looks, smiles and youthful undisciplined whiskers, some of the last being more extensive than others. There was one expression that particularly caught her eye, less smiling, more of a self-satisfied stare. She had seen it before. The man held his hands in front of him and the finger and thumb of one hand grasped a signet ring on the little finger of the other. Mina gave a sudden shiver. 'Mr Vardy,' she said.

'Vardy?' exclaimed Richard. 'Not —?'

'Yes. The husband of Mrs Vardy. The lady who is the widow of Mr Holt.'

'How do you know him?'

Mina paused. 'I — have had dealings with Saltmire and Vardy the porcelain company.' Fortunately, Richard seemed to accept this explanation and Mina continued. 'This picture is very interesting. We have here in all probability Mr Sutherland, who advised the fraudulent company on investments but was not thought to be involved in the fraud, and also, and this may or may not be a coincidence, he is the owner of the yacht from which Mr Holt vanished. But if he is in the picture, I don't know which one of the gentlemen he is. There is Captain Bulstrode, one of the notable directors of the same company, who was undoubtedly innocent, and was probably the means to attract the other notables. Then we have Mr Cobbe the banker who was tried for the fraud but acquitted. And we have Mr Vardy.'

Richard stared at the picture again. 'So that means three of the men in this picture were involved in this fraud?'

'Three at least. Some might have been the actual culprits who planned it, others were simply drawn into the scheme and acted in good faith.'

'How do you know so many things?' asked Richard. 'How do you remember them all?'

'I am older than you, my dear,' said Mina comfortingly. She was hardly more than a year older than her brother, but he didn't argue.

'I've brought you this as well,' said Richard, taking another picture from his pocket, this one printed on paper. 'There were a number of copies made. You said you would like to see one.'

Mina stared at a portrait of a seated man, and there was no doubt in her mind as to its subject. It was a grim picture, taken quite close so as to figure only his head and shoulders, the lines of the face deep and shadowy, the brow heavy with pain. 'This is the man in the police office.'

'The very fellow.'

Mina studied it carefully. 'It is a little dark, but I suppose the light was wanting. Poor man, he looks very neglected. If he is Mr Holt, then he has been shifting for himself as best he can these last few years. But I can see from this that it would be very hard, even for someone who knew him well to say whether or not it is he, what with that great thatch of hair and the beard covering most of his face.'

'Have you seen him before?' asked Richard, hopefully.

'I would not want to swear on a Bible that I have. If he was bathed and barbered, there might be a better chance of knowing who he is. The newspapers say he still languishes there. Poor fellow!'

'Yes, well if he is Mr Holt, he is a criminal, and if he is not, he is a lunatic. Either way he has to stay there for his own safety. He is not claiming to be a ghost so I didn't expect it would interest you so much.'

Mina thought it best not to bring out the collection of papers she had been lent by Mrs Vardy while Richard was there or he might let slip to her mother that she was taking on too much, and she would never hear the end of it. After her brother had gone to dinner, Rose brought up a tray, and Mina was able to extract the papers from her desk and place them on the table by her side. She was then able to compare the picture Mrs

Vardy had provided with that of the man claiming to be Mr Holt, but hard as she tried, she found it impossible to tell whether or not these were pictures of the same man.

Mrs Vardy had been quite certain after a single visit that cannot have taken long that the man in the cells was not her former husband. What had made her so very sure? A man with no distinguishing marks, a man undoubtedly changed with time and privation, a man no longer tidily groomed. How Mina would have liked to have been at that confrontation, watched Mrs Vardy's face, and heard her voice. Did she lift her thick veil to see him, or did she view him through the fabric? Did she ask him to speak? What did her brother have to say? Who else was present at that meeting to observe her reaction?

Mina looked at the two portraits once more, but the main difference she saw between them was the eyes. Mr Holt in the family portrait was proud and confident and looking directly into the camera. The man held by the police was devastated and crushed by circumstance. His eyes were vacant, devoid of hope. He was a man nourished only by pain.

Mina composed two letters to be sent immediately. The first was to Mr Phipps:

Dear Mr Phipps

I am not sure if you were aware of this, but I have discovered that three of the gentlemen whose names were mentioned in connection with the Maritime Queen Insurance Company fraud were at one time members of the Brighton Yacht Club. They are Captain Bulstrode, Mr Sutherland, and Mr Cobbe. The club premises was located in Old Steine, where the Company also maintained an office. I don't know if the Club or its records still exist, but I do have the loan of a photograph of its members

which may be of assistance. Perhaps the senior partners who recall the case
might like to see it,
 Yours faithfully
 M Scarletti

Mina's second letter was in response to a piece published in The Brighton Gazette, which caused her some annoyance:

MR HOLT'S CREDITORS RIOT IN BARTHOLOMEW SQUARE

The Town Hall Square witnessed some shocking scenes this week as a great crowd of men, numbering several hundred, all assembled demanding to enter the police offices and see the man being held there under the name of Jasper Holt. At one point your correspondent was nearly trampled in the rush and assaulted with walking sticks. The two constables guarding the Town Hall were unable to restore order and it was left to Mr Livermore, a hotelier, to calm the rioters. The excitement was a result of the rumour that the lady known as Mrs Vardy has privately concealed assets of substantial value, which would enable Mr Holt's creditors to make a claim on the estate. As to the truth of this rumour we are not in a position to comment, but it has become the subject of energetic debate in town.

Mrs Vardy has refused to make any statement to the Gazette. Mr Holt remains in custody and will shortly appear before the magistrates to answer a serious charge of attempted fraud.

Meanwhile we must make an earnest appeal to Miss Mina Scarletti the noted spirit medium and sensitive, whose powers have been commented upon by no less a personage than Viscount Hope, to pay a visit to the Town Hall and settle the dilemma once and for all.

She wrote to the editor of the *Brighton Gazette*:

Sir — *please could you publish the following notice.*

Miss Mina Scarletti wishes it to be known that despite allegations to the contrary made by uninformed persons, she is not a spirit medium or a sensitive and has never claimed to be such or practised as such. Residents of Brighton are therefore entreated not to contact her either directly or indirectly with demands for her to provide any assistance in the case of the individual currently in police custody under the name of Jasper Holt.

CHAPTER TWENTY

Sometimes Franklin Holt thought he was dead. He was not sure what being dead felt like, so he could not be entirely certain. Would death mean that he could float about in the air, drifting though the world wherever he pleased? Or would he soar up to heaven to be with the angels? Both possibilities felt pleasing, desirable, in fact far better than his present earthly existence. Maybe, he thought, next time the witch gave him the poison, he would swallow every drop of it, even ask for more, and then at last, he would find some peace.

In some of his dreams however, death was very different. His soul was still trapped in his body, which lay in a coffin, his flesh rotting, until all that was left was a skeleton. If that was true, then one day, he would be found in his miserable grave and dug out of the soil to make way for another corpse, and the gravediggers would tell jokes about him and use his leg bones to tap out their doleful music on his grinning empty skull. Perhaps, he thought, after all, it was better to endure his present ills than escape to something that might prove to be far worse.

Matthew wasn't there anymore. He had been sent away to another school, but Franklin didn't know why. Mother and Mr Vardy and Aunt Marion walked about the house whispering, although much of the time Mother took to her room. He was told she had a headache. Sometimes he could hear her crying.

There were noisy people in the street outside the house. At first, he thought he had imagined them, or if they were real, they were angry devils come to take him down to regions of fire. But when he was properly awake, which he was when he managed to spit out the witch's potion, he was able to look outside and then he saw that they were only men.

'Why are there men outside?' he dared to ask Aunt Marion one afternoon. She had brought him some books of lessons to keep him busy,

which she dropped with a thump onto his little writing desk. 'I can hear them talking. Why don't they go away?'

'They want to see your mother, but they won't,' said his aunt, throwing down an exercise book and some pencils.

'What about?'

'Oh, you're full of questions today!' she snapped. 'They've come about your father, if you must know!'

'But — but father is dead. What do they want with him?'

She laughed. 'Oh, this is the child who imagines he has seen his father's ghost,' she said derisively. 'Well, I have some news for you, and when I have told you it, I want all this silly ghost nonsense to stop. Do you understand?'

She had her witch face on, and he nodded. There was nothing else he could do.

'Your father isn't dead at all. He's come back but you'll never see him again, because he is a very wicked man. He has done some bad things, and he has been locked up. He's nothing more than a criminal, and he will be in prison for the rest of his life. And if you don't behave yourself, that's where you'll end up!'

She walked out.

Franklin started to sob, but no-one came to comfort him.

Since Mrs Vardy had been unable to attend the most recent séance due to illness, Mina had not expected to hear from her. She was especially pleased therefore to receive a letter from Mrs Vardy, although less so when she read the contents.

Dear Miss Scarletti

I do hope this finds you well.

Forgive me for not writing to you sooner, but the recent terrible events have left me quite devastated.

I am sure that you have heard the news that a man claiming to be Jasper has appeared at the Town Hall. The poor soul must be deluded, and I have the greatest of sympathy for him. I did go to view him, and it wanted barely a minute of my time to advise the police that he was not Jasper. That was perfectly clear to me. How can a wife not know her own husband?

But it seems that I am not to be believed. The horrible letters that have arrived at my home making the cruellest accusations have quite undermined my health. Only yesterday we were obliged to summon a policeman to urge a crowd of particularly vociferous individuals standing outside our house to depart peacefully. And poor Franklin, who we have done our best to protect from all this has heard them talking, and now he is more distressed than ever. My sister is doing her best to keep him calm and reassures me that when these dreadful events are past and forgotten, he will recover.

I believe more strongly than ever that Franklin is in touch with his father's spirit, which is unable to be fully at peace in the heavenly realms until his earthly troubles are resolved. I would do anything in my power to relieve his troubled soul, but poor Jasper is unable to tell either Franklin or myself what it is we must do. That appears to be the nature of spirits, they seem to exist in a region where all is indistinct, and they cannot think in practical terms as we do or even as they once did when alive. Mrs Barnham has explained all this to me. That is why the messages we receive from our departed loved ones are often couched in the vaguest of terms. Materialists who refuse to believe in these communications complain that they are so general that they say nothing at all, but I beg you, do not listen to them. The spirit world is not like ours, but they cannot comprehend it.

Silas has informed me that he paid a visit to you as he was concerned that you were in danger of suffering a relapse if you continued your enquiries, and he implored you to desist. Naturally the last thing I wish is to be the instrument of any harm to you, and in view of these recent events you would be well advised not to continue, or you may find yourself *similarly assailed by the outspoken and ignorant rabble. I do not feel it would be wise for me to visit you again, and this may be the last letter I will write to you.*

Please therefore, do not trouble to reply, and if you must have an object to which to devote yourself then it should be the pursuit of good health.

With warmest good wishes for your recovery
Charlotte Vardy

Mina felt only sorrow for Mrs Vardy. The lady was understandably going along with her husband's wishes, as the thing she craved most of all was a peaceful domesticity. Mr Vardy was not someone who would take kindly to being disobeyed by his own wife. She wondered if Mr Vardy had seen and approved the letter and suspected that he had not, and it had somehow been smuggled out to the post box by a sympathetic servant. Despite the wishes expressed by Mrs Vardy Mina felt reluctant to step back. She wanted some means of contacting the unhappy lady if she was needed. She recalled that Mrs Vardy's good friend who accompanied her to the séances was a Mrs Wandle, a widow. Her late husband according to the spiritoscope, had expressed his approval of how she managed an inn, presumably the business they had once managed together. Mina looked once more in *Page's Directory* and found a Mrs E Wandle, of the Ship Inn, Seabourne.

Dear Mrs Wandle
Please forgive me for writing to you, as we have never been introduced. Your good friend Mrs Vardy has recently consulted me about matters of which I am sure you are aware. I wish there was something I could do to relieve her distress, but she is anxious that I might make myself ill in so

doing and has urged me not to write to her again. I will of course, respect her wishes.

If there is any way, however small, in which I can help her, please do write to me.

Assuring you of my good intentions,
Mina Scarletti

Mina had scarcely completed her letter and settled to some reading when Rose announced that Mr Merridew had called and begged to be allowed to speak to her. She agreed at once that he should be shown to her room.

'Dear lady,' said Mr Merridew to Mina, 'please excuse my unexpected arrival but I have news to impart which I know will interest you.'

Mina was happy to put her books and papers aside. She could see that the customary elegance of her visitor's superior wig was a little ruffled by exertion. 'I am all attention,' she said.

'Having waited for the first wild undisciplined crush to abate, I determined to wend my way to Ship Street, to see for myself the portrait of the unhappy man now languishing in the cells at the Town Hall. Avoiding pitfalls and obstacles, and the inevitable dust and dirt of the road, I saw that there was an acceptably respectful assembly outside the window of Mr Beckler's photographic shop, where a boy had been specially employed to sweep away any debris which might have discouraged potential customers. Persons of all ages had stopped to stare; gentlemen of business, gentlemen of leisure, tradesmen, ladies with their maids and nursemaids with their charges. Even quite small children were being held up above the heads of the crowds to examine the portrait of the unknown man. Rather like the observation gallery at a trial, a lively debate was in progress in the crowd, with every individual having his or her own theory.

I entered the shop and found a busy bustle of customers, their chatter almost obscuring the delicate sound of the bell, examining the sample portraits which covered an entire wall, and a display of ornamental frames. Your brother was standing behind the counter doing his best not to look bored, a task which I am sorry to say was quite beyond him.

I decided to be a moving advertisement and so adopting my most melodious voice I exclaimed 'What a delightful shop this is! I have been more than satisfied with the set of portraits I had made here.' I walked about the premises, smiling and bowing politely to the ladies and having thus charmed them, I approached the counter.

'I have come for the exhibition of cave pictures but will certainly return for another sitting,' I said. 'Also, I had to see your most famous picture — the one in the window. I can't say that I have seen the fellow before, but if the Brighton Theatre Company was ever to mount a production of King Lear, I would engage him in a trice and have him howling like a madman in a thunderstorm.'

'I hope he won't have many lines to learn,' said Richard. 'He didn't look up to it when I saw him. Is it a large part?'

'Oh no, not at all, it is mainly howling. The real hero of the play is the Duke's son, young Edgar, who feigns madness in order to protect his sovereign, defeats the traitors, and marries the King's virtuous daughter. It is a role I have long coveted.'

At this moment, the doorbell sounded again, and a small plump lady with a feathered hat entered accompanied by her maid and hurried directly to the counter like a hunting dog that had scented its quarry. 'Oh, Mr Scarletti!' was her shrill cry. 'I am so pleased to find you here!'

Richard winced. 'Miss Hartop. What a — a pleasure to see you again. Have you come to make an appointment?'

Miss Hartop laughed in which she must have imagined was a charmingly girlish manner. The sound was like a series of rapid hammer blows on a badly tuned carillon. 'No, today I have come to see the exhibition of cave photographs. I have one of your pretty little advertisement cards. It promises a most remarkable demonstration. Do you know, I simply cannot stay away from this establishment? Now I wonder why that can be?' she added in a manner which left no-one in any doubt as to the answer.

'I cannot imagine,' said Richard, politely.

She leaned on the counter and gazed up into his eyes. She was wearing rather too much of a particularly strident cologne. 'But perhaps I will make another appointment, after all. A new photograph. A lady can never have too many, I think. My only question is which of my gowns I should wear for the sitting? I have such a darling peach silk with flounces, and a light blue with lace. Which do you advise, Mr Scarletti?'

'I don't know,' said Richard. 'They'll both look grey in the picture.'

Miss Hartop squealed. 'Oh, Mr Scarletti, you are so very amusing!'

Richard glanced at me helplessly and I decided to come to his assistance. 'The question to be determined, dear lady,' I said, 'is whether you wish the portrait to emphasise your complexion, in which case I would advise the peach, or the brilliance of your eyes, in which case the blue would be best. Either would be very flattering.'

'Oh sir!' she exclaimed, 'how very kind. And now I think about it, perhaps the peach would be my preference. But I must confess, although perhaps I ought not to say it, it is a little bit — just a little, you know —— it exposes the shoulders for all to see.' She gave a little squeak. 'Do you think I dare?'

'Oh, dare away, dare away!' I exclaimed heartily.

She laughed again. 'Oh, you are a naughty man to be sure! But don't I recognise you?' She stared at me, and I of course, obliged by striking a pose and offering my profile for her examination. 'Why yes, you are the great man of the theatre, Mr Merridew!'

'At your service,' I acknowledged with a bow.

'How very exciting to meet you! My poor late mother was a great admirer of yours and spoke of you so often. You were playing Romeo, I believe, and I am sure she saw you a dozen times over. She died with your *carte de visite* clutched to her bosom.'

'I — hope it brought her comfort,' I said, after a pause in which I was obliged to grope for the right words.

'It did, it did!' she said with a passionate gasp.

At this moment, Mr Beckler appeared from the rear of the shop. He wore a long plain linen apron over his suit, and a set of goggles was pushed back over his brow, making his hair stand up in tangled spikes. In one heavily gloved hand was a pair of long metal tongs. 'If you please, ladies and gentlemen,' he announced, 'I am about to perform my demonstration of the new miracle, magnesium ribbon. There is no need to be afraid, I will light just one small piece and it will be done in the open air, nevertheless, I can promise you that the brilliance of the light will be apparent and it would be best not to stare at it directly. If you would all like to follow me.'

He turned and proceeded down a corridor leading to the back of the premises. I offered Miss Hartop my arm which she accepted with alacrity, and she and her maid joined the crowd of visitors to the demonstration. Your brother remained at the desk, sighing, and I felt sure that he was thinking not of Miss Hartop, but quite another lady, and how she might have looked as peach silk cascaded from her shoulders.

The demonstration was brief but somewhat startling. A bench had been set out in the small open yard behind the shop, and there Mr Beckler clasped a piece of metal ribbon some three or four inches long in the tongs, put on the goggles, instructed the audience to stand well back, and applied the end of the ribbon to the hottest part of the flame of a spirit burner. The effect was rapid, the result a searing intense white light, followed by a plume of pale smoke which descended to the bench where it formed a heap of ash. There were loud exclamations from the onlookers and shrieks from Miss Hartop. Mr Beckler, obviously pleased with the result, assured the crowd that with a hotter flame the burn would start even more rapidly.

We returned to the shop, filing down the corridor, everyone chattering about what they had witnessed, with Miss Hartop dabbing her eyes, and laughing. 'Oh, what a wonder!'

Mr Beckler, having divested himself of his apron and goggles, joined us there and distributed business cards. Most of the crowd headed back to Ship Street, but Miss Hartop and I remained. I had, you see, taken the opportunity of making a small purchase, and approached the counter. 'I think I am due to make a payment,' I said, but Mr Beckler waved that aside. 'It is gratis, sir, as you are one of my best customers.'

Mr Beckler made a subservient bow to Miss Hartop and murmured something about how pleasant it was to see her again, but it was all politeness and no pleasure.

'I will come again soon, I promise,' she assured him. 'This is quite the most interesting emporium in all Brighton. There are such wonders to behold every day!' She looked significantly at Richard, who quickly fell to studying the appointments book.

'And what is your opinion of the hirsute fellow portrayed in the window?' I asked. 'What be he? Butcher or baker or candlestick-maker? Opinions vary.'

'Oh, I believe him to be an artist,' said Miss Hartop. 'I am sure I have seen him, or someone very like him, walking about Brighton with paper and pencils.'

Richard looked up. 'Pencils?' he said.

'Yes, Mr Scarletti. Why, you have such a strange look. What can you be staring at?' She gazed at him through lowered lashes, and pursed her lips, but he tried not to notice.

'Because — yes, I remember something now, when we took the photograph,' said Richard. 'The man's fingertips were dark. I thought at the time it might have been dirt or coal, but it could have been from an artist's pencil.'

'But he would not draw with his fingers, would he?' said Miss Hartop with a laugh.

'He might do. He might have used a soft pencil and then rubbed the paper with his fingertips to smooth out the marks. I am an artist myself, you know.'

'There may be something in that,' said Mr Beckler, thoughtfully. 'We should notify the police. They can make enquiries at the stationery shops.'

'Or go to his lodgings,' said Miss Hartop.

'Yes, that would be better, of course,' said Richard. 'But they can't go to every lodging house in Brighton. Or can they?'

'Oh but I know where he lodges,' said Miss Hartop.

'You do?' exclaimed Beckler.

'Well — not exactly.' She giggled. 'I am such a silly goose! I don't know the address. But my maid was paying a visit recently and saw him — I think she called him 'that smelly artist man' going into a common type of lodging house. Not one of my father's, of course,' she added quickly. 'Tilly!' she called to the maid.

The girl, who had been examining the array of portraits, hurried to her side. 'Yes, Miss.'

'Do you remember when you saw that artist going into a house?'

'Oh, yes, Miss.'

'Would you be able to point out the place?' I asked.

'Yes, sir. I didn't see the address, but I was on North Road and I saw him go down Foundry Street. It was a house by a beer shop.'

'Then we must act at once,' said Beckler. 'Scarletti, mind the premises. I shall conduct Miss Hartop and her maid to the Town Hall. And after that,' he gave a smirk of satisfaction, 'I shall alert the *Gazette*.'

CHAPTER TWENTY-ONE

In the following days, the newspapers proclaimed the solution of the Brighton mystery and Mina eagerly studied their accounts. The *Gazette* was a fount of local information, and the *Illustrated Police News* carried an abundance of sketches, but *The Times* seemed to find the whole affair disappointingly unoriginal.

THE HISTORY OF THE WEEK

From the Gazette's own correspondent at the scene: The mystery of the man being held in the cells at the Town Hall police office has finally been solved thanks to the sharp eyes of Miss Hannah Hartop daughter of Mr Henry Hartop a Brighton property owner. Miss Hartop was paying a visit to the Ship Street business of photographic artist Mr Beckler to view the new exhibition of magnesium photography when she saw displayed in the window the photograph that he had made of the unknown man who is currently at the Town Hall under arrest for attempted fraud in the name of Jasper Holt. She at once saw the resemblance between this picture and a man she had seen on the promenade, armed with pencils and sketchpad, drawing pictures of the sea. She also recalled that her maid had once seen him entering a low grade of lodging house and alerted Mr Beckler to her observation.

Mr Beckler at once conducted Miss Hartop and her maid to the Town Hall to tell their story to the Chief Constable.

We are sorry to mention that our correspondent was not permitted to enter the police office to be present at the interview, but he next saw a constable leave the Town Hall accompanied by Miss Hartop and her maid. They proceeded to Foundry Street, and there the maid was seen to point to a common lodging house situated next to a beer shop, saying that she felt sure it was the one the man had entered. Miss Hartop was most especially insistent that this lodging house was not one of her father's establishments, which are of a far superior order, and we will not disagree. Miss Hartop and her maid were then allowed to return home, and the constable knocked at the door and was admitted to the house. Some minutes later the constable emerged, this time in the company of an elderly lady whom he conducted to the Town Hall.

Our correspondent quickly ascertained from the general servant of the house that this lady was Mrs Ellison the landlady of the lodging house. He also learned that an artist lodged there under the name of John Chantry, and he had lived alone for several years. He was a very quiet individual, who often kept to his room, and it was therefore not at all unusual not to see him for a week together, which must have been why his landlady had not been aware that he was missing.

Our energetic correspondent then hurried to the Town Hall, and after a short while, Mrs Ellison emerged, and he was able to obtain an interview. He was advised that she had viewed the man in the cells and was certain beyond any doubt that he was her lodger Mr John Chantry, whom she had last set eyes upon on the same morning that he had decided to approach the police. She stated that he was a very quiet man and had never given any trouble either to her or the other residents. He only went out in order to sit by the sea and make his drawings, and as far as she knew, he had never received any visitors. She also expressed the belief that it was all the recent gossip about Mr Holt following the news of his widow's remarriage that had disturbed her lodger's mind and led to his strange imaginings. Asked if Mr Chantry was to return to his lodgings, she said that she understood that for the time being he was not to be permitted to return home as it was felt that a doctor ought to examine him and see what should be done with him next.

Next, Mina read a piece in *The Illustrated Police News*.

PORTRAIT OF THE BRIGHTON MYSTERY MAN

We publish on our front page an engraving which has been most faithfully carried out by our artist, taken from a photograph of the man being held at Brighton Police Station whose identity has until now been a mystery. (The photograph was provided by kind permission of Mr Beckler, photographer of Ship Street, Brighton) The prisoner had claimed to be Mr Jasper Holt, who vanished and was presumed drowned in 1864, but who had either been alive all that time, or had risen from the dead, but it now seems that he was in reality an artist of unsound mind, a Mr John Chantry.

Our sketch artist was kindly granted permission by Mrs Ellison the landlady of the lodging house where Mr Chantry resided, to enter the private abode of Mr Chantry, and he has depicted for our pages the humble lodgings complete with all the paraphernalia of his calling. It was Mrs Ellison who formally identified the prisoner and she is also portrayed in our newspaper together with a picture of her lodging house about which a small crowd of interested persons has collected. Mr Chantry rarely sells his drawings which are all scenes of the sea, and are of moderate skill, but he has never failed to pay for his rent and provisions, since he is in receipt of a monthly postal order from an unknown benefactor.

We also provide portraits of Miss Hannah Hartop, whose keen eyes noticed the resemblance between the portrait in the window of the photographer's shop and the mystery man, of the shop front crowded by visitors, and its proprietor, Mr Beckler.

On making further enquiries it appears however that many of the residents of Brighton remain unconvinced that the identification of Mr Chantry solves the mystery, since they feel that it is possible that he might be Mr Holt after all, who has been living under a false name in humble circumstances to avoid arrest. His recent actions are considered by some not to be the result of sudden mania, but an attack of conscience, his crimes having weighed on his mind to the extent that he felt a sudden desire to confess. All that is known about the postal orders is that they come from a London address.

And finally, *The Times*.

THE BRIGHTON MYSTERY: A SAD DELUSION

So it seems that the Brighton mystery is over, and a pathetic and commonplace answer it has turned out to be. The man in the cells of the Brighton police office is not the walking corpse of Mr Jasper Holt, or even the living Mr Holt, but a Mr John Chantry, a man whose state of mind can only arouse our sympathy. We must hope that he has relatives who are able to take care of him.

We must also observe with some sorrow that many of the residents of Brighton, and those being not the idle or curious but men of the business class, who surely ought to know better how to behave themselves, have been gathering in the street outside the home of Mr and Mrs Vardy, demanding an interview. It appears that they are labouring under the delusion that there is money to come to the creditors from the Holt bankruptcy. All our enquiries on the matter suggest that this is not the case, and these gentlemen should cease their baseless demands and return to their proper business. The editor must inform his readers that all further correspondence on this case is now closed.

Mina also received a letter from Mr Phipps.

Dear Miss Scarletti

How extraordinary that you discovered a photograph of the members of the Brighton Yacht Club, and a hitherto unsuspected connection with the Maritime Queen fraud! I would be very interested to borrow the portrait and show it to the senior partners.

I have made some enquiries and have established that the club is no longer in existence, however there are some papers in the possession of the widow of a former member which I have examined. The papers include a list of members of the Brighton Yacht Club, as of December 1862. This is of course before the creation of the Maritime Queen Insurance Company, which took place in the following year. Those members who were resident in Brighton were the founder, Captain Bulstrode, Mr William Cobbe, Mr John Taylor, Mr Walter Randall, and Mr Henry Westbury. I believe Mr Westbury was originally approached to see if he would act for the company, but he declined to be involved, a decision for which he was no doubt profoundly grateful later on. Since he does not appear in the photograph dated 1863, perhaps he left the club in that year.

There were three other gentlemen members who were resident in London, Mr Sutherland, whom we know about, and also a Mr Bertram Briggs and a Mr Frederick Chantry, all three of whom owned and sailed yachts. I have made enquiries and Mr Briggs who is now sixty years of age, was a partner in a manufacturing company who has retired and currently lives in Worthing. Mr Chantry, who was an investment broker passed away three years ago aged sixty-five, so he cannot be the gentleman in the police cells, although he might possibly be a relative. In view of their ages, neither Mr Briggs nor Mr Chantry can be in the photograph.

You will have noticed the names Taylor and Randall whom I mentioned in my earlier correspondence, and as far as I have been able to discover these are the same gentlemen who were almost certainly the prime movers in the Maritime Queen Insurance Company fraud. It would appear that while the Club did have members who were genuinely interested in yachting, like Captain Bulstrode and the three London gentlemen I have named, there were others who used its meetings to conceal their fraudulent activities and make the acquaintance of men of the profession and class they sought to inveigle into their schemes. The address of the Club rooms and the Maritime Queen Insurance company are the same.

Yours faithfully,
R Phipps

Mina immediately had the photograph sent to Mr Phipps and received a note by return of post.

Dear Miss Scarletti,

I have shown the photograph of the yacht club members to the partners, in the hopes that they might be able to identify the gentlemen, but apart from Mr Bulstrode and Mr Cobbe they could not be certain. I will however retain it for the time being.

Yours faithfully,
R Phipps

CHAPTER TWENTY-TWO

Dr Hamid packed away his stethoscope in his medical bag and poured glasses of his herbal aerated water for Mina and himself. 'As you may know,' he said, 'I am often consulted by the police regarding the state of health of a prisoner. I am called to the Town Hall to examine both men and women held in the cells there; those injured in affrays, some who have fainted from lack of sustenance, others who were suffering the effects either of too much alcohol or the withdrawal of the same, and those who found it convenient to feign illness in order to find somewhere other than the streets to spend the night. This morning, however, was different, since when I went to the Town Hall I had not been summoned by the police. I had decided to volunteer my services.'

'That was very kind of you,' said Mina.

'To be truthful, I was wondering as I went there just why I had made this decision, and I was obliged to admit that there was only one reason that I ever do anything out of the ordinary and that reason is you, Miss Scarletti. You are at once the most worrying, the most annoying, and the most unreasonable of all my patients.' It was said in a friendly tone in the manner of an indirect compliment, and Mina smiled.

He took a deep draught of the comforting water. Mina knew too well where his thoughts were tending. Memories of his eldest sister Eliza, who had been so severely afflicted by scoliosis, were always present. He had occasionally spoken of the long hours that he and Anna had sat by their sister's deathbed as her damaged and constricted lungs struggled for breath and how finally, bravely and almost peacefully she had given up the battle. Mina realised that more recently he must have feared attending on another such distressing scene. 'I went there because anything I could do to satisfy my difficult patient's insatiable thirst for knowledge and boundless curiosity would help preserve her life. But I now find myself in a dilemma, since the news I bring might be too stimulating for an invalid, even one in recuperation. I hesitate to say more.'

Mina folded her arms in a very determined manner and narrowed her eyes in a firm stare. He smiled and began his story.

As I entered the reception hall, the sergeant greeted me in a friendly manner, opened his record book, and ran his gaze down the daily list, 'Good morning Dr Hamid, who have you come to see?'

I was obliged to admit that I had not been called in any official capacity but had come to offer my services gratis for the man known as Mr John Chantry. 'All that I have heard of him' I explained, 'excites my sympathy and suggests that he would benefit from a doctor's examination, but it also leads me to doubt that he can pay a doctor's fee.'

'Well, that is very good of you, Dr Hamid,' said the sergeant, making a note. 'You know' he chuckled, with a warning shake of a finger, 'you will never be a rich man what with all the work you do for the poor.'

'I fear not.'

'He is still in the cells at present, as we don't want to turn him out until it's safe to do so. We don't think he is dangerous, and I doubt that he would run away even if he had the chance, but there is some concern about his state of mind. We don't want him wandering about on his own. We have made him as comfortable as we can seeing as he is now not charged with anything, and there is a gentleman with him, a London solicitor, from the firm that has been sending his monthly postal orders. He read about Mr Chantry in *The Times* and came straight down to see him. He is presently seeking to make some arrangements for new accommodation. He thinks it wouldn't be wise for Mr Chantry to go back to his old lodgings what with all the attention he has been getting, and I have to agree. But I'll get a constable to take you down there, and you can see him for yourself.'

'You are quite sure of the man's identity? There are no doubts now that he is not Mr Holt?'

The sergeant gave a rueful smile. 'We're as sure as we can be. We have asked him many times, but he doesn't say anything. He has certainly kept us busy, though. There were about a hundred or more letters we received here, people with their own suggestions, you know how it is. Women mainly — wives, mistresses, sisters, all hoping he was their missing man, but of course he wasn't. And then there were Mr Holt's creditors demanding to speak to him, but we didn't allow that because I don't think they meant him any good. We made a thorough search of his lodgings and there was little enough there, certainly no documents to prove who he is, but we did find one thing — an old newspaper, a copy of *The Times*, with a mark made on it beside the notice of a wedding. A Miss Ann Chantry who was married to a Mr Albert Fenwick about seven years ago. A sister, we assume. But whoever he might be, our man is not Mr Holt; the solicitor has confirmed that absolutely. The gentleman may look fifty which would be Mr Holt's age if he was alive, but he is actually rather younger in years and has not taken great care of himself.'

'That information, coming as it does from a reliable source will be a great relief to many people, although a grave

254

disappointment to others,' I said, 'I hope that a statement will be made to the newspapers to enlighten the town. There is too much speculation and supposition in the newspapers and not enough actual news.'

'I believe that is being done,' said the sergeant, 'and the sooner the better in my opinion.' He summoned a constable to conduct me to see Mr Chantry.

'Is he still under lock and key?' I asked as we descended the narrow stairs to the basement cells.

'Yes, sir,' said the constable, 'it's for his own good really. And we are very careful about who comes to see him, what with all the disturbances and the allegations. There are men out there who still believe that he is Mr Holt and think that the police have plotted with him to hide the truth.'

'Mrs Vardy was quite certain that he was not. People accused her of lying in order to save her reputation, but now I hope that anyone of sense must accept that she has been exonerated.'

'Oh yes, she just took one look at him and that was it.'

The constable remained impassive, but I could not conceal my surprise. 'Really? She didn't interview him or question him? I would have thought she might have asked him the names of places or persons that only Mr Holt would know.'

'No, nothing of that sort, sir.'

'And her brother, Mr Saltmire? He would have known Mr Holt well. What did he say?'

'I don't think he said a word. He just nodded.'

At the bottom of the stairs we reached the high gated entrance to the murkily lit corridor which houses the seven cells allocated to male prisoners. Men do not usually remain there long but are held overnight to sleep off the effects of drink for their own and others' safety, sometimes after arrest for petty crimes before being taken upstairs to court to be fined. Very occasionally the cells hold more dangerous prisoners under serious charges waiting to be remanded and transferred to gaol. The constable unlocked the gate and we entered the vaulted whitewashed corridor. All was quiet, which suggested that either there were few prisoners, or those who were there were asleep. A bored looking attendant was taking the opportunity to swab out the empty cells with a large mop dipped in a bucket of some pungent disinfectant solution.

The policeman looked through a spy hole in one of the heavy oak cell doors, and nodded, then turned the key. Inside, a little light was allowed to filter in from the corridor through a high grating. The amenities offered are no more than might be required for an overnight wallow in misery, a plain wooden bench fastened to the wall. Prisoners are not usually afforded even the luxury of a slop bucket or any item that might be used as a weapon. The necessary facilities are on the floor below, where inmates are conducted by a constable at request. You may not have heard of this incident, but the memory of Henry Solomon, the Chief Constable who was murdered in his own office by a prisoner who seized the poker from the fireplace, was still very much in evidence. Mr Chantry, however, due to his elevation in status from prisoner to lunatic, had been provided with the comfort of a blanket, a cup of water, and some bread and cheese wrapped in paper. He sat on the bench looking indifferent to all of these.

At the far end of the bench was a well-dressed gentleman with a leather case of documents, and an expression of extreme distaste. I have smelt many far worse odours than the body and clothes of Mr Chantry, but I doubted that the solicitor had.

'Mr Robertson, this is Dr Hamid, who has offered to examine Mr Chantry,' said the constable.

Mr Robertson rose to his feet, looking surprised, but nodded. 'Thank you, Doctor. I have no reason to believe that my client has any illness, but there has been a long period of self-neglect. I am content for you to examine him.'

Mr Chantry did not stir. He slumped silently, his eyes closed, only the slow rise and fall of his chest showing that he was not an awkwardly posed corpse.

'I understand that he is to be found new lodgings,' I said.

'Yes, that in itself should not present any difficulty, but given recent circumstances I feel extremely reluctant to allow my client to live alone, or we might have a recurrence of this unfortunate event.'

I sat beside the torpid man. 'Mr Chantry, I am a doctor and I am just about to make a brief examination to check that you are well. Is that in order?'

Mr Chantry said nothing, neither did he stir.

I was hesitant to proceed and glanced at the solicitor. 'He didn't say no,' said Mr Robertson. 'I'll take responsibility. He's not dangerous.'

'What can you tell me of his medical history?'

'Only that he suffered a breakdown some years ago. Not in his bodily health, but his nerves. There were serious business and domestic reversals which deeply affected him.'

'And you can confirm absolutely that he is not Mr Jasper Holt?'

'Absolutely, yes.'

'Do you know his age?'

'He is about forty, I believe.'

'Then he is much too young to be Mr Holt. You are not a relative of his?'

'No. I act for the family. There are no close relatives, but one gentleman was willing to instruct me. They are respectable and would prefer it if he was not confined to an asylum.'

I proceeded with a general examination, which I did very carefully and gently, asking the patient's permission at each stage, and receiving no objection, noting the respiration, and the pulse, checking for fever, studying the hands, the eyes, the ears. 'Well, Mr Chantry' I said at last, 'I can see no immediate reason to be concerned for your health, but I would recommend a bath, new clothes, new shoes, a visit to a barber and a better diet.' I addressed the solicitor. 'If you wish to engage an attendant for him, I can recommend some suitable persons. But that does depend on whether there are funds available.'

Robertson nodded. 'I will write to his family and see what can be arranged. Your advice would be appreciated.'

'Once Mr Chantry is more himself, I can also offer him an afternoon in the steam baths of which I am proprietor. A pleasant and soothing medicated vapour bath and oriental massage with healing herbal oils. Many of the most respectable residents of Brighton come there to refresh themselves. There will be no charge.'

'You are too kind. But I insist that you send me an invoice both for this visit and any treatments you provide.' There was the usual exchange of business cards and I departed.

'So there are funds available for the support of this poor man,' said Mina.

'There are. Not limitless, I believe, as I have been given to understand that the family is not especially wealthy, but he did have some resources before his illness, and there is sufficient to ensure that he is not confined to an asylum, which I am glad of, as I do not think that would be beneficial. His best chance of recovery is to live somewhere quiet and as near to being a proper home as can be arranged.'

'And we have the word of a solicitor that he is not and cannot be Mr Holt,' said Mina. 'Which means that Mrs Vardy can be trusted to recognise her own husband. I do hope she is given the news without any further delay and a public announcement made. I do have to wonder,' she added, with a shake of her head, 'at the three supposedly respectable and intelligent gentlemen who said that he was Mr Holt. They should be ashamed of themselves; it was nothing but self-interest.'

'In fairness,' said Dr Hamid, mildly, 'Mr Chantry does look nearer to fifty than forty, and he was disguised by so much hair and beard. We must be charitable and say they made a mistake.'

Mina paused for thought. 'Did the solicitor say anything more to you about Mr Chantry? Did he give any details of his personal history, or how he came to be in the position he is in? You say that Mr Chantry did not speak during your examination. His family have shown some concern for him — they are providing his living expenses — but they have not cared for him enough to ensure that he did not neglect his health. Didn't his landlady say that he never received any visitors? Are his relations in some way ashamed of him? Or did they just feel that having arranged for his postal orders to be sent they had done their duty?'

'That is very possible. I have known closer relatives to do far less.'

'Does he perhaps have a criminal past?'

'I was not advised of that.'

'I assume that the postal orders arrive addressed to him under the name of John Chantry. But the only document we have to confirm his identity is the newspaper report of his sister's wedding. Assuming of course that she is his sister. Did Mr Robertson confirm that Miss Chantry was his sister?'

'He never mentioned the report at all, or the name of the family. I assumed that the surname was Chantry. All he was able to say was that his client was not Mr Holt. In fact —' Dr Hamid looked thoughtful. 'This may only have been his way of speaking, but I do believe he never once referred to him by name. It was always "my client"'

Mina was deep in thought. Her mind was examining all the fragments of information she had gleaned. It was as if the answer she needed was there, but it had been broken up into little pieces and scattered widely in all directions. They lay in many different places, places that had no connection other than that she was possibly the only person who was in possession of them all, and able to see them for what they were and assemble them.

Dr Hamid sat silently and watched her think.

At last, Mina spoke. 'Richard told me that when he was at the Town Hall, Mr Chantry recognised Mr Cobbe. He actually addressed him by name. And it was obvious that Mr Cobbe knew him and was not pleased to see him.'

'He is a bank manager; I suppose that is not too surprising.'

'It's not surprising that Mr Holt might know Mr Cobbe, but what about Mr Chantry? How would he know Mr Cobbe? I doubt that he has a bank account.' Mina made a decision. 'I wish to sit at my desk.'

Dr Hamid jumped up. 'Oh — but I can bring you what you need.'

'No,' she said very firmly. 'I wish to sit at my desk. You may assist me if I require it.'

He smiled and nodded. 'It is a brave man who would stand between you and your papers. Very well. Take care and I will be here to assist if needed.'

Mina laid aside the blankets that covered her, and rose to her feet, steadying herself on the arms of her chair. She had no idea what her shrunken form might look like in her long nightdress and dressing gown and could only hope that she did not resemble something risen from a recently dug grave. Dr Hamid offered his arm and she reached out and placed her hand on his wrist. Slowly but with increasing confidence, she moved to stand by the chair that was set in front of her desk. 'I would be obliged if you brought my cushion, she said, holding on to the back of the chair. He fetched the little wedge-shaped cushion that enabled Mina to sit upright and put it in place then assisted her to sit comfortably.

She smiled. 'And now,' she said, 'I feel am myself again.'

'What was it you wished to see?'

'A letter I received a little while ago, which included a name that at the time did not appear to be important.' Mina opened her box of correspondence, and a brief search discovered the letter she was looking for, one from Mr Phipps. She re-read it and nodded. 'I was not mistaken. You didn't happen to see that newspaper of Mr Chantry's did you? The one with the wedding announcement.'

'No, I have only told you what the sergeant told me.'

'That a Miss Chantry had been married to a Mr Albert Fenwick.'

'Yes.'

'Is it not a coincidence that a man who has delusions of being Mr Holt, should have in his possession a report regarding the wedding of a Mr Albert Fenwick, when that is the name of the former business partner of Mr William Sutherland? If he is the same man, would that not explain why Mr Cobbe was horrified to see him and why Mr Chantry recognised him?'

Dr Hamid looked puzzled. 'I'm not sure I follow you. We know that Chantry is not Holt.'

'No, he is not, and Mr Holt was never a member of the Brighton Yacht Club but Sutherland and Cobbe both were.'

'But what is the significance of Miss Chantry?'

'In 1864 Mr William Sutherland was engaged to be married, but there is no record of any marriage taking place. I know this because —' Mina realised that she had better not reveal too many details. She had learned this from Mr Handley's report which was in the bundle of papers lent to her by Mrs Vardy which Dr Hamid did not as yet know she had. There was still a danger of her being accused of doing too much too soon. 'Well, never mind how I know.' She brought out a more recent letter from Mr Phipps. 'In 1862, a Mr Frederick Chantry, a man then aged about sixty, was, like Mr Sutherland a member of the Brighton Yacht Club. Both were professional gentlemen living in London. If I am right, and this is a guess, but I think it is a good one, Miss Chantry was Mr Frederick Chantry's daughter and the lady who was once engaged to be married to Mr William Sutherland, but who instead married his business partner Mr Albert Fenwick.'

'This Frederick Chantry might have been Mr John Chantry's father, or uncle,' said Dr Hamid cautiously.

'Or a future father-in-law,' said Mina.

Understanding blossomed in a brief silence. 'Then you are saying that Mr Chantry — '

'Mr John Chantry is William Sutherland.'

Dr Hamid stared at Mina. 'You cannot be sure of it.'

'No, not yet, I need more proof.'

'And he calls himself Chantry because —?'

'Sadness, perhaps, from the lost romance.'

'But why would Mr Sutherland say that he is Mr Holt?'

Mina opened her desk drawer and gazed once more at the portrait of the man in Brighton police station. 'Guilt,' she said.

'Guilt? Guilty of what?'

'The death of Mr Holt,' said Mina.

Dr Hamid stared at her. 'Are you suggesting that Holt's death was not an accident? That it was due in some way to Mr Sutherland's neglect?'

'That is possible.' Mina chose not to speak the word 'murder' but it lay in the air between them.

'And it has played on his conscience and made him a broken man? That this fault, this guilt, is the source of his delusions?'

'Can it have such an effect?'

Dr Hamid, who had been standing by her chair was obliged to sit in the armchair she had just vacated. 'It depends on the man, but I wouldn't dismiss the idea. But why would he claim that he is Holt? Is it a ruse? Or does he really believe it? If he is dissembling, then he is doing it better than any man I have ever encountered.'

Mina examined the photograph once more, the crumpled face, the vacant eyes like wells of misery. 'It is hard to enter into the mind of a deluded man. Perhaps it seems to him that the only way he can mend the situation is to deny that it happened, and to do that he had to make Mr Holt live again.'

'At the expense of being punished for Holt's crime?'

'He seemed to think he deserved it. But I need your opinion on what to do next.'

'Do? Is there anything you should do? There is such a thing as leaving well alone. Or had you not considered that? The man is being looked after as best as can be achieved. If he is deluded then he is not fit to be questioned and cannot be held to account for his faults.'

'But I am thinking of him. He was well once, and surely, he could be well again. Is it right to allow him to live in his dream? How do you think he would respond if he was challenged with being Mr Sutherland?'

Dr Hamid looked thoroughly alarmed at this prospect. 'That is impossible to know. There is a danger we cannot ignore, of driving the delusions still deeper. Alternatively, it might result in a cure, but I cannot imagine that it would be easy or quick to achieve. It could take months or even years. I am far from being an expert in this area. But nothing can be done without proof. I could try writing to the solicitor and see what he is prepared to tell me and suggest that the family seek the help of someone like Dr Fielding. But then, he might well be under instruction not to reveal anything.'

'Of course, knowing the fate of the real Mr Holt might also help,' said Mina with a smile.

'True, but I doubt that we will ever know that for certain.'

Mina realised in a sudden bright glow of insight, that there was almost nothing she liked better than a seemingly impossible task.

CHAPTER TWENTY-THREE

Dear Miss Scarletti,

I hope this finds you well.

Thank you for your kind letter and also your concern for Charlotte. She has spoken very highly of you and all the assistance and good advice you have given her. If she had not felt that Mr Vardy did not approve of her consulting you I am sure she would have been anxious to see you again. I have often felt that the visits she has paid to Mrs Barnham have not always been to her benefit, but she says she does rely on them in order to be able to converse with her late husband.

If you are able to receive visitors I would very much like to call on you for a private interview.

Assuring you of my good wishes,

Emily Wandle

The renewal of Mina's ability to sit at her desk like an adult person and manage her papers for herself had been a pleasurable adventure and it filled her with a fresh determination. An hour before the visitor was expected, she insisted that Rose should help her to dress. It was with much silent grumbling that the maid complied. At least Mina felt that the process was more like arranging her for a living portrait than a last memento. She was therefore able to receive Mrs Wandle dressed in her day clothes, with her hair arranged under a nice lace cap, while seated before her desk. There she perched on her own chair, with her little wedge-shaped cushion, facing the armchair placed in readiness for her visitor's comfort, and with a table by her side for the accommodation of tea.

It was apparent on Mrs Wandle's arrival that she was in the grip of a dilemma. The lady was as Mr Merridew had described her, in her late sixties, stout and strong, plain but not uncomely, and clad in practical clothing. She had the broad shoulders and capable hands of a woman who had spent all her life in hard work. Something, however, some terrible deep trouble, had etched into what Mina judged to be her visitor's natural confidence. She looked wearied and in need of easing her anxieties.

Mina asked Rose to bring a large pot of tea and any cake remaining from the earlier incursions of her mother and friends. Her mother, she had noticed with some relief, was considerably improved in spirits ever since the regular tea gatherings had been reinstated. According to Miss Cherry, these occasions afforded Louisa Scarletti the opportunity to describe at great length the wonderful achievements of her younger son, pointing out the photographic portrait she was convinced he had executed, which was on prominent display.

Mina gestured Mrs Wandle to the armchair and she sank into it with some relief. 'Thank you for agreeing to see me.'

'I am grateful for your visit,' said Mina. 'I have only met Mrs Vardy on two occasions, but she struck me as a concerned mother who has had many trials to endure, for none of which she can be blamed.'

Mrs Wandle nodded emphatic agreement, but she had a distracted look which Mina's comment did nothing to diminish.

'If there is anything I can do,' Mina continued, 'given that she has been — shall we say — advised neither to call on me nor write to me nor receive my letters, then please do let me know how I might help her.'

Mrs Wandle took a deep breath and puffed it out. 'It is on my own account that I am here. I am in a terrible position, and I really cannot decide what to do.'

'I will help you in any way I can,' said Mina, gently.

Mrs Wandle gazed at her inquisitively as if wondering how so small and slender a person could be the forthright individual who her friend had described to her. 'But it does concern Charlotte,' she said. 'In fact — oh I don't know where to start or even how much I can say.'

At that moment, Rose arrived with the tea tray, and conversation ceased while cups and plates were distributed. 'Thank you, Rose,' said Mina. 'I can manage the rest.'

'That's a large pot,' said Mrs Wandle. 'I'll pour if you like.' This at least was something with which the visitor appeared to be comfortable. Rose left them to their refreshments, and Mrs Wandle's brawny arm made light and expert work of the tea-pouring. The tea was very fresh and hot, and Mina was only able to sip it carefully, while Mrs Wandle took it without blinking. 'But — you must promise me,' she went on, 'I have to beg your absolute confidence before I can say a word. A friendship is at stake. My friendship with Charlotte. It has been a source of great comfort to us both. We may be different in many ways, different in family and in age, but we understand each other, almost like sisters. I don't want to injure my friend, and I don't want to lose her regard. But I'm afraid of doing both.'

There was a long pause. Mina felt she was required to say something. 'I promise faithfully,' she said at last, 'that I will say nothing to anyone of our conversation without your express permission.'

Even then, Mrs Wandle hesitated.

'Please take as much time as you need,' said Mina.

Mrs Wandle poured herself a second steaming cup of tea, and when it was half consumed was sufficiently invigorated to proceed.

'My husband Tom died ten years ago. We used to run the Ship Inn together. After I lost him, people said I couldn't manage the business on my own, but I did. It was hard, but I showed them. There's many a woman in my position, and we are better at business than we are usually given credit for.

It was July 1864 when the man came. It was a quiet day; we don't get many people on holiday excursions round Seabourne. It's mainly trade customers. Fishermen. There's a small harbour. No piers or amusements. Nothing fancy. It was getting dark, and I was thinking of closing the doors as the last customer had gone. He was a stranger to me. His clothes — they weren't like business clothes, more like a gentleman might wear in the country. They were good ones, but they were crumpled like they'd been wetted through and then dried while he was wearing them. He smelled of the sea. Somehow — I don't know why — I felt I could trust him and so I let him in.

He told me that he had been out sailing earlier in the day when his boat had overturned and he had struggled ashore. There was an old dinghy drawn up on the beach, set aside for repair and so he climbed into it and rested to get his strength back. I gave him hot food and drink and some of Tom's clothes to wear. I asked about sending a letter to his family so they would know that he was safe, but he said there was no need. He told me he had no family. And then he broke down and confessed that he had sailed out to sea in order to end his existence but once he was in the water some instinct had taken over and he had decided to save himself. He half swam half floated into the shore. He had no injury apart from a bruise on his face which he said he had got when bumping up against the hull of the boat.

As we talked, I could tell that he was an educated man. I thought he must have been a man of business who had once lived a comfortable life but had lost his fortune. He knew failure. He didn't want to speak of his past and I didn't press him. He told me his name was Henry Brown and asked if he could stay awhile, only he had almost no money and nowhere to go. So I told him he could lodge in a room upstairs and if he was willing to work for his keep he could stay. And he did.'

Mrs Wandle looked more at ease, and Mina thought that this was because she must have realised that thus far into her story there could be no going back.

'He was quiet and respectful and did his work without complaint. He kept himself to himself most of the time. Hardly anyone noticed him. If asked, I said that he was a cousin of mine from Newhaven, because I do have family there, and no-one questioned what I said. But I felt that he was waiting for something, that he had a secret he had not shared with me. He was especially anxious to see the most recent newspapers. When I commented on it, he explained that a friend of his had been very ill and he expected to read of his demise at any moment. All was well until a week or two later when the newspapers carried a story that caused him terrible distress. The story of how Mr Jasper Holt was thought to be a fraud and a cheat.'

Mina thought she might risk an interruption. 'You must have read the papers yourself?' she asked. 'What of your customers, did they not talk about the disappearance of Mr Jasper Holt?'

'Of course, and I admit that since I had seen him when he first came in his good clothes, which my customers had not, I did suspect that he was indeed Jasper Holt, but I didn't like to ask him about it directly. I felt — I suppose I hoped that in time that he would feel the need to confide in someone, and that person would be me. I did make comments in general conversation, as so many did, but while there were people who made cruel remarks about Mrs Holt, I declared that I had only sympathy for the wife and children who were suffering so much uncertainty. And then one day he did tell me. He confessed that he was Jasper Holt.

I told him that I wouldn't blame him for his actions, as I couldn't look into his mind, and didn't know all his circumstances, but I implored him to tell his wife and family that he was alive and well. He said that he had left a message for his wife, so she knew that he was alive and safe.'

'A message?' Mina exclaimed, perhaps a little louder than she had intended.

'Yes.'

'Did he say what was in the message?'

'No, I thought that was a private matter between husband and wife, so I didn't enquire. I admit, I did once ask Charlotte if she had ever had a note from him, but she said not. Of course, she might not have wanted to say, so I didn't press her.'

'No, of course not,' said Mina, disappointed to see this vital piece of information elude her. 'I wonder, did he mention Shoreham at all? He told Mr Sutherland, the owner of the yacht, that he wanted to go there.'

'He did pay visits there from time to time. I asked him why; did he know anyone there, and he said he didn't, he just — he just liked the sea view.' Mrs Wandle's lips trembled. She pressed a hand to her mouth, and Mina could see that she was close to tears.

A third cup of tea was consumed, and two large pieces of cake were made to vanish before equanimity was restored.

'Did you ever receive a visit from a detective who was looking for him on behalf of the family?'

'Yes, a few weeks later there was a man came asking questions about any strangers coming in July. I think he'd been going round all the villages. I didn't know he was from the family, I thought he might be a policeman in plain clothes. Or from a creditor after Jasper's money. People remembered Henry arriving about then although I was the only one who knew the date for sure, and in any case, he was understood to be my cousin. The man went away, and I didn't hear any more.

But poor Jasper — Henry I should call him — he was now in a terrible position; one that he had never expected. His deception had been uncovered and he couldn't go back home to his wife and children because he would be arrested for fraud. Since Charlotte was suspected, too, he thought she was being constantly watched in case he was to ever to try and see her. He was quite adamant that Charlotte had known nothing of his intentions, but while one can prove that a thing is known it is much harder to prove it is not known. For himself, he believed that he could endure being put in prison but if he was it would bring shame and disgrace to the family. And what if Charlotte was charged with being his accomplice? She might find herself in prison, too, and the children would be without a mother. At the same time, he needed to know that his sons were well and being looked after. So he asked me — in fact he pleaded with me to help him.'

Mina understood. 'And that was why you joined the Barnham circle?'

'Yes. It was the place where he knew that I would meet Charlotte and make her acquaintance. I went once a week, and

271

there was always some conversation between the sitters, some more than others, and then Charlotte would receive messages from the spirit of her deceased husband saying that he was happy in the heavenly realms. And all the time he was alive and calling himself Henry Brown and working as my pot man.'

'I imagine,' said Mina, 'that the source of the messages Mrs Barnham passes to her sitters is the mind of Mrs Barnham herself, providing what she thinks they will find believable and comforting. Did Mrs Vardy ever reveal to you or anyone else, in any way, that she knew that her husband had not died in the accident? Not even the smallest hint?'

'No, in fact she was most convincingly certain that he was deceased. Whatever he had written to her — and of course I could never reveal that I knew of it — I think she chose instead to believe the supposed spirit.'

'You were never tempted to enlighten her?'

'I was, often, but I had promised Henry not to do so. The spectres of prison and disgrace were more to him than anything. But I was able to let him know that his boys were being well cared for by their godfather, who had been as a second father to them, and that was a great comfort to him. The one thing I had not expected to result was the close friendship that arose between myself and Charlotte. We are united in sympathy. '

'There is one small question you might be able to answer. Mrs Vardy, when she visited the police cells to view the man held there was able to confirm that he was not Mr Holt with barely a moment's glance. Did she enlighten you as to the reason?'

Mrs Wandle smiled. 'Jasper Holt, at the time he disappeared was, like so many men do at that age, starting to lose his hair. It was then just a small round patch the size of a penny on the crown of his head. He was able to hide this from acquaintances by artfully combing the remaining hair, which was very thick, but he could not conceal it from Charlotte. She would have known that after more than seven years missing the loss of hair would be more pronounced, but the man in the cells had a very full head of hair. And whatever the sellers of potions might like to claim, there is no cure for baldness.'

'How simple! I should have thought of that,' said Mina, especially, she reflected, after Dr Hamid had mentioned the scalp massage offered to gentlemen who feared losing their hair. Mina had another question to ask, although she already knew the answer. Mr Merridew had, she recalled, spoken of Mrs Barnham's message concerning Mrs Wandle's late pot man Henry.

'Mr Holt — he — I am assuming that you can tell me his story now because he is no longer in danger from the law.'

Mrs Wandle nodded. 'Yes, sadly, Jasper Holt is no more. He had been in poor health for some time, and last December the doctor told me that he had not long to live. It was his heart. His father had suffered in the same way. When he knew that he was dying he asked me that once he had gone, I should give his watch, the only family heirloom he possessed, to his older son, Franklin. It was something he had once promised the boy. He urged that it should go directly to him, and so I made sure that it was delivered to the boy's school.'

'When did Mr Holt die?'

Mrs Wandle took a paper from her reticule. 'I have the certificate of his death. 25 January under the name Henry Brown. He is buried in the parish church.'

'Mrs Wandle, I must ask you, since Mr Holt can no longer be charged with any crime, do you intend to tell Mrs Vardy all this story? Judging by what you have said, it does clear her of complicity in the attempted fraud. I appreciate that in view of this message he left her, she could be questioned about protecting him from the law, but I think that would be dealt with sympathetically.'

'I am struggling with a terrible dilemma!' exclaimed Mrs Wandle. 'Charlotte told me that Franklin had been very unhappy when Jasper was declared legally dead, and even more so when she remarried. The poor boy was so disturbed that they had to hire a nursemaid to watch over him, though that at least is no longer the case. I thought that if he could be told that his father had cared very much about him, so much so that he stayed away at great pain to himself rather than bring shame to the family, that he would get some comfort from that, and be able to visit his father's grave. And Charlotte — she too would find peace at last by knowing the whole of the story right to the end. But —' Mrs Wandle was too agitated to continue. The tea was gone, and Mina offered her a glass of water, but unable to speak, she waved it away.

'But by telling her,' said Mina, you would be confessing to having deceived her all these years.' It had not escaped Mina's notice that Mrs Wandle had several times referred to Mr Holt by his Christian name. She wondered if there had been more to their years of residing at the Inn together than she liked to admit. More than she would want her good friend to know about.

Mrs Wandle dabbed her eyes with a large and serviceable looking kerchief. 'Yes. And I would thereby lose a dear friend. I had thought perhaps I could write her a letter of explanation to be passed to her after I am gone, together with proof that Henry Brown was her husband. Is that cowardly of me?'

'You have proof?'

'Yes. Undeniable proof. He wrote a loving letter to Charlotte and the children shortly before he died. Then there are the clothes he arrived in. I still have them. I would have buried him in them, but they wouldn't have fitted him of late, he had grown much larger about the waist, although I always thought it looked well on him, and there was a photograph, a family picture. He had it wrapped in oilcloth and wore it next to his heart.'

'I think Mrs Vardy would be deeply moved to see those. I have another question. Did she tell you of her intended second marriage during Mr Holt's lifetime?'

'She told me that Mr Vardy had made an offer, and that she had decided to accept, but they had not yet set a date. I received an invitation, but I could not leave the bedside of a dying man. He expired soon afterwards.'

There was a long silence during which Mrs Wandle gazed at Mina expectantly, and Mina realised that she was supposed to provide the answer to her visitor's dilemma. It was as she considered the facts placed before her that she recalled that there was something she herself ought to impart.

'Mrs Wandle, there are many persons who would be greatly affected by your story, including one you may not have thought of. There is an individual who has been suffering terrible consequences of what happened on the day Mr Holt disappeared.'

'Oh?'

'Mr William Sutherland, the owner of the yacht. I don't know exactly what happened on the day Mr Holt was thought to have perished, and we may never know, but it is my belief that ever since that time Mr Sutherland has been tormenting himself with guilt over Mr Holt's death. Unnecessarily, as it now turns out.'

Mrs Wandle looked shocked. 'I — I had no idea. The poor man. It seems that so many of us have suffered needlessly from that day. But I have now told you all that I know. Please, Miss Scarletti — advise me! What should I do?'

'I cannot tell you what to do,' said Mina. 'I can only listen to your story and comment on your difficulty. But I hope that now you have spoken all the facts aloud, and have the additional information I have provided, your conscience will tell you which course is the correct one.'

Mrs Wandle's expression told her all she needed to know.

The next morning, Mina received a letter from Mrs Wandle.

Dear Miss Scarletti

I am extremely grateful to you for listening to me with such sympathy and earnest attention. I am still considering what I must do, but I am beginning to feel that I must gather my courage and speak the truth, even though I may suffer by it.

The situation is even more complicated than I had thought. I have carefully preserved in my papers the invitation to Charlotte's wedding to Mr Vardy and find that it took place on 24 January, that is the day before her first husband expired. Of course, no blame can attach to either party, and I am sure that that difficulty may be quietly smoothed over.

Yours with great gratitude,

Emily Wandle

CHAPTER TWENTY-FOUR

'As I took my seat for Mrs Barnham's next séance,' confessed Mr Merridew after greeting Mina, 'I did so with more nervousness than I had ever experienced before the curtain rose on a new play. In this case, there were few lines to learn, and performance was all, my appearance was for one night only, and there could be no rehearsal. So much depended on timing and chemistry, and chance, and most especially on little Maggie, who knew what she had to do, because I had schooled her, and whose courage and resolve and intelligence I could see gradually emerging from the fear and gloom of her unhappy existence, and beginning to shine in the light of hope.'

Mr Merridew proceeded to recount his experience of the previous evening:

I greeted Mrs Barnham and Miss Stone with the politeness that I knew neither of them deserved. I could not help thinking that it only wanted one more female of equivalent wickedness to complete the coven and stir the cauldron of their horrid deeds. I did feel, however, that apart from the unspeakable Mr Cobbe, none of the sitters, those who had come in good faith, with their own private griefs and anxieties, hoping for answers, knew of the evil to which their hosts would stoop.

That night, I made sure to be the first of the guests to arrive so that I might sit closest to the fire. When Miss Stone went to tend to the coals, I quickly rose up, made a little bow and pleaded to be allowed to assist her. She was surprised, but quietly agreed to such a gentlemanly offer, and withdrew. By this means I was able to arrange the coals in the way that suited my intentions.

Mr Eve arrived with his usual muttered grumbles, Mrs Anscombe billowed in on her cloud of camphor, and Mrs Vardy and Mrs Wandle sat together conversing in sisterly familiarity. Mrs Vardy was wondering if it was wise for her to leave the house as she had been so ill of late, and was beginning to regret being persuaded, but Mrs Wandle replied that she thought the air and the company would do her good. And there was, she added, something she wished to arrange. She wanted Mrs Vardy to pay her a visit at the little inn at Seabourne. How earnestly she reassured her friend that her home, though humble was respectable, and that her friends while appearing at first glance to be a little rough and ready were honest hardworking fisher folk. Images of the good hearted Peggotty family from *David Copperfield* in their quaint seashore home, were being conjured up as she spoke.

Mr Cobbe strode in, and it was only now, knowing what I knew that I saw the avaricious gleam in Mrs Barnham's eyes as she greeted the banker, and his mouth twitch in suppressed anticipation as he eased into his chair.' Mr Merridew sighed. 'What a world we live in when there are those who find pleasure and satisfaction only in harming those weaker than themselves, and creatures like Mrs Barnham who assist them for money.

The séance proceeded, with the sliding of the mysteriously propelled table, the spiritoscope disk turning in its smooth oily fashion, and the cold pointing metal finger spelling out fates for all. That evening I received another message from the late King William confirming that his dear consort Adelaide was with him in heaven, and that she also gave her blessing to my literary endeavours. There was no message from the late King

George IV which was as well, since in view of his notorious life this might have led the sitters to be concerned that the spiritoscope could communicate with less elevated regions.

I watched the proceedings with care, deciding to ignore the action of Mrs Barnham's hands, to which she always drew attention in order to demonstrate that it was impossible for her to influence the movement of the table, but looked instead to see if there was any opportunity for her nether limbs to be employed. I have heard of mediums and magicians who are so dexterous with their feet that they can slip off a shoe and manipulate objects with their toes as if they were blessed with another hand, but Mrs Barnham's age and stiffness of limbs might prevent her from doing so. Recently however, I spoke to a man who constructs stage machinery, describing the spiritoscope, and as a result I entertained the thought that there was underneath the table, well hidden by the medium's skirts, a lever that could easily be operated by her knee. Since Mrs Barnham was seated across the table, any movement of her lower limbs was undetectable, and I was unable to form any conclusion beyond that it was a possibility. Like yourself, Miss Scarletti I have no objection to a medium providing a useful service and a pleasant evening for little or no remuneration. I have no desire to expose mechanical trickery any more than I would give away the secrets of a conjuror, which as you know is quite forbidden.

The other sitters enjoyed the usual messages, with the shade of Mr Holt assuring Mrs Vardy that all her troubles would soon be at an end, and she would at last know peace and harmony. The consumption of tea and bread and butter followed, and Mr Cobbe, with darting fingertips, ate and drank rapidly and cleared the plate. Once again I volunteered to tend the fire which I did with very great care, and Miss Stone took away the tea things. When she returned, it was time for the concluding act of the drama. I thought as we sat with eyes closed and sang a hymn how horrible it was that the mask of piety should be used to conceal wickedness.

At last, we were permitted to look. Maggie, and there could be no doubt in the world for anyone with eyes in their head that this was she, stood veiled and trembling in the darkened room. The company held its collective breath, some of which was let out in little gasps of wonder.

Mr Cobbe called out to his daughter and extended his arms, urging the child to come forward, but this time, to his surprise, she did not move. Frightened as she was, and she sent a rapid glance in my direction to gather her courage, she stood firm on her spot. Instead, the thin arms of the gauze draped figure reached towards Mr Cobbe and beckoned. 'Come,' whispered the apparition, 'come to me.'

There was some murmuring and concerned shifting of bodies, as this was not at all what Mrs Barnham and Miss Stone had tutored Maggie to do, but all seemed to be going well and thus far they could see no reason to intervene.

Mr Cobbe rose from his chair, and tottered forward, and there was a groan as he clasped the apparition to him. There were sounds of masculine sobbing which almost masked other noises, which would be better not described.

Then came the cry that I had been waiting for, a single word from Maggie, 'No!' I hoped most fervently that the child would remember my instruction to close her eyes.

Then I moved as fast as I had ever done in my life, throwing the strip of magnesium ribbon which I obtained from Mr Beckler onto the hottest part of the fire, and simultaneously turning the covering brass guard so that it stood like a shield between the sitters and the fire but exposed the blaze to the centre of the room. Since I was nearest to the conflagration, I quickly held my hands before my eyes.

There was a sudden brilliant explosion of white light from the fireplace provoking screams of terror from the sitters. Mr Cobbe gasped and automatically raised his hands to protect his eyes, as the brightness which illuminated the room as if it had been day, made his horrible proclivities all too plain to behold. Maggie, released from his clasp, stepped away, pulled off the filmy draperies that had covered her linen shift and threw them to the floor. In the lighted room they no longer glowed like heavenly garments but looked dull, grey and commonplace.

I turned to the other sitters who were cowering both from the glare and the dreadful spectacle. I pointed at Maggie. 'This is no ghost!' I announced. 'This is the ill-used maidservant, an innocent who has been forced by these women to take part in their diabolical scheme, and she has been treated most abominably by that evil man!'

Mrs Vardy leaped up screaming 'Oh, the poor child!', then the cloud of ash that poured thickly like white smoke from the fireplace as the magnesium ribbon burned drew a merciful veil over the scene of Mr Cobbe's shame.

Knowing that all would be plunged into semi darkness again once the ribbon had burned away, I ran forward and turned up the gas lamps. As I did so there was a sudden cry and a loud thud like the falling of a sack of potatoes. The lamplight revealed the prostrate form of Mr Cobbe lying on the floor, having tripped and fallen over in an effort to reach the door. Quite what he had stumbled upon was unclear, but Mrs Wandle had risen from her chair and there was a gleam in her eye which suggested that one of her boots had been involved. Mrs Anscombe, showing herself to be very capable of moving quickly if the situation demanded it, strode over to the fireplace, picked up the poker, and with a cry of 'you monster!' started belabouring Mr Cobbe with more enthusiasm than accuracy, aiming chiefly at those portions of his anatomy which are not usually discussed in society circles. Mr Cobbe bawled loudly as each blow fell, while Mrs Vardy hugged Maggie protectively, making sure the child's eyes were turned away from the scene of violence.

There was nothing Mrs Barnham could do or say, and she remained speechless and immobile, her eyes staring and blank. She appeared to be in a trance, a situation which I disdained to believe. Miss Stone had simply thrown a kerchief over her face and was refusing to look at anything. Mr Eve meanwhile had got to his feet with an expression of outrage. Mr Cobbe was trying to crawl across the floor towards the door to evade Mrs Anscombe's vigorous ministrations, screaming for someone to get 'that woman' away from him, which no-one was inclined to do. Mr Eve crossed the room quickly and stood in his way. 'We must not let this foul beast escape!' he cried. 'I have had my suspicions of him for some time, but I could not believe it of a man in his position. Now I have the evidence of my own eyes and the eyes of a host of respectable witnesses, and I shall send for the police.'

Mr Cobbe managed to get to his knees and did his best to plead a simple misunderstanding, wailing to Mrs Anscombe to stop, but her aim improved enough to catch him a glancing blow across the head with the poker and he slumped forward with a moan, and lay half stunned on the floor, a stream of blood pouring down his face.

'Thank you, Mrs Anscombe, you have done enough,' said Mr Eve, raising his hand towards her. She desisted, but with noticeable reluctance. 'I do not want this man killed, that would be too merciful a fate. He must be brought to justice and I promise that I shall see it done. I believe the man who occupies the ground floor apartment has a reliable manservant who I will send to fetch a constable. Mr Merridew, would you kindly ensure that our prisoner does not leave this room?'

'With pleasure,' I said. 'And if he has had enough of the poker, he will be sure to suffer the tongs.'

Mrs Vardy was shaking with rage. 'So,' she said to a wilfully silent Mrs Barnham, 'it was all a sham. Dressing up your maidservant as a ghost and subjecting her to things I would be ashamed to name. I hope you won't try and pretend that this poor child was to blame. Look how she trembles! And what else was a sham, I wonder? The messages from beyond? Were they false, too? Perhaps they came from no further than that machine. We shall not remain in his infamous house a moment longer. How I regret the time I have wasted here!'

'You can be sure of one thing, Mrs Barnham,' said Mrs Wandle calmly to the medium, 'this will be your last séance.' She turned to Mrs Vardy. 'Come, Charlotte, let us take the child to safety.'

CHAPTER TWENTY-FIVE

'And so I once again found myself at the Town Hall,' said Dr Hamid, as he and Mina enjoyed a light luncheon brought to them on a tray on the day following Mr Merridew's report. 'Have you ever encountered Mrs Barnham?'

'I have heard of her and her curious machine and select circle. But of course she would never have admitted me to her séances.'

'And yet, whenever there is some drama in Brighton concerning a medium exposed as a swindler, I cannot help thinking that you have had a hand in it in some way.'

'I don't believe I have anything to confess,' said Mina, helping herself to cheese tart and cold roast chicken. 'But do tell me how the fraud was found out.'

I was summoned to attend to Mr William Cobbe, the banker. He had been attending a séance at the home of Mrs Barnham and was being held in the cells. Mrs Barnham and her servant a Miss Stone, were also there. They had been brought in by a Mr Eve, one of their circle, who had called for the assistance of a constable. It was hard for me to make out precisely what had occurred, although I imagine the newspapers will report it in due course. The two ladies were being held in separate cells in the females' corridor. My task was solely to examine Mr Cobbe, to see if he was fit to be interviewed. His face was bruised and bloodstained, and for reasons best known to himself he was refusing to sit down. He was shaking with the indignity of his position and claimed at first that he suffered a fall.

'This is a remarkable injury from a simple fall,' I observed, since my immediate impression was that he had been struck with a weapon of some kind, but was unwilling to admit it.

'Oh it was more than just one fall,' said Mr Eve. 'There'll be marks on his body too.'

'Well if you must know, it was that horrible woman Mrs Anscombe!' exclaimed Mr Cobbe. 'She made all sorts of allegations against me and then attacked me with a poker! Has she been arrested? She should be charged with assault and battery! I shouldn't be here, I am the victim of her crime!'

'He is confused, of course,' said Mr Eve, with a shake of his head. 'There were reliable witnesses to the event, of whom I am one, and we all agree on the facts. Mr Cobbe tripped and fell against the fire irons. In trying to pick himself up he stumbled and fell again. Several times.'

'That is an outrageous lie!' Cobbe retorted. 'I demand to be released at once! Where is my solicitor? I have friends in high places, and they will be notified of this! It is a conspiracy against my good name!'

'The solicitor is on his way,' said the constable, 'and once the doctor has finished you can tell everything to the Chief Constable.'

I cleaned and dressed the wound on Mr Cobbe's head and was able to satisfy myself that it was unlikely to prove dangerous. 'You have been fortunate. There will be a great deal of swelling and bruising, but no serious damage. Now then, where are your other injuries? Your back or your limbs? Or elsewhere?'

Mr Cobbe went even redder in the face. 'Never mind about that!' he barked.

'Come on then, sir,' said the constable, 'the Chief Constable will see you now.'

'Are you sure this is necessary?'

'This way, sir.'

Mr Cobbe, still protesting loudly was conducted from the cells and led upstairs to the offices. 'You'll see!' he exclaimed, turning and shaking a fist at Mr Eve, 'I'll be out of here within the hour! I know things! I know things that they'll be very pleased to hear! I know all about the Maritime Queen! And then I'll come after you all!'

'I hope they didn't set him free,' said Mina.

'No. He'll be appearing before the magistrates first thing tomorrow morning. I have no details of the charges, but Mr Eve told me that Mr Cobbe behaved in a most outrageous manner and cannot hope to escape a conviction. He also told me that your friend Mr Merridew was there and had some means of throwing light on a situation which had previously been hidden in darkness. But Cobbe claims to have secret information which he will try to make use of to reduce his punishment or escape it altogether. The name Maritime Queen was mentioned quite often. Mr Cobbe seemed to think that the police would be very interested in that.'

A letter from Mr Phipps was delivered to Mina that afternoon.

Dear Miss Scarletti,

You will be interested to know that I called on Captain Bulstrode recently and showed him the photograph of the members of the Brighton Yacht Club. His memory was very sharp indeed and his eyesight no less so. It was not a period in his life that he wished to recall but he was able to identify all the men in the picture, including the club secretary Mr Sutherland, and a Mr Vardy who was at the time employed by Mr Westbury senior as his confidential clerk. As we know Mr Westbury senior resigned from the club over concerns about the Maritime Queen Insurance Company, but Mr Vardy did appear there from time to time, and was friendly with Mr Taylor who it is believed is a distant cousin.

Incidentally, Captain Bulstrode expressed a considerable dislike of Mr Cobbe. According to him Cobbe has always professed to be a virtuous and charitable individual, but Bulstrode had a strong impression that the opposite was the case. There was some scandal in the past about his patronage of an orphanage. No details ever emerged, and nothing was ever proved, and it seems that the matter was regarded as settled when Cobbe resigned. Bulstrode speculated at the time whether funds had been embezzled, but he had no information to share,

Yours faithfully

R Phipps

CHAPTER TWENTY-SIX

Mrs Charlotte Holt, the lady formerly known as Mrs Vardy, sat with Mina Scarletti, holding a handkerchief over her eyes, the tea and cake that had been Rose's best efforts at consoling the visitor's distress, remaining on the table at her side, untouched. She had arrived barely holding back her tears, and once in Mina's company had finally allowed herself to sob lengthily and without restraint.

Slowly, she recovered her composure. A small glass of sherry was offered and accepted, and after a while Mina's patience was rewarded and Charlotte began her story.

All was damp and grey and cold in Seabourne churchyard as I stood at the foot of my husband's grave. Mrs Wandle had shown me to the place. She had not entered the graveyard, but stood at the gate, maintaining a respectful distance. At that moment I could not bring herself to look at or address my erstwhile friend. My mind was reeling from the things I had been told, my husband's second life, and the gross betrayal by a woman for whom I had once felt such a sisterly affection.

There were no longer any doubts in my mind. The pain of not knowing was gone, but only to be replaced by the pain of knowing the truth, and I realised that this could be just as great if not more.

I had read the letter Jasper had written to me on his deathbed, in which the writing although weakened by illness was certainly his, the contents an additional confirmation. He had asked forgiveness not only for himself but for Mrs Wandle, who, he said had only kept his secret because he had begged her to; Mrs Wandle, whom I had come to call Emily, the woman who had befriended me under false pretences, spied upon me, harboured my missing husband in secret, and failed even to bring me to his bedside when he lay dying. Could any of those acts truly be forgiven? Mrs Wandle had pleaded with me, even as I touched the very garments Jasper had worn the last time I saw him, and which had been carefully preserved, and the crumpled photograph he had once held against his breast. She had asked me to believe that although our friendship had not begun as such things ought to have done, it had become in time as genuine as any friendship could be. There was another thing that I could not bring myself to speak of, the sense that this woman who spoke of Jasper with such gentleness and affection, had during the seven years and more that they had lived together, become as a second wife.

And so there I stood, friendless, and newly widowed, and a single woman, since the date on the death certificate clearly proved that my marriage to Silas Vardy had been a sham. And as that thought crossed my mind another thought followed. It had always been a sham.

To think how I had looked forward to this visit! I had even set aside a whole day for it, but now all I wanted was to do was get away. Hard as it was, I would have to break the news to Silas and the children without any delay. There was a pony-trap at the cemetery gate which would take me to the railway station, and I would be home within the hour.

I had a small posy of spring flowers gathered from the garden at the Ship Inn, and now I placed them on the grave, turned and walked back to the cemetery gate. I passed Mrs Wandle with neither a word nor a glance, boarded the small vehicle and gave orders to be taken to the station. Mrs Wandle climbed in, asking to be taken back to the Inn. We travelled in silence.

All the way home, I felt impelled to weep without stopping, but I knew that there would have to be another time for that. All that mattered to me now was my children, and I had to be calm for them. Matthew was at his new school where he had been sent to protect him from the attention of the press and the taunts of boys who knew the family's history, but Franklin was still at home being cared for by my sister. My intention was to take him aside and very gently reveal what I knew, then I would speak to Matthew that afternoon and finally break the news to Silas on his return home from the office. I hoped I was equal to the task. But there was no alternative. I had to be.

When I returned, the house was very quiet. Franklin, I knew, burdened by exhaustion, often took a long nap after luncheon, although one could never predict how he would be on his drowsy awakenings. He was less afraid to sleep during the hours of daylight, less afraid of dreaming. I decided not to disturb him until he was ready for his tea, and instead, went the parlour to sit for a while and think of what words I could best use to tell him about his father. The most important words were those of the letter in which Jasper had expressed his great affection for his children and his wishes for their future. That, I hoped, would heal many wounds.

As I pushed open the parlour door —

Here, Mrs Holt stopped, and almost gave way to tears again, but her face was not crumpled with grief but distorted by anger. Another glass of sherry was offered, but she shook her head.

'I do not wish to shock you, Miss Scarletti, but you should understand me and the course my life has taken. When I opened the door I was met by a sight I could never have imagined. It was a tableau, a picture of depravity, like a scandalous painting that had been banned from public view, but it was real. There was Silas seated in the armchair by the fire, and my sister Marion was sitting on his lap. For a moment I tried to delude myself that her sister was ill or distressed and that Mr Vardy was only comforting her, and all would be easily explained, but that was only while my shocked mind sought to reject the truth. No innocent explanation was possible ¬— their arms were about each other, their lips pressed together in an exercise of mutual affection.

My cry of horror alerted them, and my sister, not nearly as embarrassed as she ought to have been, slowly rose to her feet and smoothed her skirts. Silas, looking unrepentant, remained seated. Neither made any attempt to comment on the discovery.

For a moment I felt lightheaded, on the verge of fainting but then I clasped the door jamb firmly and steadied myself. I thought of Franklin and Matthew and that gave me the courage and strength I needed. 'Marion,' I said, 'you cannot remain in this house a moment longer. I only hope my poor children have not been subjected to scenes such as this.' I stepped aside from the open doorway for her to exit.

Marion appeared to be considering her options, but I stood firm, and hardened myself against any pleading. Above all, I knew that if I remained strong, I had the upper hand. Had Marion's poor deluded husband, Mr Norbert, suspected infidelity, he would have put her aside in shame and poverty. We stared at each other for a while, then Marion actually gave a smile. 'I'll go,' she said. 'I have had all I can stomach of your insane son. He should be beaten until he comes to his senses, that's what I would do, but no, you won't allow it. Him and his ghosts and demons! He will end up in a madhouse, that's for sure!' Uncowed and unashamed, she left the room and I closed the door on her without regret.

Silas stayed where he was and calmly lit a cigar. 'I suppose you want to know how far this has gone,' he said.

With an effort I held on to both my courage and my dignity. 'I do not. I have no interest in the subject. You may do as you please.'

We heard the voice of Mrs Norbert in the hallway loudly ordering the servants to pack her box and arrange for a carriage to the railway station. I sat down facing the man I had once called husband. 'There is something I must tell you, but I will wait until Marion has left the house, then I will fetch Franklin and we will talk.'

'Very well,' said Silas. He continued to smoke, in a slow and untroubled manner. I gazed at him. He was a stranger to me now, a man I had never really known. We remained in silence for a few minutes, and then the parlour door was pushed open and Franklin appeared, his clothes rumpled, his eyes dusty with sleep. 'I heard a noise,' he said. 'What's happening?'

'Your aunt is going away,' I said, and there was no mistaking the relief in my dear boy's reaction to this news. 'But come and sit by me, Franklin, I have something to tell you both.'

Franklin edged forward, glancing nervously at Silas, who took no notice of him, and sat down near to me. I was moved almost to tears at how thin he looked, how much younger than his fourteen years. What had I missed? What had I been blind to? Whatever happened I would not allow anyone other than myself to care for him now.

Silas casually took out his pocket watch and examined it. 'So what is this about?'

'As you know,' I said, 'I paid a visit to my — ' the word 'friend' the one I might once have used stuck so deeply in my throat that I could hardly breathe — 'my acquaintance Mrs Wandle in Seabourne this morning, and I have learned something of great importance. It concerns Jasper. I have a letter, one which he wrote to me shortly before his death.'

'And this has only just appeared? After all these years?' demanded Silas, incredulously.

'Not years, weeks.'

'I — don't understand.'

I spoke as clearly and as steadily as she could. 'Jasper did not die when he fell from the yacht. He was able to reach the shore, where he found a home in Seabourne. He did not come back because of the scandal over the insurance fraud. But he wanted to come back, he wrote in his letter about his great affection for me and his beloved children, and how desperately he wished to be with us again, but he knew that if he did return, he would be put in prison and bring shame to us. So he lived out a humble life at an inn. He died in January of a weak heart.'

Silas grunted and pulled at his cigar. 'Flim-flam!' he said.

'It is true. The letter is in his handwriting, I have no doubt of it, and there is other proof, a family portrait he always carried with him, and the clothes he wore on the day he disappeared.'

Franklin gazed up at me and his eyes, the lids swollen with fatigue, were open wide like caverns filled with wonder. 'So — father didn't drown?' he whispered.

'No, Franklin, he didn't,' I said gently. 'You remember what a good swimmer he was? He won prizes for it when he was younger.'

'But — the ghost told me — it showed me —' murmured Franklin, confused.

'My dear, the ghost was not real, it was made up out of your fears. It was your fears that spoke to you and made you have all those dreams. We can read the letter together if you like. Your father speaks to you in it. He loved us all.'

'What has this Mrs Wandle got to do with it?' Silas interrupted.

'She is the landlady of the Inn at Seabourne where Jasper lodged. It was she who sent Franklin the watch. When Jasper knew he was dying he asked her to pass it to him.'

Silas grunted again, but this time expressing a grudging acceptance. 'Well if it's true it's about time it all came out. Once all the excitement dies down it'll be a good thing. There are too many of those idlers and newspaper types outside the house, but that should stop soon. We'll have a solicitor make a statement, and if they don't go, we'll call the police again and this time there'll be charges.'

I rang for my maid. Franklin gazed at me, then tentatively extended his hands towards me and gratefully I clasped them. 'My dear,' I said, 'I would like you to leave us alone for a while as I have to speak to Mr Vardy. But I promise that I will come and see you in a few minutes and then we will look at the letter and talk about your father.'

He nodded. Little Maggie appeared, looking brighter and more content than she had during her time with Mrs Barnham, and took Franklin back to his room with the promise of milk and biscuits.

Soon afterwards, there was the sound of a box being taken downstairs and a carriage drew up outside the house for the conveyance of Mrs Norbert. We heard her depart, slamming the door defiantly behind her.

'So what is this all about now?' said Silas.

'I mentioned that Jasper died a few weeks ago. I have seen the death certificate in which it is noted that he passed away on 25 January. That was the day after our wedding.'

I was briefly surprised, although when I think about it now, perhaps I ought not to have been surprised, when Silas laughed. 'Well, there's a thing!' he said.

'Indeed it is a thing,' I said, 'a thing which means that we are not legally husband and wife. Of course, we married in good faith so there can be no blame attached to either of us, but still, that is the position.'

He shrugged. 'Well, I shouldn't trouble yourself about it, that is soon mended. You are now both legally and in fact a widow and therefore free to remarry. We will have a quiet ceremony and set things straight. We can call it a re-dedication if you like. No-one but ourselves needs to know the real reason. Your reputation will remain intact, and the business will come to no harm. That Mrs Wandle, she can be paid off if necessary, to keep her mouth closed. And even if someone was to find out, it would be a nine-days wonder, soon forgotten, and we would be properly married by then. I'll see about a licence this afternoon.'

A shiver of distaste ran down my spine. Pressed close to my breast I held the last letter my dear Jasper had written, a letter full of longing and affection, deeply felt. He had been a flawed man, but fundamentally a good man, and he had done what he thought was best out of love, and I had loved him. And now this creature, this reptile, had the effrontery to dally with my own sister behind my back and then assume that I would be willing to marry him.

I should have been angry but instead a cold calm settled upon me. 'There will be no wedding,' I said.

'What do you mean?' he exclaimed. 'We have been living together as husband and wife. Do you want the world to know the true state of affairs?'

'I care nothing for the world, not now,' I said. 'The world has thrown at me all it can, and yet I am still here. I care only for my boys, and it would be best for them not to have such a stepfather as you.'

'Oh, that little peccadillo, that was nothing!' he said dismissively.

'The mere fact that you treat it as nothing says everything about you.'

His brow furrowed in annoyance and he leaned forward earnestly. 'Now you listen to me, Charlotte. When we met you had been abandoned by your husband and were dependant on the charity of your brother. I have given you and your sons a home, respectability and a position in society. Have you no gratitude?'

'It is hard to have gratitude when I know that this supposed marriage was in effect a business arrangement, with you as the main beneficiary, and myself just an inconvenience that you were obliged to endure.'

'There are many worse marriages than this one!' he snapped.

'This is not a marriage,' I said. 'It never was and never will be. The only question is, since we can no longer respectably live together, which of us will leave the house? I have my two boys to care for, and you have no responsibility towards them, therefore it would be more convenient for you to depart.'

'Convenient!' he shouted, stubbing out the remains of his cigar in an ashtray. 'You have the temerity to demand that I leave a house which is rented in my name, with my money? I will not do so!'

I stood. 'Then I will go. I will take Franklin and Maggie and call at the school for Matthew. I am glad that he has been spared this scene.'

'You will stay here! As my wife!' he demanded.

'I will do neither.'

I turned away but before I could reach the door, he leaped from his chair, clasped me roughly by the arm, pulled me about to face him, and shook me hard. 'I will not take this disobedience from you or any woman! If you try to leave, I will prevent it!'

'Let go of her!' exclaimed Franklin, who had just burst through the door. 'Let go of my mother!' He ran forward and clasped his arms about my waist.

Silas turned to the boy, his face red and fierce with rage. He raised his hand. 'Get out of my way!'

'How dare you!' I cried, my hand curling protectively about my son's head. 'Do not strike my child!'

'Your child should be locked away as a lunatic!' Silas seized Franklin by the arm and began to drag us both to the door of the parlour where he stopped as he saw Maggie gazing at the scene of violence. 'Don't just stand there girl, get the keys to the nursery and we'll see both of these put away!'

'If you please sir,' said Maggie, 'there are two men at the door. It's the police, and they're asking to speak to you.'

At this Mrs Holt broke down again, and Mina comforted her as best as she could.

'The police spoke to him and then they took him away,' Mrs Holt said, when she was finally able to speak coherently. 'I don't know what it was all about. Not the marriage, not that, I am sure of that much at least, that was done in good faith, and no-one can accuse us of bigamy, but there was something else, something I didn't know about, in his past. And — I suppose I ought not to say this — but when I saw him go, I felt so relieved!' Mrs Holt wiped her eyes. 'I am so sorry to give way like this. I have tried to be strong for my boys, but I only have so much strength to give.'

Mina sipped her tea and said nothing. Knowing when to say nothing was an important skill she had worked hard to cultivate.

'And now I have received a note from him. He is at the police station begging my help, my forgiveness. I don't know what to do!'

'So many people ask me what they ought to do,' said Mina, 'but in matters of the heart or conscience I am reluctant to give advice. If only because the answer is already within them. You are a good woman, Mrs Holt. You know what is right.'

CHAPTER TWENTY-SEVEN

The next morning, a fresh article had been published in *The Times*.

THE BRIGHTON MYSTERY

Nothing in this world should ever surprise us. We comment here on the latest revelations about the man who was recently held in the cells at Brighton police station, since we are given to understand that he is no longer there having been removed for his own safety.

What next, we ask ourselves?

One moment he confesses that he is the earthly form of Mr Jasper Holt, strangely recalled to life, but no, it then appears that the genuine Mr Holt is indeed no more and the unfortunate man is in fact an artist called John Chantry who had been over-exercising his imagination. And just as we thought the mystery was settled, there comes a new wonder. An arrival in Brighton, a London gentleman, Mr George Sutherland has identified the man as his cousin William; not only that but we are astonished to hear that Mr William Sutherland is the very individual who accompanied Mr Jasper Holt on his final fatal voyage.

While the family would prefer Mr William Sutherland to have nothing at all to do with the press, a sentiment which we wholly understand and approve, if only concerning the sensational papers, an official statement has been issued through the family solicitor, which is said to be the very last word on the subject. We trust that it may be, as we are not sure if we can tolerate another surprise in this surprising story.

Mr George Sutherland advises us that in 1864 when his cousin was secretary of the Brighton Yacht Club and owner of the yacht Ocean Breeze, he was a partner in a small but promising London firm of stockbrokers and engaged to be married.

The accident to Mr Holt and the cruel allegations that followed resulted in Mr Sutherland suffering a complete breakdown in his nerves. He was unable to conduct his business and his engagement was broken off. Despite being blameless in the death of Mr Holt which was due entirely to Mr Holt's failure to follow his good advice, Mr Sutherland remained possessed by guilt, haunted by the feeling that he could have done something to prevent the accident.

Doctors advised him to live quietly somewhere. His great love was the sea and he also amused himself by drawing. Although Brighton was in one sense, the scene of his destruction he found himself attracted to it, as he felt that only there could he expiate his guilt. He never sails, and the yacht has been sold, the proceeds being used for his support, since he is quite unable to apply himself to any occupation, but he spends much of his time by the seashore, with his pencils and notebooks. Those who passed him by scarcely noticed him, but if they did, formed the opinion that he was simple-minded but harmless. Such was the disintegration of what had once been a fine intellect, that he was unable even to manage his own finances. His solicitor sent him a postal order once a month, and his landlady supplied weekly provisions.

And so, Mr Sutherland lived quietly, adopting another name to avoid comment, troubling no-one until the recent remarriage of Mrs Holt stimulated a great deal of gossip in the town. There was much raking over of old coals and unfortunately fresh speculation, some of it extremely cruel, as to the fate of Mr Holt and Mr Sutherland's part in it. This was too much for an already tormented mind, and it precipitated another breakdown with the result we have been discussing.

The identification of him as Mr Holt by three prominent members of Brighton society must now be put aside as a mistake. The man looked older than his years and a profusion of hair and beard did not assist the matter. We are told that he has been reintroduced to the art of the bath and the barber, and a photograph of him in his younger days has also recently appeared in which he is readily identifiable.

We have not been told of his present address and we have not desired to know it. All that we do know is that he is able to live in modest comfort with the help of a male attendant.

And there we must let the story end.

Mrs Holt came again to see Mina. Many tears had flowed since their last meeting, but she was calm and resolute.

'I decided that I would have one last meeting with Silas, but first I consulted my brother who agreed to accompany me. Gordon is a gentle kind soul. Many people, and I think Silas was one, sometimes see him as being weak and malleable, and try to exploit his good nature. When I first met Silas he seemed so strong and manly beside Gordon. What a fool I was. Oh, I know, in fact I always knew that there were reasons other than affection for the marriage, and it was such a beneficial arrangement for all concerned, especially my boys, but I had thought — supposed — indeed I had been purposely led to believe that Mr Vardy had some tender feelings for me.

You know that Gordon is godfather to my boys, and that he and his wife have no family of their own, which they would dearly have liked to have had. But they came to regard my sons as the children they were never blessed with. Gordon is very much my senior — he is fifty-nine and I am nearly forty-seven. He wanted to provide for Franklin and Matthew, especially after Jasper — especially after that. Naturally, it is far too early to say whether the porcelain business would suit them, but its value is considerable, and the business must be kept alive and flourishing for them. Gordon made a will in which he divided the business. One third went to Mr Vardy and the remainder to my boys, to be held in trust for them until they reach full age, and Mr Vardy was appointed trustee. It was an eminently sensible arrangement. Jane, Gordon's wife will be very well provided for, have no concerns about that, she will have the house and all its contents and a handsome annuity and be very comfortable.'

Mina nodded approvingly, in a manner she felt would encourage more revelations.

'However,' Mrs Holt continued, 'this bounty to Mr Vardy came with two requirements. Gordon is not strong and while he very much hopes to be still living when the boys come of age, and he can see them become the fine men they promise to be, he wished to secure their future if he is not. As a condition of the bequest Mr Vardy was tasked with ensuring that when the boys reach the age of eighteen, they are to be offered a position in the company in order to learn the business and a more senior post when they come of age. The other requirement was for him to marry me. I am sure Gordon believed it to be for the best; he felt the boys needed a father figure who was more youthful then himself.'

There was a long silence. Mina pushed her visitor's teacup closer to her and at last Mrs Holt lifted it to her lips and drank like one parched, to whom delicate sips were a lost refinement. 'But you say that you knew of this at the time?' said Mina. 'It was not something you discovered later?'

'I did, but I also thought that there was some sympathy between us. All too soon I found that I was wrong. Miss Scarletti, the marriage was not more than a few hours old when Silas — Mr Vardy — revealed that he had no fondness for me at all. In fact —' she swallowed back a gulp of shame, 'he made it very clear that my person was not pleasing to him. More than that I am not prepared to say. He said that he would do his duty by me and the boys under the terms of Gordon's will, but that was all. It was a commercial arrangement to him, nothing more. My boys were clothed and fed and schooled, but he was not the father to them that I or Gordon hoped he would be. The kindness he showed to them when he was courting me was all pretence. It ended on our wedding day. He would never give me any grounds to divorce him, of course, he dared not since his inheritance was dependant on our marriage, but that was all I could expect.'

Mina refreshed the teacups. 'But as it now turns out you are not married.'

'Yes,' said the newly minted Mrs Holt in a firmer voice. 'Gordon has engaged a solicitor to look at the will, but he feels sure that the current situation means that its terms have not been met, and should he pass away tomorrow, Mr Vardy would inherit nothing. That is why, when Silas discovered that we were not married, realising at once that this meant that he was not after all entitled to the inheritance, his only comment was that the matter was easily put right and we should make arrangements to marry at once. He seemed quite unable to comprehend how I might regard the offer. He thought I would be grateful that he was willing to regularise our relations.'

'I trust you will not be induced to consider it?' Mina paused. 'I am sorry, I should not intrude into your private business and I realised that I have overstepped — '

'Oh, please do not concern yourself about that,' said Mrs Holt, almost lightly. 'I will never marry that man. It was a mercy that the police arrived when they did. As soon as he had gone, I packed a few possessions and walked out of the house. I took Franklin to his godfather and then I came to you. But my interview with Mr Vardy yesterday was brief. We had our solicitor with us, who reminded us that since I was not legally a wife, I would not be prevented from giving evidence against Mr Vardy at a trial, though I do hope it will not come to that. I really think he imagined that I would come to see him alone and he would wheedle me with soft words. He was very shocked to see that I came armed and resorted to argument and bluster and threats none of which did him any good. And when I saw my dear brother together with the creature Silas had become, and almost certainly always had been, I recognised what true manliness is. I will never see Mr Vardy again, and I told him so. It seems he is to be charged with some financial crime, but he will have no help from me. I owe him nothing.

'My sister Marion, who came uninvited to care for Franklin — I can barely bring myself to speak of her. Franklin has told me about how she had been treating him and I was appalled at the harshness and insults my poor child had to suffer. I believe she fed him some soporific mixture so that she — so that she and Mr Vardy — well, I will say no more of that. She has gone back to her family and they are welcome to her.'

'Where are you living now?'

'We are all with Gordon and Jane who have made us very comfortable. That is myself, Franklin, Matthew and our new maid, little Maggie who has proved to be such a treasure. Did you know, I was obliged to rescue her from the clutches of that dreadful Mrs Barnham? The things I learned about that woman you would never believe.' She shook her head. 'There is such cruelty in the world.'

She gave a sudden smile. 'Miss Scarletti, forgive me, I have been so wrapped up in my own woes that I have not said how pleasing it is to see you so much better in health. I hope that taxing you with my troubles has not delayed your recovery.'

'Not at all,' said Mina. She almost said, 'rather the opposite,' but decided not to.

CHAPTER TWENTY-EIGHT

The next day's post brought more revelations. First was an article in *The Times*.

CHARGES OF FRAUD

There has been a surprising new development in the Maritime Queen Insurance Company case, which we last heard of in 1863. Our readers will recall that this company was established with the sole intention of extracting funds from its investors and was wound up to the distress and ruin of many.

Mr Silas Vardy, who is currently a manager in the Saltmire and Vardy Fine Porcelain Company of Hove was placed under arrest yesterday and charged with conspiracy to commit fraud. He is being held in the cells at Brighton Town Hall and will come before the magistrates today. It appears that a prominent bank manager of that town, Mr William Cobbe will be the principal prosecution witness. Mr Cobbe has already been acquitted of all charges in relation to the fraud but is currently in custody on another unrelated charge about which we have no information.

In 1863 Mr Vardy was a clerk in the accountancy firm of Westbury and Co. He was acquainted with the other gentlemen suspected of conspiracy, in particular a Mr Taylor who was a cousin, and one of the main instigators of the fraud, who absconded abroad while on bail, and is suspected of having murdered his partner in crime Mr Randall.

It has been alleged that Mr Vardy's skills were brought into play in forging the documents used in the fraud which were so nicely done that the most knowledgeable man would never have detected their falsity. We have been privately informed that Mr Cobbe retained in his possession some documents which will prove without a doubt Mr Vardy's role in the conspiracy. Why he has not chosen to produce them until now is a question that we hope will be revealed in due course. It is being widely speculated in the town that Mr Vardy had some power over Mr Cobbe since he knew some of that gentleman's secrets. The rumours have taken quite an indelicate turn, such that we have taken the decision not to print them here.

It also appears that Mrs Barnham the spirit medium and her servant Miss Stone are also in police custody where they are being questioned in connection with the charge against Mr Cobbe. Our Brighton readers will be well aware that whenever trouble falls upon the head of a spirit medium of that town a Miss Mina Scarletti inevitably has something to do with it, however we are told that Miss Scarletti has recently been indisposed and confined to a bed of sickness, and therefore cannot possibly have had anything to do with these recent events.

Mina had also received a long letter from Mrs Holt.

Dear Miss Scarletti,

Franklin, Matthew and I continue to reside with Gordon and Jane who are kindness itself. Their house is quite substantial, in fact rather larger than they require, and they have decided to convert a portion of it into a separate set of apartments for us. We are all very content with the arrangement.

When I told them of the good advice you had given me, they revealed that they had read about some of your earlier exploits in the newspapers. As a result, they are very eager to meet you. We really must arrange something when you are feeling stronger and are able to pay us a visit.

I thought I would write to apprise you of recent circumstances which have come to my notice and which have gone a long way to improving Franklin's state of mind. Last week I invited Mr Merridew the celebrated actor to take tea with the boys and myself. I am not sure how much you know of this, but he was once quite briefly a member of Mrs Barnham's circle. He it was, who was clever enough to see though her trickery, something which had long deceived the rest of us. Although he is a theatrical, he is also a very respectable and gentlemanly sort of person, and I wished to thank him for opening my eyes to the dreadful trade that Mrs Barnham had been practising for so long, from which I believe she has appreciably lined her purse.

As soon as Mr Merridew arrived, I saw Franklin looking at him most particularly, but when he presented me with a portrait of himself costumed and bewigged for his most recent performance, Franklin at once became very excited and addressed our visitor as 'Hamlet'. Now I was aware that not so long ago the school had taken a party of pupils to the theatre to see a classical play of great renown, but I had quite forgotten its title, and so had not appreciated that Franklin had actually seen Mr Merridew's acclaimed performance as Hamlet. I am not acquainted with the play, but I have since learned that it concerns a melancholy prince who believes that his uncle has murdered his father. Well, I will not go on but while it may be instructive, and I believe the quality of the authorship is very good indeed, I am not at all sure that this is a suitable play for children to see performed, especially a sensitive boy like Franklin. The play actually has scenes in which Hamlet is confronted by the ghost of his father. The father is also called Hamlet, so that must be very confusing, but he reveals to the prince that he has been done to death by his own brother.

All at once I realised that this play was the origin of certain of Franklin's morbid imaginings, which happened at a time when he was already very unhappy for reasons of which you are already aware. It was only after he saw the play that Franklin began to imagine he saw ghosts everywhere, especially the spirit of his father which he claimed actually addressed him and said he had been killed. I am sure that the origin of the messages came from my poor child's own fears and general upset, and now that he knows the messages were not true, I believe he is coming to understand this.

When I mentioned this to Mr Merridew, he at once appreciated my difficulty, and he was very sympathetic about it and apologised so very profusely that I was obliged to protest that I attached no blame to him as he was only engaged in his profession. He then kindly offered to conduct my boys and myself on a tour of the theatre to see what happened behind the scenery as it were. We went on the visit yesterday and it was quite remarkable. We met a number of the actors and the men who build and paint everything, and they were all so very friendly.

Matthew became extremely excited and alarmed me very much by picking up a sword and waving it about, and I had to beg him to put it down, but then I found out that it was only painted wood and was much relieved. He was also interested in all the machinery of the stage and was especially fascinated by the trapdoor which worked by some curious mechanical device that enabled the actor who was playing the ghost to appear and disappear as if by magic. Really if I had not brought him home, he would be riding up and down on it still.

Franklin is normally such a quiet reserved boy, but he was very taken by the costumes. It was quite wonderful to see him looking at the painted material of the ghost's draperies and seeing for himself that it was all make-believe. What a strange profession the stage is! Franklin also gained great amusement from the court costumes, the gold trimmings and brocades and velvets, with their paste jewels. I think it was the bright colours that attracted him, and he spent more than an hour trying them on and walking about in them and putting paint on his face. Mr Merridew was patience personified.

The result has been that ever since we came home Franklin has been talking about the visit without stopping. He has started lurking in the shadows draped in a bedsheet or jumping out suddenly with flour on his face, and trying to frighten the servants, but I hope he will grow out of it. He is not yet entirely cured of his late disturbance and still has the occasional nightmare, but I do feel that he is making good progress. His sleeping is easier, and Jane has kindly begun to tutor him in reading and arithmetic with a little history and geography, so he will not fall behind in his studies, and I am hopeful that he will soon be recovered enough to return to school.

Little Maggie is coming along very well. In fact, despite her youth, she is the only maid who has not been startled by Franklin's impersonation of a ghost as she says very robustly that there are no such things.

I know now that Emily Wandle called on you before she confessed all she knew to me, and I thank you for your guidance on that occasion which gave her the courage to enlighten me. I was of course dreadfully upset at what she had to say, and at first, I could hardly bear to speak to her, and had determined never to meet with her again. Since then I have given the matter considerable thought, and I think I can understand her reasons for the dissimulation. At least she did what she did for good reasons and not, as in the example of the reprehensible Mrs Barnham, for the love of lucre. I have therefore decided to forgive her, and we have met again with the intention of mending our friendship. It appears that Emily was convinced that I knew all along what Jasper's plans were, and when she told me that he had left a message for me, I was quite mystified as I had seen no such message. I mentioned this to Gordon and he confessed to me that on going through Jasper's papers, something I felt quite unable to do at first, he had seen a note that Jasper had left for me, but he judged from the wording that my poor husband was declaring his intention to make away with himself. He therefore destroyed it, as any suggestion of suicide would have invalidated the insurance, not to mention the distress it would have caused us all.

Gordon thought he could recall the words of the message which were 'I am going to where the world ends. We will meet again.' When Jasper and I were courting we liked to go on short trips along the coast in fine weather and look at the beaches and the little boats and quaint cottages. There was one place in Shoreham where we stopped and looked out across the sea, which seems to go on forever. I remember we said to each other that it was the place where the world came to an end. But what we meant was, it was the old world coming to an end, and we were looking at the future when we would be united, and it would be a new and better world. It was a private time between us, and I suppose I had not thought of it for a while. Poor Jasper, he was not talking of any heavenly region, but of course Gordon was not to know that.

   Trusting that I find you in good health,
   I am most gratefully yours,
   Charlotte Holt

CHAPTER TWENTY-NINE

When Mr William Sutherland was in better health, he consented to tell his story to selected witnesses, one of whom was Dr Hamid, who apprised Mina of the details as accurately as he was able to.

I, William Sutherland, being in possession of my senses, and fully aware that I am the William Sutherland who was formerly a partner in Sutherland and Fenwick, stockbrokers of London, have been recently apprised of the fact that Mr Jasper Holt of Brighton, who was thought to have died on 18 July 1864, in fact survived his fall into the sea and did not pass away until 25 January 1872.

I now wish to make a full and truthful statement of the events that took place during the last occasion on which I sailed my yacht Ocean Breeze.

Prior to the voyage I had only a slight acquaintance with Mr Holt through the purchase of wines and spirits from his shop on St James's Street, Brighton. On learning that I was a member of the Brighton Yacht Club and was in possession of a yacht he became very interested and asked if he could join me on a voyage. I agreed and told him that in view of my forthcoming marriage to Miss Ann Chantry I was considering selling the yacht. Mr Holt then said that he might be interested in purchasing it. He also said he had been advised by his doctor that sea voyaging was good for the health, and he had two sons who might enjoy sailing.

It was on that agreement that Mr Holt joined me on the yacht on 18 July 1864. I had no notion then of his true intentions and if I had I would have refused to sail with him.

Shortly after we left Brighton, Mr Holt asked to be taken to Shoreham. I thought at first that he just wished to make a short visit, but he then said that he wished to be put ashore there and told me that I must to return to Brighton without him. Not only that but he asked me not to reveal where he was. I thought this an extremely strange request and said I could not do this without being told of his reasons.

After a lot of hesitation Mr Holt confessed that if I did not help him then he would be a ruined man as his business was, through no fault of his own, failing, and he was deeply in debt. The shame of bankruptcy would be intolerable, and his family would be thrown out of their home and reliant on the charity of relatives.

I remonstrated with him. I said that running away would not cure the situation. He replied that it would if he was dead. I was appalled as I thought he intended to make away with himself, but he reassured me that that was not his intention as his insurance company would not pay out if he took his own life. I demanded to know what he meant to do, and he eventually revealed to me the planned fraud. He had recently taken out a substantial policy of insurance on his life on which he had paid the first instalment. His intention was to disappear without trace in circumstances where he would be assumed to have died. He expected me not only to assist him in this, but to tell people on my return to Brighton that he had perished in an accident. It was essential for his purpose that I should state, under oath if necessary, that I had seen him fall over the side with my own eyes, and sink below the waves, as that would be proof that he was deceased.

He planned to reappear after a sufficient interval of time, under another name, with changes to his appearance, and remarry his wife. A more desperate and foolhardy exploit I could not imagine.

I was deeply shocked by this story, not the least because he expected me to collude with him in a serious crime. I pointed out how much grief his wife and children would suffer when they thought he was dead, but he told me that he had left a note for his wife so she would know where he was and that he was safe. Once the accident was no longer newsworthy, he would write to her more fully.

I was extremely annoyed at being placed in this position, and made it known to him that I could not under any circumstances be a party to a criminal deception. Holt then said that if I helped him, he would pay me a large sum out of the proceeds of the insurance. This I regarded as an insult. Naturally I refused, and said that I would return to Brighton forthwith, hoping that we would have some further conversation on the way, and that I could persuade him of the folly of his plan.

I began to turn the yacht around, but Holt suddenly became desperate, and tried to take over steering the yacht. The result was a violent struggle. I should say that I did not feel in imminent danger as his object was to wrest the steering from me and not subject me to any personal harm. However, I was angered by his actions, most especially by his easy assumption that I would be a party to his plans and pushed him away. He made a second attempt on the steering and this time, I am ashamed to say that I struck him. I fear that I did so a little too strongly. He staggered back and not being an experienced sailor, he lost his balance, and fell out of the yacht. I did what I could to save him but saw him sinking and assumed that my blow had rendered him unconscious and he had drowned.

I was now in a horrible position. I was potentially open to charges of manslaughter or even murder. My career could be ruined if I confessed. I did not want to say that Mr Holt had taken his own life, as that would be a terrible stain on his reputation which would be an unnecessary and lasting grief to his family. I therefore determined to report the death as an accident. I was aware of course that in a sense I was conniving with his intended fraud, but I believed that once the truth of his finances emerged, there would be sufficient doubts that his plan would never come to fruition, and so in fact it transpired.

I had not anticipated the suspicion that would attach to me, and the disastrous effect it would have on my business, especially following the dreadful Maritime Queen case, in which I did no more than offer the usual professional advice. My partnership with Mr Fenwick was dissolved, and

Miss Chantry asked to be released from our engagement. It was not very many months later that Miss Chantry became Mrs Fenwick. I entered a kind of wilderness of the mind. I became a hermit who avoided all society. I had hoped that the Holt affair had been forgotten, but then it came back like a ghost to haunt and torment me.

I must offer my most sincere and frank apologies for all the distress and inconvenience I have caused others.

Signed: W. Sutherland

Witnessed: D Hamid, M D, R Phipps, solicitor, Captain H Bulstrode, (retired)

After Dr Hamid left, Mina was disturbed by a cacophony of noise. There was a percussion of boxes and baggage, and the thunder of running footsteps, with accompanying shouts and cries, and general sense of turmoil. An all-too brief interlude of peace was followed by a loud bumping sound and vociferous exclamations which suggested that a laden trunk was being taken downstairs. Minutes later she heard a carriage drawing up outside the house.

It was sufficiently alarming for her to ignore Dr Hamid's instructions and leave her bed unassisted, a task to which she found to her delight that she was more than equal, but she had not yet reached the window when Rose came in, and firmly but quietly moved her to the chair and tucked some shawls about her shoulders.

'Rose, what is happening?' Mina demanded. 'Is someone dead? Or is this to do with Richard? Or both? What has he done this time?'

'No, Miss,' said Rose, dryly. 'You just rest there, there's nothing that needs your attention, and Master Richard will be along soon.'

Mina was obliged to wait in a ferment of anticipation wondering what had led to the upset. It was only Rose's easy demeanour that told her it was not a disaster. When Richard sauntered in with a smile, she at once insisted on knowing all the truth.

'Oh, it's nothing to be alarmed about, really,' he said airily, throwing himself full length upon the bed. 'Mother has had to run off to London to be with Enid and her first granddaughter.'

'The child is born?' Mina exclaimed.

'Last night. Mother received the telegram this morning.'

'But it was not expected for a month or two. Are they well?'

'Oh yes, Enid for all her protestations, has Mother's constitution. In full health she could fell an ox if she set her mind to it. She is doing well, and the child if a little undersized is also robust and likely to live.'

Mina could not repress a profound sigh of relief. 'I hope,' she said faintly, 'that Enid did not take any dangerous measures to bring this about.'

'None were required. It was only necessary for her to peruse a letter from Mr Inskip. Her husband wrote to advise her that he is now restored to what passes for good health in his case, and since the snow in the mountains has abated sufficiently for travel, he has set out for home. Given the date of the letter he is expected to darken his own doorstep in about a week. The news alone was sufficient to throw Enid into paroxysms and the child was born only hours later.'

'I am concerned,' said Mina, 'that there will be a rift in the marriage when he returns. Will he not harbour suspicions?'

'You can rely on Mother; she already has her plans laid. She was making them as Rose packed her trunk. You know how adept she is at plotting her way out of anything that doesn't suit her. Remember, the twins were born a little early and they were not large although they have made up for it since, as they now both resemble boiled puddings and like to roll everywhere. It is therefore hoped that Mr Inskip will not find the size anything to complain of, especially if he is told that Enid was pining so much during his absence and fearing for his health that she was unable to swallow more than a spoonful of broth a day. That is to be the story and we must all adhere to it.'

'Then Enid's reputation and her marriage will be safe, and we must trust that she does not risk them again,' said Mina, with an exhalation of relief. 'Richard?'

'Yes, my dear?'

'No more talk of trying to marry me off. Not to anyone.'

EPILOGUE

Sunlight was spreading over the calm sea in a warm flush of gold, highlighting shallow wave tips. The cool spring finally retreated, leaving behind it the promise of a warm summer, with the May sky as brilliant and clear as only Brighton could offer. In her first venture out of doors since her illness, accompanied by Dr Hamid, Mina Scarletti was where she most liked to be, on the promenade, smelling the salt scented air, and gazing into a distant blue.

'I would like to take a walk,' said Mina.

'Are you sure?' asked Dr Hamid.

'Very sure. My lungs are clear, and I feel so much stronger. Miss Hamid has been so helpful with the exercises — who knows, if I am diligent, and I intend to be, I may become better than I was before I was ill.'

'One step at a time,' said Dr Hamid, warningly. He assisted her from the bath chair in which he had wheeled her down the incline towards the sea and helped her to stand. She leaned upon his proffered arm and they walked slowly along the promenade.

'Did you see in this morning's newspaper,' said Mina, 'Mr Hope has been forestalled. Dr Livingstone has been found alive by a Mr Stanley who no-one has ever heard of. It happened last year, but the news has only just arrived in England and been confirmed. So unless he can find another adventure to justify the expense of his journey he must come home again.'

'We must trust that he stays away from Brighton,' said Dr Hamid. 'He has disgraced himself enough here.'

'People have short memories, and his supporters of whom I know he has many will hear nothing against him, so he may yet appear. He also has his protégé to encourage, although I understand from Richard that Mr Beckler's experiments to create a photograph of a ghost have not been successful, so if we are fortunate, Mr Hope may tire of him and turn to something else.'

Mina looked out to sea and reflected on the events of the months of March and April, and how so many of her concerns had been resolved, and the stories that had started up then come to a conclusion. Her petulant sister Enid was recovering well from the early delivery of a daughter, who had been christened Gwendoline. While the infant was considered somewhat undersized for a nine-month child, Enid's husband, Mr Inskip who was finally home from his prolonged absence had been so charmed by this addition to the family, that he had accepted the manufactured explanation without question. His business abroad had been highly successful, and this must have effected a change in his mood since it was reported that he and Enid were on far better terms than previously and she had not complained of him once.

Mrs Barnham, exhausted by the indignity of her arrest, and denied the support both of Miss Stone and her rum punch, had quickly declined in health. Following a pathetic appearance before the Brighton magistrates, she had collapsed in her cell before she could be remanded to gaol, suffered a fit, and passed away shortly afterwards.

Miss Stone had fared rather better. When interviewed by the police she strongly denied any knowledge of wrongdoing, admitting only to her part in preparing the servant child for what she described as 'a harmless masquerade designed to comfort a bereaved father' and this, at the behest of her employer. No charges were made against her and she was released. Under Mrs Barnham's will she inherited all her employer's property including the spiritoscope, with which she continued the séances. These were advertised in the *Brighton Gazette* at 6d per person, and met with some moderate success, although she did not promise to produce bodily manifestations.

Mr Cobbe, who had been hoping to reduce or even entirely escape punishment by revealing Mr Vardy's crimes, discovered to his cost that Mr Vardy could retaliate with his own counter-accusations. Denial proved useless, as the scandal proceeded rapidly like a fall of dominoes. Those persons who had remained silent before, for fear of counterattack, loss of standing or disbelief, now felt able to join in the general outcry, and the banker's image of stout respectability and charitable deeds quickly disintegrated. Both he and Mr Vardy were currently in Lewes Gaol awaiting their trials at the next assizes.

The last chapter in the Maritime Queen affair had come to an end with the announcement that Mr Taylor, the only one of the culprits in that business still free, had been arrested in France and charged with the murder of his accomplice.

Mrs Holt, as she now called herself, having divested herself of an uncaring husband and a treacherous sister, applied herself with energy and dedication to the welfare of her children, assisted by her new maid, Maggie. She often entertained Mr Merridew to tea, where he amused the company with readings from plays. Franklin, still a strange fragile boy, but now almost free of his previous nocturnal torments, always requested to hear speeches from *Hamlet*.

Louisa Scarletti was now permanently settled in Brighton, which she much preferred to London, and was busily making the rounds of tea parties. She was promised a visit from Enid and all her family as soon as the new mother and child were able to travel.

Mina had received a letter to say that her good friend Nellie would soon be home from Italy. She was pleased to report that her maid, Zillah, who had recovered from her earlier aversion to food, had regained her appetite and was looking rosy and plump. Mina decided that she would not yet mention Nellie's return to Richard, who had somehow managed to stay out of trouble.

Almost as surprising was the recent announcement in the *Gazette* of the betrothal of Mr Ronald Phipps to Miss Adeline Cherry.

All was well. All was calm. Far away, little white wave tips scudded into shore, and Mina well knew how these could grow and burst over the promenade in a sudden storm. But not yet, she thought. Not just yet. Not today.

HISTORICAL NOTES

The Barnum Effect
The name Mrs Barnham is a reference to the Barnum effect where vague personality readings are perceived as tailored to the individual and therefore given a high accuracy rating.

Insanity
I am indebted to the lectures of Dr George Fielding Blandford on insanity and its treatment, published in 1871.

Brighton Town Hall
Completed in 1832, this substantial building is located in Bartholomew Square, Brighton. In 1872 it housed the police offices and cells. The Brighton police courts, which dealt with minor charges, and coroner's inquests were held here.

The front steps described in the book are now no longer there but can be seen in this image **http://regencysociety-jamesgray.com/volume9/source/jg_09_051.html**
The cells now form a part of the Old Police Cells Museum which conducts regular tours. **https://www.oldpolicecellsmuseum.org.uk**

On 14 March 1844 Brighton's Chief Constable (then called Chief Officer) Henry Solomon, was murdered in his own office, struck on the head with a poker by a prisoner. **https://en.wikipedia.org/wiki/Henry_Solomon**

George White was the Chief Constable of Brighton from 1853 to 1876.

Seabourne
The village of Seabourne and the Ship Inn are fictional.

The Spiritoscope

This was devised in the 1850s by Robert Hare, professor of chemistry at the University of Pennsylvania. Having attended a number of table-tipping séances, he was convinced, following the pronouncements of Professor Michael Faraday in 1853, that the phenomenon was the effect of unconscious muscular movements of the sitters while their hands touched the table.

The spiritoscope, which took a variety of forms, was designed to show whether spirit messages could be received independently of any action of the medium. Hare was undoubtedly the eminent man of science mentioned by Mrs Barnham, since he was converted to spiritualism after attending séances using his spiritoscope. He described the apparatus and experiments in *Experimental Investigations of the Spirit Manifestations* published in 1855.

The Brighton Poisoner

The 'poisoning woman' mentioned by Richard was Christiana Edmunds one of Brighton's most notorious murderers. Sentenced to death in January 1872 she was reprieved after being declared insane. She spent the remainder of her life in Broadmoor.

Stethoscopes

The stethoscope was invented in 1816 but was a single tube, and the doctor could use only one ear. The binaural stethoscope was first commercially available in 1852.

The Indian Doctor

I have been gently criticised for including an Anglo-Asian doctor in my novels, as this was felt to be unlikely at that period, however the character of Dr Hamid was inspired by the multi-talented and innovative Sake Dean Mahomed (1759-1851) who first established an Indian medicated vapour bath in Brighton.

The School of Reform: *or How to Rule a Husband* by Thomas Morton, (1764-1838)

This was performed at the Theatre Royal Covent Garden in 1805.

Monetary value

In 1860, £1 had the purchasing power of approximately £59 in 2017. (Source: The National Archives currency converter)

Franklin Holt's sleep disturbances

The transitional period between sleep and wakefulness either when falling asleep (hypnagogic) or waking up (hypnopompic) can be a time of disturbing phenomena.

Hallucinations can be experienced which can take a wide variety of forms; visions, noises, tastes, smells and being touched. There may also be a sensation of falling or flying. These hallucinations are not the same thing as dreams and can seem very real and frightening. Many people experience sleep paralysis, a temporary loss of the ability to move which can be accompanied by a sensation of pressure on the chest and difficulty in breathing.

Manager of the Brighton Aquarium

The Times of 9 March 1872 reported that Mr John Keast Lord the naturalist had been appointed manager of the new Brighton Aquarium. The Aquarium opened on 10 August and Lord died on 9 December aged fifty-four.

The Married Women's Property Act 1870
Mentioned by Mina, this enabled married women for the first time to legally own the money they earned and also property they inherited from next of kin, including money up to a sum of £200. Since Charlotte Saltmire married Jasper Holt before 1870 any property she had then owned would automatically have become his.

The Medical Thermometer
This has a long history, but it was not until the late 1860s that an easily portable design was available, that could take a patient's temperature in about five minutes. By 1868 research had established the normal range of human temperature using readings taken from the underarm.

Changes to Shakespeare's plays
In the mid nineteenth century the plays of Shakespeare, especially those published for young people, were sometimes rewritten so as to provide happy endings to the great tragedies such as Hamlet and King Lear, and they were often adapted in burlesque (i.e. caricature) form.

The Theatre Royal, Brighton
Opened in 1807 in New Street Brighton, and redeveloped by the actor manager Nye Chart, in the 1870s it produced plays, operas and pantomimes. It is now a Grade II listed building, and still a successful theatre.
http://theatreroyalbrighton.com

Porcelain mourning brooches
Often in the form of lockets, these could include portraits of the deceased or plaited locks of hair.

Old Steine
A wide thoroughfare with gardens surrounded by handsome buildings, including one built for King George IV's mistress Mrs Fitzherbert. The location of hotels, fashionable businesses and club rooms. The Brighton Yacht Club is wholly fictional.

The Maritime Queen fraud
This is loosely based on the Monarch Insurance Company fraud. The company was launched in 1869, and charges of conspiracy to commit fraud were made against the directors in 1870. Two of them absconded and the individuals who stood bail for them were unable to pay and were imprisoned.

Divorce law
In 1872 a man could divorce his wife for adultery alone, but a wife's options were more limited. She could not divorce her husband for adultery unless another offence was proven such as desertion or cruelty.

Page's Directory.
This included Brighton, Hove, Cliftonville and Preston and was published annually by Thomas Page, bookseller and stationer 173 North Street, Brighton.

The Young Woman's Companion
Published by Ward & Lock in 1863. The quotations in this book are taken from that volume.

Flash photography
For the history of the use of magnesium in photography I am indebted to the article 'Art of Darkness' by Chris Howes in *New Scientist* 23/30 December 1989.

It is often stated that Victorian photography required long exposures, and this was once the case, however by the 1870s more sensitive coatings on the glass plates meant that exposure times had been brought down to a second or two in bright sunlight. My description of the studio and the photographic processes are taken from contemporary publications on the art of photography, notably *A History and Handbook of Photography* by Gaston Tissandier, published in translation in 1876.

A NOTE TO THE READER

Dear Reader,

Thank you for taking the time to read this third adventure of the indomitable Mina Scarletti. I hope you had as much fun reading it as I did writing it and will want to see what she and her family and friends do next! I love exploring the stranger and more colourful areas of Victorian life and beliefs, and for this book I researched the techniques and careers of the slate-writing mediums, and read studies of people who reported seeing spectres of the living as well as the dead. For more details of the actual persons and places mentioned in the book, see my Historical Note below.

Reviews are so important to authors, and if you enjoyed the novel I would be grateful if you could spare a few minutes to post a review on **Amazon** and **Goodreads**. I love hearing from readers, and you can stay up to date with all my news via **my website**:

Linda Stratmann

lindastratmann.com

Sapere Books is an exciting new publisher of brilliant fiction and popular history.

To find out more about our latest releases and our monthly bargain books visit our website:
saperebooks.com

Printed in Great Britain
by Amazon